Talent for Trouble

The Blake Brothers Trilogy

Book Two

Susan Sey

Other Titles by Susan Sey

MONEY, HONEY

MONEY SHOT

KISS THE GIRL

TASTE FOR TROUBLE

For my family, because they know that I disappear and they always come after me.

For the dear, patient friends who know that I talk too much but invite us to parties anyway.

For Serena, who accompanied me to Cheese Fest when nobody else would. Being a writer's friend is full of burdens, but sheep's milk butter is not one of them.

For Bryan, who didn't say a word when I papered the dining room wall with sticky notes and left them up for weeks and weeks.

And for Claudia and Greta, who understand that happily is the only decent way to end a story.

Chapter 1

Going on the lam wasn't as easy as they made it look in the movies but Audrey Bing thought she was getting the hang of it. Okay, yes, her little disappearing act had gotten off to a rough start. She'd been evicted (three times), fired (twice), and dumped (spectacularly). And that was just the first three months. But the second three months? The three months she'd been keeping house for the Blake brothers?

Nothing but smooth sailing.

It was, she thought as she dragged an old wooden ladder out of the Annex's garden shed, something of a miracle. These were the men who'd made such a hash of her life on the lam, after all. She hooked the ladder over her shoulder and strode along the crushed-shell path to the plantation house's massive front porch, her breath hanging in icy puffs on the January air. The lost jobs and broken leases? Her fiancé's hasty decampment? All courtesy of one Blake brother or another. Usually Will. If somebody had told her even four months ago that she'd be taking care of these men on a full-time, live-in basis, she'd have suggested rehab, pronto.

And yet here she was, cheerfully dragging a ladder around their estate, taking down the holiday garlands that she herself had hung the month before. It was quite possible that she was humming leftover Christmas carols while she worked, too.

She opened her ladder under an elegant sweep of garland and climbed up. She snipped through a twist of wire and caught the evergreen rope that dropped into her hand. So she hadn't had a decent night's sleep in over six months. Big deal. She was *safe*, and that was all that mattered. She and her niece were finally safe.

Well, Jillian was safe, anyway. Audrey's own safety was a trickier proposition, and she figured it probably would be until she no longer shared a roof with William Blake. She shivered. She told herself she was cold but she wasn't. Will made her feel a great many and complicated things. None of them, unfortunately, was cold.

But she stayed out of his way and he let her, so that was working out as well as could be expected. And the other two brothers didn't give her any trouble at all these days. Drew in particular had launched a charm campaign that had won over even wary little Jillian. James had an edge or two, but she had to admit that he'd been more than fair to her in their business dealings. And his girlfriend Bel? She was the closest thing Audrey had had to a true friend in ages, and that was a blessing she'd never thought to look for. A small stroke of luck in a largely luckless year. And Audrey was grateful.

No, she was more than grateful. She nudged her ladder over to the next loop of garland and climbed up, still humming. She snipped another wire twist, and then another and then another, and by the time she'd finished the entire porch, she'd made a shocking discovery.

She wasn't just grateful. She was happy.

For the first time in recent memory, Audrey Bing was genuinely happy.

Perhaps that was why, when a strange car rumbled up the drive, she didn't immediately drop her garland and run. Perhaps that was why, when it slowed and parked next to the porch, she only blinked expectantly at it, a warm *welcome to the Annex* smile on her face. Perhaps that was why, when the car door opened, she found herself somehow expecting a pleasant surprise to step out rather than the disaster that had been chasing her for months.

But only disaster smiled with such dangerous white teeth.

"Hey, Audi-girl." Jem Bing shut the car door with a sharp snap and a blinding grin. "Long time, no see."

"Hey, Dad," Audrey said bitterly.

Yeah, happiness.

Her mistake.

Chapter 2

William Blake left the Annex with nothing but a tub of butter in his track pants pocket and a great idea. He didn't even bother with a coat, just took off across the lawn toward Hunt House at a jog. He didn't generally get all worked up about fancy dairy products—that was Bel's department—but he knew a killer opportunity when he saw one.

Or tasted one, as was the case with the butter.

And opportunity, as Will knew better than most, wasn't patient or generous. You got one chance, and that was if you were lucky. Hence the coat-free jog to the mansion next door. Because Will doubted very much that *Kate Every Day* had been the only lifestyle show to receive a sample box from Redemption Dairy of Devil's Kettle, Minnesota. A sample box that he and his brother Drew had mowed through like prisoners of war. At a certain point, they'd dispensed with the crackers and started scooping cheese and butter and whatnot straight out of the tubs with their fingers.

Jillian hadn't said a word, but the little girl had made it plain that she disapproved of their manners. Or lack thereof. Audrey insisted that the kid had only stopped talking six months ago, and if that were true, Will had to be impressed. She'd mastered the art of the damning silence, and in a very short space of time. Or maybe it was a skill that came down the bloodlines, because Audrey was no slouch in the ugly silence department herself. It didn't seem to bother Drew, but then the Bing women disapproved of Drew less than they disapproved of Will.

A lot less.

Will had earned every ounce of that disapproval, however. He'd done it the old-fashioned way, too, being a righteously drunken asshole. But he was sober today, and

4

there was nothing to be gained dwelling on the past. So he just let himself into Hunt House where Belinda West—the woman who would surely become his sister-in-law one of these days—was shooting promo spots for the upcoming season of *Kate Every Day*.

He jogged across the softly gleaming foyer of the gracious, pink-bricked manor house that millions of at-home viewers would recognize on sight and slipped quietly into the kitchen set at the end of the hall. He picked his way over the maze of cables snaking across the floor and stopped next to one of the cameras to watch Bel do her thing.

"...so join me right here weekday afternoons at four—three central—for a fresh twist on the classic *Kate Every Day* formula. The good life but for real families this time."

She grinned at the camera, dimples digging deep, and Will couldn't help grinning along with her. Bel had been Kate Davis' on-air baking maven and heir apparent for three long years, the tidy personification of Kate's chilly idea of domestic perfection. Then Bel's made-for-TV wedding had imploded in spectacular fashion, and just like that she'd been out of a job. Watching her take the reins now of the show she'd almost been denied was deeply satisfying. Nobody deserved a happily ever after more than Bel.

"Okay," somebody said, "let's break for lunch. We'll do the west coast spots this afternoon."

Bel said, "Thanks be to God." She retrieved a bottle of water from beneath the massive island counter that anchored the kitchen set. "It's like the surface of the sun out here."

"Hey, Bel," Will said, joining her under the klieg lights where it was, indeed, as hot as eternal damnation.

"Will!" She blinked at him. "What are you doing here?"

"My job. I'm your agent, remember?" And it was still a shock to remember that. He wasn't just responsible for James' career anymore; he was responsible for dozens of careers, Bel's included. And it was all thanks to the unfathomable last will and testament of the late Bob Beck, sports and entertainment agent extraordinaire. "How's the promo going?"

She grinned suddenly. "Awesome. And you know

why?"

"Why?"

"Because I have a show, Will." She danced her way to his side of the island counter. "A show of my very own!"

"So I see." He tried not to grin but didn't quite manage it. Kate's retirement had been, as they said in the domestic diva business, a very good thing. For Bel *and* Kate. As had been the decision to leave Bel in charge. "But you're not, you know, dancing like that on camera, are you?"

"Heck no. This is a private celebration. Plus, dancing is Ellen's thing. I'm staking out my own territory here." She polished off her bottle of water and handed it to one of the dozen or so aides that circled her like gnats.

"Yeah," he said. "I heard your new tagline. The good life for real families, huh?"

"Yep."

"I like it."

"Me, too." She sighed happily. "So, what brings my favorite agent to the set today?"

"Sheep."

She paused. "Sheep?"

"Sheep." He pushed his hands into his pockets and rocked back on his heels. "How do we feel about sheep, Bel?"

She tipped her head and considered this for a long moment, her hair a sleek swing of maple under the broiling lights. Finally she said, "Braised or stewed?"

Will pulled the little tub from his pocket and slid it onto the counter between them. "Milked."

Bel pounced. "Sheep's milk butter!"

"You've had it before?"

"Once." She pried the lid off, lifted it to her nose and inhaled enthusiastically. She exhaled on a happy sigh. "So sheepy." Then she stuck in a finger and tasted it. Her eyes crossed. "Will," she said faintly. "I'm in love."

Will's brother James materialized from the blackness beyond the island of blazing light. "You sure are," James told her, his brows drawn low over that same beaky nose that Will saw in the mirror every day. "With me."

He put an elbow into Will's ribs and made himself a space at Bel's side. Will refused to grunt but, Jesus, the guy had elbows. Probably explained why the DC Statesmen paid a couple million a year for his presence on their side of the soccer field.

Or maybe it was because Will was one hell of an agent. Hard to say.

"James," Bel said, her hands cupped reverently around the little tub. "Look."

James leaned in, his shaggy blond head glowing nearly white under the spots. Will took the opportunity to rub his ribs. "Is that...butter?"

"*Sheep's milk* butter."

James shrugged easily and poked a finger into the tub. You didn't live with Bel for any length of time without learning to just taste whatever odd thing she put in front of you. He licked his finger clean and said, "Whoa." He went back for seconds but Bel snatched the tub away. He drooped. "Aw."

"Will," she said, the butter cradled to her chest like an infant. "Where did this come from?"

"Redemption Dairy. Heard of it?"

"Never."

"It's in Minnesota. They sent *Kate Every Day* a sampler box."

"A sampler box?" She narrowed her eyes. "This is one teeny tub. Where's my cheese, Will?"

"Drew was licking the wrapper when I left."

"Aw." This time she and James said it together.

"It was better than the butter."

She closed her eyes and made a small, pained noise.

"Hey, Bel?"

She opened her eyes.

"You're going to Minnesota."

She blinked. "I am?"

"Yep. You're about to become America's favorite tastemaker, kiddo. And you're starting out with the best butter nobody ever heard of."

"In Minnesota," she said. "In January."

7

"Wait, what's this now?" James glared at him. "You're putting her on the road? Damn it, Will! She just got home at Thanksgiving!"

"And if I'm not mistaken, you just got a national team call up," Will told him. "Which means it's January camp for you. Go make that World Cup roster, buddy. We'll see you in February." He didn't take his eyes off Bel. "What do you say, Bel? Minnesota?"

She frowned thoughtfully down at the butter.

James said, "I was hoping she'd come with me."

"Come with you?" Bel's head snapped up. "To January camp?"

Will laughed. "Right. I've been to January camp, Bel. Believe me, the sheep farm's going to smell better. It'll definitely have more intelligent conversation." He turned to James. "And as for you? January camp isn't take-your-girlfriend-to-work week. Cripes, James. The World Cup is less than six months away and the US finally landed in a decent draw. Let's have a little focus here, huh? A little discipline?"

"I'm focused." He smiled down at Bel, all slow and hot. "I'm very focused."

"Is that so?" she murmured, taking in that smile.

"And if it's discipline you're after—" He slid his arm around her waist and began to reel her in. "—Daddy can provide."

Will pressed his fingers to his forehead. "For God's sake, James. You're in public."

"Don't listen to him," James murmured in Bel's ear. Her very pink ear. "That's just jealousy talking."

"Jealousy? Who's jealous?" Will snorted. "Drew didn't eat that cheese by himself, you know."

"Full belly, empty bed." James nuzzled at Bel's ear. "Recipe for bitterness if I ever heard one."

Will wanted to snort again but he couldn't quite manage it. Because James had a point. Half a point, anyway. Will's bed *was* empty. Remarkably empty. But it wasn't his belly that was full. It was his imagination. His imagination was extremely full, and of the woman who wasn't in his bed.

That impossible face? Check. That silver-blonde hair? Yep. A set of curves like to break a man's heart? Right there. And those eyes? Present, and how. Wide, heavily lashed, and so deeply blue they were almost purple. And filled with cold dislike.

Will's imagination was nothing if not accurate.

Oh, cry me a river. Are you listening to yourself, you self-pitying pussy?

His imagination also excelled at channeling the voice of the late Bob Beck, the man who had—in the non sequitur of the century—bequeathed him a goddamn company, thereby propelling Will from the manager of one to the agent of dozens.

Because I am. I'm listening, and it's turning my stomach. And I'm dead, *Will. It's hard to turn a dead guy's stomach.*

Will would take that one on faith.

James is a lucky bastard, no question, but that's not why he's got a pretty girl in his bed and you don't.

I know why I don't have a girl in my bed, Bob.

Will wondered vaguely when he'd starting talking back to the voices in his head. Wondered if it was a sign of an imminent mental breakdown or if he was just indulging in talk therapy for the terminally introverted.

Your bed's cold and empty because you're an asshole, Will.

I know, Bob. Thanks for the news flash. Now shut it, will you?

Bob shut it. Will sent up a brief prayer for his sanity. He wasn't the praying sort but figured it couldn't hurt. Chatting with a dead guy, Jesus.

Then he shoved the Bob situation aside so he could seize control of the rapidly devolving Bel-and-James situation in front of him. Because this was a business meeting, damn it, and James was canoodling. There was no canoodling in business.

"Bel, come on. Minnesota? If this is a go, I want to get an exclusive lock on this Redemption Dairy guy before somebody else tastes that butter."

Bel studied him with those shrewd dark eyes of hers, then turned her face up to James. "You know," she said slowly, "it might not be a bad idea to take a little time apart."

"Time apart?" James scowled down at her. "You just got back, Bel! You've barely been home a month."

"Which means we've known each other a grand total of, what, four months?" She gave him a brave smile that Will didn't quite care for. James looked positively alarmed. "Take out the three weeks I spent playing personal assistant when Bob was sick and, well, it's kind of soon to live together, don't you think? Maybe a little space—"

"Oh, for the love of Pete." James sighed, snagged her wrist and yanked her in for—yikes. Will blinked. For a kiss that didn't exactly leave anything to the imagination. Cripes, they were canoodling again.

"Come on, you guys." Will cleared his throat awkwardly. "A decision on Minnesota? Please?"

"For God's sake, Bel." James drew back to rub a gentle thumb over her cheekbone and Will had to look away from the tenderness in that little gesture. He started to ignore the jagged surge of bitterness that came with it, too, but forced himself to look at it instead. Forced himself to own it.

James was right. He *was* jealous, and of his own brother. Not because of Bel, though. Will liked Bel just fine but had no desire to repeat the one disastrous kiss he'd pressed on her a few months back during a particularly egregious episode of poor decision making. No, if he was jealous, it was of James' easy, open affection. Of that affection being received without surprise or suspicion, and by a woman with impeccable judgment and the highest of standards. Will was jealous of *that*.

Good boy, Bob said.

"Haven't you heard a word I've said to you since Thanksgiving?" James asked Bel. "*I don't want space.* I hate space. I want you. Every day. Always. In my house, in my bed, in my heart."

"For crying out loud," Will said. "I'm still standing right here." Was that desperation in his voice? Very likely. "Where I can hear you."

James ignored him handily. "You're my family, Bel. The only thing missing is the ring, and I'm tired of carrying it around anyway, so—"

"Oh my God," Will said, alarm snuffing out jealousy in a sudden rush. James was happy, and Will was happy for him. Truly. But there was a limit to what Fate could ask of a guy. Wasn't there? "You're going to do this now?"

Bel said, "Ring?"

James shoved a hand into his pocket, came up with a pretty velvet box and held it out to her. "Ring." He looked a little sick, Will noted faintly. That made him feel better. Marginally. "For you."

She reached for the box and set it on the flat of her hand, unopened. "What, um—" She looked a little faint herself. "What kind of ring?"

"What do you mean, what kind of ring? It's a diamond solitaire, Belinda." He scowled at her. She gazed back, eyes huge. "It's an I-love-you-for-the-rest-of-my-life ring. An I-might-barf-if-you-don't-put-it-on-soon ring. It's a *marry me* ring, okay? Is that clear enough for you?"

Bel launched herself into his arms while he was still scowling, and kissed him with an open-mouthed enthusiasm that had Will spinning hastily away from them.

"You know what? We can talk about Minnesota later. I'm just going to—" They didn't hear him. He didn't care. He located the exit and punched through it with a sigh of relief.

And mowed down Audrey Bing in the hallway.

He stood there like a complete fool and watched her go down in a glorious swirl of moonlight hair and movie-star curves. She landed on her world-class rump in the hall, and stared up at him, her violet eyes wide and startled. Then they narrowed with dislike. Her beauty was, as usual, a short-armed punch to the solar plexus and Will's mouth went desert-dry.

Unfortunately, it didn't go silent.

"Hey, Audrey." He heard his own voice with a sort of horrified surprise. "Fancy running into you here."

There was a knowing smirk in his voice, he noted with

a sinking dismay. As if he were subtly accusing her of lurking in hallways in the hopes that she might accidentally-on-purpose plaster herself up against him.

It was an automatic thing at this point, he knew. Some kind of knee-jerk defense mechanism that his desperate nervous system had dreamed up to neutralize the disabling blast of sexual awareness that Audrey Bing always wrenched from him. To an extent, it worked. She hated him, deeply and truly. And only a self-destructive ass would make a move—a doomed move—on a woman who'd rather see his head on a pike than his hand on her knee.

Good thing you're not a self-destructive ass, Bob said. *Oh, wait...*

She gazed up at him, and he was suddenly and viciously aware of how he must look to her. The sharp elbows. The skinny chest. The Adam's apple ratcheting up and down his pencil-neck while he groped for even an ounce of the sunny charm or easy coordination that came so naturally to his brothers. While all that groping came up empty. Again.

Rage flared to life inside him, familiar and fierce, urging him toward war. Toward bloodshed. Toward making those eyes look elsewhere. If he couldn't be admired, at least he wouldn't be pitied.

Easy there, cowboy. Bob's voice inside his head was both weary and amused. *Maybe we could wait for a warning shot across the bow or something before we fire the cannons.*

Right. Will swallowed with a small click and wished with all his blackened heart for a drink. When none materialized—it never did—he pulled a slow hand down his face and pushed the reset button on his temper.

"Jesus, Audrey, I'm sorry." He held out a hand to the woman still sprawled at his feet. "Are you all right?"

"I'm fine." She ignored his hand and rose with a fluid grace that made his blood beat in his ears. She brushed off her jeans, and he waited for the scorched-earth special of her glare. It didn't come. In fact, she didn't meet his eyes at all.

"You don't look fine."

"Nice. Thanks, Will." But she still didn't meet his eyes.

He leaned in, frowning. "What's wrong, Audrey?"

"Nothing." She folded her arms and brought her eyes deliberately to his. Will braced himself for the crazy-ass thrill ride of spills and chills and fuck-the-hell-out-of-you that summed up eye contact with Audrey Bing. He got nothing but a whole bunch of remote politesse, and it landed in his stomach with a hollow shock. He might actually prefer the fuck you. "I just need to run something past James. He in there?" She nodded toward the kitchen set.

"Yeah, but—"

She walked off while he was still talking. Walked? Hell, she practically ran but he didn't stop her. He just stood there and watched those small brave shoulders until they disappeared behind the kitchen set's heavy, sound-proofed door. It whispered shut, him on one side, Audrey and her mysteries on the other.

Mysteries that she clearly wanted to keep to herself. But unfortunately for Audrey, Will didn't tolerate mystery well. Or, you know, at all. That was just the price you paid for a photographic memory and a genius level IQ. That and getting your ass handed to you on the playground every day of your childhood.

Good idea, Bob said. *Let's make this about you.*

It was a point.

Plus? Screw mysteries. That girl's got a problem, Will. And you owe her a solution.

Will didn't argue. There was no question on that score. He'd damaged Audrey Bing, deliberately and often. It hadn't been personal, though he doubted that counted for much. His life had simply become an untenable shit hole of bitterness and regret, the only solution to which was total destruction. So he'd built his bombs, laid his charges and looked around for a handy trigger. Audrey had been the unlucky soul he'd spotted first.

He'd turned things around recently—thanks be to Bob—but Audrey had been understandably resistant to any attempt at making amends. At this point, all she wanted from Will was a solid twenty-yard perimeter. And Will, given his unruly fantasy life, was only too happy to oblige.

At least he had been.

But that was about to end, because Audrey Bing did have a problem. He knew it, even if he didn't know *how* he knew it. And Will owed her a solution. He owed her a hell of a lot more than that, honestly, but if a solution was what she needed, a solution was what she'd have.

And he'd be damned if she got it from his brother.

His stomach clenched like a hot fist at the very idea, but he decided not to examine the whys of that situation too closely.

Coward, Bob said.

Straight up. Will knew his strengths. Fighting, yes. Ruthlessness, absolutely. Name that emotion? Not so much. But this wasn't a complicated scenario, nor did it require much thought. Bottom line? He was sick of breaking shit. And he was sick to death of wandering endlessly through the wreckage of the shit he'd broken. He was ready to *fix* something. And he was going to start with Audrey Bing.

Whether she cooperated or not.

Chapter 3

Audrey Bing put the door between her and Will with a sigh of relief, but panic still pitched and twisted inside her. Because what the *hell* had just happened out there? Will had been treating Audrey like his own personal no-fly-zone for months now. Months! And suddenly, today, when her life was collapsing like the Hindenburg, he decided to get chatty?

This, she realized darkly, was no accident. This was Will. He'd probably smelled the disaster on her from half a mile off, and that big brain of his had come to point like a blood hound. Now he'd hammer away at her without mercy—*what's wrong, Audrey? What are you not telling me, Audrey? Why do you look like hell, Audrey?*—until she finally just put a nice shiny bow on her family dysfunction and handed it over. Along with her privacy, her autonomy and possibly her liberty, depending on how strictly Will planned to interpret the law.

She wondered if she could avoid him for the next few hours. She'd been doing it for months now; surely she could manage a few more hours. Just long enough to put her emergency exit plan in motion.

Which meant she needed to find James and Bel. Now. So she could lie to them.

And if that thought put a hard knot of regret in her stomach, she wasn't going to worry about it now. There would be time to mourn later for trashing the trust of her almost-friends. When Jillian was safe.

She squinted toward the brilliantly lit kitchen set in front of her. No Bel or James there, damn it. She peered into the shadows around it but after the nuclear-bright glow of the set lights it was like trying to see through tar. She closed her tired eyes to speed up the adjustment, and God it felt good. Jillian had screamed the house down twice last night. At some point, Audrey had given up on her own bed and just crawled in with Jillian. And was reminded every twenty minutes or so that, for a smaller-than-average second grader, the kid had a damn impressive donkey kick. Audrey had reflected on this unhappy fact until dawn, at which point she'd abandoned sleep for the charms of caffeine.

And happiness. Stupid, stupid happiness.

She peeled open her gritty eyes before she dozed off and searched the darkness again. This time, she found them. Bel and James were deep in the shadows beside one of the deserted cameras. They were—

Oh boy. They were wrapped around one another like wisteria vines. Lots of hands and tongues and...whoa. That was one hell of a sparkler on Bel's ring finger.

In spite of everything, satisfaction tugged deep inside her. Bel and James were the PB and J of couples as far as Audrey was concerned. They just went together and it was about time James made it official. Crashing their engagement after-glow with her crisis *du jour*? Not going to happen.

Time for Plan B, then. Time to develop a Plan B, certainly. She'd get right on that.

Audrey silently reversed out the door she'd just come through, praying like hell that Will had taken the hint and moved along.

But no, of course not. There he was waiting for her, all tall and angular, arms crossed over his chest, pale eyes shrewd, one fair brow arched knowingly, just like always. And something inside her yearned, just like always.

Stupid, she told herself. *So stupid*. Like this was really the time to indulge her libido's favorite wild card? But she'd always had a thing for brains, and Will had them to spare. His mind was some kind of high-performance engine, and the sight of it spinning behind those pale, watchful eyes staggered her every single time. Even when he was being reprehensible. So she tried not to look too often. It wasn't healthy, this weird fascination. And it damn sure wasn't safe.

Even poisonous snakes were pretty, she reminded herself. That didn't mean you ought to touch one. So she forced herself to look away, and focused somewhere over his left shoulder instead.

"Hey, Audrey." His voice was low and careful, like she was a bird and he was worried she'd fly away.

"Hey, Will." She clamped down on a weary sigh. *Now* he was careful with her, when it was far, far too late. The universe just couldn't throw her a bone, could it?

"You find James?"

"Yep." She glanced back at the door. "Bel, too. They were...otherwise occupied."

"Still?" Those thin, elegant lips of his curved ever so slightly upward, and she stared, dumbfounded. He was smiling. William Blake, the bitterest of bitter men, was smiling. Reluctantly, yes. Faintly, to be sure. But also...tenderly? Like he'd suddenly developed a soft spot for romance? What the hell? "Could be a while before you get any face time with either of them."

"Looked that way." She shrugged and tucked her shoulder so she could edge past him. "I'll catch them later."

"Audrey."

She froze, automatically obeying the command in that low voice. He wasn't a yeller, Will. He rarely raised his voice beyond the mildly pissed range. But something about him made people pay attention. Or maybe it was just her. Who knew? She didn't risk eye contact but said, "What?"

"Let's just say that James and Bel are off the grid for a while, okay?"

She shrugged. "Fine." She tried again to scoot around him but he caught her elbow.

"For pity's sake, Audrey. Will you stop a minute?"

She stiffened in an electrified rush. Even through her bulky sweater, his touch sizzled. His palm was wide and warm and ridiculously alive, and the feel of it on her sleeve sizzled straight up her arm to fry her neocortex. She sucked in one startled breath, held it for a moment, then let it out. Slowly. She pivoted on one heel and dropped her eyes deliberately to his hand before bringing them back up to his face. He popped open his fingers like she'd singed him. He eased back, palms up and open. Harmless, see?

Harmless, her ass. He'd done her more harm in the past six months than anybody had since her parents. And half of it was her own stupid, self-destructive fault for caring.

"What?" she asked with icy calm. "What do you *want*, Will?"

"For you to stand still for two damn seconds. That'd be a nice start."

"Why? So you can take aim again?"

He took a moment to absorb the blow, and regret twisted in her stomach. She'd never worn cruelty with any ease.

"No, Audrey," he said quietly. "I know I earned that, but no."

"What, then?" She folded her arms over the ache in her gut and forced herself to meet his eyes with steady contempt. "You're sober? You're sorry? We've been around those bases a couple times already, and I think I've made my position pretty clear. I don't actually care what you are, Will. I just want you to leave me alone so I can do my job. Which doesn't seem like a whole lot to ask, considering. So if you don't mind, I'm just going to—"

"It's not a lot to ask, no." He sighed and pinched the bridge of his nose. His *prodigious* nose, she noted with satisfaction. Guy had a schnoz. It didn't fix anything but it proved there was *some* balance in the universe. He had bushel baskets of brains and all the money in the world but at least he wasn't pretty. "At least it *wasn't* a lot to ask." He dropped his hand and gave her a level look. "It is now."

Nerves jittered into her stomach. "Now?"

"We're not ever going to be friends, Audrey. Believe me, I know that." He smiled, a harsh twist of sardonic amusement that looked way more at home on his face than the tenderness. "I like a stretch goal as much as the next guy but I'm not delusional." He frowned. "I don't think." He gave that a moment's consideration, then shrugged it off. "But *you* might be if you think you're walking out of here without spilling whatever the hell is making you look like—" He stopped and circled a finger toward her face. "—that."

She looked away. "Lovely. Gosh, Will, this has been so much fun. I don't know why we don't chat more often."

"I do." He smiled grimly. "It's because you hate me, and you have every right. But you're part of our family now, so—"

She dismissed that with a soft huff. "I'm the housekeeper."

"House manager. And you live in. It makes a difference."

"How so?"

He waved a hand toward the house next door where they all lived. "The Annex? Blake Brother Central?" he said. "It's your home now. And anybody who lives under our roof is ours. Which means that *you*, Audrey, are...ours."

"Yours." She didn't make it a question, but the skepticism came through loud and clear.

"My brothers'," he clarified. "And, yes, mine. You and Jillian both. Sorry." He gave a shrug that didn't look remotely apologetic. "It was in the fine print."

She arched a brow. "What fine print?"

"Check your employment contract. I amended it when you and Jillian asked to live in."

She rolled her eyes but it occurred to her suddenly that Will *had* written the contract she'd signed. He wrote every contract that pertained to James in any possible way. How thoroughly had she read that thing? It was entirely possible that he'd slid something in there she hadn't caught. Even something as ridiculous as extending the definition of family to include the help.

He spread smug hands. "You are—as per said contract—now covered by the Blake Family Credo."

"Family first," she murmured, unwillingly fascinated by the direction this conversation was taking. An ember kicked to life inside her, small and warm. What would it be like to let somebody take care of her? To have somebody who wanted to even try?

"Precisely." He didn't even attempt a smile. Family was

19

deadly serious business to the Blake brothers, Audrey knew. To each and every one of them. "What we have we share, Audrey." He eased closer as he quoted the Blake brothers' battle cry, his voice low and implacable. "Your fight is our fight now. So why don't you lay it on me?"

She gave herself half a second to indulge in a rose-tinted daydream in which Will suddenly found his humanity, lost his razor-sharp edges and slayed all her dragons. Then she reminded herself that this was *Will* and pulled herself together.

"Yeah, I don't think so." She backed up a step and bonked gracefully into the wall. Eyed the door and adjusted her trajectory. Because she was getting the hell out of here. Will couldn't solve this one. She doubted anybody could. So she'd be damned if she'd hang out her dirty sheets for his inspection. A girl could only be expected to lie down for so much. "This is one fight you're not getting your hands on."

He stepped up and cocked that supercilious brow again. "Ah. So there *is* a fight."

She blinked. Oh, damn. He'd been guessing. Humiliation after humiliation. Her cheeks burned, and she cursed her English ancestors and their rainy-climate complexions. "I have to go." She gave up on subtle and bolted for the door. For escape.

He bird-dogged her all the way to the foyer. "Damn it, Audrey, let me help you. If not for your sake, then at least for James'." She snatched up her coat while he put his back against the door, leaned there and watched her with those *eyes*. Cripes. "No? How about for Bel's sake?" She ignored him and jammed an arm into a sleeve. "No? Not even for them?" He gave a sharp laugh. "For the love of sweet tea, Audrey, get over yourself. Find your compassion, why don't you?"

She paused, startled. "My *compassion*?"

"James and Bel are happy. They worked like hell to get there and I didn't help. At all."

"No kidding."

"But they did it. They're happy and they've earned it. Don't we who love them owe them the chance to bask in the glow a little?"

She scowled and groped vainly for her other sleeve. "Of course we do. That's why I'm going to figure this out myself."

"I believe you. Only—"

"Only what?"

He tipped his head and studied her while she continued to stab blindly behind her for her damn sleeve. "You're no whiner, Audrey. You're not one to run for help unless you need it."

She spotted the trap he was building and scowled harder even as she admired it. Because what was she going to do, argue? *No, actually I* am *a self-indulgent crybaby who likes other people to solve her problems.* Right. She continued silently flailing at that elusive sleeve.

"You wouldn't be here if this was something you could take care of yourself." He made an impatient noise and came off the door to hold her coat. She finally—thank you, Jesus—located the other sleeve hole and shoved her arm into it. "So I'm forced to conclude that you have a serious problem on your hands, Audrey. You need help."

He lifted the puffy down jacket up over her shoulders and for one airless moment, she thought he might slip his hands under her hair and free it from her collar. Her lips went numb and she hung there in an electric panic. But he only lifted his hands again—open and harmless, see?—and put himself back against the door. She blinked stupidly at him for three solid heartbeats.

"And I get that you don't want that help to come from me," he said quietly. "But it doesn't have to be personal. Why not think of it as doing James a solid? Letting somebody else deal with whatever it is his staff requires so that he can mack on his future bride without imperiling the clockwork-like function of his household?"

She took a moment to pick her way down the garden path of all that vocab then dredged up a derisive smirk. "Mack on?"

"When there's such a perfect phrase to describe a situation, it's a crime to go generic." He shrugged. "I like precision. So sue me."

"Precision." Ah, hell. Will didn't do charm. She knew that. Appreciated it, even. Will was smart and sharp and dangerous, yes, but he had no game. No patter. He did, however, have a tremendous vocabulary and she was such a sucker for the well-chosen word. "Right."

"So what do you say?" He offered her a winsome smile and Audrey was struck by how badly it sat on that face of his. Most folks got personalities; Will had gotten a handful of razor blades. Watching him take persuasion out for a spin? Pure fascination. "How about letting me tackle this one? For James?"

Chapter 4

For one treacherous moment, she was tempted. She was so tired. She just wanted to lay this whole mess at the feet of somebody stronger, smarter and meaner than she was. She was so damn tired of running, of hiding, of trying and failing. If Will could fix this, why *shouldn't* she let him?

Oh, right. She remembered now. Because those razor blades of his worked just as well *on* her as *for* her.

"No." She jammed her zipper together and dragged the pull up to her chin. And she yanked her hair free of her collar herself. "Not a chance in hell so just drop it, okay? I'll deal with—"

The kitchen door swished open, spilling James and Bel and their tangible, sunshiny happiness into the hallway. Damn, they all but glowed, and it wasn't just because of Bel's new sparkler or the beard burn on her throat.

They stopped four steps out, as abruptly as if they'd smelled the conflict smoking between Audrey and Will.

"What?" Bel asked, her dark brows winging down, her face downshifting in a split second from happy-happy to no-bullshit-and-don't-even-try. "Deal with what?"

"Ah—" Audrey shot Will a look that said *don't you dare*.

He said, "Audrey's got a fire, and she's trying to stamp it out alone." She glared at him and he shrugged. "What? You do. You are."

"Because it's *my* fire, and not even a very big one." She shoved her hands into her pockets and lifted her eyes to the ceiling. It was easier to lie if she didn't have to look him in the eye. "Not that it's any of your business."

James shook his head sadly. "Now, Audrey, that's not the Blake brothers' way."

23

"Yeah, about that. I'm not sure you've noticed but I'm not actually a Blake." She threw her arms to the sides, inviting a good look. "Or a brother."

"Hard to miss," Will muttered but his eyes skittered away from her.

"Doesn't matter." James patted her shoulder fondly. "You're ours now, hon. Your fight is our fight."

"No, it's not." Audrey stepped back, panic simmering inside her. "Seriously, it's—"

"Oh, honey, save your breath." Bel arrived at Audrey's other shoulder and gave her arm a bracing squeeze. "It's in the contract."

Audrey looked from one face to the other, and saw nothing but a whole lot of implacable wearing friendly clothes. She shoved her hands deeper into her pockets and pushed back against a sudden and mortifying tightness in her throat. "Why does everybody know about this contract but me?"

James gave her that sunny grin of his. "Don't feel bad. You were unaware of the bone-deep nature of Will's sneakiness at the time of signing. It's one of his more endearing qualities." He paused, cleared his throat. "Once he's, ah, on your team, anyway."

She closed her eyes, rubbed her pounding temples and tried to put the words *endearing* and *Will* in the same mental sentence. She stopped before her head exploded. Or the temptation to take a nap overwhelmed her. She dragged both hands down her face and bore up under the ugly weight of defeat.

"Come on, Audrey." Will's voice was right there in front of her, just on the other side of her closed lids. Low, rough, a little stern. "It's time. Hand it over."

She opened her eyes and looked at him. Just looked. His back was still against the door, one big hand on the knob like it was his choice whether she came or went. His mouth was a thin, determined line under that aggressive nose, his eyes pale and serious and stubborn. This man was not moving. And she was flanked by his foot soldiers, one on each shoulder. Outgunned, out maneuvered, out of options.

Damn, damn, damn.

Audrey looked away and let the silence spin out. She didn't think she could speak, and had nothing particularly useful to say anyway.

Finally Bel said, "Okay, family meeting. Annex kitchen. Ten minutes?"

"Good by me," James said.

"Fine," Will said. "Audrey?"

She didn't look up. She kept her head bent and her eyes on her boots until she was sure she'd swallowed back any trace of the tears and fury clogging her throat.

"Ten minutes," she said but didn't meet his eyes. Wasn't sure she could without screaming. "Let me just make sure Jillian's still okay with Drew."

"If by *okay* you mean happily judging his cheese consumption, she's good," Will said. "Golden, actually."

Audrey ignored this. She had ten minutes to salvage her great escape, and she wasn't going to waste even one of them chatting.

"I'll go put on the tea kettle," Bel said.

"And the coffee pot?" James said hopefully.

Bel wrinkled her nose. "Only because I love you."

"Cookies?"

"What do you take me for, a savage?" She frowned at him. "Who has a family meeting without cookies?"

"Right." James relaxed. "Sorry."

Will gazed at Audrey for a long searching moment. Then he twisted the knob and opened the door for her. Finally.

"Ten minutes," he said.

She nodded shortly and stalked out.

Chapter 5

She cut through the massive garden that James had planted earlier that fall between the Annex and Hunt House. He'd reunited the two yards, restoring the estate to its originally intended glory and winning Bel's heart all in one grand gesture. Audrey loved every inch of these gardens and yet avoided them when she could. Because every time she set foot to one of those winding paths, she lost half an hour at a bare minimum daydreaming about hollyhocks and kitchen gardens.

It wasn't a problem today. Today she simply steamed through the arbor and its curtain of skeletal grape vines, sidestepped the hedge maze and let herself into the Annex through the glass doors leading into the ballroom. She clipped across the cavernous space, her boots squeaking on the polished floor. She navigated a series of pretty parlors, powered through the *Gone With The Wind* foyer and hit the ridiculous curved staircase at a jog. She took the stairs two at a time, anxiety climbing in her chest with each step.

Which was stupid. She knew that. Jillian was upstairs, safe and sound. Of course she was. Audrey hadn't rushed off to warm up the proverbial get-away car without arranging for supervision, after all. Maybe Drew wasn't the most mature twenty-two-year-old on the planet—Audrey felt positively ancient every time she remembered that they were the same damn age—but when it came to babysitting, Drew had skills. The guy could keep track of an eight-year-old for an hour.

They were probably programming a computer or playing cribbage, Audrey told herself while her pulse thudded in her ears. Or maybe watching that enormous TV—*How It's Made* or *Survivor* or something. She could only hope it wasn't some iteration of the *Real Housewives* franchise. She'd been valiantly introducing the concept of age-appropriate entertainment for months now but Drew wasn't having it.

But even if they were having a trash TV marathon in there, Audrey wasn't going to complain. Because inappropriate supervision was still supervision. Nobody was going to waltz in and snatch the kid away on Drew's watch, not even Audrey's dad.

She hoped.

She hit the upper landing with dread in her throat, and finally just gave in to it. She swung around the carved newel post and sprinted down the hall to a pair of solid-oak double doors. She rapped once, then let herself into the suite of rooms that Bel called the Man-Child Cave.

A massive TV hung blankly on the wall to her right, attached via a mish-mash of cables to every video game console known to man and a few Drew was still Frankensteining together. There was an obscenely huge sectional holding down the center of the room, hugging a square coffee table covered with old newspapers and magazines—mostly *Sports Illustrated,* naturally—anchored by empty beer bottles and old coffee mugs. A loose scrum of sporting equipment, computer guts, and abandoned socks littered the floor. And there, serenely in the middle of it all, sat Jillian.

Audrey's heart squeezed once, hard, then released and overflowed. *Safe.* She gave herself a moment, held onto the knob and let the dizzying rush of relief pass. She clicked the door shut behind her, nudged aside a sneaker of ridiculous proportions and picked her way across the room to her niece, who sat on the couch frowning down at a Scrabble board perched atop a minor mountain of papers between her knees and Drew's. Some kind of computer language covered the pages, Audrey saw, and she wondered vaguely if Jillian could read it. The kid had her issues but lack of brain power wasn't one of them.

"Hey," she said softly, and cupped a palm over the curve of her niece's shiny blond head. The girl's hair was just a shade or two lighter than her own, Audrey knew. It was as straight as rain and as light as air, and the warm silk of it under her palm comforted her.

Jillian didn't answer and Audrey didn't expect her to. Nobody did. Aside from screaming the house down every night, the kid hadn't said a word for months. But she gave Audrey a sweet smile in welcome then went back to frowning at the Scrabble board.

Drew sat across from her, all lanky and tan, his hair a thick sheaf of nut-brown every-which-way while he studied the board. He dragged both hands down his face and looked up. "Audrey, you're here. Thank Christ. This kid—this vicious word shark of a child—is killing me." He scowled at Jillian, who grinned back at him unrepentantly and played all seven of her tiles. Drew leaned in to examine her move. "Oh, nice. Very nice." He splayed his hands and glared up at Audrey. "You see this? You see the mouth on this kid?"

Audrey cocked a brow and tipped her head to see what Jillian had spelled. She grinned. "Used all her tiles, too, for the fifty point bingo."

"That's all you're going to say?" Drew sank back into the cushions and spoke to the ceiling. "Oh, the humanity." He sat up, shot a finger Jillian's way. "Okay, potty mouth. It's one thing to know a word. It's something else to use it properly. I defy you to use that word in a sentence."

Jillian shrugged and picked up the little notepad she had taken to carrying. She scrawled something and showed it to Drew.

"Oh, Christ." He fell back as if shot. "She has context. I need to go bleach my eyeballs." He shoved to his feet and wandered to the mini-fridge in the corner. "Is it too early for a beer?"

"Yes." Audrey held out a hand for the notepad. Jillian passed it over. Audrey winced. "Probably." She looked down at her niece's innocent face. "Where *did* you pick this one up?"

The kid's deep blue eyes moved to Drew and back again. Audrey snorted.

"He said *that*? Out loud?"

Jillian pointed toward an e-reader tucked carelessly into the couch cushions, one of Drew's many.

"Right." She blew out a breath. "Drew?" She picked up the e-reader and waggled it. He abandoned the beer fridge and came back to fire up the tablet.

"Hmm. Oh. Heh. Whoops." He worked the touch screen with quick competence, then offered Audrey a sheepish grin and handed the reader back. "All kid friendly again. And as a gesture of my deepest regret, I just downloaded Tolkien's entire oeuvre for her. Dwarves, yes. Orcs, sure. Profanity, no." He slid Jillian the side eye. "Unless you're fluent in Orcish. Are you?"

She shook her head solemnly.

"Do you plan to be by dinner?"

She shrugged.

Drew turned appealing eyes on Audrey. "What can you do?"

She gave a huff of laughter and pressed her fingers to her weary eyes. What *could* she do? Learn Orcish to keep up? She'd never read Tolkien. She leaned more toward science fiction than fantasy, and her efforts to stay ahead of Jillian's reading in that category had stalled out on *Harry Potter*. God, she was out of her league with this kid. And at eight years old! What the hell was she going to do with her at twelve? Or—God help her—sixteen?

Fear slid up inside her, not the bright panic of moments ago but a dark slick of sullen menace. Future failure looming. Nice. But she put on a smile and fluffed Jillian's hair. "Drown her in Tolkien, I guess." She put the e-reader in her niece's eager hands.

"Death by Tolkien!" Drew picked up a pillow and mashed it into Jillian's face. She obligingly rolled off the couch and onto the floor in a dramatic pile of skinny arms and legs. Drew dusted his hands. "Excellent. I do love vanquishing the enemy by noon."

Jillian sat up and cast a significant glance at the Scrabble board.

"A knife-twister." Drew put a hand to his heart, pained. "You're raising a word shark and a knife-twister." He shook his head sadly. "It's a shame how this kid is turning out. I'd consider trading her in if I were you."

Audrey's heart gave a worried bump inside her and she glanced quickly at Jillian to see how she was taking Drew's brand of affection. The kid all but glowed, her hair a shiny ball of static cling floating around her delicate face.

Audrey murmured, "I think I've got all the performance I can manage from the current model."

"Well, something to think about." Drew clapped his hands cheerfully, putting paid to that conversational gambit. Then those dancing brown eyes narrowed on her face and his brows shot up. "So. What's doing?"

"Family meeting," she said. "Kitchen."

"Now?"

"Yeah."

He tipped his head toward the couch. "Midgets included?"

"Nope. Grownups only."

Jillian looked up sharply, and Audrey's heart broke at the quick flare of anxiety in those huge blue eyes so like her own. Hated that it was so well-founded. She reached out and smoothed down the fly aways, let her knuckles brush the girl's thin cheek. "Nothing to worry about, Jilly bean. Just boring grownup stuff." She smiled while she lied. "You just concentrate on learning to swear in Elvish."

"Orcish," Drew said.

"Does it matter?"

Drew and Jillian exchanged a speaking glance. Evidently it did.

"Orcish, then." Audrey resisted the urge to rub her eyes again. "Just please stay here until Bel or I or one of the guys comes for you, okay? If you need us, text Drew. You know how?" She handed over her cell phone. Jillian pulled up the text message app and turned the screen to show that she'd cued up Drew's contact info. "Good. Stay here?"

Jillian—already back at Tolkien—nodded vaguely, the phone glowing beside her knee.

Audrey wanted to touch that shiny head one more time but stuffed her hands in her pockets instead. She looked up to find Drew's eyes on her, friendly and sharper than anybody ever expected.

"Ready?" he asked.

"As I'll ever be."

"Sometimes that's all you get."

She sighed. "Tell me about it."

Chapter 6

Will took a cookie he didn't want from the pretty basket Bel had placed in the center of the Annex kitchen's island counter. He set it on one of the pretty napkins she'd dealt out along with steaming mugs of coffee. Whatever was in her own mug smelled like boiled orange rinds but Will didn't judge. He'd spent five years pouring copious amounts of scotch down his throat and making an ass of himself. If Bel wanted to boil the compost and drink it, who was he to object?

At least your poison was top shelf, Bob said wistfully. *I miss scotch.*

Yep, Will thought. *Me, too.* Figured he always would so he just let himself miss it and watched the door like a faithful retriever. He was rewarded within moments when it swung open and delivered Audrey into the kitchen, Drew on her heels.

He stood automatically. James' brows popped up and Drew grinned openly. Even Bel blinked. Audrey just took the stool he offered her like the sight of Will minding his manners made no impression at all. She propped her elbows on the cool granite counter, and Bel slid a mug of coffee between them. Audrey wrapped slim hands around the mug and inhaled the steam with weary desperation.

"Yikes," Drew said. He hooked the cookie basket with a finger and put it under her nose. "Somebody needs a cookie."

Will eased back down onto the stool beside Audrey's and frowned at her bent head. She appeared to be attempting to absorb the caffeine via her lungs, as if she didn't have the energy required to drink it. The last of his doubts disappeared. This girl needed help, and fast. Because

Audrey's energy was epic. Fierce. Unstoppable. It swirled around her like an invisible ocean, its waves lapping at the beach of his brain until he heard her in his dreams. Sometimes he even heard her when he was awake.

"You look like hell," he blurted.

Nice, Bob said. *Good start.*

Then again, he heard a lot of weird things these days. He spared a moment to wonder exactly how abnormal this might be, then put it on the back shelf of his brain to worry about later. Because Audrey really did look like hell. No easy feat given her breath-stealing, mind-shattering beauty.

"Gosh, thanks, Will." She ignored the cookie basket and lifted the coffee with hands so thin he could see each individual tendon flexing and releasing. He nudged his own cookie toward her. She ignored that, too.

Drew gave Will a disgusted look behind Audrey's back and patted her shoulder. "Hey, so catch me up, huh? Jillian was spanking me at Scrabble while Chapter One of whatever this is was going down."

James shook his head. "For Pete's sake, Drew. I told you not to play Scrabble with that kid anymore. Her vocabulary is—" He broke off for a contemplative bite of cookie. "Well, I don't actually know a word that fully describes her vocabulary."

"Which is why she spanks you at Scrabble, too," Will pointed out. "You could try reading a book every once in a while."

James sniffed. "I read."

"The sports section doesn't count."

"Of course it does."

Will turned to Drew. "And you! Getting spanked by an eight-year-old, cripes."

"What?" Drew polished off cookie number three and— evidently just warming up—reached for number four. "I read all the time."

"Porn doesn't count, either."

He snapped off half the cookie in one bite. "I prefer the term *erotica*. I like a good storyline to go with my smut."

Will made a skeptical noise.

"And that's not *all* I read." He popped in the other half and swallowed heroically. "I just downloaded the entire collected works of Tolkien, I'll have you know."

Will narrowed his eyes. "For Jillian, I'll bet."

"Well, sure." Drew smiled sunnily. "But that doesn't mean I won't enjoy it, too. We're going to learn to swear in Orcish."

Will frowned at Audrey. "Drew's not in charge of homeschooling, is he? I mean, you're on top of that, right?"

Audrey barked out a laugh. "Yeah, I've got that tiger by the tail, all right." She pressed thin fingers to her brows and Will met Drew's worried eyes over her head. Okay, enough stalling. Time to pry this story loose. He opened his mouth to get the party started—somebody had to—but Bob said, *Not you. Anybody but you.*

Will snapped his mouth shut. Right. Right, because it was spill-your-guts time, and she wasn't going to like that. But she'd truly hate it if he was the one who pulled her cork. And hate him for it. Hate him *more*, if such a thing was even possible. He shot a look at James—his house, his employee, plus he was the one she'd been after from the get go. James should open this can of worms.

James took the cue, bless him. Bel's elbow in his kidney probably helped. Will smiled at her, faintly, but her subtle eye-roll said she caught it.

"Okay, Audrey," James said. "Let's have it. You're under our roof, and under our protection. Anything we can do for you, we'll do. But you have to tell us what's going on."

Audrey blew out a breath and lowered her hands. Slender, white and helpless, they lay on the counter like abandoned evening gloves. "Thank you," she said finally. "That means a lot to me. Honestly, though, all I really need is a couple days off to deal with a little family situation." She gave James and Bel a rueful smile. "I hate to even ask. You've cut me so much slack already." She looked at her fingers. "You gave me a job when I demanded one, you didn't peep when I asked to live in. You didn't so much as give me the side eye when I brought Jillian into the mix."

She lifted her shoulders. "I know it's a big ask but if you can spare me for two days—three, tops—I think I can straighten this thing out." Her fingers twisted together on top of the granite, knotted there until Will wondered why they didn't just snap off.

"Those weren't favors to you," he said abruptly. "The job, the slack, whatever. Those were favors to me." Audrey didn't look at him. But she didn't tell him to put a sock in it either, so Will went on. "Anything James gave you was to replace something that I took from you. You don't owe anybody anything. That's my debt to pay, not yours."

She ignored him. "Two days," she said again to James. "Three, tops. If I can just have—"

Will said, "No."

"What?" This time her head did snap around, and she stared at him, her eyes full of vivid dislike and just a touch of...was that guilt?

"I said no." Will's voice was stronger this time. He'd taken himself by surprise the first time he'd spoken. That *no* had zipped straight from his gut to his mouth, bypassing his brain entirely. But this one he had time to consider, had time to taste, and it tasted right. "You're not asking for time off," he said slowly, feeling his way. "You're leaving. You're running. You're taking Jillian and you're getting the hell out of here, aren't you?"

Now they were all staring at him. Audrey recovered first. He had to hand it to her; the girl could take a punch. Her mouth snapped shut, then her eyes cut down and to the side. When they came back to his, they were all sneering bravado.

"That's ridiculous," she said. "I don't know what you're even—"

He cut her off. "And this two—maybe three—days? That's your head start. That's giving yourself a window to get gone before anybody thinks to look for you."

"Good heavens, Will." She chuckled, but patches of color blazed on her cheekbones. "Don't be—"

"Don't lie to me." Anger growled low inside him and he clamped down on it. "I know running when I see it. But I'm confused here, Audrey, because you're not the run-and-hide type." He tipped his head and narrowed his eyes, considering her. "You don't go looking for the fight, no, but when one comes to your front door, you don't hide in the cellar, either. Not you. No, you're all dukes up, chin out, fuck all y'all and let's do this thing. It's one of my favorite things about you."

Her eyes flew wide for one startled instant, then she scoffed. "Oh, please. Like you know me or something? Like we're BFFs? You don't know me, Will. You don't know the first thing—"

"I know enough." He smiled wryly. "I know you pack one hell of a punch and I know you hit what you aim at."

She lifted her chin, all offended hauteur. "I've never punched anybody in my life."

"Laid me out easily enough."

"That's true, actually," Drew mused. "And it was a pleasure to watch. Both times."

"I count three," James said.

"She's got two-point-five according to my tally," Will said, his eyes never leaving hers.

"Well, hell. I missed one?" Drew leaned back, frowning.

"Just a half," Will said.

"Huh." Drew said, "Okay, so there was that first time, when Audrey was waitressing that fancy party we had to go to back in the fall, remember? Bel's first day on the job?"

"That was my favorite," James said fondly. "Our boy Will went after poor Audrey for blowing off your advances—"

"—my perfectly respectable and well-intentioned advances," Drew put in.

"—and she peeled off his hide in front of God and everybody." James grinned at the memory. "Good times."

"It *was* a thing of beauty," Drew said.

"He got Audrey fired, though," Bel put in. "Not so beautiful."

"But the way she IDed and called out his every character flaw? And in public?" James sighed happily. "Priceless."

"Okay, so that was one." Drew ticked off a finger. "Number two was—"

"—when he destroyed her engagement party." James paused. "And her engagement."

"I'd forgotten that one." Drew frowned. "I was thinking more about the time—"

"—that he laid an unprovoked and unwelcome kiss on my fiancée?" James glowered across all that gleaming granite at Will. "I think about that one sometimes, too. I still owe him a punching."

"Wait, your fiancée?" Drew's brows shot up. Bel wiggled her ring finger across the table, beaming, and Drew bounced to his feet. He rounded the island, snatched Bel off her stool and dipped her foolishly, finishing it up with a smacking kiss on her lips.

"Hey," James said mildly. "That's my future wife."

"Which makes her my future sister," Drew returned. "I get a freebie." He grinned down at Bel. "Thanks, sis."

"Oh. Sister." Bel's eyes went shiny and James leapt up now, too.

"What, first you kiss her then you make her cry? Jesus, Drew! Those are my jobs!" He snatched Bel out of Drew's arms and plopped back onto the stool with her on his lap. She put her arms around his neck and dropped her head to his shoulder.

"Brothers," she whispered. "I hadn't quite gotten that far yet." She lifted her head and beamed across the counter at Will, her huge heart swimming in her eyes. She reached a hand over to him, and he took it. He took a moment to savor the scent of sugar cookies before letting her go. He had no desire for James to remember that he deserved a punching, after all. She gurgled a watery laugh and looked at Audrey. "I have brothers!"

"Yeah." Audrey's smile was beautiful and miserable. "You do."

"Audrey." James' voice was still light, still amiable, but he'd hit the implacable register. They all heard it, and Audrey was no exception. "Spill it. And I want the truth this time."

"Ah, hell." Audrey pushed away her coffee, folded her arms on the counter and lowered her head to them.

And cut loose with a horrifying, gut-wrenching sob.

"Oh, nice." Drew glared at Will. "Nicely done."

"What?" Will shot off his stool, backing away from Audrey like she was a ticking time bomb. Weeping women terrified him. So did children, dogs and roundabouts, all of which operated either outside logic, or to an unfathomable inner logic. Dangerous shit for a guy whose toolbox contained nothing *but* logic. "What did I do?"

"You made her cry!" Drew patted her back gently. "There now, Audrey, don't cry. We'll fix this. Don't take on so."

"I did not make her cry." Will caught himself backpedalling like a naughty kid and forced himself to hold his ground. "James did. I never make her cry. I make her furious and extremely dangerous, verbally speaking. But I do *not* make her cry."

That's true, actually, Bob mused. *Not even at your most asshole-ish. Why is she crying now? Wait,* is *she crying now?*

Will paused, struck. He tipped his head and leaned down toward Audrey's trembling shoulders. Drew all but bared his teeth but Will ignored him. Listened.

"Well for fuck's sake." He plopped back onto his stool, unsure whether he was relieved or pissed. "She's not crying. She's laughing."

Chapter 7

Audrey made an almighty effort to gain control of the ragged laugh/sobs tearing at her throat while Drew continued to pat doggedly at her shoulder. Humiliation slid into her stomach, and twisted gleefully into the hilarity and anguish already going after each other in there like the Jets and the Sharks. Only with less dancing.

"You're such an ass, Will," Drew said above her. "She's totally crying." He paused uncertainly. "Isn't she?"

"You know, I'm actually not sure anymore," Will said above her other shoulder. He paused to give her mortifying braying another beat or two under his mental microscope. "She might be trying to do both at once." She sensed rather than saw his head come down, his ear tipped to better catch the snot-fest going on inside the safe haven of her folded arms. She could picture his face, the vague distaste for her messy display of gear-grinding emotion in the skeptical arch of that damn eyebrow. It gave her the strength she needed to contain the last hysterical bubble rising in her chest. Finally.

After a beat or two of tense silence, he said, "Audrey?"

She didn't lift her head. "Yes?"

"Are you all right?"

"Fine, thank you." She swiped her cheeks on either sleeve then forced herself to sit up and meet his gaze. His eyes were guarded, like he was concerned for her but had one finger on the trigger just in case. Which was sort of his signature emotional state, now that she thought about it. How exhausting. She'd been on her guard for only six months and felt utterly threadbare. What would it be like to tackle your entire life with that kind of constant vigilance? "I don't plan to indulge in any more hysterics, at any rate."

"Is that what we're calling it?" Drew asked.

"Hysterics?"

Audrey shrugged wearily. "Sometimes I have a hard time deciding whether to laugh or cry."

"So you do both?"

"I can't really help it." She fitted her fingers together on the counter in front of her and studied them carefully. "It doesn't happen very often. Certainly not at the kitchen counter. When it can't be avoided, I aim for privacy."

"Good call," Will muttered and renewed humiliation lapped gently at her already-flaming cheeks.

"Geez, Will," James said. "Easy."

"Right. Sorry." Will held up an apologetic hand. "I just meant, if it were me, I'd want to lose it in private, too."

"Who wouldn't?" She gave him a bitter look. "But when have you ever allowed me even an ounce of privacy? In the brief history of our acquaintance, when have you ever left me well enough alone?"

He returned her look with a level one of his own. "Never," he said. "I've never done that, and I know it. I'm sorry for it. I'd like to do it now but I'm not going to. You have to know that."

"Yeah, I do." She sighed, and for one startling moment wondered if she was deflating. Because suddenly all the anger and hurt and energy drained out of her and she slumped, utterly defeated. "God, you're like a dog with a bone."

"That's our boy," James murmured. "We figure God gave him all those teeth for a reason."

"Ever the optimist."

James just smiled. Patiently. Audrey drew in a breath and held it. Waited for a return to width and substance and form. But no, she remained paper-thin and disconcertingly fragile. She gave up, let the breath go.

"Okay, fine. You want the truth? You can have it." She glared at her knotted fingers on the countertop. "Will called it, okay? I was going to run." An actual chill wafted off Will beside her. She ignored it and forced herself to meet James' eyes across the huge expanse of polished granite instead. "I was going to take Jillian and run."

James gazed back at her, his eyes green and warm and calm. Pure sorrow crawled up her throat this time, no laughter involved. She swallowed it down.

"Oh, honey," Bel sighed. She took James' hand and leaned forward. "Why?"

"My dad wants her. Jillian. And I'm not going to give her up. Not to him."

"Is he dangerous?" Will asked. The chill flowing off him intensified suddenly. "Has he hurt her, Audrey? Or you?"

"Oh, God," Bel murmured.

"What? No!" Audrey glanced at him and automatically drew back from the black menace on his face. "Will, no. It's nothing like that." His forearm lay tensed and corded on the counter next to hers, and she touched it without thinking. An aura of violence had descended on him like sundown, and the need to lift it was instinctive. His skin was warm under her touch, shockingly so given all that cold purpose shimmering almost visibly around him. She snatched her hand back hastily. "He's never touched her." Those pale eyes searched hers and she added hastily, "Or me. He's not violent. Not at all."

"Then why are we afraid of him?" Drew asked.

"We're not afraid of him," Audrey said, her gaze flicking back to James. He just watched her, compassion in his eyes, his hand in Bel's. "Not exactly. It's just that, well—" She paused. This was the part she'd never quite figured out how to explain to people. It was why she'd never had a lot of close friends. And dating? Forget it. "He's just not exactly stable."

She looked around the counter and found a palpable *"and...?"* looking back from every face. That, and a whole lot of affectionate concern. The sort you felt for friends in trouble.

Friends. Had she made friends? Dismay tightened her throat. Oh, hell. She had. She'd gone and gotten attached. How on earth had this happened? She hadn't allowed herself to get attached to anybody in years! Nobody but Jillian. Or so she thought. But evidently, she'd just joined Tribe Blake.

Or it had joined her. She wasn't totally sure of anything at the moment, except that her heart felt like it was shredding inside her.

"Not stable?" Drew prompted gently.

"Emotionally speaking," she clarified lamely.

"Are we talking about actual mental illness?" Bel asked.

"Not exactly." Audrey tried an apologetic smile. "It's sort of a long story."

James and Bel exchanged a look. "We've got time," James said.

"Right. Okay." She gave up on the smile and pressed cold fingers to her eyes. Best start at the beginning. "It all comes back to my mom. She was a Whitechurch, see—"

Bel blinked. "Of the Boston Whitechurches?"

"Those are the ones." Audrey met her startled eyes. "And my dad was a plumber."

"A plumber?" James' brows disappeared into his shaggy hair.

Will said, "Well, that's underplaying it a little."

She risked a look his way and found him leaning forward, elbows on the counter, studying his linked fingers absently. But Audrey knew better. Will wasn't absent. Will was listening. He was taking her words and feeding them to the great machine inside his head, where they'd be chewed up, broken down and rearranged in myriad permutations, each one to be assessed with ruthless speed and precision until he'd arrived at some conclusion nobody else would arrive at for days, if not weeks. If ever. Even in the midst of her pain and humiliation, she was fascinated. And, oh hell, envious. Every speck of her own value-added was right there on the surface, no deeper than her bones and the skin stretched over them.

He said, "He might've been a humble plumber once upon a time. But today her dad is Jason Martin Bing, Jr., of the JMB corporation."

"The JMB Corporation." Drew tipped his head like a perplexed dog. "Why do I know that name?"

"It's printed on every faucet and toilet in this house."

"Huh." James glanced toward the sink. "Is it?"

42

Drew got up for a look. "It is." He sat back down. "Why is that?"

"Because, oh, maybe eight or nine years back good ol' JM, Jr.—Jem to his buddies—took out patents for a series of low-flow toilets and faucets that actually work. Revolutionized the market for high-end environmentally friendly construction." Will slanted a look at Audrey. "Rich people have their eco-ethics, sure, but make them choose between the environment and decent water pressure? No contest. So Jem secured his patents, revolutionized the market and took the company public shortly thereafter. Retained a nominal role on the board but essentially retired to sit on his billions and invent shit."

Audrey stared at him. "Why am I surprised that you know this?"

"Hell if I know." He shrugged. "You work here, Audrey. In our house. You think I'd let you move in without performing due diligence?"

"Of course not. I just..." She sighed. "You have a file on me, don't you?"

He said nothing, just returned her look with one of his own.

Drew said, "Can we please get back to the story? Pick it up where the princess ran away with the plumber."

"The princess and the plumber." Audrey gave him a wry smile. "You make it sound like a fairy tale."

Will said, "Somehow I don't think happily ever after is where we're going with this."

"We're not."

"Uh oh." Drew sobered. "What happened?"

"Exactly what you'd expect to happen when the high-maintenance princess runs away with the poor but ambitious plumber."

"True love?"

"Try bitter disappointment." Audrey gave a weary laugh. "I think they did love each other, at least in the beginning. But to Mom, love was being cherished, tended, petted. To Dad, love was having somebody to kiss goodnight after another long, frustrating day of toilet design. Ten years, two kids, and no patents later, Mom gave up on true love and decided she was ill."

"Decided?" Will asked.

"She developed headaches. Terrible ones. I don't know if the pain was physical or psychosomatic, but it hardly matters, does it? She hurt." She shrugged as if her own pain weren't still a hard black knot inside her. "She tried everything, and I mean everything. Pills, IVs, massage, acupuncture, meditation, religion, alternative religion, exorcism—"

Drew gave a short laugh. "Exorcism? Really?"

"Really." Audrey pressed her lips together. "It didn't work."

"Imagine," Will said.

"Nothing worked, of course, because the problem wasn't her head. It was her marriage." She linked her fingers carefully together on top of the counter again. "She wanted—needed—more of her husband than he was giving her. And when Jem wouldn't—or couldn't—pony it up, she tried to *take* it." She paused. "The exorcism was probably one of her more effective attention getters, actually. Jem nearly blew a gasket when he came home to a houseful of chanting priests. I'd never seen Mom so happy."

"Which wasn't, I imagine, lost on good ol' Jem," Will said.

"It wasn't," Audrey told him. "Jem's no dummy. After that, he pretty much washed his hands of the situation."

"And by *the situation*, you mean your mom?" Bel asked.

"Yep. He simply refused to engage after that, and things disintegrated pretty predictably from there. My dad had something else to love but Mom had nothing. Nothing but the disappointment, and I think it poisoned her. She'd never been strong, emotionally speaking." She studied her fingers and kept marching down this well-trodden path. "I was thirteen when she killed herself."

"Oh, Audrey." Bel's voice was thick with pain and sympathy.

"How?" Will asked suddenly, as if the method were as

important as the result. She blinked up at him, startled. Nobody ever probed for details when she told this part of the story. It was indelicate.

"Morphine." It took her a moment to dredge up the word, but that extra moment wedged a small, unexpected space between her and the pain. She filled her lungs for the first time in what felt like minutes and wondered if he'd thrown her off-script on purpose to allow exactly that. "She used morphine." He nodded, apparently satisfied, and she went on. "My dad took it hard. He blamed himself, of course."

James said, "I don't know if I'd go *that* far but—"

"—but it's a fair enough point, I know." Audrey let out a slow breath. "He's been obsessed with her ever since."

"And she's not even around to enjoy it." Drew shook his head. "Ironic."

"Well, that's where things get sticky," Audrey said. "My dad's not actually convinced of that."

"Of what?" Drew goggled. "That your mom's dead?"

"No, she's dead. He knows that." She met his eyes. "He's just not convinced that she's gone."

Chapter 8

"Oh cripes," Will said and palmed his face. "He believes in ghosts, doesn't he?"

So do you, Bob said inside his head. Smugly.

I do not.

So what am I?

The unholy love child of rehab, a high IQ and a shitload of regrets.

Please. Your IQ only wishes it were this high. And you're sober but you're not that sorry.

I am so. I'm extremely sorry.

You're sorry she hates you. You'd do the rest again tomorrow.

Can we please have this conversation later?

Bob laughed. *I'll be here.*

Will figured that for the stone-cold truth, so he pinched the bridge of his nose—hard—and focused on the clarity and simplicity of pain.

"He thinks your mom's spirit is hanging around, doesn't he?" he asked Audrey. "That his neglect drove her to suicide, and now she's punishing him via eternal stalking. And she will until he finds a way to make amends."

"That's the rehab talking," Drew said, *sotto voce* to James and Bel across the table. Like he was a theater patron rather than a participant in the conversation. "When did he ever say shit like *make amends* before rehab?"

"Bingo," Audrey said to Will, and Drew's jaw dropped. "How do you *know* this stuff, anyway?"

Will shrugged uncomfortably while Bob cackled in his head. "Educated guess."

"Well it's bang on target. He still throws a bunch of money at eco-friendly plumbing design, and does more than his fair share of philanthropy, but that's just a smoke screen."

"For what?" Bel asked cautiously.

"Paranormal research," Audrey said. "Any yahoo with a faraday box and a neat proposal can count on a little chunk of change from my dad."

"Faraday box?" This time it was James leaning over to Drew.

"Shielding device," Drew whispered back. "So you can isolate the EVP."

James' brows lifted. "EVP?"

"Electronic voice phenomena." James blinked blankly and Drew sighed. "I'll explain later."

Will ignored them. "And I'll bet every ghost whisperer east of the Mississippi knows about this, don't they?"

Audrey's lips twisted. "Including Hildy Wise."

"Hildy Wise?" Drew's eyes went huge. Evidently this was a name Will should recognize.

He leaned around Audrey to Drew. "You know of her?"

"You don't?" Drew shook his head in wonder. "Dude, do you even *have* the internet? Hildy's awesome. She looks like your regular old middle-aged housewife, right? All tidy hair and sensible shoes. Even wears a little gold cross. But she sees dead people. Or maybe she just talks to them? I don't know. Her thing is *making the bridge*."

"The bridge to what?" Will asked, unwillingly fascinated.

"The Great Beyond."

"Which is?"

"Who knows? Hildy specializes in getting earth-bound spirits across the bridge. She doesn't talk to them once they're over."

"Huh." Will pondered that one for a moment. Wondered if Bob had any interest in whatever lay across the bridge.

Fuck you.

Guess not.

"And this Hildy Wise," Will said to Audrey. "She has her hooks in your dad?"

"Yes." Audrey's face was set, hard. "I didn't realize she was in the picture until I came home this summer."

"From college?" Bel asked.

"Ah, not exactly." Audrey frowned at her fingers. "I graduated in January. I spent the spring doing, um, a secondary program overseas."

"A secondary program?" This sounded suspiciously vague to Will's ear. "What kind of secondary program?"

"Just a certification," Audrey muttered. "It's hardly important right now—"

"A certification to do what?"

Her cheeks pinked but she met his eyes directly enough. "To butle."

"I'm sorry?"

"To butle," she said clearly. "I'm trained as a high-end butler."

Drew laughed delightedly. "You are?"

"I hold a certification from Smythely and Harkis, along with a provisional endorsement from the Guild of British Butlers," she said. "You have a yacht, an estate or a high-rise penthouse, and I can run it for you." She shrugged. "I'm supposed to apprentice under an experienced butler for a year or two before they'll remove the provision from my endorsement. So I came home to look for a placement."

Will stared at her. "You were working at a strip club when we met you."

"As a waitress," Drew said quickly.

"Not as a butler," Will snapped, "that's for damn sure. Because we haven't been rich all that long but if it were possible to hire a butler who'd wear a Dolly Parton wig and a skirt the size of a cocktail napkin, believe me, we'd have had one."

"That's true, actually." Drew eyed her speculatively. "I don't suppose you'd consider—"

"No," she said.

He shrugged. "Worth a shot."

"And yet that *is* what you were wearing when we met you," Will said. "If memory serves."

And his memory did, indeed, serve. Will's brain was a

bitch for details and it wasn't giving up the image of Audrey Bing's otherworldly beauty all wrapped up in a barely-there pastiche of sequins and spandex. Not ever. He knew exactly *what* she'd been wearing the first time he'd laid eyes on her, right down to the thread count of that heart-stopping skirt. He just didn't know *why* she'd been wearing it. And he damn well wanted to.

Drew rolled his eyes. "Okay, Mr. Judgy Pants, I think it's time to get over that whole you-worked-in-a-strip-club-so-you-must-be-trashy thing. The money's good, and the hours are flexible. Plus she *wasn't stripping*. Plenty of girls—"

"Not Audrey." Will folded his arms and maintained eye contact. And waited. Patiently.

Now it was Audrey's turn to palm her face. Will expected the blackest of her black scowls when she met his eyes again. Deserved it, probably. He wasn't handling this with any finesse—

Damn skippy, Bob said.

—but he wanted an answer on this one. How the *hell* had Audrey Bing—of the Boston Whitechurches, thank you very much—ended up slinging drinks at a strip club?

"I'm getting there," Audrey told him from behind her hands. "Just listen, okay?"

"Listening."

"So I came home to look for a job and found the Hildy situation in progress. Which was bad enough, right?" She dropped her hands to her lap and Will started at the pure weariness etched on that perfect face of hers. "Then my sister turned up."

"Jillian's mom?"

"Yep." Audrey sighed. "Olivia."

"And Olivia is your..." Will's brain did math in the background without permission all day long, and today was no exception. A split second of automatic calculating later and dismay clutched at his chest. "Your older sister?" Please?

"What? Oh, yeah." She waved a vague hand. "Three years."

Will did the math deliberately this time. Audrey was twenty-two, so Olivia must be twenty-five. And if Jillian was eight... "Pregnant at seventeen?"

"Sixteen." A smile ghosted over her face. "She delivered at seventeen."

"Christ."

"She had Jillian the year your mom died," Bel said softly and Will jolted. Evidently he'd checked out before his brain had gotten to the relevant math.

"Yep," Audrey said, her mouth tight. "First Mom died, then we had Jillian, then Dad's patents came through. It was a banner year for the Bings."

Bel shook her head. "I don't suppose Olivia considered abortion or adoption?"

"Hell, no." She laid her hands palm-up on the counter, and Will's heart squeezed at the helpless defeat in them. "She loved being pregnant. All that attention, you know? And when it was over, she figured she'd have this adorable little baby to carry about like some kind of living purse. It was win/win as far as Olivia was concerned. Then she had an actual baby."

"Oh boy," Bel murmured.

"You know how some kids are born with a built-in timer? They know when to wake up, when to go to sleep, and that they need to eat every four hours?"

"Yeah."

"Jillian wasn't that kid."

"Oh."

"Right. I spent every night of the six months leading up to my fourteenth birthday on the floor next to her crib."

Drew blinked. "Why you?"

"I loved her." She shrugged again. "And Olivia slept with ear plugs in."

"And you slept when exactly?" Will frowned.

She smiled faintly. "During algebra, usually."

"Oh, honey," Bel said.

Audrey waved off the sympathy. "I was never much of a student anyway." She shook her head. "Band stung, though. I liked music."

"You failed *band*?" Drew's face was half admiration, half shock.

"Oh, don't panic." Audrey waved him off, too. "It was just six months. After that it got better." Her face darkened. "Jillian got cuter. Cute enough that Olivia decided to try her hand at parenting. But by then it was too late."

"Too late?" Alarm bells started ringing in Will's head. "What does that mean?"

"It means I was in love with a baby who wasn't mine. But worse? The baby was in love with me. And she hardly recognized Olivia."

"Which does not go over well with the baby-as-accessory set," Drew said.

"It doesn't." Audrey gave him a rueful look. "It really, really doesn't. And I was fourteen. I was fourteen and in love with a baby. I had no game."

"Particularly not against an attention whore," Bel said. "I might hate your sister. Is that all right?"

"It's fine. She's my sister and I love her but she is what she is." Audrey's face went dark. "She spent the next six months threatening to take Jillian and move somewhere far away. Her fresh start, she called it."

"Bitch," Bel murmured.

"Then she actually did it."

Bel's mouth went hard. "*Bitch.*"

"Right." Audrey shook her head. "Turned eighteen, came into her trust fund and that was that. She just up and disappeared while I was at school one day, no forwarding address, no call-you-when-I-get-there. Not even a post card. Just...gone. Her and Jillian both."

"Oh, honey." Drew touched her shoulder. "That blows."

"Thank you. It did." She patted his hand. "But I got over it. Or thought I did. If you can't have something, you can't have it. Years went by. I went to Switzerland for high school—we were rich by then, remember—then North Carolina for college—"

"You got into butling?" Drew suggested.

"I got into butling," she confirmed, though she offered nothing else. Will wondered what was in the gaps she was skipping over. "I came home expecting a job search and got side-swiped by Olivia's hit-and-run special instead. Next thing I knew she was off crewing yachts in the Mediterrean and it was just me, Jillian, my dad and Hildy Wise at home. Oh, and my mom's ghost."

Chapter 9

"Your mom's ghost." Drew's voice was carefully nonjudgmental. "You...saw her?"

"Me? God, no. I don't believe in any of that garbage." Audrey rubbed her eyes. "I don't know what the hell my dad and Hildy were up to in that regard. I was too busy trying to get a job and get the hell out to pay strict attention to the situation. Plus I didn't want to get attached to Jillian again." She smiled bitterly, and Will's heart broke a little at the self-recrimination in that smile. "Nice, huh? Throwing an eight-year-old under the bus to protect my twenty-two-year-old feelings?"

Drew patted her hand encouragingly. She shot him a crooked smile that filled Will with black envy.

"But something definitely happened when I was too busy being uninvolved to notice," Audrey went on. "Something bad. So bad that Jillian either can't or won't talk about it. Or talk, you know, at *all*."

"Oh hell." James rubbed his jaw.

"So I went to Dad and Hildy, who gave me some story about Mom refusing the bridge and getting vengeful. About Jillian getting caught in the cross-fire." She waved a hand. "I didn't pay strict attention to that either as it was just another variation on the same old ghost-story crap I've been listening to all my life. So I explained that while they could build all the spirit bridges they liked in private, they would henceforth keep that crap away from the under-aged and impressionable. They said no." She smiled grimly. "We then engaged in what might politely be called a scene."

A beat of silence ensued in which Will assumed everybody was doing what he was doing: extrapolating their personal experience with Audrey's temper and filling in the blanks around that wholly inadequate word *scene*. He imagined it had been something worth seeing.

"So I took Jillian," she continued. "And we got the hell out."

"Of course you did," Bel said stoutly. "Thank God."

"To a strip club, though?" Will asked. Bob made a disgusted noise inside his head—unnecessarily, of course. Will didn't need the cue. He knew he wasn't doing himself any favors by continuing to hit this note. But something wasn't adding up here, and Will's brain would *not* let it go. "Where was *your* trust fund?"

"After the Olivia fiasco, my dad decided to change my age of access to twenty-five." She gave him a smile that was all teeth. "At which point I would presumably be better able to make good decisions about a significant sum of money."

"Said the guy with a staff of ghost-busters hunting his dead wife's spirit via his granddaughter," Drew said.

"Tell it to the judge." Audrey gave a bitter laugh. "My dad is fabulously wealthy, philanthropically inclined and—unless you view it through a particularly skeptical lens—a darn solid citizen. His eco/green fan base covers the tri-state area at the very least, and he throws a lot of money at grief-based causes to boot. Counseling for orphans, support for families of suicide victims, you name it, he's donated. The paranormal research is a relatively small—and very low-profile—aspect of his charitable portfolio." She shook her head. "In short? Jem Bing is not somebody you'd want to tangle with when it comes to custody of an abandoned blood relative. Not when you're young, single, unemployed and looking for live-in work that requires you to be on-call 24/7."

"But if she stopped talking while in his custody—" Drew started.

"Oh, but that's only because her mom abandoned her," Audrey said. She huffed a small laugh. "Poor kid. Parked with relatives she barely knows while her mom crews yachts all over the Mediterranean. Swore she'd be back by August, but when September came and went we had to assume she'd signed on for the Caribbean season as well."

"Well, how long does that run?" Drew asked, outraged.

"Does it matter?" Will asked. "The point here is that any emotional trauma Jillian is currently suffering can be plausibly laid at the feet of her mother's abandonment, and not on Jem and Hildy's witch hunt."

"Exactly." Audrey sighed. "And Jem's made it abundantly clear than he'll unleash his cadres of lawyers all over my ass if I try to argue otherwise."

"Cadres." Will blinked. "Good word."

"Thank you." She smiled, and his heart fell into a stutter step. Good God, she was smiling at him. At *him*. "When the perfect word exists, it's a crime to go generic, you know?"

"I do," he managed. He didn't smile back though. He didn't smile well. Every time he tried, people backed up, and Will didn't want that. Not from Audrey.

"So I really had no choice." She linked her fingers together on the counter and stared determinedly at them. "I had to get Jillian out of that situation, and I couldn't do it through normal, proper channels. We had to disappear."

"Hence the strip club." Will's brain stopped churning and gave a sigh of relief. Finally. An answer. Unanswered questions were the bane of his existence.

"Hence the strip club," Audrey agreed. "It's like Drew said. The hours were flexible and the money was good. Plus my dad would never think to look for us there." A corner of her mouth flickered. "The Dolly Parton wig was kind of a bonus, actually."

"Tell me you sang *Jolene* into a hairbrush before you left the dressing room every night." Drew put his hands together as if praying, pressed them to the center of his chest and closed his eyes. "You did, didn't you? It would be a crime if you didn't."

"I'm not answering that," Audrey said.

Drew opened his eyes and leaned in. "Is there any chance of an encore performance—"

"No."

"Ah, well." He smiled. "Always worth a shot."

"So how did he find you?" Will asked. "Your dad. I assume he *did* find you?"

"Sure did." Audrey didn't smile at him this time. The look she sent him was pure malevolence. "Evidently, my engagement party back in October caught his attention."

"Oh." Will's chest went tight and hot. *Shame*, Bob whispered. *That's shame right there, buddy. Go ahead, roll around in it. You earned it; you might as well enjoy it.* "Oh, Audrey, I'm sorry."

"For what?" She eyed him. "For torpedoing my gold-digging ways? For assuming I *was* a gold-digger? For judging me? Or just for telling my fiancé, his mother and their entire social circle that I was your favorite stripper?"

"Yes," Will said. "All that."

"Oh, hey." Drew shifted uncomfortably. "It wasn't like that."

"Sure it was." Will didn't look away from Audrey's contempt. "Maybe it wasn't all like that, but it was definitely like that."

"Wynton Quist was a douche, Audrey," Drew said quickly. "You have to admit to the epic scale of your fiancé's douchery—"

"Do I look like I'm denying it?" She lifted her brows. "But the Quists are one of the only families in this town with the social standing and the bank balance to put my dad to bed should he ever decide to take me to court. So when the opportunity to marry into the Quist family arose—" She paused and colored faintly. "—I took it." She shot Will a scowl and again he had to wonder what she wasn't saying. "Tried to, anyway."

"Well, water under the bridge," James said and patted the counter with an air that said he was finished with back story. "I think we'd be better served now dealing with what's currently on the table."

"Right." Audrey dialed back the scowl and put her hands on the counter, too, though hers were fisted, Will couldn't help noting. "Long story short: I had no job, no resources, no sugar daddy and no home. I did, however, have an extremely bright and troubled kid in my care who needed a safe haven. Thanks to Will, you guys owed me a favor." She sent him a sour look. "Several, actually. So voila, instant live-in housekeeper, via the famously amended contract. I've been pretty careful about staying out of high society's sight ever since, but high society came to me at least twice."

"The Fox Hunt Ball," Bel murmured. "We hosted it here."

"Yep." Audrey met her eyes. "And Bob's funeral." She shook her head. "I managed to stay mostly in the kitchen at the ball but somebody must've spotted me at the funeral. Because my dad and Hildy Wise showed up this morning."

"They came here?" Will felt his own hands fist up, but kept them under the table. "To the Annex?"

"Yeah."

"What did they want?" James asked, while Will wrestled a heady surge of blood lust to the ground.

"What do you think they wanted?" Drew made a disgusted noise. "They wanted Jillian." He turned to Audrey. "Didn't they?"

"They did."

"Is that so?" Now it was James' turn to sound dangerous. You might not have caught it if you didn't know him, but Will knew him. And so did Bel. She blanched and put a hand on his forearm. He just continued to gaze at Audrey. "What exactly did they say?"

Audrey must've picked up on the violence under that sunny charm because she tried a tentative smile. "Hildy didn't say a word. My dad did the talking. And it wasn't what he said so much as what he didn't."

"What did he imply, then?"

"That Jillian was a sensitive and special child. That she was incredibly gifted and so very precious."

"Good so far," Bel said warily.

"And that as a result, she needed a very special environment in which to discover and explore her many gifts. A rich, stimulating, stable environment in which she could feel safe enough to challenge herself, to stretch and grow."

Drew rolled a hand. "I'm waiting for the hatchet drop here." Will just held his breath.

"An environment that, despite my very best intentions, I

am simply not qualified to provide." Audrey sighed. "He has all the respect in the world for my intellect, mind you. But there's no denying that, from a certain point of view, I'm nothing but a band-failing, drink-slinging housekeeper whose most recent work history includes a strip club and moving in with a trio of over-funded men-children whose public shenanigans were epic enough to land them a damn nanny."

"Life coach." James slung an arm around Bel's shoulders. "We like to think of her as a life coach. Best bad decision of my life."

"Like there was just the one?" But Bel leaned into him with unmistakable affection. She did, however, exchange a look with Audrey that Will didn't even try to interpret.

"All's well that ends well," James said placidly.

Audrey, Will noticed, didn't comment on this. Probably because nothing had ended yet, well or otherwise. Not for her. Will understood this even if James didn't.

"All of which is to say," she went on, "that to an impartial third party—like a judge, for instance—it might appear that a child as special as Jillian would be far better off with somebody brighter." She smiled brilliantly. As if hearing that from her own dad didn't even touch her, much less hurt like hell. *Bullshit*, Bob said, and Will had to agree.

"He wrapped it up by politely inquiring as to whether or not she's begun speaking again. Because if my tender care were sufficient, surely she would be speaking after six months of it."

"Well, ouch." Bel sat back with a frown. "Like kids heal on a timetable."

Audrey gave a jerky shrug. "At no point was legal intervention mentioned outright but it was definitely there between the lines. It wasn't a conversation so much as a preview of the custody filing."

"Call them," Will said. All heads snapped his way and Bob said *For Christ's sake, use your indoor voice.* Will modulated his tone. "Get them back here," he said more calmly. Or at least more quietly. "I want a sit down."

"What does that mean?" Audrey asked, alarm flaring in

those wide, purple eyes. She looked around the circle of faces at the island counter. "What does he mean, a sit down?"

"He means you ought to call up your dad and his minion and get them over here. Will's looking to negotiate." James smiled, slow and satisfied. "And Will doing a deal? That is always a sight worth seeing."

Chapter 10

Two days later, Audrey found herself in the heart of DC's business district, trailing Will down K Street at a mincing trot. It was the best she could do given her sky-high heels, Will's long-legged stride and the teeming throng of cubical dwellers grabbing lunch via this particular sidewalk. In the half block since they'd left the parking garage, Audrey had already taken a briefcase to the midsection, dodged a clutch of power-walkers, and hurdled a homeless guy, all while wearing footwear designed for show ponies.

"How much farther?" she asked. *Show no fear, acknowledge no pain*. Christ, her feet hurt.

"A block."

"One block?" She could do a block.

He squinted at the skyline. "Maybe two."

"Two?" Her heart sank. "Maybe?"

"Block and a half?" he offered. Like they were negotiating. "You going to make it?"

"Of course."

She gave him a tight smile and glared down at her weeping feet. Where she was promptly distracted from the pain because, damn, they were great shoes. Stylish, smart, and very, very tall without even a whiff of stripper. It was a tough combination to find but crucially important to women who topped out at five-three and needed to be taken seriously from time to time.

She stifled a whimper and rededicated herself to pacing Will, who strode easily along in a pair of shiny wingtips. Bitter envy filled her. Not that she wanted to wear wingtips—heaven forfend—but why did looking good and walking always have to be such an either/or proposition for women? Lord knew men didn't have to choose. The proof was striding along ahead of her on classic, comfy shoes, filling out a thousand-dollar suit far better than his skinny ass had any right to.

And there was the bitter envy again, along with a hefty dose of resentment and a bright streak of panic. Because while it was a truth universally acknowledged that a well-cut suit did good things for every man on the face of the planet, it had been something of a shock to discover that Will was one of those guys who returned the favor.

In track pants and a t-shirt he was so average, Audrey reminded herself. Maybe a bit south of average, truth be told. Tall. Skinny. A little awkward, and saddled with a face too sharp and cruel for everyday use. None of which gave a girl any reason to suspect that a few yards of Italian silk was going to transform him into six-plus feet of smoking hotness. Certainly she hadn't been prepared.

She'd been waiting for him in the Annex foyer, updating the weekly grocery order via her cell. She'd heard him jogging down that ridiculous curved staircase—the Grand Promenade, Bel called it—looked up and promptly lost anything resembling brain function.

He'd hit the landing and stopped. A shaft of golden light kissed his brow, and she wondered for one wild second if dark angels signed their work. "Hey, Audrey." He'd shot a cuff, checked a heavy silver watch and said, "Right on time. God, I love the women in this house. We ready?"

And had she answered him? Had she managed even a simple yes or no? She had not. She'd just stood there gaping at him like an accident victim. It was possible she'd spent a good thirty seconds or more simply staring. Because, holy Moses, that face of his matched the suit, line for scalpel-sharp line. And she'd realized on a jagged pulse of dismay that Will wasn't average, or anything like it. He was just out of context in daily life.

But this wasn't daily life. This was war. A civilized war, to be sure, but war nonetheless. The kind of war you fought in exactly this sort of suit, with words and will and those sharp, sharp teeth of his. Will was going to battle, she realized. No, not just going. Eager for it. Hungry. Amped.

And suddenly all the tensions and contradictions that made Will so damned uncomfortable to be around shifted, pulled tighter, went higher. And then clicked into a kind of harmony. It wasn't easy-listening, not by any means, but it was compelling and once she heard it she couldn't stop hearing it. It was like his exterior had finally stopped fighting his interior, and he suddenly snapped into focus for her with his whole being. She didn't know for sure. All she really understood was that it made for one hell of a sucker punch when you weren't expecting it.

"Audrey?" Oh, damn it, then he was giving her the single eyebrow. He looked like a spread from *GQ*. Not the American version. The European one where editors understood that men didn't have to be pretty to make women pant. She pressed her knees together and prayed for mercy. "Do you need a minute, or—"

"I'm ready." She'd leapt to her feet and pasted some professionalism over the panic. He'd ushered her out the front door and into something sleek and low that smelled like leather and speed. She spent the drive into the city trying to figure out what the hell was *wrong* with her. Because she'd seen him dressed up before. Of course she had. He'd been wearing a tux when he'd cost her a job, a waiter-version of the same when he'd cost her a fiancé, and full-on Civil War-era breeches during the Fox Hunt Ball. And she'd been *fine*. So why was she having a heart attack over seeing him in a business suit?

It was the sobriety. Had to be. It was the only variable in play. She'd never seen him both dressed up *and* sober. Who knew it would make such a difference? Evidently it did. It took her back to the focus thing. If drinking was an effort to keep the uglier edges of life blurry, Will had been doing a bang-up job. He'd blurred his very *self*. And now that he was sober, his edges were coming back, crystal-clear and viciously sharp. And Audrey had a thing for sharp and shiny. Oh, God help her, she dearly loved shiny things that cut. This was not good news.

So she'd closed her mouth, wiped her chin, and forbidden herself the luxury of looking. She'd spent the rest of the drive with her face resolutely turned toward the window, her lips pressed relentlessly together, and every ounce of her strength turned toward defeating this horrible, persistent awareness.

But it was impossible to trail a guy down a crowded sidewalk without looking at him. Plus it was weird. It would draw suspicion, and the very last thing on God's green earth that she wanted was Will turning that big brain of his her way, and wondering what was up.

So when he said, "Okay, here we are," in front of a looming black-glass monstrosity of a skyscraper, she gave him a rueful smile and said, "Oh thank Christ. My feet had about half a block left, and then I was going to swallow my pride and ask you to piggy back me."

He laughed. Spontaneously and with every appearance of genuine amusement. Which shocked her even more than his facility with high fashion. She stared at him, startled to find him grinning back at her. Like he was...happy. *Happy.* Will was the angriest, most dangerous guy she knew. Or had been, pre-rehab. What he was since he'd emerged was still an open question as far as Audrey was concerned but whatever it was, she hadn't expected any permutation of the man currently grinning at her, his coat open to the January wind like he didn't even feel it.

"Good God," she said and swallowed hard. She forced her attention to the black-glass tower in front of them. "This is where you work now?"

"If I want to. It's where Bob officed, and the lease is good through June so..." He shrugged.

She tipped her head and considered the curb appeal. "It looks like the sidewalk is giving us the finger."

Will snorted out another laugh. Good lord, she was two for two. "I think that's sort of the point," he said. A doorman dripping epaulets and gold cording pulled open a twelve foot tall door for them and Will gestured her ahead of him.

She preceded him into the lobby. Glass panels soared three full stories, enclosing a small nation's worth of black marble and polished brass like one of those bell jars you put on top of African violets. A massive water sculpture in the center stretched nearly to the ceiling, water sheeting down its stark, angled surface, reflecting yet more light until even the weak winter sun bounced blindingly around the space. The water murmured discreetly, as if it, too, were chatting into a tiny phone just like all the important people in expensive suits swarming the lobby.

"You did this on purpose, didn't you?" She cast him a glance over her shoulder. "You thought meeting here would scare Jem and Hildy more than meeting at the Annex."

He led her past the reception desk—a hexagonal hive of activity the length of a city bus—and keyed a code into a number pad next to a bank of elevators. "Oh, Audrey. I don't want to scare them." An elevator opened with a low chime and Will's hand was suddenly on the small of her back, nudging her toward it. She leapt forward.

"You don't?" she asked, before Will could focus too hard on her hopping away from his touch like a panicked rabbit. "Why not?"

"Fear breeds resentment. And resentful people are dangerous. Sneaky. You have to keep your eye on them." He followed her into the elevator and they watched the doors slide shut. "If you're going to fight a war, you want to take on an army," he said. She realized she was breathing through her mouth. Like she was afraid she might smell him. Or jump him. "Armies stand and fight by a well-established and traditional set of rules. Guerillas, on the other hand, are unpredictable, amorphous and undefined, which makes them impossible to defeat. We don't want that. We want a win here."

She nodded sagely, like she talked tactics all the time. "*Never start a land war in Asia*," she murmured.

He shot her a sideways smile. "Or go up against a Sicilian when death is on the line?"

Again with the smiling! She suffered a brief wave of dizziness. The suit, the face, the smile. God.

"I wouldn't have figured you for a *Princess Bride* fan," she managed.

"It's Drew's favorite."

"Of course it is." That *did* make more sense, actually.

"So...Jem and Hildy. You want them to stand and fight?"

"Like men of honor, yes."

She eyed him as the elevator moved smoothly upward. "And how do you propose to do that?"

"I'm going to piss them off."

"Piss them off." She gave him a dubious look.

"It's a strong suit of mine." He didn't smile this time.

She opened her mouth, then closed it. Because she couldn't really argue. He *was* good at pissing people off. Had sort of a genius for it, actually. But something about the way he shouldered the role bugged her. It sat in her stomach like iffy leftovers, the kind you kept down but regretted eating nonetheless.

The elevator glided to a halt while she was still frowning, and the doors parted. She stepped through them into a hallway that smelled of lemon polish and expensive carpet. And promptly lost her balance when the carpet tried to swallow her entire foot. She stumbled and Will caught her elbow. She suffered another punishing crackle of heat. Damn and double damn.

"My God," she said, eying the carpet distrustfully. "It's like walking on a mattress."

"I know." He looked positively delighted. "The whole building's like this. It just oozes money."

He was close enough now for her to catch his scent, damn it. All that breath-holding in the elevator, wasted. But his scent, oh wow. It wasn't anything like she'd expected. It was better. Will smelled like ink, she realized. Like good books and fresh air and losing her balance. Want and panic tumbled together inside her but she pushed them aside and tugged experimentally at her arm. Will released her with respectful alacrity. She almost wished he'd go back to smirking at her the way he used to. Provoking her. Insulting her. Screwing with her life. That way she could lay the tangled mess of conflicting impulses inside her at his door, dust her hands and be done with it. But no. Suddenly Will was Mr. Hands-off, and she was stuck with a gut full of what-on-earth and nobody to blame for it. She seriously could not catch a break these days.

She gave him a disgruntled frown only to find him watching her with a face full of polite expectation. Oh, crap. Clearly it was her turn to say something. What the hell had they been talking about? Ah. The carpeting. The building. Both of them oozing money.

"And you felt this would make an impression on Jem," she said. "Your money-money office. An impression that would work to our advantage?"

"Yes." He smiled, and this time she saw the shark teeth. "Because after his experience with the Whitechurches, I'm guessing that Jem hates rich people. And not rich people like James who have a sense of humor about it and keep their *Gone With The Wind* décor just for fun. He hates rich people who put down carpet that makes people who can't afford such things feel small and off balance and stupid for even venturing into a world they don't belong in."

She stared at him, startled by the accuracy of his analysis. She realized suddenly that Will might have been her enemy, but she'd never been his. Because if he'd truly taken aim at her, she'd be nothing but a spot on his luxurious carpet by now.

"You're scary sometimes," she said slowly.

"I know. Thanks."

"I'm not sure it was a compliment."

"I know that, too. It's okay."

He started down the hall and she followed him thoughtfully, the carpet swallowing the sound of their footsteps with eerie ease. Every few yards the walls sprouted a console table upon which rested a single vase of fresh flowers, each one identical to the last petal. Not a drooping bloom or mote of dust sullied the table tops. It wasn't exactly attractive—a little too regimented for her taste—but she had to admit there was some seriously good butling at play here. She wondered who the head of housekeeping was.

Will stopped in front of a darkly polished door with no sign, no address, no identifying information whatsoever, and entered another code. He pushed open the door and gestured her inside.

Chapter 11

The waiting room was just that. A waiting place. It held a few more acres of carpet, some bold slashes of color in frames, and a few square arm chairs that Audrey suspected swallowed people like boa constrictors. Unless they were built like line backers. Which, she realized suddenly, most of Will's clientele probably was. Bob had been heavy into athletes. Sports careers were brief and cruel. You wanted to keep earning those millions? Best cement that broadcasting career before you blew out your knee. Which was likely why James had signed with him. Soccer super-stardom wouldn't last forever, and Audrey had no doubt that Will had hand-picked Bob to lay the groundwork for his brother's career beyond it.

She dropped her purse into one of those enormous chairs and sure enough, it disappeared entirely. She tossed her coat after it—what the hell—and strolled the perimeter of the room, absorbing the feel of the place. She wondered if she could get away with taking off her shoes. She'd bet this carpet felt awesome under your bare feet. She stopped in front of one of those starkly geometric paintings, cocked her head and studied it.

"Severe," she decided, and shot him a glance over her shoulder. "No reception desk, no phone, no signage." She found him giving her the same careful consideration she was giving his office. Her pulse jumped, a low thud that she felt in the palms of her hands and the tips of her ears. "How long will you make them cool their heels out here?"

"An insultingly long time." He crossed the office and keyed open the single door on the far wall. "I want them good and pissed by the time we open negotiations."

He went through the door, and she followed, curious.

"Good God." She stared at a massive teak desk and the matching credenza behind it. "That thing's the size of an ocean liner!"

"I know." Will dropped into a tall leather chair behind the desk and swiveled to face the wall full of windows. "And there's the White House."

Audrey looked. Okay, she might've gaped. No matter how many times you saw it, the White House was damned impressive. "That's quite a view."

"Yep." Will gave it a casual glance. "It's even better from the Dr. Evil chair." He half-rose, his brows up. "You want to try it?"

"Maybe later." He dropped back into the chair with a very Dr. Evil-like noise of proprietary satisfaction, and she chuckled. "But we're not intimidating them or anything."

"Nope." He did get up this time, jacked a hip up on the edge of his desk and gave her some serious eye contact. "We're making a real put-the-plumber-in-his-place move here, and if I've got a handle on your dad, he's not going to appreciate that. In fact, he's probably going to come back at me with guns a-blazing. And then?" He grinned, and it lit up his entire face with an unholy anticipation. "It's game on."

She blinked, a little startled, then found herself smiling back. She couldn't help it. She wasn't one for open warfare—not when it could be prevented—but he looked so happy at the prospect of bloodshed. And she needed a soldier. How could she judge him? Especially when his blood lust had just plain old garden-variety lust uncurling slow and hot in her belly?

She was a sick woman. She needed therapy. She'd get some.

Later.

"Well, damn, Will. I wish you'd mentioned sooner that we were shooting for anger rather than fear." She shifted on her feet. "I'd have worn more comfortable shoes."

His eyes drifted down the nubby wool of her black-and-white suit, over the smart little peplum jacket that slapped some class on curves that resisted it. His gaze slid slowly down the fitted skirt, drifted over her calves, lingered on her ankles and landed—finally—on her shoes. Her beloved shoes. They were a pair of severely simple Mary Janes with a discreet platform, a four-inch heel, and a button-detail instep strap. They were, no question, amazing shoes. But her calves and ankles felt extremely naked all of a sudden. Heat bloomed low in her stomach and she reminded herself not to call Will's attention to her bare skin in the future. That laser-beam focus of his made the hair on her nape stand up at the best of times. But when directed at her bare skin? That was...not good. Or very good. Too good. Dangerously good.

Finally he said, "Your dad has a fear of...buttons?"

She yelped out a startled laugh. A little hysterical but not bad. Trust Will to notice the details. "No. Tall people."

Will's eyebrows popped up. "Really?"

"That might be overstating it a little." She sort of wished she had her coat back. Covering up felt like the prudent move all of a sudden. "But Jem's five-six on a good day."

"And you're, what? Five-four?"

"Five-three, but thanks."

"And in those shoes, you're...five-six?"

"Five-seven. Possibly five-eight."

"So you were going to glare down at your father with magnificent disdain from the tower of your shoes?" He studied her. "That was your plan?"

She shrugged. "Hildy's short, too. I could've done them both together."

He rose from the desk. Slowly. He rounded the corner and her breath hitched in her throat because suddenly there was nothing between them but air, and it was rapidly disappearing. She wanted to back up, told her feet to get moving, but that ridiculous carpet had them in some kind of ninja grip and she was nailed to the floor. And Will just kept coming. She couldn't look away. His shoulders were huge, wide, all but eclipsing the windows as he moved closer, step by inexorable step. He finally stopped when his wingtips all but kissed her Mary Janes.

She stared at the half-inch of carpet between them, fascinated, her pulse pounding in all sorts of interesting places.

"Audrey." His voice was low and firm. But something in it was hot, too, and it dragged across her nerves with a friction that made her itchy and needful.

She didn't look up. "Yes?"

"Look at me."

"No."

"Please?"

Oh, shit. A request. In *that* voice. A voice that didn't do requests. A voice that gave orders and cut like a knife. But he wasn't telling her; he was asking her. She should say no. It was within her rights. She didn't have to look at him if she didn't want to. And she really didn't want to.

Then suddenly, she did. She wanted to see him. Wanted it more than her next breath. More than she wanted to sink her toes into the damn carpet. She wanted to look up and see what was in those eyes, to see if it matched the voice. All that command twined together with that little bit of please. Jesus, it was hot in here.

She looked up. And he was right there, the cut-glass cheekbones, the hawkish blade of his nose, the cool pale eyes that wavered between blue and gray. And that mouth. That fine, thin mouth. So talented, so cruel. But sensitive. She suffered one of those stunning blasts of insight, and suddenly understood that Will's mouth was all those things. Hard. Dangerous. Elegant. Gorgeous as a fencing foil. A miracle of form married to function, and Audrey understood just as abruptly that she wanted to know what it felt like. She knew how well and how deeply it cut. Now she wanted to feel the other side of that blade. Wanted to know the beauty and the art of it. Now she wanted to know if he could use it with a surgeon's delicate precision, if he could heal and nurture and create with it, not just destroy.

The heat wasn't sudden this time. It didn't take her by surprise and she didn't fight it. This time it was a slow uncurling that slid through her veins like honey. Sweet, sticky, delicious.

His hands came up to cup the balls of her shoulders and she stopped breathing. Because his mouth, oh dear God that *mouth* was within range. All she'd need to do was grab those lapels, boost herself up onto her toes—thank you, platform Mary Janes!—and help herself to a taste. A long, slow, lingering taste. She was only taking the one so she'd make it a good one. It would have to last her.

"Audrey," he said again.

"Yes?" She didn't look away from that mouth. Jesus, it was pretty.

"Are you afraid of me?"

"No." It was automatic, that *no*. Just popped out of her subconscious so easily that she knew it was true. She might've been afraid of him once but she wasn't any more. She had a healthy respect for those cutting edges of his but she wasn't afraid.

"Are you angry with me?"

"No," she breathed.

"Of course you're not. Because the looming thing?" He gave her shoulder a bracing pat. "It's for amateurs." He took a step back and suddenly she could breathe again. "We can do better than that."

"Oh." Color rushed into her cheeks as awareness came back on line and she realized what she'd almost done. Humiliation and horror mixed with that persistent lust, and the whole thing went curdled and bitter.

"Plus," he said, "we're two city blocks from the parking garage."

"Believe me, I know."

"Those shoes probably hurt you more than they'd ever hurt Jem."

"I know that, too. I do now, anyway." She fluttered her hands at him in a waspish little *back up*, which he did. Easily. "I'm sorry I wore them, believe me."

"Oh, I believe you." He hitched a hip on the barge of his desk and slid his eyes back to her feet. Little flames of lust licked her all the way down. God, she was an idiot. "On behalf of men everywhere, however, let me thank you for your sacrifice."

"Oh shut up," she muttered and stalked to the window.

Will let her go. She was pissed at him, and that was as it should be. He sat on the desk and linked his fingers loosely over one knee. He hoped they weren't trembling. Because oh Jesus God he'd almost kissed her. He'd only wanted to demonstrate that the looming thing was overrated, especially by short people.

Then he'd found himself six inches from all that curvy determination packed into some kind of suit that made her look like she belonged in one of those black-and-white detective flicks. The kind where a dangerous woman wandered into a guy's office, cried a few pretty tears and turned the entire world upside down. Next thing you knew it was all gunfire and cigarettes and mobsters and back stabbings.

And Will wanted a taste of that. Of her. Desperately. But he wasn't going to take it. Not now, not ever. That ship had sailed. Not that it had ever pulled up to his dock anyway. He knew what he looked like, and a girl like Audrey would have to go slumming pretty hard to get all the way down to Will's dock.

But even if he set that aside, there was also the fact that Audrey was wired like a stick of dynamite. She had no subterfuge, no strategy, no game. She was determination in human form, and she was *good*. Look what she'd gone through to protect a kid. Hell, look what she must have gone through as a kid to protect herself. She focused, she took aim, she took her shot. And she shot straight. She didn't apologize or work around. She simply located the target and threw herself at it with honor and integrity.

And a guy like Will, whose one talent in this world seemed to be playing dirty? He had no business putting his greasy fingerprints on that kind of straightforward goodness. Literally or figuratively. The best thing he could do for Audrey Bing—the only thing, really—would be to use his dark gifts to help her keep a kid's innocence intact. And then leave her the fuck alone.

Glad we have that straight, Bob said inside his head. *Now get your ass off my desk.*

Right. Will stood up. He assessed his current level of

self-control and risked a look at Audrey. She was still standing at the window, frowning darkly at the view. Will thanked Christ that he hadn't taken a flier and kissed her anyway. He had no desire to meet Jem and Hildy with a black eye. He'd lay good money that Audrey had one hell of a swing on her.

He checked his watch. "You should try out the Dr. Evil chair," he said. "I'll go watch for Jem."

She nodded shortly but didn't move. Probably didn't want to get any closer to him than she already was. Guess it was too much to hope that she hadn't smelled the longing on him. Will stepped into the waiting room and closed the door behind him.

He was so screwed.

* * *

Will had been sitting in his own waiting room for nearly 45 minutes when the door opened and Tom Cruise stepped in.

Will blinked.

Okay, that wasn't Tom Cruise. That was Jem Bing. But Will did wonder for a second if the guy had considered work as a stunt double, because the resemblance was uncanny. Dark hair (fashionably shaggy), a set of blindingly white chompers, and a whole bunch of barely-leashed something that he supposed you could read as either charisma or crazy. Will had met enough famous people over the course of James' career to know how blurry the line between crazy and charisma actually was, but it looked to him like Jem was leaning toward crazy.

The moment for popping politely to his feet came and went, and only then did Will unfold himself from the depths of his chair. Leisurely. It wasn't looming, but it was looming's classier cousin, and he wondered if Audrey would be pleased that he'd worked it in. "Jason Bing?"

"Call me Jem." The guy all but rushed him. He seized Will's hand and squeezed it like he was trying to crack a walnut. "Jason's my dad." He gave a few booms of hearty laughter.

"Of course." Will heard his own knuckles grinding and

welcomed the pain. This, at least, he understood. "William Blake."

Jem released Will's hand—what was left of it—and stepped to the side to reveal a small round woman. "Hildy Wise," Jem bellowed. "My associate."

"Pleased to meet you, Mr. Blake." She dimpled up at Will with palpable warmth.

"And you," he said automatically, a little stunned. Because where Jem's knuckle-crunching had singularly failed to impress him, the warm-bosom, open-arms vibe pouring off this woman arrowed straight to Will's orphan heart. Good lord. He studied her carefully. In a dark woolen coat, a neat gray bob, sensible shoes and minimal makeup, she was exactly as housewifely as Drew had said. If an apple pie ever decided to take on human form, Will was certain it would look just like Hildy Wise. He felt instantly and inexplicably at home with her, too, as if he could say anything from *nice to meet you* to *hey, will you look at this mole?* and she'd take care of business without twitching a lash. He wondered if she had this impact on everybody, or just people who still missed their moms like they'd miss their right thumbs.

"Thank you for coming," he managed.

"Oh, dear, it was our pleasure. Thank you so much for inviting us." Hildy leaned in and gave his arm a little squeeze. "The situation has gotten entirely out of hand," she said, her voice lowered confidentially. As if Jem weren't standing right there, all white teeth and crazy eyes, listening intently. "High emotion, you know." She patted his arm and stepped back. She clasped her hands in front of her coat and beamed around the waiting room with an air of deep satisfaction. "It was such a good decision to bring everybody to neutral ground, Mr. Blake. Very compassionate and wise. I have a very good feeling about today. And about you."

He just blinked at her. She blinked back, then gave him a critical up-and-down. He resisted the urge to straighten his tie. "Yes," she said finally. "I think you'll do very nicely."

He cocked a brow, a reflexive bit of arrogance his own mother would've twisted his ear for. "Will I?"

She smiled, and this time it was a small, secret smile. The kind that said *I know you better than you'll ever know yourself so don't bother trying to put one over on me, young man*. "I think you will."

"You'd better," Jem said, his teeth flashing. "Otherwise I rearranged my damn Thursday for nothing."

Will flashed his own teeth, one shark to another. "Why don't you both have a seat?" He waved a hand at the massive chairs that would surely eat Jem and Hildy alive. He'd have to winch them out of there if they leaned back too far. "I'll let Audrey know you're here."

Chapter 12

Audrey shot to her feet the instant Will walked through the door. Oh dear God, they were here. Jem and Hildy. It was happening.

"What's wrong?" She gripped her hands together hard enough to hurt and stared at Will, who frowned absently at the desk between them. "You're all grim. Why are you grim?"

"I'm not grim," he said but didn't meet her eyes. He just kept studying the desk like it was a museum piece. Or maybe like he was trying to figure something out. Like how to tell her bad news. "My face is always like this."

"I know what your face is like, believe me." She scrambled around the desk for a better look while panic tugged at the edges of her composure. "And this is grim, even for you. Why are you doing your grim face?" She stopped, alarmed. "Oh my God. Did they bring the police? Am I under arrest? Or—" She seized his arm. "Do they have Jillian? Did they take her?"

"What?" His head snapped up and he finally met her eyes. "Jesus, Audrey, no. It's nothing like that. Jillian's fine. Relax."

"Relax." She let go of his arm and stepped back, terror deflating within her in a great gush. "Relax?" Fury sparked, hit the terror vapors and went up in a massive fireball. It propelled her forward again and she gave him a solid shot to the shoulder. He fell back, astonishment chasing the grim right off his beautiful face. She followed him, welcoming the anger, relishing the way it burned away the panic. "Don't you tell me to relax, you jerk! I've been sitting here for an hour all by myself, imagining every possible scenario! Every one of them was worst-case, too, if you were wondering, and

I'm in here just drowning in them, and where are you? In the waiting room! Like I'm contagious or something!"

He held out staying hands. "Easy, Audrey. I don't think you're contagious."

"Liar." She slapped aside his hands and shoved him again.

He didn't fall back this time but held his ground. Narrowed his eyes. "Stop that."

"No." Because something was boiling over inside her and she was helpless to turn down the burner. And because every time she shoved him, whatever this was between them thinned and stretched and chipped. And she suddenly wanted to break it. To break *him*. To break herself *on* him like a wave smashing itself on the rocks. She lifted both hands for another shove.

His eyes went hot and he said, "I'm warning you, Audrey—"

She shoved him.

He moved faster than she'd have thought possible. He didn't resist the shove, just flowed with it like water. She stumbled, caught off guard by the lack of resistance, but there was no time to wonder about it because then her hand was folded into his fist and she was spinning under his arm. Almost like they were dancing, she thought wildly, if dancing came with consequences.

In the next heartbeat, she found herself bent over the desk, one hand splayed on all that shiny teak, the other still trapped in Will's fist and pinned to her opposite shoulder. She saw his free hand on the desk, too, big and hard as he held her there, the edge of the desk biting into the front of her thighs, the wide expanse of his chest curled hotly over her back, the sharp press of his knees angled into the backs of hers, those long thighs cupping the curve of her bottom. The unmistakable thrust of his growing arousal.

"I'm going to say that again," he said, and his voice was low and rough, a study in strained control. "Stop pushing me."

"Why?" Her voice shook, and she prayed he'd read it as anger and not the horrible lust it truly was. Because, God help her, she liked this. She liked him like this, trembling on the razor-sharp edge of his control. She wanted to push him right off it, then tumble with him into whatever handy pool of damnation waited to swallow them below.

Yeah, she wanted that. Badly. She could acknowledge it, too, if only to herself. Because that was healthy. No point lying to herself. But should she do it? Hell no. She had responsibilities. She had Jillian. She couldn't get lost in whatever Will was, whatever he could do to her. Because she would lose herself. She knew that without question or reservation. And she'd worked too hard to find herself to indulge her inner submissive now.

Besides, she *wasn't* submissive. Not at all. She was a feminist, damn it. And given the genetic hand she'd been dealt, she'd fielded every possible come-on from every possible type of guy, too. So she ought to know by now if the ultra alpha approach turned her on. It didn't. At least it hadn't in the past. So surely it was a stress-induced aberration that she was melting all over the desk for Will. Her body was getting a stern talking-to at her earliest possible convenience.

"Do you get off on hurting women?" She threw the words out even as she fought not to press herself back into the heat of his body. To arch her back and offer herself up. His jaw was right there over her shoulder, nearly touching her cheek, and the scent of him filled her lungs. *Paper and books*, she thought. A wave of lust crashed over her head and she bore up under it helplessly. "Is that what you like?" she forced herself to ask. "Is that why you're so screwed up?"

His hand twitched on the desk and heat streaked up her thighs and landed in her core. Oh dear God was he going to—

His hand left the desk. Slowly. She turned her head to track it but he checked the movement with his jaw against her cheek like a stallion covering a mare. She heard the rasp of invisible stubble against her skin even as she felt it and she gripped the edge of the desk with desperate strength. But she obeyed the silent command and stopped trying to watch his hand. Because now she could feel it.

It was there on her hip, the warmth of his palm leaking through her heavy wool skirt like a stain. She wondered if she'd have a handprint there later. He smoothed it down the side of her hip, along the edge of her thigh, to the vulnerable skin at the back of her knee. Then he started back up. She could feel the heat of his hand, still politely on the outside of her skirt, and even so it had want blooming at her center. Her breath hitched in her throat. She concentrated with her whole being on the slow progress of his hand conquering the back of her thigh, inch by aching inch. Her heart hammered wildly in her chest until suddenly the curve of her bottom was cradled in his big palm. At which point her heart gave one more desperate strike then just stopped.

And that was him touching her *over* her skirt. She wondered what would happen if he ever touched her bare skin. The very thought sent her heart lurching back onto the job and she gulped in a harsh breath.

Evidently Will interpreted this as distress because he said, "I'm not hurting you, Audrey." His voice was like his hand—hot, commanding, and utterly assured—and she concentrated on breathing more normally. "And I won't. Not ever. But it looks like we're going to be working hand-in-glove here for a little bit, so there are a few things you ought to know about me."

"Okay," she managed.

"I've got a real thing for you, Audrey. Won't deny it."

"Yeah." She gave an involuntary squirm but froze when she encountered the thrust of his arousal against her bottom. "I noticed."

"You caught that, did you?" She felt him shrug. "Not a surprise, I'll bet. I'm a guy. And you're...well, look at you." He gave her bottom a fond squeeze and a rush of heat slid down her legs to weaken her knees. "My dick thinks you're the cat's pajamas. Can we blame him?"

"Oh, Will. You say the sweetest things."

"Don't I just?" He barked out a harsh laugh. "So there's that. Then there's the fact that I also like a good fight."

"What does that have to do with—"

"I'd tell you if you'd shush."

She stiffened. "You did *not* just shush me."

"Sure I did." He rubbed her bottom again and her outrage was snuffed out by crashing desire. As was any impulse to chat. "See, I spent a lot of years resenting the hand I was dealt. That James got all the talent and Drew got all the charm, while all I got was test scores that made my peers want to beat the shit out of me and a mouth that sealed the deal. The fact that I got a funeral for two and custody of my brothers for my eighteenth birthday? That pissed me off some, too. I'd been looking forward to college."

A surge of sympathy surprised her. Will wasn't the kind of guy you felt sorry for, but the past six months had given her some real boots-on-the-ground experience with the whole instant family business. It was no picnic. And a brain like Will's missing out on college? It boggled the mind.

"I'm sorry you lost your parents," she said. "That blows. But you have a photographic memory and a computer for a brain. Forgive me if I don't weep bitter tears over how fate shafted you."

"No, see, that's my point. I've spent years trying to pretend like I'm only mean because James and Drew used up all the nice. But I wasn't a drunk because I loved scotch, you know. Some people are, but not me. No, I was a drunk because I loved the way scotch helped me tell that particular lie. But I'm done with that. I'm playing *my* hand now. And as it happens, I got dealt a whole bunch of sharp and mean, along with the occasional fight card. I'm smart, I'm ugly and I like to split my knuckles sometimes. A black eye or a bloody lip? That's like routine maintenance on my inner villain. It's just what I am, figuratively and literally."

"So, what, you're saying you like it rough?" She arched a brow he couldn't see. "That you want to spank me or something?"

"No, Audrey, that's not what I'm telling you." His breath was warm and sweet against her neck and she suppressed a shiver. "What I'm telling you is that I'm not precisely stable where you're concerned. You're like crack to my libido, and I'm already nursing an above-average attraction to...let's call it interpersonal friction. So when you take a swing at me? When you come at me with all that heat and courage packed into that curvy stick of dynamite you call a body? Spontaneous combustion is a very real possibility. I'm keeping my shit to myself out of respect for you, and to make amends for my previous and well-documented assholishness. But I'm not super human. You pull my cork, you're probably not going to like what happens next." His mouth dropped to within inches of her ear and goose bumps broke out on her thighs. "But I will. I'll like it a lot."

She swallowed. Or tried to. "Why are you telling me this?"

"Forewarned is forearmed," he said simply. "I don't go around dropping truth bombs on people for the hell of it—I try to keep that on a need-to-know basis—but you shoved me. I took it twice but number three saw you bent over the desk, my hard-on snuggled into your very pretty bottom. And I won't lie—I have half a mind to see what's under your skirt." Audrey's core gave an abrupt flutter and she choked down a small moan. "So unless you want me to move forward with that happy plan, you're going to want to cool it with the pushy-shovey, you feel me?"

"Yeah, I feel you," she said. Because, Jesus, did she. She felt him everywhere. On every inch of her skin, with every beat of her heart. Definitely against her ass. But worse, she felt him inside herself. It was like every cell in her body had zeroed in on that dangerous harmony of his and was having a goddamn sing along. "Kind of hard to miss you at this point."

"Yeah." He released her and stepped back, and the heat of him abruptly receded. She registered a quick pulse of loss—of insanity, really—before the relief rushed in. "Sorry about that."

She straightened slowly, and took a moment to smooth the wrinkles from her skirt. Took another to smooth the lust from her face. Then she turned, and there he was, all cool arrogance and brutal beauty, hands tucked easily into pockets. Like he'd given her tax advice instead of bending her over the desk and setting her on fire.

She wanted to shove him again.

Fire licked through her at the thought. She really, *really* wanted to shove him again, if only to find out what would happen next. She bet it would be worth the consequences.

Before she could follow through on that little bit of insanity, the door rattled on its hinges.

"Knock knock, kids!" Her father's voice sawed through the heavy oak with determined cheerfulness. "You planning to join us at some point, or should I go try to salvage some fraction of my work day?"

Audrey's hand froze mid-air. It had already come up for the shove, for crying out loud. She and Will stared at each other in tense silence, the air between them thick and unresolved.

"Looks like we're trying Jem's patience," Will said finally.

She shifted course, touched her hair instead of giving him that shove. As if tucking back the fly aways had been the plan all along. Then she leaned back against the desk, gripped the edge until her fingers hurt and met Will's cool, wary eyes.

"Are you ready for this?" she asked.

"Are you?"

She shrugged. "Your show."

He shrugged back. "Your life."

"Yeah." She studied him. Wondered again where he hid all that damn heat. "Keep it in mind, will you?"

This time, he reached out. Slowly. Plenty of time to move if she wanted to but she didn't. She simply sat there, frowning but still, and let him smooth a stray hair away from her temple.

"Always, Audrey." His voice was quiet, his touch light. Something shifted inside her, came unmoored. "Count on it."

Chapter 13

It wasn't exactly his film noir fantasy, Will thought five minutes later, but it was darn close. He had a pair of suspicious characters in the chairs across from his desk and a curvy blonde perched on the corner of it. The two across the desk wanted something from her, she wanted something from him, and he definitely wanted something from her. And every one of them had murky motivations that needed sorting out.

Everyone except him, that is, since he'd just laid his motivations out on the table, face up. Which had included laying Audrey Bing out on the desk underneath him, face down.

Should have been game over, right there. Will knew that. Just like he knew that she was still very much in the game. She hadn't said much while Will was doing the big reveal. Hadn't said anything, really. But that ocean of energy, the restless music of her that filled his ears all the time? It had shifted unexpectedly as he'd played his cards. Gone from wary to...interested? No, that was too strong. That ocean of hers was complicated and dark, and it concealed more than it exposed. But if it hadn't been exactly interested, at least it hadn't been fuck you very much. Or not *all* fuck you very much, because this was him and Audrey they were talking about. There was always going to be a little bit of that between them.

And you like that shit, don't you? Bob sighed. *You're so bent.*

Will supposed he could argue but why bother? First of all, he *was* sort of bent that way. Hadn't he just said as much to Audrey? It was a fair point. Plus he'd recently made it a policy not to argue with his own imagination.

For Christ's sake, I'm not your damn imagination.

Will didn't bother to argue with that, either. Because why waste time arguing with his *imagination* when there was a far more interesting point on the table?

Audrey Bing was still unmistakably in the game.

And after what he'd said, after what he'd done? After what he'd *wanted* to do but hadn't? Audrey's continued presence on the pitch was a minor miracle.

The fact that she'd gone on to perch her curvy little behind on the corner of his desk and was now staring down at her dad and Hildy like she and Will were a team? A unit? A fighting force to be reckoned with? That was major miracle territory right there.

And the fact that he had both a fight to win and a girl to save? A girl who'd just gone eyeball-to-eyeball with his inner monster and hadn't blinked? Good God. He might start whistling here in a minute. He was just that happy.

Not, of course, that he looked happy. He looked like a mean, ugly bastard, just like always. Not his fault, just something about his face. He'd never been grateful for that before, but he was now. He gave Jem some good, hard eye contact across a vast sea of polished wood and wound up for the opening pitch.

"So, Mr. Bing—"

"Jem!"

Will inclined his head but didn't correct himself. He wondered if the guy had any volume south of a hearty bellow. "I understand you dropped by my home the other day to threaten my employee with legal action."

Jem chuckled. "Is that what she told you?"

Will gave him the dead eye and some cold silence.

Jem's laugh lines were deep and movie-star handsome but his eyes were frigid. "Since when is it a crime for a father to drop in on his own kid?"

"You were just in the neighborhood?" Will returned the smile politely and just as warmly. "Thought you'd drop in for coffee and a little catch up?"

"Something like that." Jem leaned back in his chair, propped an ankle across a knee and studied Will. Will studied him back. "I didn't realize she'd be required to clear her visitors through security and a background check. You doing something out there in the country you don't want folks seeing?" He grinned again, a thin smear of friendly over a display of fangs. "I've heard stories, you know. About what goes on out at that place of yours. You and your brothers haven't been exactly low profile around here. Word gets around."

"Does it?"

"Sure does. Lot of talk about you Blake boys."

"Is there?" Will leaned back himself, interested. He'd been through countless tense negotiations in his career, both as James' manager and as a wildly unprepared eighteen-year-old head of household. Enough to know that veiled threats, implied blackmail, and general character assassination were nothing but prologue. Nothing Jem had said so far surprised him in the least.

But how he said it? That was pretty interesting. Because there was something between the words, underneath the words. Something invisible but palpable. A frequency, a supersonic buzz, a hive of furious bees. Like one of those whistles only dogs could hear, but somehow Will was picking it up.

He wondered with a quick flare of worry what the hell was going on with his brain these days. First it was conversations with dead guys, then it was Audrey's ocean. And now Jem had bees?

Those aren't bees, Bob whispered inside his head. *That's fear. You can hear it? Funny. I always smelled it. Make him spin it out. Keep him talking.*

He reminded himself of his decision not to engage his imagination in conversation anymore. It couldn't be healthy. But still...fear? Interesting idea, that.

I'm not your fucking imagination, you ungrateful dickwad. I've seen your imagination. It's not this good.

Will paused, convictions forgotten. Bob had seen his imagination?

I'm inside your head, idiot. What do you think I look at all day?

85

Will didn't want to even think about that.

Yeah, that's right. Because you are *a bent bastard. I know all about your sweaty little dreams—*

Will's eyes flicked automatically to Audrey.

Exactly. You want my opinion—

I don't.

—you don't have a chance.

I know, thanks.

But feel free to take a swing. Everybody needs a dream, even you. And I could use the laugh because despite what you might think about your IQ, it's not actually very interesting in here. Jem's the most fun I've had in weeks. So will you do me a favor and focus? I want to enjoy this.

Right. Will dragged his attention back to Jem. But he caught Hildy watching him with an inscrutable smile on the baby-doll bow of her lips. It made him feel a little naked so he focused on Jem. "You've heard rumors, have you?"

"Sure have. Word is you're trouble. All of you boys, but you especially. Got a real talent for trouble is what I hear, Mr. Blake."

"Is that so?"

"Trouble to the tune of a six week dry-out over at Magnolia Hills recently if my little birdie has it right. And Magnolia Hills isn't cheap. Sounds like some serious trouble to me." He flicked a speck of lint off the knee of his trousers. "The kind of serious that makes a man real nervous about it brushing up against his granddaughter on a live-in basis."

"But not his daughter?"

"Her, too. Of course." He showed Will all those fangs again but that weird inaudible buzzing didn't abate. It filled the air around the guy like a swarm of killer bees. And those eyes that crinkled so chummily? They were cold and black. *And afraid*, Bob said. *He's fucking terrified*. Will agreed. "I came by to express my concern."

"I see. And you felt that offering to savage your daughter in court was an appropriate method of expressing said concern?"

"For crying out loud." Jem chuckled again, though it sounded more like he was gargling gravel than having a laugh. He turned to Hildy. "Hildy, you were there. Did I ever, at any point, threaten to savage anybody in court when we visited with Audrey a few days ago?"

"Of course not." Hildy gave his arm a reassuring pat. She was a toucher, Will noticed. He filed that away. Forewarned really was forearmed. "But you could have been gentler."

"Gentler!"

Jem made a rude noise which Hildy serenely ignored. She turned to Will, leaned in and lowered her voice. "Jem has a very forceful presence. You might have noticed."

"Is that what we're calling it?"

"It's a great asset, and has made him very successful in a business setting. But personally and emotionally?" Hildy gave a tiny sigh. "Well, it can be something of a handicap."

"Jesus, Hildy," Jem boomed. "I'm right here. I can hear you."

"I know, dear." She patted his arm again, a bit absently. She didn't break eye contact with Will. "Jem's intentions are sincere and well-motivated, Mr. Blake. But his execution can be a bit...brusque."

"He called me a stupid stripper and a jumped up maid," Audrey said clearly. And Will's blood gave a sudden hungry surge that he heard even over Jem's bees. Everything in his veins just leapt up and crashed into his eardrums like a rogue wave. It drained away just as suddenly, leaving behind nothing but the jagged urge to rip out Jem's throat.

Jesus, Bob said inside his head. *That's some temper you've got there, buddy.*

I know, thanks.

Will eyed Jem thoughtfully.

You got a grip on that thing?

Relax. I'm not going to eat the guy.

Not ever? Because that was some nasty shit he said to our Girl Friday.

There was another surge inside his head, the beast that lived in his mental cellar stirring and shifting. Growling.

Okay, Bob said. *Jury's still out. Got it. Just checking.*

"A stupid stripper," Will said softly, his eyes fixed

unwaveringly on Jem. "A jumped up maid."

"Oh for Christ's sake." Jem shifted uncomfortably. "I said *stripping* was stupid."

"I never stripped!" Audrey snapped. "I just—"

Will cut her off with a sharp wave, his eyes never leaving Jem's. She subsided with a hiss, and Will knew he'd pay for that little bit of high-handedness later on. But he didn't soften it or apologize. She'd defend herself to this asshole over his dead body, and if she tore a strip off him for it later, well. His blood jumped again at the idea, only hotter than before. Everything came with a cost. He'd pay this one. Gladly.

He arched an eyebrow at Jem. "You were saying?"

Jem scowled. "Just that I didn't pay a Swiss boarding school bushel baskets of cash to turn out a goddamn maid." He narrowed his eyes and shot a finger Audrey's way before she could interrupt. "And I don't care what your fancy job title is. You pick up dirty socks for the likes of this joker and his brothers? You're the maid." He snorted, and now Will heard something new inside all the buzzing bees. This was pride, and it rang like a hammer off tempered steel. "You're a Bing, for Christ's sake. Find your dignity."

"Dignity?" Audrey's back went stiff and her hands went to fists on her knee. But she didn't jump up. Will knew it must have cost her, that restraint. "Dignity? Yeah, guess what? I had to sell that along with everything else you ever gave me to buy therapy for your granddaughter."

"Therapy?" Jem's brows snapped down. "Therapy?" He came forward in his seat. "She's talking? Has she said anything—"

He broke off, glanced at Hildy who gave her head a tiny shake.

"About Mom?" Audrey gave a bitter laugh. "Or *from* Mom? Isn't that really what you want to know?"

"Don't you sneer at me, young lady," Jem barked. "You have no idea what we're dealing with here, and if you did—"

"I'd be the one taking you to court, because no judge on earth would give you custody of a kid if they knew what you wanted her for."

"You have no idea what you're talking about," Jem said again, and the buzzing around him intensified. Will wondered what exactly had him so frightened. "*No* idea."

"That's right," Audrey sneered in direct defiance of Jem's *no sneering* edict. God, Will liked this girl. "Because I'm just a stupid stripper and a jumped up maid."

"Oh dear." Hildy leaned across Jem, neatly cutting off whatever nastiness he had cued up, and beamed all that compassion Audrey's way. Will watched closely but Audrey didn't seem even a little bit fazed by it. Maybe it didn't work on girls? He'd have to ask her later if she caught some kind of mom-high off Hildy. "That was such a hurtful thing for your father to say. And untrue. You're a bright and sensitive young woman. He knows that, and somewhere between all the badly chosen words, I hope you could hear the love and pride motivating them."

"Oh, yeah," Audrey said. "Couldn't miss it. It was right there between *stupid* and *stripper*."

Hildy smiled sadly. "That must have been terrible to hear."

"It wasn't exactly a newsflash, Hildy." Audrey stared her down. "Nor was it the first time he'd aired his opinion of my intellect and my career choice."

"Butling!" Jem snorted and sat forward abruptly. Caught Will's eyes with his laser beam of crazy. "Do you know how many languages they make them learn in Switzerland? And instead of going to goddamn diplomat school or working for the UN or some shit, she decides to *butle*? Jesus." He threw up his hands and glared at Audrey. "Maybe *you're* the reason your mom's so pissed. She's a Whitechurch, you know. Probably dying of shame."

"I'm sure." Audrey folded her arms tightly over her chest. "Except that she's *already dead*."

Jem's brows were a black line of disapproval. "Your mother is not at rest."

"Says her." Audrey waved a hand Hildy's way. "Speaking of jumped-up maids." She rolled her eyes. "What are you paying her, anyway?" She leaned around Jem to speak to Hildy. "What kind of salary do you pull down helping selfish assholes make amends with the wives they neglected into suicide?"

Jem shot to his feet, quivering with rage. "You shut your mouth."

Audrey shot to her feet. "Make me."

Will came to his feet leisurely, rounded the desk and touched Audrey's stiff elbow. He leaned down and murmured into her ear. "I didn't know you had that much bad cop in you. Color me interested."

She jerked back to glare at him, her ocean a furious froth in his inner ear. He held her gaze until he heard the slow retreat from whitecaps to rolling waves. Finally she sighed. "What, am I stepping on your lines?"

"Let's just say I've got it from here." He nudged her toward the Dr. Evil chair and took her place on the corner of the desk. He let Jem stand there, looming. Short guys loved to loom, after all, and Will had nothing to prove. He linked his fingers together and looped them casually over his knee.

"So," he said easily. "Now that the pleasantries are out of the way, let's get down to business, shall we?"

Chapter 14

"I have no business with you," Jem snarled, his eyes still pinned to Audrey. She crossed her legs and ignored him. Something warm bloomed inside Will—pride?—and Bob said, *Good for her. I really do like that girl.* Will did, too. He really, really did.

"Oh, I think you do. You see, Audrey is employed by Blake Brothers International. And I, as the Chief Operating Officer of BBI, oversee all contracts pertaining to it."

Jem raised a skeptical brow. "Including the maid's?"

"I wrote it myself." He smiled just enough to remind Jem that he wasn't the only one with fangs. "As it happens, Audrey is contracted to a full-time, live-in position as James Blake's household manager." He spread his hands. "Even if she were inclined to leave her position at this time, which she assures me she isn't, we aren't inclined to release her from her contract."

"So don't." Jem waved a dismissive hand that had Will's monster whispering sweet nothings about throat ripping again. "She wants to take out your trash and keep your whites nice and bright, it's a free country. I can't stop her." Jem canted forward, lowered his voice and pushed the words through bared teeth. "But I will have my granddaughter."

Will smiled pleasantly. "No."

Jem blinked. Evidently he wasn't used to his scary face missing the mark. "Excuse me?"

"I said no." Will put his smile away. "That option isn't on the table at this time, nor will it ever be. Jillian remains in Audrey's care and under Audrey's constant supervision. That's non-negotiable. Now if that's a deal breaker for you—" He shrugged. "—we'll just work this out in court.

But if you choose that route, understand this. Audrey Bing is a valued employee and a cherished member of our household, as is Jillian. Why, they're just like family to us. And family—as you've likely gathered, given your taste for gossip—is one of the only things we Blake boys take seriously."

"Family." Jem snorted. "Strippers and top-shelf scotch is more what I heard."

"We do enjoy a good time," Will said easily. "And nothing spells *good time* to us Blake boys—outside of strippers and scotch, that is—like a nice, bloody brawl. So if you think the prospect of a bare-knuckles lawsuit is a deterrent, you're sadly misinformed, Mr. Bing."

"*Jem.*"

"And if you think we'd ever, in any incarnation of the universe, hand a woman and child under our protection over to a pint-sized, delusional bully? Well. You're beyond misinformed. You're a fucking moron."

The color drained out of Jem's cheeks with comic abruptness, then roared back in ugly splotches. His mouth worked but no words emerged. Triumph slid hot and lazy though Will's veins. First blood was delicious. He leaned in and lowered his voice. Spoke while Jem was still gargling venom. "You'd be most unwise to underestimate how far we'd go to protect what's ours." He smiled. "*Jem.*"

Jem glared at him, and Will could hear the man's fury pulsing like a heartbeat under the wild buzz of his fear. "Yours, huh?" He slid a speculative look at Audrey, all but lost in Will's massive leather chair. "You heating up more than the leftovers, Audi-girl?"

Audrey returned her father's gaze silently and without perceptible emotion while Will's monster lunged against its chains. Will concentrated on breathing. Blood was like scotch. One taste was never enough. Even Hildy made a pained noise.

"What?" Jem snapped over his shoulder at her. "It's a legitimate question."

"Oh, absolutely," Audrey said. "Because the only reason a man would go to this much trouble for me is if I were blowing him and his whole family on the side. Nice, Dad. Thanks."

"Oh, Audrey." Hildy waved a hand in the air, like she was erasing Jem's ugly words from a blackboard. "He doesn't think that. It's just that he's your father."

"Yeah," she said sourly. "I know."

"And his experience is of men." Hildy gripped her purse and leaned in earnestly. "Think about it. Construction, plumbing, entrepreneurial endeavors? He lives in a very masculine world, and it colors the way he views—"

"Christ's sake, Hildy, enough psychobabble," Jem boomed. He turned that glare on Will. "I know what men are," he said. "I know what they want and how they think. And I know what they think when they look at a woman like her." He hooked a thumb Audrey's direction. She flinched— a tiny flinch, really, barely perceptible—but Will caught it. His monster lunged against its chain again, and the clash and gnash of it was deafening.

"A woman like me," Audrey murmured. "What do they think, Dad? When they look at a woman like me?"

"You know what they think," Jem said, his eyes never leaving Will's. He made the words an accusation, one Will couldn't deny. He knew what he thought whenever he looked at Audrey. "It's a legitimate question, Blake," he said softly. "And if it comes down to it, I'll bring it up in court. Don't think I won't."

"You'll do what you think best, of course." Will rose, and tucked his hands carefully in his pockets so he wouldn't accidentally put a fist through the guy's jaw. He rounded the desk to hold Audrey's chair while she rose, too. As if demonstrating some manners would pound them into Jem's thick skull.

Then again Will's mom had pounded manners through his own thick skull once upon a time but his anger and fear had buried them so deeply he'd only recently uncovered them. It occurred to him to wonder if maybe that was why he could suddenly hear Jem's fear and pride. He'd finally put his own buzzing fury to bed. His ears were clear for the first time in years, and suddenly he was hearing other people.

People who are not your goddamn imagination, Bob said inside his head.

He ignored that and wondered idly who Jem might be when he wasn't flooded with that weird, angry noise all the time.

"Fine," Jem snapped and spun for the door. "You want a war? You can have one. My lawyers will be in touch. Come on, Hildy. I told you this was pointless."

"Jem, stop." Hildy came to her feet, folded her hands in front of her and drilled him with a mom-look that Will was grateful she hadn't turned on him. He was a mean bastard but he couldn't promise he wouldn't cry like a baby under a look like that. All loving disappointment and betrayed expectation. Jem scowled and hunched. But he stopped moving toward the door. "We didn't come here to fight," Hildy announced. "We came here to solve this."

"Like I can solve anything when she's holed up behind her guard dog?" Jem rolled his eyes. "They won't even negotiate!"

"I didn't say we wouldn't negotiate," Will said. "Only that Jillian's custody is not now and will never be on the table. She belongs to Audrey."

Jem threw out a hand. "See?" he said to Hildy. "See? They're keeping my granddaughter from me!"

"Damn right I am. Because you're crazy." Audrey slapped her hands on the desk and leaned in. Fury lit up her face and towering waves crashed in Will's ears. "And because your brand of crazy scared your precious granddaughter to the point that she doesn't even talk any more. So, hell yes, I'm keeping her from you. I don't know what you two did to her but it's not happening again. Not ever. Not as long as there's a dollar in my bank account and a breath in my body. So sue away. You're not getting her. Not ever."

Jem opened his mouth hotly but Hildy snatched his arm. "You see?" she said to him. "This has all been a misunderstanding!"

Jem muttered, "Misunderstanding, my ass." But he subsided. Sulkily. Will's hands went to fists in his pockets but he kept his face cool, impassive.

"Has it?" he asked, his voice bland.

"Yes, of course." Hildy smiled and turned to Audrey. "You see, dear, your father and I? We didn't do anything to Jillian. We've been trying to do something *for* her. We've been trying—quite desperately—to protect her."

Audrey cocked a brow. "From what? The burdens of communicating via speech?"

"From your mother."

Audrey sat back down and covered her eyes. "My dead mother." It wasn't a question. Will lowered himself to the edge of the desk and settled in. This should be interesting.

"Yes, dear. Your dead mother."

"Who is not," Jem put in darkly, "at rest."

"We believe that your mother's earth-bound spirit has attached itself to Jillian," Hildy said, as if this were a commonplace event. Something unpleasant but not out of the ordinary, like head lice or the stomach flu. "It's not harmful, physically speaking, this kind of psychic co-existence. But it's an extremely unsettling experience, even for an adult, let alone a child of Jillian's obvious gifts. She must be terrified, the poor thing."

"Not that she's mentioned," Audrey said bitterly. "And thanks very much for that."

"If we'd had any idea that Jillian was at risk, we'd have taken protective measures," Hildy said, Audrey's malevolence sliding right off her. "Unfortunately, Cece— that would be Audrey's mother," she told Will, "turned out to be more wily than I anticipated."

"Wily?" Jem snorted. "She's insane!"

"It's been an unusually difficult case," Hildy admitted.

"How so?" Will asked.

"Well, most earth-bound souls aren't complicated," Hildy said. "They can't be. The bridge to the hereafter enacts a tremendously powerful pull on a soul once it's been liberated from its mortal shell. Resisting that pull requires an incredible amount of energy and an unwavering focus. Anything less, and the soul is simply pulled across the bridge whether it desires to go or not. That's just how we're designed."

"Handy," Audrey murmured.

"Isn't it?" She smiled. "We are indeed fearfully and wonderfully made. And the human heart is so full of contradiction and paradox. Force a soul to acknowledge even one of those contradictions, and over it goes." She spread neat hands. "All it takes is a single moment of inattention, a small lapse in focus."

"And you couldn't break Cece's focus?" Will asked, unwillingly fascinated.

"I'm afraid that at this point, all Cece *is* is focus." Hildy pursed disapproving lips. "All those lovely contradictions that make up the healthy human spirit? Cece has none, and I should have anticipated that. A young mother doesn't commit suicide without an overwhelming burden of bitterness and pain, after all. And a soul doesn't resist the bridge as long as Cece has unless that burden is so enormous that it drowns out every other note in her soul, including love. Throwing off the bonds of love—even the love she bore her own children and grandchildren—has allowed her the strength and the focus to pursue her ultimate purpose without conscience or remorse."

"And what purpose is that?" Will asked.

"Revenge." Hildy sighed. "Jem refused to acknowledge or legitimize Cece's pain during her life so she's bound and determined that he should experience it after her death." She shook her head. "It's become something of a *raison d'être*, I'm afraid."

"*Raison d'être*," Audrey mused. "Can you even use that phrase when you're talking about a dead person? Or is it absurd to talk about a non-being's reason for being?"

"A fascinating existential question," Will said. He might be in love. "Ms. Wise?"

"Fascinating, indeed. And well above my pay grade," Hildy said. "I don't philosophize or judge. I simply make the bridge and encourage earth-bound souls to use it." Her lips flattened. "Unfortunately, Cece was beyond encouragement. She reacted rather badly."

"No shit." Jem shook his head. "She was supposed to

cross over, not hijack the nearest warm body."

"Hijack the nearest—" Audrey stared. "You mean Jillian."

"Which is why," Hildy said hastily, "we need her to come home."

"Come home? Why?" Audrey rolled her eyes. "So you can perform an exorcism or something? I thought Dad was down on those. He was when Mom held one, anyway."

There was a guilty silence in which Hildy and Jem exchanged speaking glances and Audrey's heart sank.

"That was supposed to be hyperbole," she told them.

"Hyperbole," Will murmured from somewhere off to the side. Like he was tasting the word. Enjoying it.

"But you're for real on this." She slid a glance her father's way, then went back to Hildy. They both returned the look impassively. "You want to do an exorcism."

"It's not an exorcism, *per se*," Hildy said quickly. "It's a simple ceremony. Absolutely harmless. Everything you're thinking? The demons, the chanting, the judgment? It's not that at all."

"Then what is it?"

"Some light guided meditation, some essential oils. A little massage." Hildy clasped her hands as if in prayer. "Above all, though, it's *gentle*. Some children actually fall asleep."

"You've done this before?" Will asked.

"Several times." Hildy didn't look away from Audrey. "It's not uncommon. Children are so chaotic, emotionally speaking. They offer a great deal of energy to an earth-bound spirit looking for the strength to resist the bridge. What I do is teach how to withhold that energy." Hildy offered a tentative smile. "I can help Jillian create a certain stillness in her mind and body. This interrupts the flow of energy to the invading spirit, of course—"

"Oh, of course," Audrey murmured.

"—and when Cece's strength is at low ebb, I simply make the bridge and extend the invitation." She paused. "Perhaps a bit more forcefully this time."

"Easy peasy, lemon squeezy," Audrey said. "Sounds delightful."

"Wonderful!" Hildy gave a happy clap and beamed. "When can we expect—"

"But no." Audrey rose and flattened her hands on the desk. "I'm sorry. No. Jillian's a little girl. And fate dealt her a shitty hand. Crappy mom, selfish grandparents." She sent her father a sharp smile. "Impulsive aunt with stripperish tendencies who makes decent men think indecent thoughts."

"Audrey—" Will stepped up, took her elbow. She shook him off.

"No. She's not going back to that house," she said flatly. "She's not going anywhere without me."

"Of course not." Hildy opened her arms like she was inviting a hug. "You come home, too."

Chapter 15

"Like hell," Audrey snapped, dumbfounded.

"Temporarily," Hildy said hastily. "Not forever, just for a few days. A week, tops." She gave Audrey the big, soft eyes again. "Please. We want you there. We need you there. You're an incredibly strong presence, spiritually speaking. So determined." She beamed. "You're very like your father that way."

Audrey cocked a brow. "If you're trying to flatter me, you're going the wrong direction."

"Audrey." Will was still there beside her, tall and stern, his hand back on her elbow.

"I'm serious," she said to him. She kept her voice level but panic welled up inside her. Because she knew that face. It wasn't his grim face, but it was close. It was his *let's do business* face. And any business that put her back under her father's roof, back in her mother's darkened bedroom? Back where the normal rules for what was real and what wasn't had been suspended longer than she could remember? Just the idea sent icy shards of terror straight to the center of her soul. She'd lived through that. She'd put it behind her, and didn't care to repeat any piece of the experience. And she'd be damned if she'd expose Jillian to it.

"I'm not going back there, Will. They want to do their little ceremony, fine. They can do it at the Annex. But Jillian and I are not going back there."

"I'm afraid we can't do that," Hildy said softly. "Oh, sweetheart, I'm so sorry. We would if we could." To her credit, the woman did sound genuinely sorry. She was good, Hildy Wise. Very, very good. Audrey would have to remember that. Be on her guard. She'd been without a mother for a long time. Far before Cece's suicide, truth be told. But she'd done just fine on her own and Hildy Wise could take the damn memo on that. She didn't need a substitute mommy.

"But it has to be at home," Hildy went on. "*Her* home. Cece's. She won't step out into the unknown or the unfamiliar. The separation of spirits needs to happen at the site of the original entanglement."

Will's hand was on her elbow. He frowned down into her face and she stared back at him, willing him to understand. Because she didn't want to say it out loud. Didn't want to give voice to how badly the thought of going back to that damn house and into her mother's bedroom terrified her. *Please, Will*, she thought desperately, leaning hard into the eye contact. *Don't make me do this.*

He held her eyes for a searching moment, almost like he was listening to her mental screaming. Like he could hear the panicked static in her head. Then he turned to Hildy and Jem.

"We'd like a moment in private, please."

"Of course!" Hildy chirped. Jem frowned blackly but didn't resist when Hildy looped her arm through his and towed him toward the door. "We'll just step out to the reception area!"

She hustled him through the door and clicked it shut behind them. And Audrey realized that Will's hand was still on her elbow. Warm. Solid. Reassuring. Which was strange because she didn't generally care for being touched, particularly not by men who wanted something from her. And Will definitely wanted something from her. She remembered the desk situation quite clearly.

But he wanted something apart from *that*. She could feel it vibrating in the air between them. Something in that sharp-edged face said negotiations weren't over. Not nearly.

"Seriously, Will." She held up her hand between them like a goalie, ready to deflect his shot. "I won't go back there so don't ask it of me. I won't ask you to stand behind me on this—"

"You don't have to."

"—nor do I expect you to wage legal war on my

behalf—"

"I like waging war."

"—plus I'd never ask you to spend that kind of money or go to that kind of trouble—"

"Why not? I have plenty, and I like trouble."

"—but I am going to ask you to stall them."

"Stall them?" He frowned. "Why?"

"So I can grab Jillian and get the hell out of here. If you can just buy me enough time to get home and—"

"Audrey." His other hand came up, and suddenly he had her by the upper arms. Gave her a gentle shake. Not enough to hurt her, or even rattle her. Just enough to cut through the panic and stop the words falling from her mouth, faster and faster, like a rockslide or something. "Hey. Audrey. Stop, okay? Let's just take a minute here." His grip shifted and suddenly he wasn't holding her. He was rubbing her. Sliding his open palms up and down her arms. He was...comforting her. Calming her. *Petting* her. And it was working. Something thick and warm slid into her veins, eased the highest spikes off the panic and fear. "Breathe, honey," he said softly. "Breathe, and we'll talk in a minute."

It was, she decided later, a mark of how truly desperate she was that she didn't argue. She just took those gorgeous lapels of his, one in each trembling fist, and laid her forehead against his chest. And breathed.

"There you go." His voice smoothed over her skin like warm oil and his hands slid over her back in slow, small circles. The heat of them seeped through the textured wool of her jacket, and made her feel...safe. And good Christ, when had that ever happened? When had she ever felt safe in William Blake's presence? But his palms were huge. The two of them together probably covered ninety percent of her back, and it was hard not to feel protected with your forehead pressed to a guy's tie, his cologne in your lungs, and his two hands shielding your spine.

She stayed there—couldn't force herself to leave actually—for an embarrassingly long time. Well over a minute, probably. Which wouldn't be very long if she'd been, say, surfing the internet. But she was allowing herself to be...cuddled, and by a dangerous man. By *Will*. A minute was an eternity.

Not that he seemed to mind. He stood there, solid, steady, and still, his hands moving in lazy circles over her shoulder blades. They moved like the tide, those hands of his, and with a care she'd never expected of him. She found herself catching his rhythm, leaning into it. Her breath slowed, deepened. Her heart crawled out of her throat—reluctantly—and settled back into her chest where it belonged. When her fingers stopped tingling and she regained feeling in her lips, she forced her fists to open and her feet to step back. Will didn't try to hold her.

She took another second to gather her strength, then lifted her eyes to his. She should have braced herself. That wicked beauty of his was a lot to take when your knees were already iffy. He slipped his hands into his pockets and watched her closely in return.

"You're good?" he murmured.

"Yeah." She blew out a breath and glanced away. Call her weak but she needed a respite from the impact of that face. Then she forced her gaze back to his, and found his eyes filled with an unholy tangle of concern and left-over bloodlust. She didn't know how one person could simultaneously feel both of those things but Will was a mixed bag. Always had been, always would be. It tugged on something inside her, though. Something unexpected. An answering contradiction, maybe. She didn't know, but she wished his complications didn't appeal to her so much. Be a lot simpler.

"Yeah," she said again. "I'm good."

"Good." He eased one hip onto the edge of his massive desk and gave her a very direct look. "Because it's time to deal, Audrey."

"Oh, hell." She dropped into the Dr. Evil chair and scowled. "I knew you were going to say that. But why should we? When they walked in here, it was all *give us the kid and nobody gets hurt*. We've got them down to *let us borrow the kid for a few days, oh, and you can come with her if you want*. Why do we have to deal at all? Why don't we just finish them off?"

"For exactly the reasons you just pointed out. They've already given up a lot. A hell of a lot. So much that Jem's probably out there right now wondering if it wouldn't be better to just pull the trigger on that ugly lawsuit he's so fond of threatening us with. We want them to stay in the game, Audrey. Giving them a little something will ensure that they do."

"This isn't a damn game, Will." She pressed cold fingers to the ache between her brows. "Somebody could get hurt."

He shrugged. "*Life is pain, Highness. Anyone who says differently is selling something.*"

"Oh my God." She dropped her hand to stare at him. "*The Princess Bride* is your playbook here? Please tell me your next move isn't developing an immunity to iocane powder."

He grinned, and the sight of genuine amusement on that difficult face arrowed through her, landed hard and sharp in her belly. A twinge of dismay landed right behind it. Because this thing, this *want,* was getting out of hand. "No time for that, unfortunately. Plus, if I ever get to take out your dad, I'm doing it the old fashioned way. Poison would be wholly inadequate to my rage at this point."

His rage. Shit. Shame lapped at her and she sighed. "Yeah. Sorry about that."

"Sorry?" He frowned at her. "About what?"

"About my dad being horrible to you."

He waved a dismissive hand. "Eh. Garden variety trash talk. *You're a drunk and you pay for sex. Your family is trash, and your mama wears combat boots.*" He made a rude noise. "It was a bit of a disappointment, frankly. I figured your dad would land a better punch."

"You did?" She studied him. "Why?"

"Because yours is awesome, verbally speaking. You must get it from your mom." He shrugged and Audrey grappled with an unruly rush of pleasure. He thought she had an awesome verbal punch? "No, your dad didn't slide out of bounds until he called you a stupid stripper and a jumped up maid. He didn't piss me off until he dismissed you and degraded you and implied in every possible way that you weren't—aren't—important. And even that I could've been cool with. If it had rolled off you, that is. I mean, we're all adults here, and the game is what it is." He leaned in and Audrey held her breath. "But it didn't roll off you, Audrey. He made you feel small. He made you feel dirty, and...less."

"Less?" It came out in a cracked whisper but she didn't care. "Less than what?"

"Less than you are." His mouth tightened into a razor-thin slash. Sharp. Dangerous. "Less than good. Less than principled. Less than brave and honest and right." One hand gathered into a fist on the desk beside him, and it looked hard. Effective. She wondered if he even knew he'd done it. "And that shit won't go unanswered."

The knot of self-reliance inside her loosened with a sudden slippery lurch and yearned toward him. Toward this big man and his dangerous fists and his hard face and his ridiculous belief that her honor was his to defend. So she administered a sharp slap to her inner fair maiden and glared at him. "Please, Will. I'm not a delicate magnolia blossom, okay? Yeah, my dad threw some rocks at me. They stung a little, too, I won't deny it. But I'm perfectly capable of throwing them back. I don't need anybody to—"

"Believe me, I know." He shrugged easily. "I've been on the receiving end of your temper, Audrey. I have personal experience that says you're dangerous as hell. I respect that. To be perfectly honest, it turns me on." His face didn't change in any way she could put her finger on but suddenly she was aware of every inch of her skin. "You want to take your dad on? Be my guest. Let me know, though, because I want front row seats. Watching you lose your temper gives me a serious thrill."

He did smile at her this time and she had to clench her knees together. Because suddenly her thigh muscles felt remarkably loose. Good God, this man was dangerous.

"And while I'll enjoy the hell out of that—and on any number of interesting levels, too—that's you satisfying your rage. My rage is a separate thing entirely. Before all is said and done, I'll be introducing your dad's teeth to his spleen, via my fist. And I won't be asking your permission before I do it, or apologizing after." He frowned down at his fist on the desk like he'd only just realized it was there. Opened it experimentally then shrugged and let it reform. "Jem and me? We understand each other. Or we will. The punching is just part of it."

She stared at him for a long moment. He held her gaze and didn't blink. "Oh, whatever," she muttered. "Beat the crap out of each other. See if I care."

"We'll do that."

She sighed. He looked so happy. "So how do we keep them in the game?"

He eyed her. "You ready to hear it?"

"As I'll ever be." She leaned forward, elbows on knees, fingers pressed to her lips. "What are we giving them?"

"Exactly what they asked for."

Chapter 16

On Monday morning, Audrey stood at the Annex kitchen's island counter with a cup of coffee in her hand and a frozen lump of dread in her stomach. Jillian sat on a stool ignoring her toast. She had Drew's e-reader (Audrey had diligently checked it for smut) propped up against the jug of milk, and was staring at it with the glassy eyed devotion of an addict. Evidently Tolkien was her cup of tea. She'd been through the entire Lord of the Rings trilogy at least four times since Drew had downloaded it for her not even a week ago, and had knocked off *The Hobbit* half a dozen times in between. Like it was dessert or something. And still, it absorbed her to the point that her toast lay forgotten on the counter between her elbows while her eyes slid back and forth with a speed that made Audrey both dizzy and uneasy. Because how was she going to keep up with this kid's appetite for information? How could she effectively parent a child with this kind of firepower upstairs?

She could probably start by making sure she didn't forget to eat.

"Jillian."

The girl jumped and flicked her a questioning glance.

"Breakfast."

She blinked down at the toast like she'd never seen it before.

"Man cannot live by Tolkien alone. Eat up."

Jillian lifted a toast point, bent it in half and wrinkled her nose.

"Well, it was crispy twenty minutes ago." Audrey moved over to the coffee pot and topped off her mug. Again. "When I put it in front of you."

Jillian sighed and took a minuscule nibble.

"Jilly, come on." Nerves swirled in Audrey's stomach but she couldn't be sympathetic here. The kid was skinny to the point of transparency already. "We're leaving for Grandpa's this morning, and you know you get carsick on an empty stomach. If you don't eat breakfast, you'll puke all over the floorboards. Of *Will*'s car."

Jillian wrinkled her nose again but took a more substantial bite of toast. She was chewing manfully when Bel flew in the swinging door. She wasn't running. Bel never ran. She was too organized to fly around like her hair was on fire the way Audrey did. But she did have a top gear and she was very clearly in it.

"Hey, Bel." Audrey set down her coffee mug and grabbed the kettle off the stove, glad for the distraction. "Tea?"

"Bless you," Bel said, her head already in the fridge. "I finally got James out the door to the gym but I think he's more nervous about this January camp thing than he's letting on. He was particularly difficult this morning."

"Hmm." Audrey stuck the kettle under the faucet and flipped the handle. She waited for it to fill and threw Bel a speculative glance. Beard burn on her neck and a dreamy, satisfied air sliding underneath all that bustle. "Was he?"

Bel paused, elbow deep in the cheese drawer. "Was he what?"

"Difficult." Audrey kept her face bland, her eyes innocent. "As in hard. To, you know, handle?"

"Oh, hmm." Bel pulled out a wad of butcher paper, her eyes sliding away from Audrey's. She sniffed at it experimentally. Or maybe she just thought she was hiding the blush creeping up that beard-burned neck.

Audrey sighed sympathetically. "You poor thing."

Bel finally looked up and caught the grin Audrey was fighting. She grinned back. "It's a burden. But some men need a firm hand. Lucky for James, I have one." Her grin went sly. "Lucky for me, he seems to like it when I use it."

Jillian popped up behind the e-reader like a prairie dog sniffing the air. Audrey cleared her throat meaningfully then took the kettle to the stove and fired up a burner. Bel carried her hunk of paper-wrapped something to the island counter. Jillian leaned over for a closer look. Bel was always pulling wonderful and unidentifiable things out of her magic fridge.

"My point," Bel told the child, "is that some men need more tending than others." She gave Jillian a confidential look. "Now I like tending but that's me. You'll want to choose carefully when your turn comes."

Jillian nodded wisely.

"Now then." Bel gazed critically at the mystery package center stage. "Let's talk about cheese."

"Cheese?" Audrey shot a look at Jillian who shrugged back. They both watched as Bel unfolded the butcher paper with a ceremony that suggested that she was about to reveal a heavenly choir or maybe the Ark of the Covenant. Certainly not a runny, grayish lump that smelled strongly of something Audrey couldn't quite place. If pressed, she'd put it on the scale between fish and fertilizer. "Do you want to talk about that cheese in particular, or—"

Bel leaned in and filled her lungs with cheese fumes like somebody had opened a thousand-dollar wine and she'd been offered the cork. Audrey was watching this with fascinated revulsion when Will walked in wearing another one of those gorgeous suits. Her stomach gave a hot squeeze that had nothing to do with cheese.

"Good God, Bel. What on earth are you doing?" His lip curled with magnificent disdain. "Stop smelling that thing. Botulism can be air borne, you know."

"Oh, please." Bel leaned back and sighed with satisfaction. "This gorgeous, washed-rind, hand-wrapped beauty is a Cato Corner Hooligan. That's not botulism. That's *terroir*."

"*Terroir*." Will clearly knew the word; he just wasn't buying it. But he shaped it in his mouth with a drawling ease that made Audrey wonder if he spoke French. She wanted desperately for him to say it again. The kettle sputtered into a piercing shriek and she realized she was staring. Oh boy. She tore her eyes from him and all but skipped over to the stove. She prayed he'd been too distracted by the cheese to notice her staring with fascination at that *face* of his while it moved through its usual range of emotions. Disdain, judgment, impatience.

None of which, she reminded herself as she automatically measured out Bel's favorite tea like the highly trained butler she was, spoke well of the man who habitually wore them. So why the hell did it—he—compel her so? Why couldn't she stop looking?

She had to stop looking.

She pulled in a settling breath and delivered the tea cup to the island counter. "Four minute steep," she told Bel who was still regarding her cheese with the manic enthusiasm of a kindergarten teacher on finger painting day. Jillian tapped the counter and held up her little note pad. She'd scrawled *Tear what?* Audrey hesitated and hoped Will would take the question. She knew the word, of course—Swiss boarding school had taken care of that—but she really, really wanted to hear him speak French again. That wouldn't be looking. Just listening.

"*Terroir*," Will told her, still frowning at Bel and what he clearly considered her flagrant courting of disease. Audrey suffered a wave of slow, rolling lust. Then he broke it down, syllable by syllable, letting that little trace of Texas in his speech pull the vowels out. "Tare. Whar." Audrey had to clutch the counter. Oh hell. She had to stop listening, too. "It's a French term. It means having the characteristics of the land which produced it. Usually it's applied to wine but it can certainly be applied to cheese."

Jillian digested that one and Bel leaned over again for another whiff. Audrey winced on her behalf and glanced involuntarily at Will. He met her eyes and gave a tiny shrug, the indulgent kind family members give each other when one of their own is deep in a quirk. Audrey was glad she was already leaning against the counter.

Bel actually wafted the fumes closer to her nose with a happy hum. "Smell the dairy air."

Jillian grinned and scribbled. *All I smell is derriere.*

Audrey laughed. The smell *was* powerfully reminiscent of cow butt. "Me, too."

"Yep." Will headed for the coffee pot. "I think I

changed my mind about breakfast."

Jillian gave Audrey big, hopeful eyes.

"Persons weighing under sixty pounds have no breakfast skipping options." Audrey shot a look at Bel. "We'll be out of here in fifteen minutes," she said. "Is there any way you can put your *terroir* away until Jillian's finished her toast?"

"Oh!" Bel shook herself out of her dairy-based reverie. "Right. Sorry." She wrapped up her cheese again and put it back in the fridge. "It's just that if I'm going all the way to Minnesota for sheep butter—"

"You're going to Minnesota?" Audrey asked, startled. "For *sheep butter*?"

"Didn't Will tell you?" She grinned. "I'm visiting a sheep farm in Minnesota while James is at January camp. They do this butter that I swear makes the angels sing. And if the cheese is punching as far above its weight class as the butter? My viewers will want to know about it. And how it compares to the classics like the Hooligan whose *terroir* we all enjoyed just now." Bel heaved a happy sigh at the memory. "There's been an uprising on the artisanal cheese front, you know."

"Oh, of course." Will flipped on the exhaust fan over the stove to suck the dairy air out of the kitchen. "Who doesn't know about the artisanal cheese uprising?" Bel ignored him. Jillian frowned ferociously down at her toast.

"And people are so interested in eating locally," Bel went on. "I wonder if I can get this Redemption Dairy guy to..." She trailed off, eyes unfocused and Audrey knew that the magic was happening in her head. *Kate Every Day* was off and running, and in very good hands.

Jillian looked a question at Audrey. *Get the dairy guy to...?*

"I'm sure we'll find out," Audrey told her. "Why don't you eat breakfast and let Miss Bel work?"

Jillian sneered down at her wilted toast. Will brought his coffee back to the island, and Audrey wondered if she should warn him about the motion sickness thing. Or at least make sure his sporty little bullet of a car had a bucket handy.

He hitched himself up on the stool beside Jillian's and stole a quarter of her toast. The girl blinked at him in surprise.

"Sorry, were you eating that?" He licked the crumbs from his thumb and cocked a brow. "I couldn't tell."

She gave him a glare that clearly said *You didn't want breakfast, you said so.*

He eyed the remaining toast thoughtfully. "I could eat."

Jillian snatched up a quarter of toast and shoved the whole thing into her mouth. Will stole the last quarter while she was busy chewing. She sputtered with outrage.

"Amateur," he said airily. "Hasn't Drew taught you anything?"

She frowned at him but kept chewing.

"Huh. Been holding out on you, has he? And here I thought you two were so close." He bit into his purloined toast with every appearance of relish. "Eat while it's in front of you, kid, or risk the steal. You want a leisurely breakfast? Lick everything you plan to eat. Or spit on it. Sneezing works, too, but only if people see you do it. Then you can take your time."

Her eyes went huge but the chewing continued.

"What, he didn't share his strategy?" Will shook his head. "Doesn't surprise me, I guess. Drew's fun but he doesn't play when it comes to food. He'd mow down his own granny for a piece of apple pie."

Drew ambled into the kitchen. "There's apple pie?"

"Speak of the devil," Will murmured and automatically secured his coffee cup. Then he caught Jillian's eye and pointedly set his mug on the counter between them. Drew swooped in like a hawk and was enjoying Will's coffee before Jillian even swallowed her toast.

"So," Drew said, making a production of the first swallow. "I'd swear I heard somebody mention pie."

Will reached up a casual hand and gave Drew's earlobe a sharp twist. Drew yipped and handed over the coffee.

Will said, "I was just explaining to Jillian here that you're not to be trusted when it comes to unattended food."

Drew swept the kitchen with a hopeful gaze. "There's

unattended food?"

"There was." Will leaned around Drew to smile his sharky smile at Jillian. "I ate it."

"Aw." Drew turned sympathetic eyes on her. "Mean ol' Will ate your breakfast?"

She gave him a pretty decent pathetic orphan face.

Drew shook his head. "You should've licked it."

Will lifted a brow at Jillian. "See?"

Jillian dropped the orphan routine to glare back.

"For heaven's sake." Bel cut through the by-play with an exaggerated eye roll. "Fighting over toast when we have a kitchen full of food." She shook her head. "Who wants eggs?"

Hands shot up all along the island, Jillian's included. Audrey hid a grin and turned away to tuck another few slices of bread into the toaster with a spark of wonder in her heart. Because all this good-natured squabbling in the kitchen? The giving and taking of crap while kids resisted breakfast and adults tricked them into it? All the food stealing and ear twisting and—ugh—toast licking?

It felt an awful lot like family. At least what Audrey had always imagined family felt like.

Which made it all the harder to think about going home.

Chapter 17

"You didn't have to do this," Audrey said again. It was probably the fourth time since they'd left the Annex that she'd mentioned that fact. Will clamped down on a flicker of impatience and concentrated on driving. Traffic was a bitch this hour of the morning in DC, no matter where you wanted to go. Will was rarely grateful for that, but he was today. It gave him something to focus on other than the fact that Audrey seemed deeply reluctant to share air space with him.

He didn't know what had happened, either. He was no stranger to being *persona non grata* but he could usually put his finger on his offense. He wasn't a subtle guy. When he pissed somebody off, it was out loud and unmistakable. Especially when it came to Audrey. His missteps with her were epic. But in this case, he was honestly in the dark.

He thought they'd left things in a pretty good place on Thursday. There had been rocky bits, sure. Most memorably those tense, hot moments on his desk. He'd relived those a time or two (or twenty) in his imagination since, no denying it. But he thought she'd sort of taken that whole deal in stride. He'd spilled his guts, confessed his perpetual hard-on, and struck a bargain: his hands-off in exchange for hers.

Deal.

They hadn't shaken on it or anything—appropriate, given the hands-off agreement—but he'd had the distinct impression that they'd achieved a sort of détente. A wary truce. A working relationship. The way they'd tag-teamed Jem and Hildy afterward had warmed the cockles of his cold, twisted heart but he wasn't a fool. He didn't imagine she was suddenly going to forget what a dick he'd been to her, embrace his finer qualities and fall in love—

Inside his head, Bob chortled. *You have finer qualities?*

113

He scowled. He didn't delude himself that they were even going to be friends.

Co-ed friendship? Please. That's nothing but a gateway drug to sex, and you know it.

But when he'd closed the door on Jem and Hildy on Thursday afternoon with a promise to deliver Audrey and Jillian bright and early Monday morning, he'd judged her easy enough in his company. She wasn't jumping when he spoke to her. She wasn't avoiding his eyes. She wasn't keeping her hands tucked into her pockets and a careful two-yard perimeter of his person. She certainly wasn't acting like riding in the same car with him was akin to sniffing anthrax.

So what the hell had happened?

"Seriously," she said. "I could've driven us myself. Potomac isn't exactly on the way to your office, and I—"

"—don't own a car," Will finished. "So what exactly were you planning to drive?"

Her mouth went flat. "Bel would've lent me—"

"What, her catering van? Because that's all she owns." He shot her a look. "And it's not in fantastic shape. If James doesn't find some excuse to gift her a shiny new one by March, I'll be—" He broke off with a glance in the rearview. Jillian's eyes were on him, large and interested. "—a monkey's uncle."

The kid looked out the window with palpable disappointment. Will suppressed a snort. That child had an unhealthy fascination with inappropriate vocab. Then again, if she used it to spank Drew at Scrabble... Will wondered if he knew any swears with Js or Zs in them he could let slip.

"I'd have figured something out," Audrey muttered, her eyes fixed on the glove box like it held the secrets to the universe. "You didn't need to—"

"This is my exit?" The question was a formality, of course. He had the map in his head and knew exactly which exit was theirs. But people liked to participate, whether he needed them or not. Sometimes he could still hear his mom's voice: *I don't care if you already know the answer. It's not about information, it's about input. You need people, Will. Just not for their answers.* It had taken him a number of years to figure out just what the hell *that* meant—

Bob chuckled. *What did I say about that IQ of yours?*

—but now that he had, he was working on it.

Only twenty-five years too late. Won't your mom be proud?

Will ignored the cutting edge on that one, because he knew she would be. His mom would totally be proud of him. He knew this like he knew his own name. Because if she'd been Johnny-on-the-spot with the flat of her hand up the back of his head, she'd been even quicker with the hug and the forgiveness. If you were trying to do the right thing—no matter how bad you'd screwed up first, or how long you'd spent doing it—she was behind you, cheering you on.

God, he missed his mom.

He wished he could tell her she was right. Wished he could be his eighteen-year-old self again and thank her for all the ways she'd tried to steer him away from the rocky path he'd carved out for himself with sheer, stubborn arrogance. But she was gone, he'd dug this ugly hole himself, and it was up to him to start digging his way out.

So he was asking questions he didn't need to ask in the vain hope that he could get Audrey to say something to him—anything—that didn't start with *we don't need you*.

"Audrey. Come on. This exit?"

She didn't say anything.

Will spotted a gap in traffic and shot across three lanes without the benefit of his blinker. Audrey squeaked and clutched her door handle, but if Will knew about pointless questions, he also knew about rush hour. You either seized your moment or you lost your chance. He glanced at her then at the rearview, gauging a gap sliding toward him in the exit lane. "Yes or no, Audrey."

She squeaked again. He figured that was the best he was going to get, and punched into the exit. He downshifted and they decelerated into the tight cloverleaf without a hint of complaint from the tires. God, he loved this car.

Audrey didn't speak to him again until they pulled into the half-moon drive of her childhood home.

Will killed the engine and leaned forward to take in the

view. Three stories of white-shutters-on-beige-brick perched on a golf course of a lawn, it anchored a well-tended cul de sac buried in a warren of other well-tended cul de sacs. Evidently nobody in the gated community of Billingsgate Stables wanted to live on a through-street. Nor had to. This was not a neighborhood built around navigability.

It was, Will decided, built around conformity. Because Jem's house was identical in every practical aspect to precisely one third of its neighbors. Will had to assume there were only three floor plans available to the residents of Billingsgate Stables—McMansion A, B or C, one on each cul-de-sac. Jem had chosen the biggest one, of course— nothing but the best for his new bride. Will wondered how horrified Cece Whitechurch had been when she'd faced this incontrovertible proof that her husband's promises would fall so short of her expectations. Her *needs*.

He slid a glance at Audrey. She looked resigned. Tired. Pale.

Beautiful.

"So," he said. "*Chez* Bing."

She closed her eyes just a little longer than a blink. Like she was taking a micronap. Or gathering her strength.

"*Chez* Bing," she said, and opened her eyes. "Such as it is."

He dragged his gaze back to the house before she caught him staring. "Such as it is." He got out of the car and flipped forward his seat for Jillian. The kid scrambled out and stood for a moment, peering up at the house. Will took another glance himself, took in all that brick towering against the pale wash of a winter sky and wondered what it looked like to her. The home of her crazy-eyed grandpa? The last place she'd seen her mom? The site of her own personal haunting? He pushed the car door shut and watched her watching the house. She was like a tiny, fragile version of Audrey, swathed against the cold in a thick wool coat, with about twelve yards of gold and scarlet scarf wound around her skinny neck.

"You're in Gryffindor?" he asked. Her eyes came down to his, and she frowned a *what*? "Your scarf." He nodded toward it. "Those are Gryffindor colors, right? From *Harry Potter*?"

She shrugged dismissively, and Will narrowed his eyes.

"What, you're too good for *Harry Potter* now that you're a *Lord of the Rings* freak? You're all *Oh the invisibility cloak's just a bad imitation of the Ring and the dementors only wish they were Ring Wraiths*, huh?"

Her eyes came back to his, interested this time. Will laughed. "What? I was a kid once." *A kid who could eat up thousands of pages a day, too, just like you.* "Imitation is the sincerest form of flattery. You ever hear that?"

She nodded cautiously.

"Don't think of it as ripping off," he advised her. "Think of it as paying tribute. Loving Harry doesn't make you disloyal to Frodo. You don't have to choose."

She pursed her lips and considered him. He tucked his hands into his pockets and considered her back. He could hear Audrey fussing with the suitcases, and while his inner gentleman was itching to go snatch them from her hands, he took another moment to ask a question. The rarest kind. The kind he didn't know the answer to. "Are you afraid, Jillian?"

She didn't answer. Just looked.

"It's okay to be afraid. You've got family behind you."

They both glanced at Audrey, half in the trunk now and muttering about boots. Jillian nodded but there was doubt in those wide, violet eyes and Will realized he'd have to be more specific. The kid's experience of family was a mixed bag.

"You've got Audrey," he clarified, "and she'll take care of you." He met her eyes, made sure she was looking back before he went on. "But you've got us, too. James and Drew and me. Which means that nothing bad is going to happen to you here." He leaned in, lowered his voice. She didn't move. Didn't even blink. She just took him in with those wide, skeptical eyes. "Because you're under the Blake family umbrella these days, and you know what we say in the Blake House."

She rolled her eyes.

"That's right," Will said, as if she'd chimed in with the

Blake brother battle cry. "Family first. What we have, we share. Your fight is our fight. And we Blakes are not amateurs when it comes to fighting. I in particular am the meanest bastard you will ever meet. Do you doubt that?"

She took a moment over that one, then slowly shook her head.

"Good." He reached out and flipped the end of her scarf. "Brave girl."

A smile flickered around the edge of that serious mouth.

"And you'll need to be brave, Jillian. Because I don't think your aunt is feeling great about being back here." Jillian glanced at Audrey who was now scouring the backseat for stray mittens and socks. "Family's a two-way street. She's got your back, so you have to get hers. I want you to take care of her, and text me if you think even for a minute that she needs us."

She put her open palms out to the sides, doing her best appealing orphan again. Will could almost hear the *But, Will, text you with what?* This time he did the eye rolling.

"Like you need your own phone. You're the frickin' Bilbo Baggins of cell phone thievery."

One corner of that mouth tipped up for real this time.

He reeled off his cell number. "Put that in your bear trap of a brain next to Drew's and James'. Don't hesitate to use it, either, you understand me?"

She nodded.

"Good."

Audrey finally seemed to realize there was nothing else she could possibly haul out of the car or arrange for easier transport. Will watched that realization settle on her, bow those courageous shoulders and flatten that lush mouth into a grim line. He and Jillian exchanged a look of perfect understanding, the first one they'd ever shared.

He said, "Let's do this thing."

Audrey didn't resist when Will scooped the suitcases from her hands but she wanted to. She felt naked without the bulk of them standing between her and whatever was waiting for her in her father's house.

It's just a placebo, she reminded herself as dread gripped her stomach with cold fingers. Hildy's little ceremony or whatever you wanted to call it. It was nothing more than a sugar pill for Jem's guilt-addled mind. And as Will had pointed out, a fake exorcism beat the living hell out of a real lawsuit. It might be uncomfortable, but it was a small price to pay for uncontested custody.

Will tackled the steps and Jillian followed with unusual alacrity. Audrey wondered what exactly he'd said to the child while she'd been busy stalling. Then she realized that she was stalling again wondering about it. No hesitation, she told herself grimly. Don't think, just do. Move. *Go*.

She marched up the front steps, brushed past Will and rang the bell.

Will arched a brow. "You ring the bell at your own home?"

"This isn't my home," she said. "I haven't lived here on any regular basis for close to ten years."

"Ten years?"

"High school in Switzerland, remember? Then college in North Carolina—"

"And butler school in the UK."

She nodded, acutely aware of her dampening palms. How could her fingers be both numb and sweaty at the same time?

"You don't even have a key?"

"Of course I do." She shot him a scowl. "But it doesn't feel polite to use it since this isn't my home."

He shrugged easily, as if he didn't have eighty pounds of suitcases dangling from his fingers. "So where do you call home?"

"I don't have one."

"You don't?"

"I'm a butler," she said shortly. "I live where I work."

"Which means the Annex is your home."

He didn't move, didn't twitch a muscle as far as she could see but she had the impression that he'd leaned in. Focused on her. And, as always, that focus of his was something else.

"I guess," she said.

"You guess?" He cocked a skeptical brow. "Do you ring the damn doorbell at the Annex?"

She stared at him, a little mesmerized. "Of course not."

"That's right," he murmured with unmistakable satisfaction as the door swung open. "And don't you forget it."

Audrey blinked at him then turned to the open door.

And found a total stranger standing there.

Chapter 18

"Hey there." The woman gave her a friendly smile. "You must be Audrey."

"I am." Audrey didn't return the smile. "And you are?"

"Answering your dad's door." The woman didn't offer anything else, though that friendly smile didn't budge. Audrey's brows lifted. The woman was within a year or two of Audrey's own age but had her by probably half a foot of height. She was striking rather than pretty, with a strong-boned face and sharp green eyes set off by a high, sandy ponytail. Her skin was creamy enough to suggest that she'd been hatched in an Alpine meadow somewhere, and she had a silly, elfin nose that should have looked out of place in that sharp-edged face. Somehow it looked perfectly at home. A little touch of whimsy to go with that perma-grin of hers.

Whoever she was.

"So I see," Audrey murmured.

The woman turned her attention to Will, and those eyes went bright and interested. She gave him a brief and very female up-and-down. "William Blake, I presume?"

"You presume correctly," Will said gravely but Audrey heard the laugh underneath. She wondered what the hell was so funny. "May I present Miss Jillian Bing?"

The woman dropped to her haunches. "Pleased to meet you, Jillian. I'm Meg." She held out a hand to shake. A big hand, Audrey noted nastily. Because tall girls got gorgeous long legs, yes, but they often got man hands, too.

And man feet. She glanced down and smiled in satisfaction. Yes, indeed, Meg was walking around on some serious gun boats there. Nothing in life was free. And it was nice to know how universally that rule applied.

Jillian hesitated, then looked at Audrey who hastily

dragged her attention away from petty bitchiness and back to the worried child for whom she had full responsibility.

Audrey said, "Meg...?" She let it trail off into a deliberate question.

"Wise." Meg turned that friendly grin Audrey's way, but kept her hand out for Jillian to shake. "Meg Wise."

"Hildy's daughter," Will said, and Audrey thought *Of course*. She wondered why she hadn't seen it immediately. Meg didn't look a thing like her mom but that overpoweringly friendly twinkle? That unspoken *we're going to be such friends!* vibe? It was pure Hildy. Maybe she got that undercurrent of *I'm watching you* from her dad?

Meg sent Will that laughing look of hers. "Got it in one. You really *are* smart, huh?"

"Impressed you, did I?"

Those sharp green eyes made another leisurely inventory of his person and she said, "Not yet but I'm open to it. Keep trying." Will grinned. Audrey ground her teeth. Meg turned back to the silent child in front of her. "My mom's the lady who's going to help you feel better," she said easily. "My job is to help her help you. I hope we can be friends."

Jillian glanced at Audrey again and Audrey managed a reassuring smile. So she reached out and gave Meg's hand a quick shake. Evidently satisfied, Meg stood and flung the door wide.

"Come on in," she said expansively. "No point in heating the neighborhood."

"The refrain of my childhood." Audrey lifted a brow as she sailed into the foyer. "You must be spending a lot of time with my father."

Meg laughed. She scooped one of the suitcases from Will's hand and shut the door. "If that's your subtle way of asking if I'm sleeping with Jem, the answer's no." She nodded them across the coldly impressive foyer Audrey had always hated and sent Will a sparkling look. "He's too short for me."

"He's too old for you," Will said. He might as well have added *But, hey, I'm tall!* Audrey bit down on an acidic comment.

"Oh, I'm not such a stickler for age," Meg said airily. Audrey stalked across the foyer, propelling Jillian ahead of her. Meg and Will trailed behind them, chatting like old friends. "I find that older men have less to prove and more to offer, and I appreciate that. But the height thing is important. Short people are so...short." Audrey actually felt Meg's significant glance on her back. Her jaw was starting to hurt from all the tooth grinding. "Why risk a permanent neck cramp if you can avoid it?"

"I hear that," Will said feelingly.

Outrage smoked sullenly inside her. Audrey didn't recall asking him to bend her over his desk the other day, nor any mention of neck pain when he did so. Then again, maybe she'd been distracted by the massive hard-on he'd been cuddling against her rear end.

"Also, I'm addicted to high heels, so height matters."

Will didn't respond to that but the quality of his silence was thoughtful. Audrey forced herself not to turn around to see what was in those cool, gray eyes of his. If it was speculation, interest or even appreciation, she didn't want to see it. And she didn't feel like digging into exactly why. She just felt like disliking Meg Wise intensely.

She stopped at the base of the stairs. "You can leave the bags there," she said sweetly to Will. She turned a politely inquiring face on Meg. "Did my father mention where he wanted us?"

"To sleep?" Meg pursed her lips. "I assume you're in Cece's room. That's where I set up the equipment."

Audrey said, "No."

Will said, "Equipment?"

"Recording equipment. Video, audio, electro-magnetic." Meg flicked wide, innocent eyes between them. "We never work off the record. It's just asking to get sued."

"We aren't sleeping in that room," Audrey said flatly, her stomach cold and tight.

"Sued for what?" Will asked. His voice had dropped below zero but Audrey didn't care. She wasn't sleeping in her mother's room. And neither was Jillian.

"Breach of contract, fraud, you name it," Meg told him, then switched back to Audrey. "Why not?"

She glanced down at Jillian, at her worried eyes and pinched mouth, then back at Meg. "Where are you and Hildy sleeping?"

"Not with your dad, geez. Neither of us." Meg rolled her eyes. "You're kind of obsessed with that, aren't you?"

"You can sleep wherever and with whomever you like." Audrey gave her a look that suggested her taste in both regards was likely substandard. "Your mother can, too. As for Jillian and me? We'll take the bedrooms with the connecting bath. Top of the stairs, right turn, west-facing windows?"

Meg wrinkled her nose. "Oh, right. The gothic nightmare and the library. Yeah, go for it. Mom and I are here on the main floor."

"Fine. I'll just get the beds made up." She seized the bags and gave Will a fierce smile. "Thanks for the ride, Will."

Will was still frowning at Meg. "Nobody said anything about recording equipment when we negotiated this deal."

"It's standard operating procedure," Meg said. "Mom probably felt it was understood."

"It wasn't." Will didn't budge. "Where are Jem and Hildy?"

"Upstairs. But they're—Oh, hey!"

Will had started up the stairs. Meg flew after him, squawking in protest, her friendly smile finally dented. Audrey watched them, bemused, and her irritation fled. Will had gone from banter to battle in the space of a single heartbeat. Could a person really switch gears that fast?

Then again, maybe he hadn't shifted gears at all. She frowned after him. Maybe he only had the one gear, and everything else was just for show. What if he approached his entire life like a war, and had simply learned to slap a smile over it? Or some flirty banter? It would certainly explain his habit of making conversations into battlefields, and strangers into enemies.

She wondered if he'd been born that way, or learned it

somewhere along the line. A sudden and bewildering surge of emotion swamped her: sorrow for the boy he must've been, tenderness for the man he'd made himself. Jealousy leaving the building, gratitude whooshing in behind it. Will might be complicated and he might be damaged, but he was damned dangerous all the same. And he was leading her dragon up the stairs at a run. One of her dragons, anyway. She seemed to have a lot of them lately.

She stared at the now-empty stairs.

"I don't get him at all." She looked down at Jillian. "Do you?"

Jillian shook her head.

"I won't deny it, though." She looked back at the stairs and shook her head, too. "He kind of grows on you."

Jillian shrugged noncommittally, picked up her suitcase and started up the stairs. Audrey picked up her bags and followed.

* * *

Will threw open the door Meg had raced him to and stopped short. "My God." He stared. "It's...it's..." He gave up, unable to locate the word.

"It's like a brothel and a candle factory had a baby," Meg supplied helpfully.

"A baby that barfs flowers."

Meg laughed delightedly. "I *know*, right?"

Will stepped into the room, taking it in. The walls were dark and lush, the light pink and indirect. A low, fat chaise squatted at an angle to the door, piled with pillows and draped in cashmere blankets.

A lady's fainting couch, Bob said inside his head. *Nice. Wonder where she kept the smelling salts.*

Will wondered that himself. He could use them, actually, because, Jesus, the smell. Between the thickly scented candles and the enormous vases of flowers covering every flat surface he could see, the air was barely useable.

Will switched to mouth breathing. "Window?"

"It's January," Meg said.

"Screw January. I need to breathe."

"Cece didn't believe in fresh air," she said. "According

125

to Jem, anyway. Give it a minute. You'll get used to it."

"Christ, I hope not." He continued his search for a window, but every single edge, corner or line was padded, upholstered, or draped with silk, so he couldn't quite locate one. The carpet was a deep, rusty brown, too, which sucked up yet more of the stingy light. It was nearly the color of dried blood, now that he thought of it, and thick enough to give Bob's office carpet a run for its money.

Unkind, Bob said. *I didn't pick the damn carpet.*

The room doglegged left after the fainting couch and Will turned the corner, hoping for fresh air. He found only an ocean of a bed piled with a curving archipelago of pillows, all of it tented under an elaborate canopy of silk printed like the night sky.

And flowers. More goddamned flowers, guarded by an army of candles. Jesus, the smell. It was starting to get to him.

He found a door on the wall to the left of the bed and strode over to it. He threw it open and found himself peering into a walk-in closet. He flipped a switch and yet more pink light revealed acres upon acres of clothes. Silky clothes, of course. He couldn't see enough of any one outfit to determine a style but he'd bet his last dollar on a vaguely eastern theme—new agey, drapey and about ten years out of date. Cece's clothes.

And more goddamn flowers.

Screw the smell, Bob said inside his head. *Can you hear that?*

Will stopped, struck. And listened. Behind him, Meg did the same.

After a moment, she asked cautiously, "What are we doing?"

"Listening," Will told her. "Zip it, will you?"

She shrugged and complied. Will figured that, given her upbringing, she was probably used to indulging crazy people who heard voices. Except that Will couldn't hear anything.

So pipe down and try harder, Bob said.

Will felt like an idiot.

I'd love to say it's a novel experience for you, Mr. High

IQ, but you're an idiot most days. Now shut the fuck up and listen, will you?

Will listened. He dropped his head, closed his eyes and built a mental brick wall between his back and Meg's cheerful cooperation. He tried to put Bob on the other side of the wall, too, but Bob just laughed his gravelly laugh and said *I don't think so, asshole*. So he forgot about Bob and focused all his mental energy on listening. On hearing whatever the hell there might be to hear inside this shrine to a dead woman's fashion sense.

And he heard it.

It was a faint at first. Echoey. Like the shadow of a stain you can only see in certain lights. He strained toward it, fumbling with the controls on this weird new skill of his. And suddenly it jumped out at him.

It was a scream, a cry of pain so wild and jagged and bloody that he instinctively leapt away from it.

"Whoa." Meg jumped back, too, startled. "Easy, champ."

Will shook himself like a dog and Bob said *Nice, huh*?

"Sorry," he said and blinked around the perfectly ordinary walk-in full of a dead woman's clothes.

"Did you get something?" she asked, her eyes green and interested. "I didn't know you had any psychic ability."

"I don't." But he dialed in on the frequency of that scream again. Cautiously. He found it more easily this time. Was able to keep the volume on low, too, thank God. Even so, the unhinged anguish of it threatened to take out his knees. "This place is freaking me out a little, though. Is this where Cece died?"

"I don't know." He could feel the intensity of her eyes on him. "Is it?"

"How the hell should I know?" He flicked a glance her way and, yep, she was definitely staring. Good thing he was used to being conspicuous. "You and Hildy are the psychics."

"My mom's the psychic," she said. "I'm public relations and technical support. But if you're getting a ping here, I'm sure she'd like to know about it."

"I'm not getting a ping." Because if Will had a religion, it was vocabulary. He believed in the power of words. He liked to call things what they were, and this was no ping. This was a fucking tidal wave of pain in aural form. "It's just weird, you know? Being in a dead woman's closet." He rolled his shoulders, trying to get out from under it. "It made her really *real* for a second there. Sort of brought home the kind of pain she must've been in to do what she did. That plus the flowers?" He gave her a wry look. "I'm not going to lie to you. I had a minor moment. Which I will go to my grave denying, mind you, so how about you just show me where you've set up the A/V equipment and we'll keep this between us?"

"No problem." Meg's smile was inviting, as was her hand on his arm. "We can start with what I've got on the bed."

He smiled back and let her lead him out of the closet. He let his brain automatically record the details of the monitoring equipment while he considered that scream. He wondered if Audrey could hear it, too, on some level. If that was why she refused so baldly to sleep in this room.

It would explain a whole hell of a lot, actually. Audrey owning a key she didn't use. Having a house she wouldn't call home. If he heard his mom screaming every time he opened the closet door, Will wouldn't visit, either.

And if they'd made Jillian sleep in this room? If they'd trapped her all night, every night with her dead grandma's screaming? No wonder the kid had stopped talking—

Dear God, Bob said inside his head. *You're fucking hopeless, aren't you?*

Will frowned, stung. Oh, come on. You wanted me to hear Cece's scream and I did. Not that I enjoyed it. So what the hell else do you want me to—

That's not Cece screaming, you jerk. Why would you be able to hear her? You never even met the woman. That scream? That howl? That fucking barbaric yawp of sheer grief?

That was Audrey.

Chapter 19

Audrey settled Jillian in the bedroom she herself had grown up in—the Library, according to Smiley Meg. Her lip curled automatically but then she was forced to relegate several stacks of paperbacks to the closet before she could make the bed. She had to unload the drawers of yet more paperbacks before she could unpack Jillian's clothes, too.

So, fine. She'd give Smiley Meg that one. Audrey liked books. Always had, and her childhood bedroom looked like it. So sue her. Jillian liked them, too. She'd be happy here for days. She eyed the little girl sitting cross-legged on the bed, already deep into Audrey's old copy of *The Illustrated Man*. Well, hours, maybe, given her word-per-minute pace. But nobody did sci-fi with a human twist like Ray Bradbury, and Jillian didn't seem to have any problem with re-reading. She'd be happy here. Safe.

"I'm going to make up my room now," she said to Jillian. "Just through the bathroom?" She pointed. Jillian nodded absently but didn't look up. Audrey sighed. "Be right back."

She passed through the jack-and-jill bathroom she'd shared with Olivia for the first thirteen years of her life and walked into her sister's old room. The one Meg had called a gothic nightmare. Audrey tried to summon up her sneer again but it was too good a call. She had to go with Meg on this one, too. Deep purple walls, every shade tightly drawn? Ten-year-old posters of hollow-cheeked, guy-lined emo bands staring sullenly down at her? Tubes and bottles of cosmetics still littering the vanity? Black spreads on the twin beds? This place was a cathedral to teen angst.

She stepped briskly into the room intending to snap up the shades, crack a window and get to work, but suddenly the lingering scent of pot and mascara hit her. And she was thirteen again. She was lonely and bewildered and desperate, standing in this room, in this very doorway, squinting into the darkness and the fury, looking for the sister she used to have. The sister who used to look out for her. The sister who, when Audrey caught her at exactly the right moment, in exactly the right mood, might consent to smooth eye shadow on her lids and tell her how pretty she'd be if she ever lost the baby fat.

Then, if she was really lucky, Olivia would let her curl up on the bed and watch while she demonstrated how to vamp for imaginary paparazzi, how to kiss a boy, how to pretend to take a hit from a joint when you didn't feel like getting high. At some point, Audrey would always smear her makeup, and Olivia would huff impatiently about stupid babies, but Audrey didn't mind. She ignored the words and concentrated instead on Olivia's fingers on her face—delicate, gentle, almost loving—while she repaired the damage. Because nobody ever touched her anymore, and Audrey wasn't proud. She'd take what she could get.

Audrey shook herself. Shook off the memories. She wasn't that girl anymore. She wasn't a girl at all. She was a woman, a grown up. She'd put that kind of neediness behind her. She knew better now than to go looking for somebody to fill up an emptiness inside her. She could fill her own holes and when she couldn't, she lived with the emptiness. And she made sure—damn sure—that no child in her care was ever reduced to humiliating machinations to get a simple hug.

She marched across the room, zipped up the shade and let the thin, winter-weight sunlight chase away the past. She made her bed, unpacked her bags and swept Olivia's old makeup into the trash can. And when she couldn't avoid it a single second longer she went looking for Will.

She found him in the hallway outside her mother's suite at the other end of the second floor. He was standing hipshot in the open door, his cell phone to his ear and the other hand jammed into the thick, pale spill of his hair.

"So reschedule," he said to whomever was on the other

end. "They've got this place wired to the high heavens and I don't have the time or the know-how to map it. You do. So get here." He listened for a moment. "I don't know her background. Yeah, *her*. Hildy's daughter. Evidently she does double-duty as mommy's techie." He paused to listen, then rolled his eyes. "Yeah, Drew, she's hot as hell, and I'm pretty sure she wants you. Just get your ass over here and check out her work, will you?"

He frowned and drew back to look at the screen of his phone. "What the—" He put the phone back to his ear. "James is ringing in. Yeah, I thought he was at practice too. I have to go. Get here."

He tapped the screen to switch calls and said, "James. Hang on." He put the phone on his shoulder and shot a finger Audrey's way. That thick hair dipped over his brow and Audrey's stomach tightened involuntarily. "Do *not* go into this room."

"I wasn't going to."

"Good." He pointed at the wall across from the door. "Stay. I have to talk to James, then I want to talk to you."

"I'm not your dog," she snapped. He ignored her.

"What?" he said to the phone. "Oh for Christ's sake, I don't have time for—James, I'm telling you—Oh good God, you didn't—" He pulled back to stare at the phone. "He hung up on me."

"Shocking." Audrey folded her arms, leaned back against the wall he'd ordered her to stay on. "You being so pleasant and all."

He frowned down at the phone for another beat or two, then surfaced. He turned those sharp gray eyes on her. "I'm sorry, what?"

"Nothing." She sighed. "What did James want?"

"You wouldn't believe me if I told you."

She cocked a brow. "Think about why you're in my childhood home, then say that again."

"Right." He pushed a hand over his mouth. "Right."

She pointed her chin past him, at the silk-and-opium opulence of her mother's room. "What's going on in there?"

He leaned against the doorjamb, and his shoulders all

but filled the space. "It's totally wired. It's like they're planning to film a documentary or something."

She shrugged. "Hildy's ambitious. No secret there."

"Did we know this when we said yes to this deal?"

She shrugged again. "They can take all the footage they like. Jillian's a minor, and I'm her legal guardian. Or I will be once we do this thing. If I say they can't put her on TV, it goes in the garbage."

"You're making a pretty large legal leap there, Audrey. Assumption after assumption."

"What choice do I have?"

He smiled at that, his blood-in-the-water smile. "Why don't you let me look into it?"

She studied that smile. Wondered what it said about her that it sort of turned her on to see it spread across the angles and edges of his face, transforming him from interesting to dangerous. "Don't you have somewhere to be?" she said finally. "Some ransacking to do? Some corporation to rape and pillage?"

He shrugged. "Nothing pressing."

"Liar."

"Okay, so there's stuff to do." He moved his shoulders inside that gorgeous suit and the hair fell over his forehead again in a thick comma that made him look like he belonged at some posh British boarding school. Eton or some such. If Eton turned out assassins. "I'll do it later."

"Why?" She came off the wall and moved toward him. "Why would you do that, Will? Why aren't you already out of here?"

"I told you," he said, watching her like a cobra watches a mongoose. "You're under the Blake—"

"What's in there?" She was right in front of him now, close enough to catch the clean, soapy, *wordy* scent of him. She nodded over his shoulder toward her mom's sitting room. Toward that silk-draped cocoon where Cece had insulated herself from the slings and arrows of outrageous fortune, or at least from further disappointment. Eventually from life itself. "What's Hildy got cooking in there that you don't want me to see? And don't give me another line of crap about surveillance equipment. Why am I not allowed in my mom's old room, Will?"

He didn't say anything for a long moment. Just watched her. Waited. She put one hand on his chest, prepared to nudge him out of her way, but the warmth of it startled her. He always looked so cool. It amazed her to find him so *hot* every time she laid a hand on him. His lips peeled back from his teeth at her touch, like she'd burned him but he refused to flinch. She didn't push him. Not exactly. Heat bloomed low in her stomach and slid down her legs at the memory of what had happened the last time she'd pushed him. And she was tempted—very tempted—to do it again but she didn't. She simply applied pressure and waited to see what he'd do.

He covered her hand with his, and it was her turn to hiss. He said quietly, "Why didn't you tell me?"

"Tell you what?" she asked, but she knew.

"That you were the one to find her."

She stared at him, her heart thudding, her fingers numb. There was compassion in those stark eyes of his. Compassion and pain and rage. Oh, yes, rage. There was always rage where Will was concerned. "I don't know what—"

The rage came forward, darkened his eyes like the sky before a storm. "Don't lie to me, Audrey," he said softly. "Say whatever you want, whenever you want. Tell me I'm an asshole, tell me I'm a dick. Tell me you hate me and want my head on a pike. But don't ever lie to me." He curled his fingers around hers, turned her hand over and suddenly they were palm to palm. "Please."

She tried to swallow but her throat was too dry. So she nodded instead and he nodded back. He didn't smile. She was glad he didn't try.

"Why didn't you tell me?" he asked again. He didn't let go of her hand and she didn't think about trying to pull it away. It felt safe inside his, pressed against the hard wall of his chest. He lifted his other hand and touched the ends of her hair.

"I—" She stopped, an awful pressure closing her throat. Oh dear God was she going to cry? This man dealt in casual cruelty, she reminded herself. That was why he was here. Because he had the emotional constitution of a hit man. For goodness' sake, he'd already cost her multiple jobs, a fiancé and a shitload of sleep. Had she cried then? Hell, no. It had been all dry eyes and screw you, then and ever since. So why was she thinking about watering the carpet over an odd moment of kindness now?

Low-grade panic wriggled in her stomach and she slipped her hand from his. She shouldn't let him touch her like this. Not with her needy thirteen-year-old so close to the surface, whimpering things about empty spaces and desperate loneliness. Will's tenderness, she realized, was as dangerous as his temper. More dangerous, really. Because unlike the temper, Will's tenderness came hard. He didn't want this...well, whatever this was between them any more than she did.

Oh, hell, who was she kidding? Like she didn't know what was snapping and crackling between them? Of course she did. Why else would she be dancing around it like a coward? She knew what it was; she just didn't want to name it. Unfortunately dishonesty was one more luxury she couldn't afford anymore so it was time to admit it, if only in the privacy of her own head.

She and Will were flirting—dangerously—with love.

Maybe it wasn't the kind of love that Bel and James had. Maybe it wasn't the kind that led to diamond rings and happy ever afters, either. But Audrey couldn't argue with the math: scorching lust plus aching, persistent tenderness equaled love of some sort. It just did.

But Will didn't want to love her. She didn't want to love him, either. The very idea was ridiculous. They hated each other. Or had. Now he simply regretted the damage he'd done her, and she...

Well, she didn't know precisely what she felt for Will, but she suspected that her needy thirteen-year-old was measuring him against the crater-sized hole in her soul with hungry eyes. Not that the grown-up Audrey didn't own some of the blame for that. She'd been taking advantage of his willingness to make up for past sins for days now, offloading one burden after another onto the uncompromising width of those shoulders, cramming them through the loophole that put her under the Blake family umbrella, if only temporarily.

She hadn't had a choice. Still didn't. She knew that. She had Jillian to think of, and if her inner thirteen-year-old liked Will's shoulders, she was positively ferocious about Jillian's security. If maintaining that security meant taking advantage of Will's shoulders for a little while yet, she would.

But she shouldn't touch him.

She stepped back. He didn't stop her.

"Why didn't I tell you about finding my mom?" Her voice was a miracle of even detachment. "About discovering her body?"

He nodded, his eyes steady on hers.

"It wasn't any of your business." She kept her face as impassive as her voice. "It still isn't."

He absorbed that one in stoic silence. Then he nodded again. "I know. I still wish you'd told me."

She shrugged. "Wish in one hand and spit in the other. See which one fills up first."

"I've heard that one," he said. "Only it wasn't spitting."

Her lips twitched in spite of herself. "I'm in charge of a profanity-obsessed eight-year-old. I don't curse anymore. Jem was a terrible influence."

"I'll bet."

"Then we moved in with you people."

"It explains why she likes Drew so much. Guy's a potty mouth. Always has been."

"Did you try a swear jar?" She leaned back against the wall, and let gratitude fill her. He wasn't going to push it. Will could be a dog with a bone, but evidently he wasn't any more interested in digging deeper into that odd, dangerous moment of tenderness than she was.

"They suggested it at parent-teacher conferences," he admitted. "Repeatedly. It never worked."

"Why not?"

"First off, James was worse than Drew."

"And you were probably worse than both of them put together."

He moved his shoulders. "I was eighteen and raising my brothers. I felt entitled."

"You were." She gave a heartfelt sigh. "You totally were."

"That means something coming from you. You've been there. You *are* there."

She shrugged this time.

"Secondly, though? We were too broke. What the hell good is a swear jar when you have nothing to put in it?"

She started. Somehow it always took her aback to think of Will as poor. But he had been. Dirt poor by all accounts, and for years. With responsibility for his brothers on top of it all. It had to have been crushing.

"Oh, don't look like that," he said, waving off whatever was on her face with an irritable hand. "We ate. We had a roof over our heads. And James was shining even then. He'd been offered a contract with a third-rate team in the UK right before my parents died. He wanted to take early graduation and ship out, but my mom was dead set against it. Once it was just us, though, I did the math and figured we could all eat better on what they were willing to pay him than we could crammed into family housing on campus while I took out loan after loan."

"And learned," she put in quietly. "Don't forget the education."

His lips twisted. "Oh, I got an education. I cut my teeth doing deals with the Premier League, and that's not for amateurs."

"Is that why Bob left you the agency? Because you knew your way around a tense negotiation?"

"I don't know why Bob left me the agency. I suspect Bel had something to do with it."

Fondness was no more than a thin thread stitching together his words, but jealousy spurted up in her so violently that she started again. Will wasn't in love with Bel. She knew that. Not in any purposeful way. But he clearly loved Bel and it had her inner thirteen-year-old baring her teeth and hissing *mine*.

Oh boy.

"But he did leave it to me," Will went on, clearly taking her silence as an invitation to end the conversation, "and unless I want him haunting my ass into eternity, I'm going to have to actually go to the office today. Evidently James just sent a potential client my way. An extremely talented young goalie from Spain will be sitting outside my office door within the hour, to hear James tell it, which means I should leave—" He shot a cuff and checked his watch. "—oh, twenty minutes ago. I hope to God he speaks English because my Spanish is mostly swear words. As soon as Drew gets here, I'll head out."

She nodded. "Thanks," she said. "Seriously, Will, thanks for everything. You've been..." She shook her head. "You've been—"

"Oh, I know what I've been." He moved out of the doorway and slung an arm around her shoulders. Turned her toward the suite of rooms she was sharing with Jillian. "Went to rehab for it. No need for you to come up with the perfect word. You have a tremendous vocabulary and I don't think my poor ego could take it."

"Your poor ego," she snorted through a little glow of pleasure. He liked her vocabulary. He kept saying that.

"Plus, there's no need for tender goodbyes." He steered her down the hall at an amble. "I'll be back tonight."

She stopped and stared up at him. "What? Why?"

He frowned back. "Audrey, come on. They have this place wired like they're expecting the *Real Housewives* or something."

"I know, but Drew's coming so—"

"—and nobody knows geekery better than Drew, no question. But trust me when I tell you that he's a lover not a fighter."

Audrey had to give him that. There was a reason Jillian had trusted Drew first.

"Jem and Hildy are trying to slide shit past us, Audrey, and I'm not having it." His face hardened. "You're going to have your hands full protecting the kid. You need a guard dog, and that's my department. Drew's bringing me an overnight bag."

Her mouth dropped open. "You're staying *overnight*?"

"Looks that way. Think there's room for me?" He glanced around the massive hallway, and an evil grin flickered at the corner of that hard mouth. "Hey, can you put me in Cece's room? That'll burn their toast."

She blinked. "You're sleeping here. And you want Cece's room. The one that's wired up like a reality show."

"Yep." He tucked his fingers in his pockets and rocked onto his heels with an air of deep satisfaction.

"Jem'll blow a gasket."

The grin grew into a full-on smile. "I'll be looking forward all afternoon."

"You know what?" She studied him for a long moment. "I don't think Bel had anything to do with Bob's decision to leave you the agency. I think he knew exactly what he was doing."

The smile died and Will gazed down at her, all serious eyes and sharp bones. Then he shrugged and flicked the ends of her hair. "I'm sure he'll let me know," he said improbably.

She blinked. "He will?"

"Indubitably." He turned and jogged down the stairs. "I have to make some phone calls. I'll send Drew up when he gets here. Meanwhile, why don't you let Jem know that Jillian's busy with schoolwork today and won't be able to see him until I get back tonight?"

Audrey laughed. "You really are spoiling for that fight, aren't you?"

He threw her a glance over his shoulder. "Honest to God, Audrey, it's going to make my day."

She believed him.

Chapter 20

It was nearly midnight when Will finally headed for bed. Cece's bed, as requested. He hadn't thought he'd actually win that one, but Jem hadn't so much as squawked. In fact, he'd granted Will's room request with a smug satisfaction that had Will approaching bedtime with some serious trepidation.

But the room wasn't booby-trapped. The bed wasn't short sheeted. All the cameras were in plain view, and there were none in the bathroom. Drew had been very thorough on that point.

The problem was Drew himself. He was in the bed. Will's bed. Shirtless. Looking damn comfy, too, like he might be intending to stay a while.

"What's this now?" Will asked, though he wasn't in the least confused. Fucking Jem.

"This?" Drew stroked the duvet beside him. "We call this a bed. It's for sleeping."

"I know that." Will's temper rumbled half-heartedly but he was too damn tired to even fight with Drew. He tugged his tie loose, pulled it off and tossed it toward the nearest chair. "What I don't know is why you're in it."

"Because it's almost midnight." He smiled. "And I do like a good eight hours."

"Amen." Conversations with Drew tended to move in circles—big, fat, slow ones—so Will stripped down to his t-shirt and shorts, threw back the duvet and crawled shivering into the bed. Evidently Jem's commitment to the environment included dialing the thermostat down to frigid after sundown. Luckily, Will could argue horizontally as well as vertically. Maybe he'd even fall asleep before it was over. "This, however, is my bed. What are you doing in it?"

"Oh, that." Drew sighed happily. "Meg."

"Oh no." Will gazed at the silk canopy overhead, defeat seeping into his bones. Drew was in love. "Already?"

"Have you seen her legs, Will?" Drew's face went dreamy. "They go on and on and *on*."

Will flung an arm over his eyes and prayed for unconsciousness. "She's a tall drink of water, all right."

"And her tech skills! They're superior. I spent all day checking out her set up here and I wouldn't have done a thing differently. This girl is the whole package—looks, brains, legs." Will felt his brother roll closer and dropped his arm to glare. Drew was a cuddler, and it was best to enforce the perimeter when bedsharing with him. It wasn't *that* cold. Drew didn't appear affected by the glare but he didn't breach the perimeter either.

"I know I've said this before but..." He grinned that beatific grin of his. "This might be it, Will. I think I'm in love."

"Super. Why don't you go sleep in her bed?"

"One step at a time, bro. You don't rush the real thing."

"And step one is sleeping with your brother?"

"No." Drew folded his arms on top of the sheets, carefully plumping up his biceps. "Step one is giving her every opportunity to ogle the merchandise." He aimed a melting look at the corner cam.

Will snorted and rearranged the blankets with some violence.

"Gah!" Drew aimed a kick his way. "Knock it off! It's freezing in here!"

"No kidding." Will shoved him. "Your feet are like ice."

"Yeah, well, quit flapping the blankets and maybe they'd warm up."

"It's January," Will observed. "Wear a shirt."

"And deprive Meg of the gun show? I think not."

A dark thought occurred to Will and he snatched off Drew's half of the blankets entirely. Drew shrieked like a little girl and yanked the blankets back up.

"For the love of—" He glared at Will, the blankets

bundled under his chin. "Are you *trying* to give me hypothermia?"

Will smiled. "Just making sure."

"What, that I wasn't dead yet?"

"That you weren't free-balling bedtime."

"Only in your pervy little dreams." Drew arranged his arms carefully on top of the sheet again, hissing against the chilly air. "Fuck me, it's cold."

Will smirked. "Jem's not one to heat the neighborhood."

"Billionaires," Drew muttered but he kept his arms nice and visible. "So damn stingy."

A beat of silence passed.

"You don't actually have guns, you know," Will remarked.

"Neither do you."

"Hence no gun show on this side of the bed. I know my limits. I woo women with my brains."

Drew rolled his eyes. "Yeah, how's that going for you?"

"It's not."

Drew made a sympathetic noise.

"Because I'm not currently wooing anybody." He felt compelled to point this out for some reason.

Drew ignored this with aplomb. "If you think wooing Audrey with your brains is going to work, you're not firing on all your usual cylinders."

"My cylinders are firing just fine."

"Sure they are."

"Plus I'm not wooing anybody."

"I didn't say you were. Just that *if* you were, you're doing it wrong."

"Well I'm not."

"Of course you're not." Drew closed his eyes, linked his fingers over his belly and nestled his head into the pillow. "Get the light, will you?"

Will snapped off the bedside lamp and glared into the darkness. "And if I were, it wouldn't be Audrey."

"Well, good," Drew murmured. "She's not your biggest fan, you know."

"I know."

"I figured. You being so smart and all."

"Hey, Drew?"

"Yeah?"

"Shut it."

"Okay."

As it turned out, Drew's silence was worse than his conversation. It was knowing. Smug. Will found the first minute ugly but the second was painful. The third was excruciating. The fourth broke him.

"Okay, but just for argument's sake?" he finally said.

"For argument's sake," Drew agreed happily, rolling dangerously close to the perimeter.

"Let's say I *was* going to pitch some woo."

"Pitch woo." Drew grinned in the darkness; Will could hear it as much as see it. "You should make sure to say that to Audrey. A little humiliation could go a long way toward evening the playing field between the two of you."

"This isn't about Audrey."

"Of course it isn't," he said indulgently. Will ground his teeth. "I'm just saying. Women love grand gestures, and grand gestures require significant loss of personal dignity. The best ones do, anyway."

"Women or gestures?"

"Both. Either." He waved a magnanimous hand. "Take your pick."

"How would you know?"

"I read a lot of romance novels," Drew said calmly.

Will snorted out a laugh then realized he wasn't kidding. "You do?"

Drew aimed a look at him across the bed. "You don't?"

"Uh, no."

"Oh come on." Drew rolled his eyes. "Women are *complicated*, Will. They require study. And what did Mom say about studying? What did she *always* tell us when we needed to learn something?"

"Go to the library," Will said automatically.

"And I'll bet you went to the psychology section or some shit." Drew smirked. "You really are hopeless."

"So I've been told," Will murmured. Bob snickered inside his head.

"You're looking to find out what women want? What they love? What makes them melt into soft, sweet-smelling puddles of romantic goo in your manly hands? You want the romance section, dumb ass."

"And this is where you've learned that what women really want is men who'll publicly humiliate themselves?" Now that he considered it, that *would* explain all the man chest splashed across the covers. Not that he'd spent a lot of time studying the man chest. But he did check out his own groceries and he wasn't blind. He read the tabloid headlines, too.

"No," Drew said. "This is where I've learned that the road to true love is a lot longer and bumpier for assholes."

"I'm not on the road to true love." He didn't bother to argue the asshole bit. Truth was truth.

"Of course you're not," Drew said easily. Too easily. "But just supposing you were? You've behaved badly toward the object of your manly affections, Will. Flagrantly and on multiple occasions."

"If the object of my manly affections were Audrey, sure." Will realized he was speaking through his teeth. "But it isn't."

"Oh. Well, in that case." Drew rolled onto his back, snuggled down into the pillow and shut his eyes again. "Night, bro."

Will glared into the darkness for two solid minutes, his jaw ticking like a time bomb.

"All right but supposing she were the object of my manly affections?" he finally said, hating himself. "Just as a for instance, you understand."

Drew rolled immediately back to his side. "Just as a for instance," he agreed.

"What would your exhaustive research into the female psyche suggest I do?"

"Prove yourself changed and worthy," he said promptly.

"Oh." Will considered that one. "How?"

"Let's look to the romance canon for guidance, shall

we?" He sounded delighted.

"Do we have to?"

"First, we'll need to identify what type of hero you are." He gave that a moment's thought. "I'm thinking alpha hole."

"Excuse me?"

"It's a type of hero," Drew informed him. "A mash-up of *alpha male* and *asshole*, typically referring to a guy with an exaggerated and old-fashioned interpretation of masculinity. Likes his women hot, his cars fast and his fights dirty. Doesn't play well with others."

"Alpha hole." Will let the word sit on his tongue, really tried it on for size. "I'm an alpha hole?"

"Well...yeah." Drew found Will's hand in the darkness and gave it a sympathetic pat.

"Mind the perimeter." Will punched his shoulder for him.

"Ow."

"Sorry. I'm such an alpha hole."

"That you are." Drew rubbed his shoulder philosophically. "Lucky for you, women love alpha hole heroes."

"They do?"

"Sure. Not at first, of course, but when a guy like that falls in love? True love? He goes down like a fucking redwood. Loses his shit, big time. And he's been a jerk so this is deeply satisfying."

Will considered his long and tortured history of destroying Audrey's best-laid plans for reasons that utterly failed to stand up to logic or sobriety. "I'll bet."

"All he has to do now is prove he's a changed man."

"How?"

"Well, generally speaking it involves approaching problem solving with a *we* instead of an *I*, and restricting the punching to socially acceptable occasions."

Will brightened. "There's a socially acceptable occasion for punching?"

"Of course. We're still men, are we not? Let's say some idiot takes aim at Audrey. You, sir, have just been invited to the all-you-can-punch buffet, with hero sex for dessert."

The very idea of somebody taking aim at Audrey had blood lust pacing and growling in Will's basement. He blew out a breath and reminded himself that Audrey was safely in bed at the other end of the hall. In fact, if he concentrated, he could hear her there, the soft murmur of her energy lapping gently at his mind like waves on a white sand beach. Safe. Soft. Asleep. His brain lurched toward the hero sex thing and he wrenched it away. He punched for fun and for family. Not for sex. It was too...transactional.

He said, "So if Audrey's ever kidnapped by marauding pirates, I'm golden."

"Exactly!" Drew beamed at him. "See? It's not so hard to figure this stuff out."

"Except that pirates aren't really thick on the ground this time of year," he pointed out. "Or in this neck of the woods." He paused to let that sink in. "Or, you know, anywhere at all."

"Well, no." Drew contemplated that. "No, they aren't. That's true."

"It is."

"And violence is rarely the answer," Drew admitted.

"To anything. I know."

Silence.

"Let's take pirates as a metaphor then," Drew finally said.

"Why not?" Will was ready to agree to anything at this point. This discussion was getting damn depressing, and he was wishing heartily he hadn't been stupid enough to start it. "Pirates can be metaphorical."

"They're just the vehicle anyway."

"For what?"

"For demonstrating that the alpha hole is a changed man. Jesus, Will, keep up."

Will wondered if he could get away with punching him again.

"He'll still save our heroine's bacon when they do turn up," Drew told him. "The pirates. But she might just save his, too. And instead of yelling at her for putting herself in danger, he'll accept her equality and her love. He might even say thank you."

And with that, any stray bit of hope Will had been nursing flickered out and died. Because even putting Audrey in the same sentence as pirates—metaphorical or otherwise—had his fists in knots under the blankets. And he'd be good and goddamned before he'd thank her for risking herself for him. Which meant—according to Drew and the romance canon—that there would be no happily ever after for him. Not that he'd ever expected one. He was righting his wrongs and paying his debts. He wasn't falling in love. He didn't know what the hell he was even doing in this conversation.

"That's all women want, Will. To be your beloved *and* your peer. After that, it's all hero sex and epic banging and happily ever after." He released a long, contented sigh.

Will eyed him in the darkness. "You really do read a lot of romance, don't you?"

"I read a lot of everything. But I'll admit to a soft spot for romance. My fourteen-year-old self had a lot of questions regarding epic banging and hero sex. Romance novels were extremely instructive."

"Fourteen?" That gave him a moment's pause, followed by a familiar clutch of *God, am I a shitty parent.* "I should have paid more attention to your reading habits."

"No kidding," Drew said promptly. "You wouldn't be in this mess if you'd found the romance section earlier."

"That wasn't exactly what I meant."

"I know. Lucky for me, you had your hands full. Plus, I turned out exceptionally well."

Will made a rude noise but it was mostly reflex. Because it occurred to him suddenly that Drew really had turned out pretty well. It was a puzzle, one that Will readily admitted he couldn't solve. Because Drew was smart enough to have conquered the internet when nobody was looking, and yet he was also ridiculously charming and universally beloved. How he'd pulled off that little hat trick Will hadn't the faintest. In his experience, you had to choose—smart or happy, brilliant or beloved. You couldn't be both. Will had never managed it, anyway. Evidently Drew had. He was on a different path from Will's entirely, and Will was profoundly grateful for the places—the happy, sunny places—that path had taken him. Even if Will couldn't go there himself.

"You want to judge me and my reading habits, go ahead," Drew went on blithely. "But when it comes to women, I believe my track record speaks for itself." He arranged his arms on top of the duvet for maximum lady-slaying impact and smiled for the corner cam. "As does yours."

Will's throat was ridiculously tight, so he punched his brother's arm again.

"Ow." Silence. "Alpha hole."

"Sorry. I thought you were a pirate."

Drew actually laughed, and Will's throat eased up.

"Good night, Will."

"Night."

Chapter 21

A scream split the night like a brutal fork of lightning. For a moment, Audrey thought it *was* lightning. She saw the flash of it behind her closed lids, a white blast of shock inside her head. It jerked her to her feet before she was fully conscious.

Jillian, she thought dimly and staggered toward the door. She smacked smartly into the wall instead, setting off another light show inside her head. She sucked her throbbing knuckles and pressed the other hand to her howling eyebrow. Well, hell. She wasn't at home. This wasn't the Annex. This was...home.

Jillian screamed again, and even muffled by several layers of drywall and darkness, the sound had Audrey's heart knocking hard against her ribs. Because Jillian's night terrors never sounded frightened. They never sounded thin or childish or plaintive. No, when Jillian screamed the house down, it was with a bloody, raw-throated fury.

It was Audrey who was terrified.

Adrenaline spurted savagely in her veins and she patted frantically along the walls until she located the dresser. She fumbled for the light. Oh, for pity's sake, a lava lamp? Damn it, Olivia. She ran shaking hands along the wall until she came up with an actual switch plate. Light blasted into the room and she squinted against it to locate the bathroom door. The closed bathroom door. What the hell? She'd purposely left it open so she could hear Jillian in the night.

Another howl tore the darkness and a shameful revulsion gripped her like a damp fist. Nailed her feet to the floor while terror closed her throat. She fought free of it and forced herself to move. She shouldered past the door, sprinted through the echoey, tiled darkness of the bathroom and burst into Jillian's room.

The cold was stunning—the vicious, full-body slap of jumping into a frigid lake. Goosebumps broke out in waves and convulsive shivers followed them. She clamped down on a craven impulse to hit the lights. Light only made it worse. She knew that one from bitter experience. You couldn't shock Jillian out of it; you had to ease her up from the madness with warmth and words and time.

Plus she had no desire to see Jillian's tiny body heaving and twitching in a tangle of sweaty blankets, that unholy rictus of fury twisting her face. She knew demonic possession was Hollywood bullshit but that didn't stop her nervous system from seeing all the symptoms and responding accordingly.

She forced herself to walk across the carpet calmly, murmuring soft nonsense like she was approaching a terrified horse. "Easy, sweetheart, I'm here. Audrey's here."

Suddenly the door to the hallway crashed open and a silhouette loomed into the dim rectangle of light. Shock jolted Audrey right into the air and she gave a thin, strangled screech. Then she recognized that shape—the broad shoulders, the knotted fists, the general air of barely suppressed violence. It was Will, wearing only a t-shirt and boxer-briefs, swaying slightly on his big, bare feet. He was probably still more asleep than awake, but there he was, fists at the ready, come to slay her dragons. Again.

"Holy Christ," he muttered, groping for the lights. "What the hell?"

"Don't!" She ran to him, slapped his hands away from the light switch. "No lights!"

His hands landed on her shoulders, paused at the skinny straps of her tank top, then moved on to briskly rub her chilly arms. "Jesus," he breathed. "I thought it was cold in my room."

"Jem's not one to heat the neighborhood."

"Yeah, but he could consider heating the house."

"Believe me, it's been mentioned."

She wanted more than anything to lean into the warmth of him, but another scream ripped rawly from Jillian's throat

149

and she turned. "Easy, baby," she said, moving into the darkness, into the madness. "I'm here. Audrey's here."

She eased down onto the edge of the mattress, her heart thundering inside her chest and reached across the empty air that seemed to shiver with fury and violence. She found the thrashing lump of child, and the fact of Jillian's sweaty little body under her touch abruptly dialed back Audrey's terror. The noises were inhuman, unrecognizable, but this was Jillian. A tiny, ill-used, bewildered child. A child who needed her, and from whom Audrey would not turn. Ever.

At Audrey's touch, Jillian's body stiffened. It always did. She went utterly, impossibly rigid, her spine bowing off the bed until she was a straining arc of fury. Will moved silently to the bedside. "Audrey, what—"

"Shhh," she said, as much to him as to Jillian. "Let it go now." She chafed the clawed fingers, smoothed the bramble of hair away from her damp cheeks.

Will leaned in, laid the back of his hand against Jillian's forehead. "She's having a febrile seizure." He spun for the bathroom. "I'll run a tepid bath."

"It's not a seizure," Audrey said, keeping her voice low and sing-songy. "The doctor said—"

Jillian's body went abruptly limp, as if the dream monster that gripped her had given a savage exhale and released her. The whimper that rose from her throat now was all child, as were the tears that followed. Will stopped halfway to the bathroom, his silence a question.

"The doctor said they were just night terrors," Audrey murmured while warm relief sluiced through her. "All the doctors, actually." Jillian gave a hoarse cry and leapt into her lap. Audrey clamped her arms around a trembling, sweaty bundle of precious trust and put her chin into a tangle of hair that smelled almost burnt, like whatever had just released her had been hot and smoky. Her own version of hell, maybe.

"I'll be damned if it was." Will's voice was flat in the darkness. "That was a seizure. And believe me, I know what they look like. Drew had one once. Spiked a fever north of one-oh-five while we were in Bosnia-Herzegovina for an away game. He was only twelve. I can still say *send a fucking ambulance* in Croatian."

"Sounds useful."

"It was that night."

"Took a few years off your life, did it?"

"I was just glad it didn't take any off his."

"I hear that." Audrey shifted Jillian to her other thigh. The kid's butt bones were so sharp they were going to give her a Charlie horse. Jillian gave a worried squeak and lashed her arms around Audrey's neck. "But believe me, Will, I've looked into this. We've seen doctors, consulted specialists, gotten second opinions. There's nothing physically wrong with her."

Will's silence had a thoughtful quality that assured Audrey she didn't need to fill in the blank for him. There was nothing physically wrong with Jillian, no. But emotionally? Well, that was a different story.

He came back to the bed, sank down on the edge of the mattress. Jillian whimpered again and cringed away from him. He slid immediately a few feet farther down the mattress but didn't get up. He put his elbows on his thighs and dropped his face into his hands. Gave it a weary scrub.

"Jesus, Audrey, I'm sorry."

She blinked. He'd apologized before but always with a subtle edge. Like they were still at war with each other and his apology was just the opening volley of yet another skirmish. This was the first time he'd ever simply expressed sorrow and regret, flat out, unvarnished. No edge, no motive, no bite. Just grief.

"What for?"

"I know what it is to be responsible for a sick kid, and to be too damn poor to take care of them." His eyes met hers in the dim light from the hall, and his were bleak with knowledge. "No insurance, no money, no access to care, whatever. I know what that does to your gut. It burned holes in mine I'll never fill. And I don't know if it'll do you any good to know it, but the fact that I put you in that position with Jillian has burned me a few more."

"Oh, Will." She closed her eyes and rubbed her cheek against Jillian's hair. She was very much afraid that she might cry here in a minute, and that would mortify them both. "You didn't—"

"The hell I didn't." He wasn't angry. Didn't sound it anyway. Just resigned. "You were hiding. From your dad, from her mom, from *your* mom, whatever. The bottom line is, even if you had insurance, you couldn't use it without tipping Jem off to where you were, and risking him taking her from you. And I don't care what's wrong with her, you couldn't give her up to Jem. If she were a different kid, maybe, but she's..." He moved his shoulders helplessly. "...what she is. She needed you, and nobody else. You knew it, and you knew what it would cost you to take her, to keep her. To keep her safe. You took her anyway. You took her, you got her help, and you paid for it yourself. Somehow. You paid and you paid and you paid, didn't you?" He shoved both hands through his hair with a violence that made her wince on his behalf. "And I didn't care."

"You didn't know," Audrey said gently. "How could you have known?"

"It wouldn't have mattered either way." She knew this for the truth, so she didn't say anything. Just let him spin it out. He clearly needed to, and something inside her wanted to hear it. This blunt honesty—no self-pity, no maneuvering—was sliding over her jagged edges, soothing and smoothing them. "I was too caught up in my own shit to worry about—or even perceive—anybody else's. I'd have screwed you over anyway. I was that damn angry. All righteous and wronged. Jesus." He shook his head. "So don't let me off the hook on this, Audrey. You were in a desperate situation, desperate enough to try to marry money, anyway—" He broke off and stared at her in the darkness, his eyes huge, like the full import of her brief and ill-fated engagement had just struck him. "Wynton fucking Quist," he breathed. "Holy hell. You'd have *married* him."

"Well, I didn't want to." She wrinkled her nose automatically. "But desperate times and all that."

"My God, my God." He put his head back in his hands and rocked. "Wynton Quist."

"You sort of saved me, actually." She eyed him

speculatively. She hadn't thought of it quite this way before. "I mean, Jesus. I could be married." There went the nose wrinkle again. She really couldn't help it. "To *Wynton*."

"How the hell did that happen, anyway?" He stared at the carpet, his steepled fingers against his lips. "A marriage of convenience? I thought that was romance novel shit."

She cocked a brow. "You read a lot of romance novels, Will?"

He paused longer than he should have. "Let's just say I've recently become acquainted with the genre."

"Really?"

"Drew."

"Ah. That makes more sense."

"Doesn't it?" He sighed. "So, your marriage of convenience?"

"Engagement. And it wasn't all that convenient, honestly." She shifted Jillian again. The kid wasn't under yet, not by any means, but she was on her way. Which meant she was getting heavier.

"I bet not. From what I hear, ol' Wyn is quite the catch. How'd you get him to pony up a ring on cue?"

"I've known Wynton most of my life. The rich part of my life, anyway. Kids of our socio-economic status were all farmed out to different boarding schools for the most part, but during holidays we had nothing better to do than hang out at the country club and date in incestuous little circles." She shrugged. "He took me more seriously than I ever took him."

"Evidently."

"When I came home this summer, he was waiting for me with a ring. I guess he thought we'd been going that way for years." She sighed and shifted Jillian to her other thigh. The child murmured fretfully. "I told him I had to think about it."

Even in the darkness, Will's eyes were uncomfortably sharp on her. "You considered it even before Jillian?"

"Not really. But Wyn..." She moved her shoulders. Jillian stirred unhappily. "Let's just say that Wyn has a lot of influence in this town. His mother has more. And I was

153

looking to land a position working for exactly the sort of people they have the most influence with."

"You thought he'd poison the well if you said no."

"He's got a healthy ego and it doesn't get dented that often." She shrugged. "I was planning to get a job *then* deliver the blow. Then Jillian happened and I had to reconsider my options."

"Then *I* happened, and took away those options."

"You left me one." She met his eyes in the dark. "I'm living it. And Will? It's a good one. Better than being Mrs. Quist."

"Mrs. Quist." He looked faintly ill. "God."

"Hey, you know what?" She gave Jillian a testing joggle. She moaned but didn't stir. "I think she's close to out. I'm going to put her down."

Will stood with an air of relief. "Give her to me. You can straighten out those sheets."

"I don't think she'll go to you."

"She's asleep."

"Barely."

"So we have a window. Hand that kid over and get 'er done, Audrey."

She hesitated, then blew out a breath. God she was tired. "Fine."

Will scooped Jillian from her arms with a deftness that suggested he hadn't lost his post-midnight parenting moves. Even so, Jillian murmured unhappily and flung out an arm. Audrey leapt to her feet, ready to snatch her back at the first shriek, but Will murmured too, his voice dark and low, until Jillian's searching hand clamped onto the neck of his t-shirt and she settled.

Uh oh. Audrey eyed the death grip Jillian had on that t-shirt. She'd latched on. To Will.

"Well? Go on." Will nodded her toward the tangled sheets, swaying rhythmically to the unheard beat of sleeping children. "I don't know how long she'll be happy here."

"You might be surprised," she muttered, but remade the bed with quick, practiced hands. "Okay, go for it." She held her breath while Will eased Jillian between the turned-back sheets.

"Um, Audrey?" He remained bent over the mattress.

"Yes?"

"A little help?" He pointed to his collar. "She's got my shirt."

"Oh, that." Audrey sat on the edge of the mattress. "She does that."

"Does what?"

"Holds on."

"Well, can you get her to let go?"

"Not without starting the scream cycle all over again."

Will froze. "We don't want the scream cycle."

"We don't."

"So what do I do?"

"Get comfortable," she suggested. "She'll let go when she's ready."

"How long does that take?"

"As long as it takes." She gripped her knees. "I usually just fall asleep waiting."

He shot her a narrow look. "I can't sleep in here."

"Why not?"

"Because you don't sleep in the same bed as a kid you're not biologically related to. Not unless you're an idiot or Michael Jackson."

"It's a point." She pressed cold fingers to gritty eyes.

"A good point."

"Not arguing."

"Then *do* something."

"Right. Okay." She rose. "Scoot her as far toward the wall as you can."

He eased Jillian's little body across the mattress until her grip on his collar had her arm fully extended.

"Okay, now lie down on the outside edge of the mattress."

He glared at her. "I'm *not* sleeping—"

"Do you want my help or don't you?"

He flattened his lips and stretched out on the bed, leaving a careful two feet of open mattress between his body and Jillian's. Audrey crawled over him and deposited herself in the space.

"What the—" He breathed the words into her neck. A crackle of lust raced down her legs and she sat up like he'd shocked her.

"Pillows." She snatched up the extra pillows she'd laid at the foot of the bed and shoved one under Will's head. He flopped onto his back with a startled noise, nearly tumbling off the edge of the mattress. She dropped her own pillow on his outflung arm.

"Audrey, what are you—"

"Blankets." She leaned down again and grabbed the sheets, blankets and duvet. She hauled them up with a practiced snap and scooted down between Jillian and Will. Will's biceps was under her pillow, and Jillian's thin arm was threaded through the hollow at the nape of Audrey's neck, her fingers still tight on the collar of Will's t-shirt. Heat pumped off Will's body and she shivered a little closer to him. "There," she said briskly. "Cozy. Now go to sleep."

Chapter 22

Will gave an incredulous laugh. "Yeah, I'm pretty sure that's not going to happen."

"Try." She wiggled a little in what Will assumed was an effort to get comfortable. But the sweet curve of her butt touched his hip under the blankets and want exploded inside him like a bomb. His dick came to rigid, hopeful attention and he had to suppress an actual moan of lust. Dear God, he was a sick man. There was a *child* in the bed. "It'll be a long night otherwise."

His brain offered up a high-def slide show of suggestions for making the night longer. Hotter. Sweatier. "It's been long enough already," he said tightly.

"Will, shhh."

"Right."

Silence fell, broken only by the occasional post-meltdown snuffle from Jillian and Audrey's light, even breathing.

Will stared into the darkness above him and considered the wild bang of his pulse, the heavy ache of his rock-hard cock. He must have experienced a more acute blast of lust at some point in his life, he mused. He couldn't bring it to mind at the moment but he was sure he must have. Because if this was it, if this was the most intense sexual experience he'd ever had, he was completely freaked out. There was a *kid* in the bed, for Christ's sake. Granted, he was separated from said kid by about a hundred and twenty curvy pounds of warm, sweet-smelling, barely dressed woman, but surely the Jillian factor ought to neutralize the devastating sexual impact of Audrey's round little butt making brief and accidental contact with his hip?

He thought about it.

Nope. His dick was an iron spike and he was actually trembling with the effort of keeping himself flat on his back. Because his arm was under Audrey's pillow already, taut as an unsprung trap. It would be nothing, the work of half a second to hit the trigger. He could haul her on top of him and roll them both off the bed and onto the floor before she could even squeak with surprise. Before she could say word one, he'd have her underneath him, her thighs spread, his aching cock snugged into her melting welcome. Then he'd put his mouth on every inch of skin he could reach and *move*. He'd thrust and push and slide and rock until she made those needful, kittenish noises he heard in his best dreams. And then he would die of pure pleasure.

Because he fully expected to die. Making love to Audrey would be like looking at the face of God. You didn't survive that shit, but you weren't supposed to. It was just the price you paid for glory. And Will—should he ever be so lucky—would pay that price. Happily.

His dick jumped on his belly at the very thought, and sweat broke out on his upper lip. Oh God, he couldn't breathe. His hands went to fists and he inched desperately toward the edge of the mattress.

"For heaven's sake, stop fidgeting," Audrey hissed. "You're going to wake her up."

"Is she asleep?" he managed, his voice strangled. Maybe she'd take it as his attempt at a whisper. He'd never had a very good indoor voice.

"Yes, but she won't stay that way if you don't settle down. Now *stay still*."

"I'm trying." He bit the words off coldly. Like he was in control. In hand. Like he wasn't two inches from committing a lustful felony. "It would be easier if you'd stop touching me. Didn't we talk about that? I feel certain we did."

Tone! Bob shouted it so loudly inside his head that he stopped, startled. *Jesus, watch your tone!*

Will knew tone was a problem for him. A weapon, actually. One of his favorites. Probably the sharpest, shiniest one in his vast arsenal. He'd years ago perfected the ability to speak utterly benign words in a tone that was pure contempt. It drove his brothers bonkers. Maybe that was why he'd gotten so good at it. Good enough that it had become his reflex response to potential humiliation.

And he'd just used it on Audrey, making it sound like her touch was both purposeful and kind of slutty, rather than the best split-second of his week so far.

But he couldn't think of any way to take it back without divulging certain truths that would mortify them both, so he let the silence stretch out, cold and unbroken.

Finally she said, "Believe me, I'm trying to avoid it. But it's only a full-sized mattress, and you're not exactly a small guy."

He barked out a laugh. He *wasn't* a small guy. Not at the moment, anyway.

Oh, dick jokes, Bob said inside his head. *Nice.*

"What?" Audrey snapped. "What's so funny?"

"Nothing," he said icily. Nothing he was going to say out loud anyway. "What could possibly be wrong?"

"I have no idea. Because this is such an awesome situation all around. Fun for the whole family. Highlight of my night for sure." She gave him her back and fisted the blankets tightly under her chin. "Good night, William."

"Good night, Audrey," he said, equally pleasantly. Equally coldly. Then he enjoyed a few minutes of sub-zero silence while lust shifted inside him like black-hot lava. He gave his t-shirt a testing tug but Jillian's Claw of Tenacity was still firmly engaged. He wondered how big a dick he'd have to be to make Audrey opt to trigger the scream cycle again rather than endure another minute of his company. Because holy Mary mother of God he had to get out of here.

Don't be such a jerk, Bob said wearily. *It's not her fault you're sporting the hard-on of the century.*

At this point Will didn't care whose fault it was. All he knew was that he was a few quick pumps from embarrassing himself. He didn't know if he could be any less jerky and still avoid that miserable fate.

Kid in the bed, he chanted inside his head with desperate fervor. Kid in the bed. Kid in the bed.

For Christ's sake, pull yourself together, Bob said, though not unkindly. *Come on, now. What's our new motto? What did we learn in rehab?*

Be honest, Will thought automatically. Be who you are. Live your truth. Something like that. He wasn't thinking with perfect clarity at the moment, but he thought that might be pretty close. He didn't imagine Audrey would be overly impressed should she happen to encounter his current truth against her leg, however.

Well she's sure as hell not impressed with your lies. She's doing you a goddamn favor, Will. A big one. She could have left you here with Little Miss Death Grip and gone back to her nice comfy bed, you know.

Will did know. Audrey wasn't torturing him. Not on purpose, anyway. She was doing him a solid. He got that, and was grateful for it. Profoundly grateful. He only wished she weren't doing him said solid in nothing but a skimpy tank top and a pair of frilly little shorts. Shorts that barely covered her bottom. He swallowed thickly. A bottom that could make contact with his ridiculous and unwanted erection at any moment.

A happy accident which would make your fucking year, should it ever occur.

Will couldn't argue. Bob sighed.

You're not angry at her, Will. And you don't think she's a slutty whore who rubs up against anything that crawls into her bed, either. Why would you let her think you do?

Because it was easier. He realized this with a trickling sense of shame. It was easier to let her think he was pissed off rather than incredibly turned on.

What, that's a secret now? Bob snorted. *Oh, please. If your jones for Audrey is a secret, I'm Betty Fucking Crocker. You dry-humped her on my desk not even a week ago while whispering that shit in her ear, Will.*

That gave him pause. He *had* sort of—

Sort of, my ass. That was dry-humping, son. With a side dish of dirty talk. Believe me, she knows where you stand on the matter. So seriously, enlighten me. What do you have to gain by making her feel like shit because she touched you?

Nothing. The realization came to him slowly, painfully. Projecting disdain was a reflex, nothing more. A habit. He'd learned to draw first blood years ago. That way, when his own was shed, it sort of blended into the general spillage. Camouflage for alpha holes. Nice.

Hey, there we go, Bob said. *That big brain of yours does come in handy once in a while. When you use it.*

Will sighed and reminded himself that he'd actively courted pain once upon a time. Invited it. Provoked people into giving it to him at regular intervals. He didn't need it as much since adopting brutal honesty as his watch word but he reminded himself how very clarifying pain was. And rejection, he knew from vast experience, was an extremely dependable soft-on. Put them both together and maybe he could make it through this night without getting arrested.

Way to connect the dots there, super genius, Bob said. *For a minute I thought I was going to have to do it for you. Now are we going to tell the truth and get rejected or what?*

He made it sound like a party. To him, it probably was. The afterlife must not be very entertaining.

Somebody's stalling, Bob observed.

He hated it when Bob was right.

"Audrey." He cleared his throat. "Um, hey. Audrey. Are you awake?"

Silence. The cold, vibrating sort.

"Come on, I know you're awake. I can hear you breathing."

"That's because I'm asleep," she told him, each syllable a sharp little icicle of *I hate you*. "Not dead."

"Well, that's a relief. I have my limits, you know." And he was up against them, Jesus. "I'm already in bed with a kid. I draw the line at dead bodies."

She gave his desperate attempt at humor a moment of scathing silence. Then, "If I said *please* would you shut up and go to sleep?"

His brain—dirty, foul, hopeful thing that it was— ponied up all the ways he'd like to make her say please. And Will was a visual thinker, so it played out on the big screen in full color. His dick pulsed optimistically and he had to perform some complicated mental math before he felt confident that he could continue without incident.

"Just let me say something first."

"Fine." She shifted sullenly. "Say whatever you need to say so we can—" The ruffle on her shorts brushed his thigh.

He shot out a hand and gripped her hip before she could brush him again. "You're going to have to stop touching me, though."

She froze under his hand like he'd given her an electric shock, and he found he was powerless to let her go. Even as she obligingly scooted two inches closer to Jillian he didn't take his hand back. He just savored the soft play of skin and heat against his palm like he hadn't just told her to stop touching him.

"There," she said evenly. "All better?"

"Much, thank you." It was a dirty lie but it was better than the alternative. Which was begging.

"Will?"

"Yeah?"

"Now *you're* touching *me*."

"Oh." He'd wondered when she'd notice that. He peeled his fingers from the curve of her hip with a superhuman effort. "Right. Sorry." He sucked in a harsh breath and released it. Slowly. Did a few more mathematical gymnastics.

"Well?" she said. "You had something to say?"

"Oh. Yeah. That. Okay." He had no idea how to start this.

Oh come on, Bob said. *You've got the words. You've* always *got the words. Now grab your balls and spit them out.*

"I'm having kind of a hard time here, Audrey," he finally said.

"With what?"

His mouth was unbearably dry and he wanted her to the point of pain.

"This...situation."

"I'm not exactly thrilled with it myself, Will."

"I know. Believe me, I know. It's just that—" He

162

paused. How the hell was he supposed to explain this? "I don't think I should say it out loud."

"For heaven's sake, why not?"

His hand found hers in the darkness. He lifted it and placed it flat on his chest, right over his hammering heart. The desire swirling inside him gave a sudden, wild jolt, then sucked in on itself, creating an eerie, waiting vacuum. He slid her hand lower, led it down the taut line of his belly and onto the straining placket of his shorts.

Chapter 23

She said, "*Gah*," and snatched her hand back as if he'd burned her. Because, oh dear lord in heaven, Will was nursing one hell of an erection. Not that she'd seen all that many erections in person. Girls who looked like Audrey were always one bad decision away from a permanent address in Slutsville so she'd been choosy. But she'd seen enough to know that Will was built along extremely impressive lines. Evidently that old wives tale about big feet shouldn't be dismissed out of hand.

A wild, panicked laugh edged up her throat. Oh good God. Was she really pondering naughty fables right *now*? Was this really quite the moment?

Then again, had she really just felt up William Blake?

Well, yes. Yes, she had. And she'd go to her grave savoring the memory of his hot length pressed unashamedly to her palm. She had no idea how to explain this momentary insanity. Stress? Sleep-deprivation? Love? (Oh good God.) But she decided that explanations could wait. Her first priority was ending this conversation—*now*—before she did something tragically stupid. Like touch him again.

His voice came through the darkness, all rueful amusement. "Yeah, I'm sorry about that. I'm sure it was a flagrant violation of every personal boundary known to man, but I don't know how awake little Miss Vocab is or what she'd grasp. Show and tell seemed like the answer."

She allowed herself a deep breath before trying to respond. Her lungs felt scorched and dry, and she wondered if it was his heat or hers that had done it. "I...see," she managed.

He shrugged. "I'm no happier about it than you are, believe me. I'm a dirty-minded jerk wad. And I know that. I feel bad about that. But unfortunately, I have this ugly habit of never feeling bad alone. So I've spent the last fifteen minutes being rude to you instead of just owning the real problem."

"The real problem?"

"Wanting what I can't have." He said it with a calm acceptance. With relief, even. Audrey didn't know what to make of that. "And blaming you for making me want it in the first place. Which is stupid, because even I'm not such a jerk as to think you're in any way to blame for my...current condition."

"I'm not?"

"Of course not. It's not like you asked to be ridiculously hot, or squashed into bed with a guy you hate. It's not like you thought, *hey, let's do this barely dressed, too. Fun!* But the sad fact here is that I'm in bed with a gorgeous woman and a fragile kid, and we're all one wrong move away from screaming the house down again. My gears are grinding here, Audrey, and discomfort brings out my mean streak. I'm sorry I let it get all over you."

"Oh." The shocked desire inside her deflated a bit at that. Deflated a lot, actually. Because nothing killed the moment like hearing that a guy's hard-on was nothing personal. Not that she'd heard that one terribly often. Most guys had enough game to at least pretend they were emotionally attached before putting a girl's hand on their boner. She should appreciate Will's honesty. On some level, she supposed she did. Or so she told herself, and she was sticking to it.

"So there's that," he said. "Sorry for the, uh, overshare."

"Overshare," she mused. "Is that what we're calling it these days?"

"The truth will set you free," he said solemnly. "And I can't speak for you but I do feel better."

"I don't know if it's wise for you to feel much better than you already do," she said, but to her chagrin it came out more awed than pissed. Her palm was still tingling, for heaven's sake.

"It's a point," he agreed. "But I think I've got it under control now. Talking it out is really helping."

"Oh good," she murmured. She could feel his arm relaxing under her pillow. Evidently this really was helping him. Getting the truth off his chest. Only problem? It was burning itself on her brain with the kind of searing intensity that would leave a permanent mark. And she didn't know why the hell she couldn't stop listening. "I'm so glad for you."

"Unfortunately, there's more."

She frowned at him in the darkness. "More?"

"Yeah. And brace yourself, because this is where it gets weird."

"And here we've been having such a normal night so far."

"Yeah. Maybe that's why full disclosure seems like the way to go. Or maybe I'm just a fool." He paused, as if listening. "Or, yeah, maybe there's no maybe about it. But there's something else I feel like I have to tell you. Something that's making you...complicated for me."

"Fine." At this point, what did she have to lose? "Fire away."

"I can hear you."

She waited for more. Nothing. "Um, I can hear you, too. So?"

"No, I mean I can *hear* you. All the time. Even when you're not here."

"When I'm not...wait, what?"

"I just...hear you." He lifted the hand trapped between her and Jillian and gave the air a lazy stir, all *don't ask me*. "You sound like the ocean, did you know?"

"I...no."

"You do. It's gorgeous."

She had no idea what he was talking about but decided not to interrupt him to ask. She just lay there, watching him in the darkness, letting her silence encourage him to go on. It wasn't like it was costing her anything to listen, she told herself. He might even be trying to give her something. And she was too damn curious to refuse it. Whatever it was.

She reached out before she could allow herself to think better of it and laid her hand on his chest again. He covered it with his own and released a sigh so deep she felt it in the arches of her feet.

"Most people are so still." His arm curled under her pillow and then his free hand was in her hair. He plucked out a single lock and let it run through his fingers like water. Then he did it again. A third time. Over and over and over, like he was petting a cat. She had to squint against the rush of pure pleasure. "Most people are just *there*. But you, you have this energy. It swirls around you all the time, a constant rush and withdraw. It's like waves on the beach, the rising and waning tide. It's in my ears all the time, like my pulse or the turn of the earth. I can *hear* you. And I like it. It's...I don't know. Comforting." She felt his shoulders move, like his search for the right word was a physical endeavor. She wondered when she'd managed to curl herself into his side. When her cheek had moved from her pillow to his shoulder. When she'd pressed her nose up against the hollow of his throat and exchanged fresh air for the paper-and-ink scent of his skin.

He drifted his fingers across the back of her hand on his chest, then circled them around her wrist. "You look like you'd blow away in a strong breeze," he said, and his voice was a warm rumble under her cheek. "Just float away like dandelion fluff. But you don't. No matter what life throws at you, no matter what *I* throw at you, you never do. You don't bend, you don't break, you don't stop. You're relentless."

"Like the ocean?"

"Like the ocean."

Inside her that hard knot of self-reliance gave another one of those dangerous, slippery lurches. But she didn't pull back and she didn't say a word. She wanted *him* to keep talking. She wanted to hear more about how she was Will's ocean. He traced each of her fingers carefully, like it was a puzzle he was putting together or a bomb he was defusing. Then he twined his fingers through hers and let them rest on top of his beating heart. And kept talking.

"I didn't even know what I was hearing at first. Or that

what I was hearing was you. By the time I figured it out, it was too late. It was already in my blood, in my bones."

He wasn't making sense but she nodded anyway.

"Now I need it," he said helplessly. "I need *you*. I need that ocean in my ears all the time, telling me that you're there, that you're okay. All I do all day long is come up with excuses to get next to you, Audrey. Which is kind of a challenge, considering."

He laughed softly but Audrey could hear the blood dripping off it.

"Considering?" she asked.

"Considering that I'm the last person you want to see in your daily orbit. Considering that I've given you every reason to feel that way." He shifted under her cheek in a miserable shrug. "Not that I haven't earned every bit of your hate but it's exhausting to keep coming up with work arounds and excuses. Reasons to put myself anywhere you are, reasons to stay there. And God help me, I'm tired enough already trying not to—"

He stopped short and her heart gave a wild lurch. He'd talked her right up to the edge of a cliff, she realized. No, he *was* the cliff. He always had been. He was the edge of the earth for her, a wicked, dangerous drop into the void. He made her want to abandon all sense and fling herself into it, into him and the black unknown that was his soul. She might not survive the fall—probably wouldn't—but always in the back of her mind was the possibility that maybe she wouldn't fall. That maybe she'd fly instead.

She had a sudden, vivid mental image of hot green leaves and wet new-born wings. Of possibility unfurling in the sun, aching and slow.

"Will, please." She forced herself to back up, to put a few precious inches of space between them. Because she had to stop this. Now. His words were gorgeous and forbidden, dark as chocolate and twice as delicious, but her wings weren't ready. *She* wasn't ready. Not now. Not yet. Maybe not ever. But oh God she wanted him to keep talking. Forever and ever and ever. "You don't have to—"

"Yeah. I do." Want closed its relentless fist around her,

and she fell silent with suicidal eagerness. What was wrong with her? "I owe you the truth, all of it."

"You don't," she made herself say. "You really don't. I'm fine. You don't owe me—"

"I want you, Audrey," he said baldly. "I want you all the time. Like food, like air, like books. I *crave* you."

"Oh my God," she breathed, and twisted her fingers together until her knuckles cracked. Because it was either that or reach for him again.

"I know, right?" His voice was all wry amusement, as if she'd taken the Lord's name in vain out of horror rather than pure, aching need. She'd put that careful two inches of empty space between them but suddenly it didn't feel careful. It didn't feel safe. It felt like an unlit fuse, all tight-packed potential, and his thumb was trembling on the match head. Or hers was. Hard to tell at the moment. "It's not good, that craving," he told her. "Because I don't just want your body, Audrey. I want your goddamn everything."

"My everything?"

"Hell, yes."

She had to take a moment over that one, too dizzy and star-shot to formulate a snappy come-back. Her everything. He wanted her everything? Nobody had ever wanted her everything before. Her own father looked at her and saw nothing but a face and figure that tempted men into bad behavior. But Will—brutal, harsh, uncompromising Will— he wanted more. He wanted it all.

Didn't he?

"My everything," she murmured again, heart pounding with fear and elation. Those wings unfurled just a bit farther, lifted and spread in a hopeful breeze. "Which is what, exactly?"

He chuckled, low and dark, and everything inside her went to a lovely, glowy smolder. "You want it spelled right out, don't you?"

"I appreciate clarity," she said primly. "I know you have the vocab for it. So dazzle me, why don't you?"

"I don't think dazzle is exactly the word, but if you want me to put a label on precisely what it is I want from you? I can do that." He paused and her heart slipped breathlessly sideways in her chest. Suddenly there was a tense, waiting gap inside her, ready to receive whatever he dropped into it next. "I want your body, Audrey. I won't deny that. But I also want your time. I want your attention. But more even than that? I want your answers."

"My answers?"

"God, yes. I want that most of all. You're this gorgeous, endless question to me, Audrey. The kind that looks like a snap so you dive in, then three days later you look up and think *what the hell*? Because you're deep in the weeds, making absolutely no progress, and happier than you've ever been. You're that fascinating and complicated to me, and every time I fight my way around one of your corners, I don't find anything like what I thought I would. And I love that. You *surprise* me, all the time, and nobody ever surprises me. I could try to solve the riddle of you for the rest of my life and never get bored. And you throw that on top of the epic lust I've got cooking for you? I only know one word that covers the situation."

Her mouth was dust-dry. "One word?"

"Love." He sighed. "I'm in love with you, Audrey. I'm so sorry."

Chapter 24

"You're sorry."

Will didn't know if he could breathe. His lungs were tight, brittle. Good Christ, he *loved* her? He hadn't known that was going to pop out. Three hours ago he'd punched Drew—twice—for implying that he sort of had a thing for Audrey. And suddenly he was declaring his love? To *her*? Before he gave his brothers a chance to talk him off the ledge?

"You're in love with me," Audrey said. Mused, really. She didn't sound angry. She didn't sound horrified. Just...thoughtful. "You're in love with me and you're sorry."

"Yes," he said fervently. "I'm truly and deeply sorry. Believe me, I didn't mean for this to happen. If I could fix it, I would. I will. I did it by myself; I'll figure out how to *un*do it the same way. It's not your problem, Audrey. Don't worry about it."

Of all the boneheaded, misguided, and desperately self-destructive moves, Bob sighed. *I thought we were done with that shit?*

Will scowled. Bob was the one who'd told him to ante up the truth. Now he was taking potshots?

I'm not talking about your touching declaration of love, you asshole—

Shut *up*, Bob. Will blasted that corner of his subconscious with all the bitterness and fury inside him. He could feel his control splintering, and soon there would be nothing between Audrey and his howling, doomed want. Between her and all his ugly, spewing pain. And he couldn't let that happen. He would chew his own arm off before he'd let the ugliness inside him touch her again.

"Don't worry about it? How can I not worry about this,

171

Will? You just said—"

"I know what I said," he snapped. *Tone*, Bob sang gleefully. He ratcheted his volume down a notch or two. "But this is *not your fault*." And it wasn't. It wasn't her fault that he was an idiot with delusions of grandeur. It wasn't her fault that she sang to him like the frickin' ocean. "It's nothing you asked for," he told her grimly. "This is my shit, and it's on me to fix it."

Jesus Christ on a crutch, are you listening to yourself? Are you hearing what you're saying to this girl?

Hell yes, he could hear it. He was saying it, wasn't he? Maybe he wasn't saying it with any particular finesse but look at him go, spitting out random words to the tune of *well, shit, sorry about that*. And considering that Will normally greeted a loss of dignity this stunning with bared teeth and two smoking barrels, this constituted something of a miracle. There was a lot of blood and fury swirling inside him, and he was keeping it contained. Relatively speaking. But if he was going to continue the trend, Bob was going to have to *shut the fuck up*.

Silence rang inside his head.

"For pity's sake, help me out here, Audrey." He forced his lungs to release the charred, oxygen-free air they were holding onto. "You must get this shit all the time."

"Um, no. Actually I—"

"Oh, please. Looking like you look? This is not the first time an undesirable has confessed his burning and unrequited love. You have to know how to walk us back to normal from here."

"Normal." That horrible, thoughtful tone again. Will's hands were straining fists. "That's really what you want? To go back to normal?"

"Hell, no." His lips twisted in the darkness but he wouldn't lie to her now. Not when he'd just carved the truth on his heart and handed it over. What would be the point? "What I *want* is to spend the rest of my life hearing you answer those damn questions, then asking more. What I *want* is to go to sleep every night with your head on my shoulder and your ocean in my ears. What I *want* is for God himself to perform a fucking miracle and make me somebody else. Somebody who doesn't shred everybody he touches like Edward fucking Scissorhands, maybe. Somebody who could tell a girl he loves her without having to apologize afterwards. But reality being what it is, I'd settle for finding some way to go on from here where I don't have to lie anymore but you don't treat me like a cancer patient." He laughed, and it sounded miserable even to his own ears. "Or is that asking too much?"

"Will?" Her voice was calm in the darkness, smooth as milk. But something vibrated underneath it, an odd pitch Will had never heard before. A gathering, he thought for no reason he could put his finger on.

"What?"

"Jillian's let you go."

"She...what?" He touched his collar. Jillian's hand was still there but her fingers were open, relaxed.

"She's finally under. She's let you go."

"Oh." He suffered a gear-grinding surge of gratitude and disappointment. Gratitude because a wary and brilliant child had trusted him—*him*, of all people—to stand guard while she slept, to beat back whatever monsters lurked in the dark of her unconscious. And disappointment because no matter how painfully uncomfortable this night had been, Will wasn't ready for it to end. Lying here in the warmth of Audrey's body, speaking his truth into the sheltering darkness, being *close* to her even in this doomed, humiliating way? He wasn't ready for it to be over yet.

He was so screwed.

"Right," he said. "We should probably—"

"Yes." She nudged his side and he slid obligingly— reluctantly—out of the bed. "We should."

He watched as she slipped from the sheets, then bent to tuck Jillian in more securely. She straightened and faced him. He gripped his hands together, strategically in front of his crotch. His dick was an incorrigible optimist. "Okay, well. That's that. I guess I'll just go back to—"

She curled her fingers into the fabric of his t-shirt, wadding it into a knot in her hand. Will's heart tried to leap through his rib cage to get at her.

"You'll just come into the other room here," she said, "and we'll finish this conversation."

He was sorry. It rang inside Audrey's head like some kind of echo, repeating itself each time her bare foot hit the carpet. Sorry, sorry, sorry. He loved her and he was sorry for it.

She led him toward the gothic nightmare of her sister's old room to the beat of his love and his regret. She stopped in the bathroom between the bedrooms and eased Jillian's door closed. The darkness deepened by a few degrees and she noticed that the other door, the one to Olivia's room, was also shut. She frowned at it. She'd left that one open; she knew she had. But enough light leaked in around the frame to keep her from smashing into the counter or falling into the toilet.

Which was great, because suddenly she didn't want to take Will into Olivia's old room. It was probably the best-lit space in the whole house at that moment, and yet it still seemed too dark. So she stopped right there, leaned against the counter and turned to face him. He folded his arms and leaned back against the shower door. Even in the half-light she could see that brow cocked speculatively. Arrogantly. And everything inside her yearned.

Because even with his bald confession of love lying between them, even with a miserably sincere apology lying right beside it, he could still look at her like she was a meal that would probably fill him up but wouldn't have him writing a thank you note to the chef. He might love her but he wasn't happy about it.

And she never saw that. She'd never looked into a man's eyes and found anything there but avarice and dazzled lust. Which meant they weren't looking hard enough. Because she had her issues. Lord, did she. She was sarcastic, short-tempered, impulsive and more than a little bossy. She wanted things her way, and *right now*. And that always seemed to come as a surprise to the men who claimed to love her. But she had a feeling it wouldn't surprise Will at all.

Not even a little bit. She'd slice at him, and he wouldn't blink. He'd probably *like* it.

In fact, she knew he would. Will would like it a lot.

And he thought she sounded like the ocean.

"For God's sake, Audrey." He scrubbed two impatient hands over his face. "Let's just get this over with. Hit me already."

For one wild moment, she wondered if he was being literal. Her thoughts leapt back to his desk. To that hot little scene they'd played out on top of it—her, face down on the shiny surface. Him, hot and hard against her back. The cage of his arms around her. That big hand sliding up her thigh, his blatant need pressing into her bottom. Those dark words he'd dropped into her ear, a warning tangled with a promise.

"Bring it on, Audrey." He dropped his hands. "Let's hash this out."

Lust kicked low and hard in her belly, and she knew suddenly that she hadn't brought him here to talk. He'd talked enough. More than enough. He'd talked like words were seeds, and she was his personal garden.

A damn fertile one, too. Because some of those words he'd thrown out with such shocking courage had caught. They'd pushed down roots, sent up runners, and unfurled leaves. Everything inside her was suddenly jungle green, hot and hungry. It was going to take a hell of a lot more than words to satisfy her now, but she *would* be satisfied. And Will was going to do it.

"You know what?" She gave a laugh, exquisitely aware of her nipples tightening against the thin fabric of her tank. "I changed my mind."

"Thank you, Jesus." But he frowned at her through the darkness. "Wait, about what?"

"About finishing this conversation."

Again with the skeptical eyebrow. Her knees became vaguely unreliable. "You don't want to talk this out."

"Nope."

Pause. "Why not?"

"Because you've said plenty." Had he ever. Flames licked from the tight points of her nipples straight down her thighs. "Don't you think?"

He gave a startled laugh. "Well, yeah. But I thought you'd have—"

She eased forward until the space between them narrowed to bare inches, and he broke off. Swallowed. The thin slice of darkness she'd left between them sizzled with anticipation and heat. She cocked her head, peered up at him. "You thought I'd have what?"

"Questions." He slid a measuring look toward the door, like he might be considering escape. But he was already flat against the shower. He wasn't going anywhere. A delighted laugh bubbled up in her throat but she swallowed it down. "I thought you'd have questions."

She brought her hands to his hips, and he sucked in a harsh breath. She sympathized. She wasn't getting quite as much oxygen as she might've liked herself but her heart thudded along anyway, hot and alive and needful inside her. She eased her hands over the edges of his hipbones until her thumbs found the groove in the center of his abdomen. He stopped breathing. She traced that shallow indent all the way up to the swell of his pecs, and found his heart jerking under her finger tips.

He wasn't muscular, she mused. That wasn't the right word, and vocab was important. She needed to put the right word on the fascinating animal truth of him under her hands. Will wasn't bulky or heavy. Will was...dangerous. Yes. She smiled her satisfaction. *That* was the right word. Will was hard, he was tight and he was dangerous. He was lean elegance coupled with whip-tight menace. And all that latent violence, all that bloody potential? It was leashed and trembling under her palms. He was holding it all in check. For her.

Lust squeezed like a hot fist inside her, then released in a flash-flood of want. It crashed home, overtaking her in a brutal, super-heated rush that was akin to pain. Her fingers opened spasmodically on his chest, then clenched. Not gently, either. She was suffering here. Exquisitely, yes. But suffering was suffering.

She must have scratched him because he made some

noise low in his throat—warning? Protest?
Encouragement?—but she didn't let him go. She didn't
apologize. She just gathered up the soft cotton of his t-shirt
with greedy hands until he finally came off the shower door.
Until the space between them was nothing but an aching
thumbnail of darkness. Until she had what she needed.
Almost.

"Audrey." Her name came out on an agonized groan.

"Right here." She slid her palm up, over his collar bone
and pushed her fingers into the brutally short hair at his
nape. She nearly hissed at the cool silk of it against her skin.

How long had she wanted to touch him like this? she
wondered wildly. How much time had she wasted
insisting—even to herself—that she wanted no such thing?
She had no idea. Too much, certainly. Because now, with
her hands on him, with the heat of him singeing her skin, she
wanted to touch him—to keep touching him—more than she
wanted to breathe. But even as that satisfaction raced
through her she wanted more. Now touching wasn't enough.
Now she wanted to taste him, too. She put her mouth a
heartbeat from his.

"Audrey." He closed his eyes as if pained. "What are
you doing?"

"Oh, Will." She took that last step, the one that fit her
body into his. She could almost hear the sizzle of it, and her
brain shook loose of a hinge or two. It was delicious.
"Sometimes you talk too much."

And she kissed him.

For one suspended moment, he allowed it. And she
gloried in it. Because damn, that mouth of his was
everything she'd imagined, and then some. And she had a
spectacular imagination. But even as she staggered under the
sheer weight of his dazzle, she knew there was more.
Because he stood as if frozen, letting her taste him, touch
him, shock him. He was letting her drive, she understood
suddenly, and Will wasn't one to give up the wheel.

He pulled back as if he'd heard her thoughts. Stared
down at her in the half-light, his face dark and searching and
sharp. Her heart jumped into her throat and lodged there as

she held his gaze.

"Don't play with me, Audrey." He stepped back, but came up hard against the shower door. It rattled on its frame and she lurched forward to flatten her hands on the door on either side of him. Which stopped the rattling before it could wake Jillian, yes, but also snugged her body right back into his. Electric sparks shot from her nipples all the way to her belly. She bit back a sharp moan and Will gave a ragged exhale.

"I know I deserve it," he said tightly, "but Jesus, I'm begging you. Don't play games with me right now. I can't—" He broke off, his hands in fists at his sides, and stared at the ceiling. His throat worked visibly in the darkness. "Just...don't, all right?"

She stared up at him through the inky darkness, suddenly and exquisitely aware that this was the end of *before*. What they were together, what they'd been to one another? She was balanced on the very edge of it, and it was crumbling away beneath her feet, taking her escape hatch with it. A breath, a step, a word would launch them both into the yawning new world at her feet, and she was terrified. Terrified to fall into it, but terrified not to. And it was his fault. *His* fault that she felt this way, all unsettled and uncertain. Alive and yearning and petrified.

And hungry. So hungry. She had no idea what it was going to cost her, this aching hunger. She knew only that she needed to satisfy it. Needed *him* to satisfy it. And he had no right—*no right*—to ask for safe harbor when she was so damn needful and afraid.

Fury rushed in, swirled giddily into the lust and caught fire. She curled one hand around his nape again, helped herself to a handful of that cool, silky hair. Hard. She saw his eyes narrow as she dragged him down to her again, but with what? Pain? Pleasure? Both? She wasn't sure. She wasn't sure it even mattered, because then his mouth was on hers and she was falling. She'd chosen. She'd tipped over into the void of him, and she was falling, falling, falling.

Chapter 25

He cupped his hands under her elbows and lifted her. Caught her. But how had he known? How had he *known* she was even falling? She stopped wondering almost before she'd started, because this was Will. Of course he knew. He always knew what other people didn't or couldn't. That was the miracle and the tragedy of Will. He *knew*.

So suddenly her feet were off the tile and she was airborne. Flying. She saw those wings again in her mind's eye, fierce and strong now, spread to the sun and wind, lifting her above fear and danger. Then she landed with an ungentle jolt on the cold marble counter. It slapped her out of the fever-dream of her lust, and she opened her eyes. He was a hot shadow in the darkness, black as evil, huge as pain, his hands hard and uncompromising as they circled her upper arms. Steadying her, probably, but maybe just holding her. Keeping her. Taking her. She knew one stark beat of terror because Will *would* take her. He'd take her and keep on taking her until there *was* no her. Until there was only him, and what he wanted and her aching, endless desire to be whatever that was. To be that perfect, unanswerable question that he would never tire of.

But that was impossible. All questions had answers, every desire burned itself out, every love had its limit. And when Will found his and got bored with her—because he would, oh heaven save her but he would—Audrey would have nothing left to be. She'd have given it all to him. And that would be a tragedy, one she'd promised herself she'd never play out. She'd seen that one, after all. Her mom had starred in it for years, and Audrey had had front row seats. She hadn't liked the ending.

So, no. She couldn't do that. She couldn't be that, she

wouldn't be that. She—

Then he hooked one hand around her nape and lifted her into the scorching heat of his mouth and her words fell away. They flew into the flames and drifted down in a cloud of useless ashes because oh, dear God, that mouth. Will's mouth was a miracle—hot, skilled, and punishingly precise. Just like Will himself. Heat pumped off him, his desire a fierce, sharp tang that filled the air around them. It replaced oxygen and she breathed it in. It sliced at her, twisted against her, and sparked a vicious blaze that made her previous desire look pale and undernourished.

And why? Because last time, *she'd* kissed *him*. But this? This was him kissing her, and it was like living in the center of a nuclear blast. He wanted her with a terrific intensity, the kind that melted metal and destroyed buildings. The kind that laid waste to whole cities, and opened seeds that only opened for the devil himself. It wasn't a comfortable or friendly want; it was no game. This shit was for real, and the stakes were high. The stakes were blood.

He twisted his fingers in her hair and tugged sharply. Pain bloomed brightly, then it, too, fell away, devoured by a hot, sparkling lust. Hunger roared in, and she only wanted more. More and more and more of him. She tipped her head with a greedy obedience and he slid into her mouth like he owned it, like he'd conquered it and now it was down to the sacking and pillaging and looting.

And she opened for it. Opened for him. Willingly. Gratefully. Eagerly. Her knees fell to the sides and he put himself right there. Just *there* against the center of her want, and a scouring black heat filled her head. It consumed her thoughts, her fear, even her desire to breathe. It left nothing for her but him. His mouth on hers, his tongue dancing and thrusting, seeking and finding, demanding and taking. She knew nothing but his heat, tight against her aching need, advancing and retreating to the wild beat of her heart.

And this thing he'd planted inside her, this needful hunger? It was growing. He was tending it, roughly, and it was rising. It was twisting inside her, surging higher and hotter with each maddening circle of his hips against the slippery crotch of her shorts.

But it wasn't enough. She *needed*. She needed something. Something more. She shifted restlessly under the hot weight of him, itchy and wanting and *hungry*. She pushed her hands under his t-shirt and found the smooth expanse of his back, a glorious canvas of muscle and skin. It shifted and clenched to the rhythm of this savage symphony he was playing on her body, and wrenched from her another spasm of dark-edged need. Her consciousness popped another bolt and swung there on one hinge like a broken door. She curled her nails into the animal sleekness under her palms and let that blast of need push her farther and farther into him.

He hummed and arched into her nails like a big, sleek cat, and that itchy, empty *hunger* in her ratcheted another punishing degree toward pain. Then his hand was on the hem of her tank, dancing under, up. He found one nipple with those fast, clever fingers, and an abrupt flutter seized her core. And that last hinge gave way. Suddenly she was across the threshold, control behind her, nothing but black heat ahead. She was rocking herself into him, shamelessly pushing the hungry knot of her need against him. She opened herself, arched helplessly into him. Hooked her fists over his shoulders, wrapped her legs around him and reached.

Then, just like that, she flowered for him. Hard, sharp, sudden. The tight-wrapped bud of her need burst extravagantly into bloom, petal by aching petal.

She gave a shocked gasp and tore her mouth away. She gripped his hips with both thighs, holding him hard against her lushly swollen and shuddering core. He dropped his head to her shoulder, his open mouth landing on her collar bone. The wet heat of it, the sharp edge of his teeth against her skin sent another series of mindless shockwaves though her center. The mirror was cool and slippery against her shoulders but she only twined her legs around him tighter and ground herself shamelessly against the hot thrust of him.

"Will," she said, as it went on and on and *on*. "*Will*."

He stilled. He stayed right there—rigid, hot, and trembling with effort but absolutely still while she rubbed and circled and twisted against him until that punishing sizzle inside her had died back to the subsonic rumble of overhead power lines.

She surfaced slowly, with no real idea how much time had passed. Her fingers ached. This was the first coherent thought that put itself together in her mind. Her fingers ached. She wondered why, then realized that she was still gripping Will's shoulders with a desperate strength that was probably bruising him.

"Oh!" She opened her fingers with a start. Blood tingled back into them and a number of other startling realizations flooded her sluggish mind. She was sliding bonelessly down the bathroom mirror, for one, the counter cool under her super-heated thighs. For another, she wasn't but fifteen yards from her sleeping niece. There was a closed door between them but still. Not good. Also, she had her legs wrapped firmly about Will's tight behind, and his pulsing erection was still snugged cozily up against her delighted sex. Which was, yes, still giving the occasional happy spasm.

And Will was curved over her, his body a tight, trembling arch. One hand was planted on the counter beside her hip, the other was between her head and the mirror. It was a little gesture of gallantry that she hadn't noticed at the time—she'd been otherwise occupied—but now it tightened her throat dangerously. She'd come all over him without a thought for his pleasure, and he'd kept her from giving herself a goose egg while she did it.

And *he'd* apologized for being in love with *her*.

"Oh," she managed again. Shame chased lust and terror and thrilled satisfaction around and around inside her but she couldn't make sense of any of it. She couldn't *think*, not with the pure glory of him still pulsing and pushing against her, sending little showers of lustful sparks down her legs.

She edged sideways, just far enough to pull in a decent, head-clearing breath. But that breath came with the hot scent of his want and her satisfaction, and she released it on a moan. It was involuntary but utterly sincere, and Will jumped like she'd tased him. He jerked back far enough to peer down through the darkness and find her eyes.

And Audrey forgot about trying to sort out and name the emotions twisting around inside her. She forgot about breathing. Oxygen paled next to the wild horror written on the gorgeous, harsh lines of his face.

"Oh my God." He leapt away from her and threw his hands out to the sides. He held them up and out, as if they were loaded guns and he was being careful. "Oh my *God*," he moaned, and actually sidled from foot to foot. Audrey tried hard not to stare but if his erection had been impressive to feel, it was something else to look at. Even through his shorts. She swallowed. "Audrey, Jesus, I'm so sorry. I'm so, so sorry."

She blinked. He kept apologizing. Why on earth was he doing that? She wanted to ask him but her system was still too glowy and stupid to pull it together. Any energy she could muster up was being drained off by the hope that round two was forthcoming. Because he might be a little panicked but that was a serious tent he had pitched in his shorts.

"Did I hurt you?" He slapped both hands to his face and stared at the ceiling through splayed fingers. The laugh that slipped through was harsh and jagged. "Oh, Christ, listen to me. *Did I hurt you?*" He pulled back to stare down at his own hands. "Oh my Jesus Christing motherfucking—" His voice cut out abruptly, like his throat had just closed up shop without warning. He sounded two steps away from actual tears, and concern knifed through her buzzy contentment.

She eased herself up to a sitting position—mostly—and tried to put her knees back together. They didn't want to go. They wanted to wrap themselves around those narrow hips again and get down to business. "Will?" she managed. "What are you—"

"Your *hair*," he moaned. "Your beautiful hair."

She frowned and put one hand to her head. Even her scalp tingled happily, she realized. "I don't know if I'd go with beautiful at the moment, but thanks. What about it?"

He didn't answer. Instead, he folded slowly onto his knees in the center of the room. Just sank down, beaten. Alarm shot her off the counter, put her on her knees before

183

him.

"Will, you're scaring me." His head was bent, his hands pressed together and tucked between his knees. She tugged at his tightly corded forearms. She wanted those hands in hers. She wanted to see what was the matter with them. What he *thought* was the matter with them, anyway. Because she was pretty sure he was wrong. Whatever had put him on his knees in defeat was *wrong*. "Show me, Will. Now." He shook his head but she persisted, and finally managed to free one hard fist. She cradled it between her palms as if it were a hummingbird. It shook as she peeled it open, and the hair at her temple stirred as the breath sawed in and out of his lungs.

"There's nothing here." She peered down into his empty palm, her pulse raging against her eardrums. "My God, Will, what is it? There's nothing here!"

He pulled in another shuddering breath and held it. Then he brought his eyes up to hers. Even in the darkness she could see the glitter in them. Fury, pain, resignation, sorrow.

"It's your hair, Audrey." He lifted his hand to the thin thread of light streaming around the edges of the bedroom door, turned it this way and that until she could see several long pale strands twisted around his fingers. "I pulled out your goddamn hair." He unwounded them and placed them in her palm, folded her fingers gently around them. "You let me kiss you, and I *hurt* you."

She gaped at him stupidly. He thought he'd hurt her? Because he had a few of her hairs tangled around his fingers? He rocked back, planted his butt on the floor and let his back fetch up against the shower door. He propped his elbows on his knees and jammed both hands into his own hair. Audrey—still stunned into silence—wondered idly if he was planning to tear out his own hair now in penance.

"I thought I could handle it," he said softly. "When you kissed me I thought I could just...let you. I thought I could let you kiss me and it would be enough. More than I ever expected or deserved, that's for damn sure. But nothing's enough for me when it comes to you. Next thing I knew I had you by the hair, dry-humping you on the counter like I was some kind of animal. Like *you* were some kind of animal." His hands were fists in his own hair, and it sprouted up between his fingers in sharp peaks. "And that, I feel confident, is *not* hero sex."

"I don't know, Will." She had no idea what hero sex was but her body was still clenching and glowing, for God's sake. "It felt kind of heroic to me."

He pulled his hands down his face again, gripped his knees and looked her in the eye. "I'm sorry, Audrey. I can't tell you how sorry I am."

"You're sorry?" Dismay trailed greasy fingers down the back of her neck and she shivered. "You made me come like a waterfall, Will. Why are you sorry?"

He went utterly still. "You...came?"

"Um, yes. I did. Hard. What did you think all the noise was about?"

"I—" He blinked. "You *came*? How?"

"I guess I'm just slutty that way." Hot embarrassment joined the dismay swirling in her gut and she sat back on her trembling heels. She'd opened for him because she thought that somebody had finally spotted the weird, flawed, vulnerable *her* trapped inside all the pretty. He'd said he loved her, and with such bloody reluctance that she'd gone and believed him. More the fool she. Because if he hadn't noticed the world-shattering, ruin-her-for-all-other-men orgasm she'd just had all over him, he definitely hadn't noticed anything else. Anything deeper. Any*body* deeper. No, he'd done something *to* her, not *with* her. Prepositions made all the difference, she thought wryly while shame pooled sick and oily inside her. "I come for any guy who dry-humps me on the bathroom counter, didn't you know?"

"Audrey—"

"Got to say, you've got some hidden depths. Dry-humping. Who knew?" She gave a jerky shrug. "But it totally worked for me. Guess I owe you one."

He dropped his hands to stare at her over his knees. "You *owe* me one?"

"Sure." She reached forward, circled her fingers around his ankles. He hissed like she'd burned him. She only smiled, but it felt sharp. Nasty. As ugly as the hurt and anger cramping her stomach. "You put your finger right on what I like and you gave it to me. Hard."

"I hurt you," he said, his voice flat.

"Check your back," she advised him. "*I* hurt *you*."

He took her by the shoulders, set her away from him and stood. "Audrey, please. I'm twice your size." He paced to the counter and flattened his hands on it. "I can take it. You can't. You're—"

She scrambled to her feet. "—not done yet."

"Not—" He dropped his head, stared at his hands. "I have never had a more frustrating conversation in my life, and I grew up talking to Drew. What are you *talking* about, you're not done yet? Done with what?"

"With you." She stalked to him, furious and still *hungry*. Hungry for him. Oh, the shame. She hooked him by one elbow and spun him to face her. She let her gaze drift pointedly south. "And judging from the look of things, you're not done with me, either."

"The dick is ever hopeful," he muttered. He shook off her hand and turned away, arms folded over his chest. Closing her out. "Ignore the dick."

"Like you're trying to ignore me? I don't think so." She put herself right in front of him again. "I'm not that rude."

She wasn't invisible either. She hoped. But the fear was there, always there, that she—the real, raw, deeply flawed truth of her—was utterly invisible, and nobody would ever, ever see her.

Fury rose up inside her, sent flames high into the scorching air, and she decided that Will was going to see her tonight if it was the last thing she did. See her for real, whether he wanted to or not. She wondered if his "love" would survive the dawn. She doubted it. She gave him a shot to the shoulder. Not a gentle one, either. He glared at her and lifted a hand to rub his shoulder. "Jesus, Audrey."

"You're praying to me already? I must be better than I thought." She shoved him again and he backed into the counter. Those eyes went narrow and hot.

"Stop shoving me."

"No." She stepped up, put herself right in the danger zone. "You make love like you're at war, Will. Like you're at war, and I'm the enemy. By the time you were done with me, I couldn't remember my own name for wanting you. You goddamn destroyed me." She found the wrinkled fabric of his t-shirt with her palms, slid them slowly, agonizingly up the ridged plane of his abdomen until they rested on his chest. He sucked in a harsh breath and it dropped into the chaos inside her, that unwilling noise. And it made everything darker, hotter. "And if you think you're walking out of here before you're as wrecked as I am, you're not as smart as I think you are."

"Audrey, I don't want—"

"Oh, Will. I know exactly what you want."

She planted her feet and shoved him again. Hard.

Chapter 26

Will knew what she was going to do. She wasn't a natural fighter, his Audrey, and she telegraphed her moves pretty broadly. A kindergartener could have anticipated that she was going to push him. So it wasn't that he didn't know she was going to do it. It was more that he couldn't believe she would.

But she did. She pushed him, and put all her hundred-pounds-and-change behind it, too. She pushed him in full knowledge of the fact that Will had a taste for the edgy, the bloody, the harsh. That pushing him, far from discouraging his lust, would only whip it up harder, hotter, higher.

She pushed him anyway, and with furious enthusiasm.

And he was so startled, so *stunned*, that he reeled. He actually stumbled and had to catch himself against the sink. He wondered if it was the shove that had stolen his balance or the vicious sweep of super-heated lust shredding through his veins. His knees trembled, but not with weakness. No, never weakness. It was anticipation. A black-edged, sharp-clawed intent gathered at the base of his spine. It sent hot runners out, made fists of his hands and wings of his feet. It was instinctual, primitive, and hard-wired into the most basic part of his brain's machinery.

It was time to hunt. To stalk, capture and ravage. The monster in his basement was hungry, and Will was an excellent provider.

"Audrey, seriously. Last chance. You want to walk out of here, you're going to have to knock that off."

She smiled. "Make me."

He sucked in a breath and it was hot, full of her. Full of her wild challenge and the rich musk of her satisfaction. Her *satisfaction*. He'd made her come. Like a waterfall, wasn't that what she'd said? Wonder blew through him, along with another punishing crash of pure lust. She'd come for him. Hard. He remembered the small noises she'd made against his chest, the sound of his name, rough and agonized, on her lips. He'd read her all wrong, he realized suddenly. *All* wrong. He'd been so caught up in his own unhinged shit that he hadn't even noticed how unhinged she'd come herself. And that was a mistake he aimed to rectify immediately.

He reached for her, and she slapped his hand away with a crisp, stinging crack. "Oh, fuck that." She glared at him with magnificent disdain. "I said *make me*."

His dick jerked against his shorts and he stared at her. That black intent coiled inside him dangerously and he knew a moment's hesitation. The monster in his basement was whispering bloody nothings and they were delicious. *She* was delicious but did she really understand what she was asking for?

She snorted at his instant of inaction, and spun on one heel toward the silhouette of the door. And the beast inside him said *the fuck she will*.

He shot out a hand and caught a moonlight-pale hank of her hair. He wrapped it around his fist and jerked her back. She didn't even squeak, but came like she'd been ready for it. She came with her elbows sharp and her heel driving for his bare instep. And she was laughing. *Laughing,* Jesus.

Pain radiated from the arch of his foot halfway up his shin, hot and bright, then her elbow found his diaphragm. He grunted appreciatively and spun her in the circle of his arms, trapped her there against his body. She squirmed and fought like a cat, all claws and fury. He forced her head back and took her mouth. It was a mighty clash, that kiss, full of teeth and rage and blinding lust. He tasted blood—his? Hers? He didn't know but the tang of it only twisted that driving hunger inside him tighter. Fed it and created it at the same time.

She fought her shoulders free of his grip, got an arm hooked around his neck and twisted herself around him like a climbing vine. Then her hands were everywhere, hot, merciless, devastating. She striped his back with sharp nails, unleashing a pain-tipped wave of want over his head that unstrung his knees. He grabbed the lush curve of her bottom, jerked her off the floor and into the pounding ache that was his dick. She didn't hesitate, but wrapped her legs around him, gripped a handful of his hair and forced his mouth from hers so she could feast on his throat. And oh, God, that mouth of hers. The wet, hot pull of it right over the hammer and pound of his pulse. The scrape of her teeth, the sweet sweep of her tongue soothing what she'd stung.

And he knew he had to get inside her. He had to have everything, all of her. He needed the pain and the pleasure, the demand and the generosity of her. He needed the hot glove of her body seizing and clenching around him, dragging him over the edge into insanity.

Farther into insanity. Because Christ Almighty, he was already there. He was *there*, half insane with need, and if he didn't get inside her he was going to embarrass himself. And fuck up what was quite possibly the only chance he'd ever get to have her. To get inside her—mind, soul and body. And to come inside her. He wanted to come and come and come inside her, and he would be goddamned to hell and back before he'd give up the opportunity.

A whisper of sanity tickled the back of his mind, pulled on a thread of caution, and he froze. He dropped her on the counter before him and gripped the edge on either side of her hips with desperate fingers. Oh fuck.

"Condom," he managed. He spoke to the ceiling while she continued to ravage his throat. While she jerked the hem of his t-shirt up toward his shoulders and his arms lifted mindlessly to let her. She skinned it off over his head and rewarded his cooperation by clamping her teeth onto the meat of his shoulder and sucking. Hard. His cock jerked, and the coiled heat at the base of his spine threatened to unspool itself in a glorious jet of *right now*.

"Audrey." It came out on a moan, barely intelligible. "We need a condom."

"No, we don't." She lifted her mouth from him, and he wanted to moan again. "Not unless you have some communicable disease I need to know about."

"I'm clean," he managed. "But—"

"Then I have it covered."

She hooked her thumbs into the waistband of his shorts and skinned those down, too, and a white-hot light blasted the inside of his skull. It bleached every thought from his mind but getting inside her as soon as humanly possible.

"So all we really need," she said precisely, even coolly, "is for you to shut up and fuck me."

"Right," he said. "On it."

Even as some distant fraction of his brain marveled that he could even form words, he snatched that pretty tank top right off her. He filled his hands with her breasts, with the lush, generous curves. Flicked his thumbs over the tight points of her nipples. Not gently, either. She arched into him, pushed herself into his hands and said, "Harder. Goddamn you, Will, *harder*."

She shimmied herself out of her ruffly little shorts; they drifted down to land on his foot. He hooked his hands under both her knees and yanked her down to meet him. She was slippery and hot against his cock, and his heart crashed into his ribs. He took the flare of her hips in shaking hands. She was so tiny, his mind whispered, so delicate; his fingers met each other in the small of her back. Be careful.

He hesitated for a fraction of a second, just long enough for her to slap her hands out, to brace them flat against the mirror behind her. She wrapped her legs around him and drove her heels into his ass. And then he wasn't thinking at all. There were no voices, small or otherwise. He simply gripped her hips and drove himself home. He sheathed himself in the tight, hot glove of her body and let his heart explode in his chest. Allowed it with dim satisfaction, really. He'd known making love to Audrey wouldn't be a survivable event. He was dying, and it felt like it. But he was going out with a fucking bang.

He got one forearm around her waist and bowed her body up to his mouth. Latched onto a ruched pink nipple and drew, hard. He swirled his tongue around that tight needy point and lost himself in her. In thrusting himself, deep and rough and fast, into the hot give of her body. And when that give turned into a take, into a convulsive flutter and pull, he used his teeth on her. She threw back her head on a muffled scream, hooked one elbow around his neck and grabbed his ass with the other hand. Used her nails on him while her inner muscles spasmed around him, and that small, pretty pain joined hands with the impossible fury of his want and shoved him over the edge into madness.

He came with her, came inside her. His hips pistoned mindlessly, desperately. But even as that dangerously coiled hunger inside him came unspooled, even as he came and came and came, he couldn't stop pumping himself into her. He wanted more, goddamn it. He was as close to her as he was ever going to get, he was *inside* her, for God's sake, had her nails biting deep into his skin, and yet that hunger wasn't gone. It was just...less. For now.

Oh Jesus. He was so screwed. Even as those last mind-bending shudders wracked him, even as she gripped his hair and arched into him, he still wanted more. He dropped his forehead to her shoulder and fought to control his breathing, fought to gather up the shattered bits of the public self he'd thrown off a handful of hot, sweaty, world-changing minutes ago. He willed his heart to settle, to slow. He willed himself to ignore the delicious sting of her nails and teeth, along with the possibility that a few strategically placed bruises might bloom on his skin in the morning, incontrovertible proof that this had honest-to-God just happened. He and Audrey. They'd happened. Holy Christ.

He'd cherish every bruise and mark she'd put on his body, of course, but he'd hate them, too. Because he already wanted her again. He was still inside her, and the hunger was already building. And the likelihood of he and Audrey ever happening again? Slim. Slim to fucking none. She'd met Will's monster but good this time, and he doubted she liked feeling a split in her lip or some stripes on her back come the morning after quite as much as he did.

Or, you know, at all. Most people didn't.

Then her limbs were loosening around him, her hands slipping away from his shoulders to lie on the counter, her legs unwinding themselves from his waist to dangle bonelessly to the floor. And he took his cue to step back. To whip the guest towel from its tidy ring on the wall and hand it to her. To scoop up his own t-shirt from the floor to clean himself up. To fix on his blandest game face and say, "So."

"So," she sighed. He wished he could see her face but it was too dark. "That was—"

She paused and his brain—back on line with full, demoralizing vocabulary—filled in the blank. *Violent. Twisted. Rough. Wrong.* He waited to see which one she'd pick. She never got the chance.

The door swung open, the one leading to the room where Audrey was supposed to be sleeping, and second-hand light leaked into the bathroom. His own nakedness occurred to him but only as a detail. It was Audrey's squawk of alarm that threw him into motion. He swept her off the counter, put her behind him and turned to face the light, his hands in hard fists, his mind clear and focused on protecting her from this new threat.

"Well my goodness," said a voice, all southern and amused. "What have we here?"

The bathroom light flicked on, and Will squinted into the sudden blast of it. He found a woman leaning casually against the doorjamb, all long, tanned limbs and dark, streaky hair. It tumbled nearly to her elbows, dramatic and sun-shot, and he thought, *Yachting will do that*, even before Audrey said, "Olivia."

Because of course this was Olivia. Audrey's sister. Jillian's mother. And she looked, Will decided, a lot like Jem. It wasn't a physical resemblance, though she had his coloring right down to the cold black eyes. It was more that *ignore me at your peril* vibe that poured off her. She was beautiful, no question. But the sort of beautiful that reminded him of poisonous snakes and loaded guns. Dangerous and unpredictable and nothing smart men wanted in their pants.

He remembered belatedly that he was naked, and hastily clapped his wadded up t-shirt over the essentials.

Audrey stepped out from behind him, magically swathed from armpits to knees in a fluffy white towel. Regret was an automatic pang somewhere in his gut—he'd probably never see her naked again, after all—but she slapped a second towel into his hands and regret disappeared inside some serious gratitude.

"Oh, how sweet!" Olivia murmured, her eyes sliding over his torso as he fashioned himself a man sarong. "Your little boyfriend's shy!"

Audrey didn't look at him, only regarded her sister with that same blank disdain she so often turned on Will. "So," she said evenly. "You're back."

"What tipped you off?" Olivia pushed off the doorjamb and strolled into the bathroom, her mouth a moue of jaded amusement.

Audrey sighed. "I'd ask where you've been but it doesn't really matter, does it?"

Olivia hitched herself up onto the counter in a fluid motion and hooked her ankles together. "And, really, why ask if you don't care?" She sharpened up that sly half-smile and aimed it at her sister. Will wondered if it was her default expression, because nothing else in her face or body language indicated amusement.

Audrey stared. "You are *not* the victim here, Olivia. Don't even try it."

Olivia's laugh was as bright as breaking glass. "Oh, honey, please. There's only one professional victim in this house, and it's never been me." She leaned toward Will, caught him with those frigid eyes. "I like a good time too much for that nonsense."

"That's the rumor," he murmured politely.

She let go with a low, lusty laugh. "I might like this one, Audi-girl," she said. "He's not your usual."

"No."

Will didn't know if Audrey was agreeing that he was not, in fact, her usual type, or if she was simply negating the idea that he was her anything at all. He wished he weren't so interested in knowing which it was.

"Unlike your other little boyfriends, this one's got a dick," Olivia observed. "I saw it."

Well, yes. Yes, she had. Everybody had. Lovely. Mortification gathered inside him like a cruel fist.

"And what a sight it was." She sent him a broad wink. "Look sharp, baby sister. I might have to steal this one away from you."

"You can try." Audrey's expression didn't shift. "Might find your hands full."

Olivia's eyes dropped to the rise of Audrey's breast above the towel, to—oh God—to the hickey unabashedly blooming there. Her eyebrows lifted slowly until they were practically in her hairline. "My, my, my," she murmured. "You really did hook yourself a live one, didn't you?" She flashed that naughty-angel smile Will's way. "And you! Introducing Princess Touch-Me-Not to a little whip-me, strip-me!" She chuckled and shook her head. "I suppose that comes with a smutty little thrill all its own. But, hey, you ever want to pick on somebody your own size, you let me know."

A flush started on Audrey's chest and climbed until her cheeks were blazing. Will watched it with fascination. But that flat disdain in her eyes didn't budge. "So you abandoned a yacht in the Caribbean to steal my boyfriend?" she asked. "Is that it?"

"Of course not." Olivia waved an elegant hand. "Hurricane Ivanka turned out to be a right bitch, that's all. *The Penelope*'s in dry dock until Rafe deems her unsinkable. He's such a bore that way." She rolled her eyes. "As for coming home to steal your little boyfriend? Please. Anybody who'd date you couldn't wake me up from a nap." She dropped her lashes Will's way. "Present company excepted, of course." He returned her gaze impassively.

"So why are you here?" Audrey asked again.

"Why do you think?" Olivia bared her teeth in a smile as cold as her eyes. "I came for my kid."

Chapter 27

Terror gripped Audrey hard and tight. All the oxygen left her body and her head went dangerously light. She'd known this would happen. Eventually. She'd known Olivia would come back sooner or later. Come back to take Jillian from her. Again.

"No." She stepped forward, teeth clenched, jaw aching, heart screaming. "You can't have her."

"Of course I can." Olivia gave her that toothy smile of hers, evil and delighted. "I'm her mother."

"You abandoned her."

"Hardly. I took a job, that's all." She twirled a dark lock of hair around one finger and watched Audrey with hungry eyes. Olivia loved nothing more than winding her up, Audrey knew, feeding on her impotent fury and her incoherent pain. "A job incompatible with the needs and schedules of a child. So I arranged for her to stay here with her doting grandpa while I applied myself to keeping us in rent and groceries for the rest of the winter." She gave Audrey wide, innocent eyes. "Which is what any decent mother would do, don't you think?"

"You took off with your boyfriend *du jour* to tour the seven seas." Audrey bit the words off, panic rising in her throat like vomit.

"Or I crewed for an internationally ranked sailor." Olivia's smile didn't budge. "And you can't actually be a sailor and a mommy at the same time." She paused, and something shifted behind those hard eyes. "Not unless you want to end up at the bottom of the ocean."

Audrey's heart elbowed past the terror and panic to lodge itself in her throat. "Something happened out there," she said. It wasn't a question. "Something happened out there, didn't it?" She slapped the wall beside her. "Damn it, Livvy, you have responsibilities. You have a *child*. You can't just risk your neck anymore like some stupid teenager—"

"Oh, settle down." Olivia smiled and those eyes went as blank and hard as marbles again. Audrey hated her suddenly. Hated her for dangling closeness like a little treat, then snatching it away when Audrey reached for it. Hated herself for being stupid enough to reach in the first place, which she did. Every damn time. "Nothing *happened* out there." She didn't condescend to use actual finger quotes but Audrey heard them nonetheless. "God. Get a hold of yourself." She slid a look Will's way, drifted a greedy look over the sharp elegance of his naked chest. Audrey resisted the urge to throw herself in front of him. She'd seen what Olivia did to men's good intentions, and had no desire to watch Will succumb. "Maybe you should leave this one with me and go hang out with Rafe. He's a safety freak, too."

A passionate defense of safety as a lifestyle leapt to her lips but she swallowed it down. Blanked her face and breathed for a solid three count. Talking to Olivia was like dancing. You couldn't let her lead, not unless you enjoyed red-faced screaming matches. Which Olivia did. Audrey did not.

"You could have called." She focused on breathing. Only breathing. In and out, nice and slow. "Written. Emailed. Texted. A postcard?"

"Why? To remind the kid I wasn't here?" She cocked a derisive brow. "I didn't want her to miss me."

"Well done, then." Audrey didn't break eye contact. "She didn't."

Olivia's eyes went narrow and hard. Harder, anyway. "Of course she didn't. Not with perfect Aunt Audrey in charge. Or have you got her calling you Mommy now?"

"Now?" Audrey smiled cruelly. "You mean again."

Olivia jerked like she'd been slapped and Audrey could have bitten her own tongue off. Oh, God. The one thing she could have said to make a bad situation worse, and she'd tossed it into the ring between them, right out loud. Oh, hell.

Oh, shit. Oh, damn.

"Again," Olivia said softly. "That's right." She slipped off the counter with a sailor's innate grace. "She *did* call you Mommy once, didn't she?" She crossed her arms over her waist and let Audrey remember exactly what had happened the last time Jillian had been caught calling her Mommy. Both Jillian and Olivia had been gone within twenty-four hours, no forwarding address, no note, no nothing for the next seven years. The staggering loss still rang inside her head like a distant bell when she let herself think about it, which she didn't. Not often. But she was thinking about it now. She didn't have much of a choice, did she? Not with her sister dangling that sword over her head again.

"Olivia, I—" Her lips were numb and the hand she reached out trembled.

"Forget it." Olivia brushed Audrey's hand away. "It's cool. Thanks for everything, okay? But all the same, I think I'll just wake up *my* daughter and get going."

"Livvy, please—" Audrey began again, shock and memory reeling together. *Again*, she thought frantically. It was happening again. Pain swamped her, short circuited every defense she had and swept away strategy, control, pride. So she begged. "Please don't do this. Please. You can't—"

"I absolutely can." Olivia side-stepped her and started for the far door. For Jillian. Then Will—so silent Audrey had almost forgotten he was there—blocked her path. Olivia stopped short, her eyebrows flying up. She treated him to a full-length inspection, from his bare feet to his rumpled hair. A quick spasm of lust shivered through Audrey, involuntary and reflexive. She wondered if she'd ever look at him again and not feel that.

But, worse, there was hope, too. It flared to life inside her because even wearing nothing but a towel and some bite-marks, Will didn't look like the kind of guy anybody wanted to cross. And he'd just stepped up to Olivia the Ruthless. For her.

"I don't think so," he said.

Olivia stared. "Excuse me?"

"Jillian's had a rough night," he said.

"Is that so?" Olivia's eyes wandered pointedly over his naked chest.

"It is." Authority rang quietly in his voice, as if he opened negotiations half-dressed every day. "She's sleeping and she's going to keep sleeping until morning."

"I beg your pardon." Olivia widened her eyes with outrage, but Audrey knew better. This wasn't outrage; this was delight. Back to back smack-downs were Olivia's idea of heaven. "Are you keeping me from my own child?"

Will merely held her gaze. "You'd like that, wouldn't you?"

"I...of course not!" Olivia narrowed her eyes, reassessed with the lightning speed of a veteran fighter. "But you appear to be standing directly between me and my child, so forgive me if I draw the obvious conclusion."

"Of course. If you'll forgive me for drawing an equally obvious conclusion."

"Which is?"

"You're exhausted, Ms. Bing." He gave her an impassive up-and-down of his own. "You certainly look it."

She drew back, one hand flying automatically to the sexed-up tumble of her hair, a look that Audrey knew she cultivated with obsessive care. She wondered if Will knew how well he'd aimed that little barb. She suspected he did. This was *Will*.

"And Jillian is definitely exhausted," he went on. "So while I'm all in favor of touching reunions between mothers and children, common sense suggests that we table this one until daylight hours." He paused, lifted a questioning brow Olivia's way. "Unless there's some pressing reason that you'd rather take off in the dead of the night?"

Olivia regarded him in tense silence for a long moment, then shifted gears again. "You're right." She gave a shuddering sigh and pressed her fingers to the circles under her eyes. "You're right. I'm tired." She reached a tentative hand toward Audrey. "I'm so tired. I'm not thinking straight. Forgive me?"

Audrey forced her lips to curl up into something

approximating a smile and took her sister's hand. "Me, too?"

"Oh, honey. Always." Olivia drew her in for a suffocating hug, and Audrey endured it. The scent of cigarettes (faint) and vanilla (overpowering) enveloped her but she returned the embrace with as much enthusiasm as she could manage, because if Olivia detected even a whiff of reluctance, the mood could shift again.

Will said, "Why don't you get some rest, Ms. Bing? We'll pick up this discussion over breakfast like civilized people."

"So forceful, this one." Olivia drew back to cock an amused brow at Audrey. "Are the two of you together for real?"

Audrey sighed. "The hickeys don't lie."

Olivia gave a snort of laughter. "Of course they do, sweetie. Have I taught you nothing?"

"No, you've taught me everything," Audrey murmured. "You want to join me in your old room? There's a bed free."

"Ah, memories." Olivia shot a look over her shoulder. "Are those really my posters?"

Audrey smiled. "They aren't mine."

"Cripes." She sighed and shook her head. "Okay, I'll go to bed. I'm ready to drop right here."

Audrey pressed a kiss to her sister's cheek, and her throat was suddenly tight with memories of her own. Better ones. "Good night, Olivia."

"Night, baby." She threw one last dancing look Will's way. "Night, Mr. Large and In Charge."

"Goodnight, Ms. Bing."

"Ms. Bing." Olivia rolled the words around her mouth as she sauntered toward the door. "I do like it when he calls me that." She put a hand on the jamb and sent a look Audrey's way. "Does he call you that while he—"

Audrey said, "Good night, Olivia."

She laughed. "You kids go straight to bed, now. No more bathroom shenanigans, you hear? It's late." She flicked off the light and clicked the door shut, plunging them back into the dark.

Silence. He didn't reach for the light switch, and she

was grateful. She was too raw, too vulnerable. She didn't want him to see her like this. His hand found her cheek in the darkness, cupped it with a gentleness completely at odds with what they'd done to one another minutes earlier.

"Audrey." His voice was quiet in the darkness. "Are you all right?"

"I don't know." She shrugged miserably. "What if she does it? What if she takes Jillian and disappears again?"

"We fight it."

She huffed out a weary laugh. Fight. Will's answer to everything. "She's the legal and biological parent, Will. There's no court in the country that would—or should—strip a parent of rights just because auntie thinks she can do it better."

"Of course not. But I don't think that's the war we're fighting here." His voice was flat in the darkness, utterly unemotional. But she knew better now than to imagine he was untouched. He wasn't calm; he was careful. He didn't used to be but he was now. He kept his emotional shrapnel to himself. Was she crazy for missing it? "She doesn't want Jillian."

"Jesus, Will, of course she does. Didn't you hear what she just said? She'd have taken her right now if you hadn't bowed up on her like that." She sighed. "And thank you for that, by the way. Seems like all you do anymore is fight my battles for me."

"My pleasure. And I think you know I mean that literally."

She surprised herself with a laugh. "No argument."

"Then don't argue with this, either. Your sister's not here for Jillian. She's here for you."

"For me?"

"You bet. Girl like that? She breaks hearts for fun." His pause was grim and certain. "Believe me, I know the type."

"Sounds like a story."

"For another day. Suffice it to say that I'm familiar with the breed. She learn her moves from your mom?"

"My...mom?"

"Sure. Obviously I never met Cece but everything I've

201

seen and heard leads to a mental picture heavy on the spoiled, beautiful, and poisonous. Somebody who needs a lot of attention, and doesn't care who she hurts to get it. Sound familiar?"

"Yeah," she said faintly. "It does."

"Figured it might. And then there's you."

"Me?"

"You. Defending yourself with the old lock-it-down, show-no-fear, show-no-*anything* strategy. Which is smart, Audrey. Really, really smart. Because giving up even a drop of emotion only feeds the flames. And maybe I'm leaping to conclusions here, but I bet there's nothing Olivia likes more than burning shit down. So you can't engage. At all. Which you probably learned at an extremely young age." He paused again, but she had the strangest impression of delicacy. Gentleness. Again. When had Will learned to be gentle?

"I did," she admitted quietly. "Too young, probably."

"Which is why I'd bet my 401k that you learned your moves from your dad."

She sucked in a breath while that insight detonated inside her skull like a bomb. She was like her *dad*? Oh dear lord. She was. She was like her dad. That awful dance she'd watched her parents do her entire childhood? The one where her mom acted out more and more dramatically, and cared less and less about the fallout? The one where her dad descended further and further into the stoicism that only pushed her mom further and further down the path to self-destruction? She and Olivia had recreated it, word by word, year by year.

"Oh my God," she breathed, stunned. "I'm like my dad."

He touched his thumb to the corner of her astonished mouth and said, "You think I don't see you? You think I don't know? Oh, Audrey." He sighed. "That was true once but not anymore. I see you now. I can't *un*see you. And you're as beautiful as anything God ever made, but—and I say this with great love—Jesus, you're messed up."

"No argument," she said again, faintly. "I'm like my *dad*."

"At least you're not like your sister. Because that girl is one sadistic bitch."

She blinked. "Go ahead and call a spade a spade, why don't you?"

"I will, thanks." His hand drifted from her cheek, hooked itself around her nape and stayed there, warm and strong and reassuring. "But you know what I think? I think Sailor Rafe turned out to be a bore. And Olivia doesn't do boredom, so she came looking for a fix. For a heart to break. And yours is so reliable, especially when it comes to Jillian. You're good value that way. At least you were last time."

"She's going to do it again, isn't she?" Tears thickened her throat but she swallowed them down. "That's her plan?"

"Probably." He drew her in and she went without protest. She dropped her aching forehead to his shoulder, and breathed him in. Savored the power and the fury and the *fact* of him, strong enough to absorb her sorrow and all this helpless fear. "But I'll be damned if she gets it done."

"Oh, Will." Tenderness blew through her in a cool, lovely rush and she thought *I love this man*. And she did. She loved him. Loved him for his fists and his teeth, for his tenderness and his insight. Loved him because he was so right about her, and so wrong about himself.

"She might take Jillian," he warned her. "She's the parent and that shit's hard to contest but I swear on all that's holy, her days of hit-and-run are over, at least where you're concerned. If she leaves, she's not ever coming back. I'll make it my life's fucking work."

"Oh, Will," she said again, a thin thread of shame curling through the love. Because maybe he'd seen her, but she hadn't seen him. Not fully. She'd thought that indulging his taste for pain, forcing him to share his sharpest edges with her—deliciously—was the greatest intimacy of which he was capable. But she'd been wrong. So very wrong. For Will, the deepest, scariest, rawest exposure would be love. Tenderness. Sweetness. He'd been edging up to it, trying to show it to her, and retreating time and again into warrior mode. Maybe because that's where he was most comfortable, maybe because it was all he valued in himself.

203

Maybe because it was all anybody valued in him. Even her.

He'd told her he loved her, and *apologized* for it.

That was wrong. It was wrong and she, by God, was going to fix it. She was going to prove to him that there was more to him than his teeth and his fists, that she saw it all and loved it, even if it took the rest of her life. Pray God it would.

But even as that conviction took hold, even as it cemented itself inside her soul, became the fixture around which she was going to build the rest of her life, she remained silent. Love for him bubbled up her throat but she swallowed it back down. Habit, maybe. Fear. Or just simple timing. Because, you know, time and place. They mattered.

Or maybe because, oh boy, here came the laughter. It gushed up her throat, tangled with the tears, and she snorted out one of those horrible, unintelligible laugh-sobs for which she'd become famous. She never had done strong emotion with any finesse.

"Oh God," he said. "Not this again."

"I'm sorry," she brayed. "I can't help it."

"I know." He patted her hair and sighed deeply. "It's okay. Go ahead and..."

Laugh? Cry? Snort wetly on my shoulder?

"...well, go ahead."

So she did. And fell deeper in love with every damp moment.

Chapter 28

Will hit the stairs bright and early the next morning, partly because he was a habitual early riser, and partly because he had no desire for Drew to get a load of the nail marks on his back. Will knew he would never get a repeat performance of last night, so he wanted a few days to savor the memory before Drew got his hands on it.

He would be delighted for Will, of course. Will could hear his brother now—*You and* Audrey? *That is some miraculous shit right there, bro. How the hell did you...hey, are those* bite marks?

It wasn't a discussion Will could avoid forever—this was his brother, after all—but he didn't intend to have it this morning. Which was why he'd had his tie knotted and was following the sound of Audrey's ocean before Drew even considered cracking an eye.

The stairs dumped him into that echoing showpiece of a foyer. He cocked his head and considered the sound of her inside his head. It swirled and fretted this morning, as if she were unsettled. Uneasy.

Are we surprised? Bob asked with amusement. *What do you think freaked her out the most? Olivia's grand return or the dirty sex with you? And congratulations, by the way. I did* not *see that one coming. The truth will set you free but it usually doesn't get you laid.*

Will blanched. Bob was in his head.

I'm always in your head, ass wipe.

Bob was *always* in his head? Like *last night* always?

Bob chuckled. *Oh, relax. I have other options. I can check out when you need your privacy.*

"Jesus," he breathed, his heart thudding. He really needed help. His imagination was spying on him, and he was panicking over it?

For the last time, Bob growled, *I am* not *your goddamn imagination. And I'm not spying on you, either. I checked out when it became clear things were going to get...interesting. Is it my fault you've been all about the instant replay ever since?*

Oh my God. Shut up, Bob.

Whatever. But he stopped talking.

Will took a moment to breathe, to refocus on the rush and wash of Audrey's energy inside his head. He would deal with Bob—or whatever Bob was—later. This morning, he was sort of scheduled up. And right at the top of his to-do list? Talking to Audrey. Because there were a few details of yesterday he hadn't had a chance to update her on. Details she sort of needed to know.

He assessed his options then chose a short hallway, all teak paneling and oil paintings. He wondered if that was Jem's taste or Cece's, then decided it didn't matter. He was just filling the space in his head before Bob (or whatever) filled it up for him.

He must've chosen correctly because suddenly the hall opened up into a massive kitchen. And, good lord, it was some kitchen. It was like somebody'd taken half a soccer field, then filled it with gleaming marble, custom cabinetry and stainless-steel appliances. And plunked Audrey Bing down at the far end like just another priceless work of art.

He zeroed in on her like she was wearing a homing beacon. He suspected she was. For him, anyway. He'd marked her with his teeth and his scent, with his body and soul, and she was his. She didn't know that. Probably never would. She didn't have to. He knew it, and that was enough. Would have to be enough. He'd make it enough, he told himself grimly, because he wasn't getting anything else.

Aw, Bob said fondly. *This is no time for a crisis of confidence, buddy. That's your woman right there. Go get her.*

Will sighed. His imagination had come completely unglued.

Audrey looked up and blinked. He realized he'd

stopped in the archway to stare at her like a love-struck teenager.

Or a weird-ass stalker, Bob offered.

Unkind but accurate. Not entirely unglued, then.

"Hey." It came out a little gruffly but better than the octave-skipping voice break he'd experienced under pressure clear into his twenties. He ordered his feet to move and they did. Without incident, too. It was a day for miracles, evidently.

"Hey," she said, and smiled at him. Only she didn't. He could hear it, though, the rush and swirl of her ocean shifting from a minor to a major key, just for a moment. And wasn't that...unexpected?

You're not as smart as you think you are, Bob whispered. *How many times do I have to tell you that? Pay attention, dickwad. Pay attention like you don't already know all the answers, because you don't. You really, really don't.*

Will was paying attention all right. To Audrey. He didn't—couldn't?—take his eyes off her, or the smile he could see now, if only in the clear violet of her gaze. Her hands continued to dance over the coffee pot, delicate and graceful as birds. Memory flashed, hot and sudden, and he saw those same beautiful hands curled into claws, hooked into his shoulders while she feasted on his throat. He'd knotted his tie extra high today to hide the hickey.

"Well if it isn't Mr. Large and In Charge," Olivia said.

Will nearly jumped but caught himself just in time. He hadn't seen Olivia there, and he was almost on top of her. Christ. She was sitting at a massive island counter, a cup of coffee cradled between tanned, capable-looking hands. Her hair was a glossy cloud of the blackest sin reaching nearly to the curve of her waist, close enough to touch if he wanted to.

He didn't. He really, really didn't. And he suspected Olivia could tell. She didn't like it, either. No more than she'd liked the fact that he hadn't even noticed her for staring at Audrey.

"Good morning, Ms. Bing," he said.

"Olivia." She gave him a curly little half-smile.

"Please."

"Olivia, then." He extended a hand. "William Blake. Will, since you've seen me naked."

Her eyes warmed up a little at that, and she lifted her mug as if to hide a grin. "I thought we'd leave that politely unmentioned."

Will shot a look at Audrey. "Yeah, I did, too." He shrugged. "How about we leave it between just us three?"

Olivia dimpled. "Deal." She shook his hand. Her palm was tough and square inside his, clearly no stranger to back-breaking labor. He wondered what kind of person could sweat for a living but chicken out of parenting. He had a feeling he was going to find out before all this was over.

Will took his hand back a full two pumps after he wanted to—egos were delicate things—and turned to Audrey.

"Audrey," he said. "I'm glad you're here. I need to talk to you."

"Yeah, I figured." She smiled with her whole face this time, but it was wry. Self-mocking. It was the same smile he'd seen on the face of every woman who'd ever indulged her inner bad girl with Will's monster. First came the sheepish smile, then it was all, *Well, gosh, this has been fun but...* He wasn't surprised to see that same smile on Audrey's face—far from it—but his heart sank anyway. Which was stupid, as he'd been braced for it.

Then she stepped forward and hooked a finger into his collar. Every nerve ending in his body surged toward the brush of her knuckle against his throat. She came up on her toes and peered into his collar. Sighed at the sight of his hickey. "I thought you looked suspiciously buttoned up this morning. Going to work?"

"Actually, work is coming here." He cleared the lust out of his throat. "That's, uh, part of what I needed to talk to you about."

"Mmm hmm." She stepped back, put her hands on her hips and studied him. "And the other part?"

The other part was, as she suspected, hiding under the knot of his tie. He shifted, wondering how to launch into this one with Olivia listening to every word with unabashed enjoyment. Damn. Olivia and Drew were a match made in heaven. And, shit, he hoped Drew didn't decide that same thing. Dismay clutched his gut with its usual acidic churn and he said, "I need coffee if we're getting into the other part."

"Fresh pot already brewing." She studied him for another long moment. Then she reached out with slow deliberation, wrapped his tie around her fist and pulled him down to her mouth. It was sweet and soft and tasted like blessed coffee, and Will fell into it with a shock of confused wonder. For a long, glorious moment, he was aware of nothing but her mouth under his and her ocean swirling in his ears.

She stepped back far too soon and gazed up at him, her face grave and perfect. "Good morning, Will."

"I, um—" he managed while his brain spun its wheels uselessly. Her brows rose slowly and he realized he was probably frowning at her. The same way he frowned at a really good problem or an excellent question. Only she didn't know that. She was probably wondering if he was going to say something ugly. Or dry-hump her on the kitchen counter. Neither of which was an out-of-the-ballpark possibility where he was concerned. Which she knew damn well. He cleared his throat but didn't try to smile. Smiling wasn't his strong suit.

"Every time I fight my way around one of your corners," he murmured.

"Not what you expected." She continued to regard him with that steady gravity. "I know."

"Never." He tucked his hands into his pockets.

"Which is part of what we need to talk about."

"Guess so."

She tossed a glance Olivia's way. "Privately."

"Please."

"Aw." Olivia folded her arms on the countertop. "Just when things were getting good." She glanced around the kitchen. "Now what I am supposed to do for fun?"

"You could make breakfast," Audrey suggested.

"Me?" Olivia drew back, startled. "Where's the cook or housekeeper or whoever?"

"You know Dad and housekeepers."

"He had somebody last time I was here. Chubby, gray, maternal? Heidi or Hannah or something?"

"Ah. That would be Hildy." Audrey glanced at Will. "And she's still here. But she's not the housekeeper." She hesitated and Olivia's eyes went huge.

"Oh my God. Dad's got a girlfriend? *Live in*?" She laughed delightedly. "Jem Bing, getting some." She shook her head. "I never thought I'd see the day."

"You haven't." Audrey opened a cupboard and retrieved a mug. "Hildy's not the housekeeper *or* Dad's girlfriend." She poured Will some coffee and handed it over. He took it gratefully, but kept his eyes on Olivia, and wondered how Audrey was going to play this one. "She's his psychic."

Directly. Will nodded. Of course. This was Audrey. She wouldn't dance around it. She'd just deliver the news.

Olivia set down her coffee with a sharp click. "Oh, hell, no. He's not still—"

"He is, actually." Audrey topped off her own coffee, added cream, then turned to face her sister. She leaned against the counter, mug between her palms. "And, Livvy? It gets worse."

"Worse? How could it get worse than a live-in psychic?"

Audrey paused uncomfortably.

"Right." Olivia stood up. "Don't tell me yet. I don't think I want to hear whatever *worse* is on an empty stomach."

Audrey gestured a go-ahead toward the fridge. When Olivia's head was buried in the crisper, Audrey caught Will's eye and mouthed *She cooks if provoked*. Will raised a brow and Audrey smiled smugly. Admiration filled him for the elegant strategy, the flawless execution. He wondered if maybe his heart had known something his brain didn't when it had insisted on Audrey Bing.

Something to think about, Bob murmured. *When you're*

not too busy thinking you know it all.

He continued to bask in the warm glow of Audrey's smile and thought idly, *Shut up, Bob.* Bob just laughed that sharp-edged laugh of his.

"So." Audrey's eyes danced at him over the edge of her coffee mug. "Work's coming to the house today?"

"Right." He shook off the dazzle of that smile and focused. "It is. Remember that guy James sent me yesterday? The Spaniard?"

"Sure."

Then Olivia backed out of the fridge with an armload of vegetables, a packet of cheese and a carton of eggs. "Get the milk, Audi-girl."

"On it." Audrey held up one finger to pause Will. She snagged the milk jug and nudged the fridge shut with her heel. Olivia wheeled around her to deposit her arm-load of food on the counter. Audrey bent and retrieved a frying pan from the cupboard while Olivia cracked the eggs. The moment they were all glistening in the bowl, Audrey produced a whisk from thin air and slapped it into her sister's waiting hand like it was a surgeon's scalpel.

Will cocked his head and took it in. These two weren't dancing for the first time. He hadn't doubted Audrey's word that Olivia cooked but knowing it and seeing it were two different things. And watching her and Audrey move around each other with the fluid grace of synchronized swimmers? Like they were performing a routine they'd done so many times it was indelibly grooved into their memories? That was unexpected. He shook his head. That was his Audrey, though. A surprise around every corner.

The kitchen was starting to smell like the promised land so he topped off his coffee mug and took it to Olivia's abandoned stool. Checked his watch. He had a few minutes yet. He could take them to study the Bing sisters in action.

"I knew it." Jem appeared in the doorway of the kitchen, his brows low and thick over those crazy eyes as he scowled at his daughters.

"Good morning, Dad," Audrey said. Jem ignored her. Olivia ignored them both and flipped her eggs.

"When did you get in?" Jem barked at Olivia. "Middle of the night, as usual?"

"Jet lag." Olivia looked up and offered him that semi-smile of hers, the one that suggested she was amused but not for any innocent reason. She shrugged languid shoulders. "It's a bitch."

"You'd know." Jem stumped into the room while Olivia's smile curdled. Will felt his brows shoot up and he caught Audrey's tiny sigh. Looked like this was a well-worn track in everybody's memory as well. "What are you doing here?"

"Aw, Dad, you old softie." Olivia's teeth flashed bright and sharp. "You missed me!"

Jem snorted and plunked himself down on the stool beside Will's. He caught Audrey's eye and said, "Coffee."

Audrey gazed at her father with impassive patience. He sighed.

"Audrey, darling, fruit of my loins, would you be so good as to put your expensive and extensive education to use and butle your dear old dad a cup of coffee?"

She folded her arms and considered him.

Jem gave her a smile hard and bright enough to put Olivia's to shame. "No wonder you couldn't land a job."

She didn't blink. "I'm very pleased with my current position."

Jem slid Will a poisonous look. "Bet you are."

Audrey filled a mug and put it in front of him. "Drink your coffee, Dad. You're mean in the morning."

"I'm mean all day," he said.

"Truer words."

Olivia said, "Eggs are up" at the exact moment Audrey produced a platter. Will marveled. There were companies listed on the NASDAQ that could take a lesson from the Bing sisters on just-in-time inventory. Will thought about getting up to search out plates and forks but didn't want to disrupt the flow. It was fascinating.

"Have they always done this?" he asked Jem.

"What?" Jem's nose was buried in his mug and he was inhaling caffeine devotedly.

"This." Will nodded toward the stove. Toward Audrey punching down toaster buttons and dealing out plates, toward Olivia catching the toast as it popped up and slapping butter on it.

Jem looked at his daughters. "Oh, that. Yeah. Had to eat, didn't they? And we never could hang onto a housekeeper above a month or two." He slid a look Will's way, challenge in those black eyes. "Place is haunted, you know."

Will checked his watch. "Yeah, about that." He accepted the plate Audrey slid his way with a grateful smile, and waited until all four of them were seated and served before he said, "James sent me a teammate the other day to see if I'd be interested in representing him."

Jem hunched over his plate and started shoveling in the eggs. "What does that have to do with my haunted house?"

Olivia's lips went tight and Audrey sent Will a worried look. "The house isn't haunted, Dad," Olivia snapped. "The only place Mom's still alive and pissed off is in your head." She tapped her own forehead. "In your guilty, guilty conscience, okay?"

Jem pointed his fork at her. "Yeah, tell it to your kid."

"My kid?" Olivia sat back and frowned. "What about her?"

"Dad, why don't you let me—" Audrey began, but Jem mowed over her as usual.

"Your mom's taken the kid over."

Olivia blinked. "Taken her...what?"

"Taken her over. Spiritually speaking." He waved his fork dismissively. "Hildy can explain it later. Bottom line? Mom's in there, in her little head or whatever. Scared the kid shitless. Hasn't said a word in months unless you count screaming her lungs out every night." He went back to his eggs while Olivia gazed at him in stupefaction. Audrey covered her eyes with a hand and Will just watched.

"Bullshit," Olivia finally said, faintly. An angry flush rode high on those perfect cheekbones but he was more interested in the sudden pallor underneath it. Olivia the Fearless was afraid of ghosts?

Jem shrugged. "You can take the kid if you want to, but don't blame me when your mom goes with you." He closed his lips over his fork with relish. He smiled around a mouthful of eggs. "Good luck with that."

Chapter 29

Drew arrived during the shouting. Jem and Olivia were keeping the volume at eleven without any help from Will or Audrey, and Will watched his brother pause in the doorway for one of his lightning speed assessments. Will could see it all zip through the guy's head as if in cartoon thought bubbles: family drama, coffee, unattended food. Drew's eyes lit up and he swooped silently down on Jem's abandoned plate of eggs. Then he helped himself to Olivia's. Will had never loved his brother more.

He picked up his own coffee cup—brotherly love had its limits—and waited for a lull. He didn't wait long. It was hard to sustain top volume for more than a few minutes at a time. Plus Jem had just dropped the e-word (exorcism) and rendered Olivia utterly speechless. She was staring, throat working, venom backing up and Will said, "May I make a suggestion?"

Audrey said, "Please."

Jem turned his furious smile Will's way but Olivia continued to gaze in disbelief at her father.

"Before we let Hildy try anything on Jillian, why don't we request a demonstration?"

"Demonstration?" Audrey blinked.

"Sure." Will shrugged. "You know. A show of good faith. Proof of safety, that kind of thing."

"Why not?" Jem threw up his hands. "I'm sure it'll be no problem to find some other kid possessed by the enraged spirit of her dead grandma. They're everywhere these days." He rolled his eyes. "Why don't you take your suggestions and shove them up your—"

"As it happens," Will broke in pleasantly, "I have somebody in mind."

Jem stared. So did Audrey and Olivia. Even Drew paused, a forkful of eggs halfway to his mouth. Will gave himself a mental high five. He'd dropped a bomb so good it had neutralized Drew's appetite. Temporarily.

"I believe I might've mentioned this teammate of James' I met with yesterday? Goalie from Spain by the name of Maximiliano Robledo."

Olivia blinked. "You met with Max 'The Blade' Robledo?"

"The Blade?" Audrey asked.

"Cuts off strikers like a knife," Drew mumbled around his eggs and made a chopping motion with his free hand. "Ha-cha!"

"Wait, back up," Olivia said, narrowing her eyes on him. "This James we're talking about. This is James...Blake? Of the DC Statesmen?"

"That's the one," Will said.

"Which makes you William Blake, James Blake's..." She paused, calculating. "...brother?"

"Yep. One of two."

Olivia glanced at Drew, who gave her a finger wave and went back to demolishing the eggs.

Will smiled. "That's the other one."

"My God." She shook her head. "Two thirds of the Blake brothers, in my kitchen." She said this in tones of deepest awe. Will wished he'd known earlier that she was a soccer fan. He hated going into negotiations blind. She glanced around the kitchen with a faint frown.

"Looking for something?" Will asked.

She shrugged. "I just always thought the Blake brothers traveled with strippers and scotch."

"Ah, the good old days," Drew said.

"Right. Well, we gave that up," Will told her. "In exchange for Bel."

"Bel?"

"James' fiancée."

"Aw," Olivia said with what looked like real regret. "He got engaged?"

"He did."

Drew smiled. "She's a peach, our Bel. Her eggs are even better than these, and these are stellar."

"Thanks," she said, still studying Will. "So where *is* James?"

"Right now?" Will checked his watch. "On a plane to Florida for January camp."

"Damn," Olivia said. "I was just in Florida."

"You should've stayed," Jem snapped.

Olivia gave him a poisonous smile. "And miss the exorcism?"

"Which brings us back to Max," Will said. "Goalie extraordinaire and the pride of the Spanish nation. As I'm sure some of you know, Real Madrid drafted our boy Max right out of his sophomore year of high school. In an impetuous show of gratitude, Max swore an oath of eternal loyalty to team and country right there on national TV. Vowed never to leave either one. To be fair, he spent the next seven years honoring that vow. Then the DC Statesmen made him an offer he couldn't refuse." He smiled thinly. "Evidently Spanish football fans take their oaths seriously, because they cursed the poor guy."

Jem studied him, lips tight, and Will heard that customary swarm of bees all around him but it was soft now. There was the pulse of temper, too, but controlled. Jem had his fury and his fear on the leash again. Finally. "Cursed him, huh?"

"Or so he says." Will set his coffee aside. It was getting cold anyway; Drew could have it. He leaned forward. Linked his fingers together and put his elbows on his knees. "A curse he takes absolutely seriously. This is his career on the line, and he's only twenty-two. He's got years ahead of him yet, but evidently there's been...talk."

"Talk?" Olivia frowned. "What kind of talk?"

"The *washed up, too old, should retire before we put him out to pasture* kind."

"Ouch."

"Exactly." Will smiled at her. "And Max? Max is not having that shit."

"No kidding." Olivia sat down. "That guy's a work of

frickin' art when he's on."

"Evidently he hasn't been on in some time."

Olivia shrugged. "I wouldn't know. I've been at sea."

"Yes," Audrey said. "Yes, you have."

Olivia shot a finger her way. "Do *not* start with me."

"Am I starting?" Audrey threw up innocent hands. "Who's starting? Not me."

"Well, don't."

"I'm not."

Will figured that could go on for some time so he said, "Right. Well, James sent ol' Max my way yesterday, just in case he really does need to put some infrastructure in place for a post-soccer career."

Drew pushed away from his empty plate—plates—and whistled. "Bet that didn't make him a happy Blade."

"Well, no." Will spread his hands. "But he was delighted to hear that I'm currently like this—" He held up his crossed fingers. "—with the most famous curse-breaker in the tri-state area."

Audrey studied him for a long moment and the chaotic gnash of her ocean suddenly fell into a discernible rhythm, like the puzzle pieces had snapped into place inside that head of hers and order had been restored. "You invited a cursed goalie to swing by the house so Hildy can demonstrate her exorcism skills for us?"

Will grinned at her. "I did, yeah."

Drew laughed. "Just when I think you've gone completely corporate on us." He rose and wrapped Will in an unexpected but enthusiastic hug. "I love you, man."

"Say that the next time I refuse to reimburse the receipts you never file."

Drew sighed. "We were having such a nice moment. Why would you want to spoil it with receipt talk?"

"Hey, receipt talk!" Meg wandered into the kitchen. "I love receipts. I also love coffee." She sniffed the air hopefully. "Is there any?"

Drew abandoned Will instantly. He leapt forward and took Meg's hand. "There is!" He ushered her to the stool he'd just abandoned and seated her with a courtly flourish.

"Coffee for the pretty lady, coming right up!"

He began rifling the cupboards with enthusiasm, searching out a mug. Olivia and Jem went back to sniping at each other, volume at a solid seven this time. Meg propped an elbow on the counter and her chin on her hand. She leaned toward Will. "Is he always like this?" she asked, watching Drew fill a mug like it was the holy grail.

Drew cast soulful eyes Meg's way. "Cream, fairest? Sugar for the sweet?"

Will sucked his teeth until he felt like he could keep a straight face. "Like what?"

"Cream," Meg called. "No sugar."

"Of course not." Drew's smile was brilliant. "No need."

"Like *that*," Meg whispered. "All slavish and weird."

"Only when he's in love," Audrey told her. "It never lasts, so if you're planning to take advantage, do it fast." She leaned in and offered Meg her father's smile. "But know that I'll eat you alive if you try. I like that kid."

Will couldn't have loved her more if she'd suddenly started quoting the Blake family motto. She might as well have.

"Kid being the operative word." Meg rolled her eyes. "I prefer my men to be..." She sent Will that blinding smile of hers. It really was extraordinary, what it did to her face. He had to blink a little and refocus to catch the end of her sentence. "...well, to be *men*. All grown up, you know?" She fluttered those lashes at him outrageously.

Will had to choke back a grin. God, this girl was the female equivalent of Drew. She just couldn't help herself. "Ah hmm," he managed.

"Get your own man," Audrey told her flatly. "This one's mine."

Meg cocked a brow. "He is?"

Will's jaw dropped. "I am?"

She glared at him. "Unless that's somebody else's hickey under your tie?"

Will touched the knot of his tie and studied Audrey's perfect face, the tight lips, the hot eyes. Her ocean grumbled ominously and Will wondered what the hell was going on in

219

that head of hers. First she was kissing him in front of Olivia, then she was snarling at Meg for being the same kind of knee-jerk flirt Drew was? All while her ocean twisted and shifted unhappily? Evidently she had a few more corners for him to fight his way around, and a few more surprises for him to handle before he had the answer to that one. He almost grinned just thinking about it.

"Uh, no," he said. "It's definitely your hickey."

Audrey turned her glare back to Meg. "Mine."

Meg sighed. "Pity."

Drew slid a cup of coffee under Meg's nose. "Thanks, Drew," she said and flashed him The Grin. Drew all but wriggled with pleasure.

"You're a prince among men, Drew," Audrey said stoutly and caught Meg's eye with a glance that said *break his heart and face my wrath*. Meg only lifted her coffee cup and gave an appreciative murmur.

"So." Drew sank down on a stool beside Meg and propped his chin on a fist. "You're a fan of receipts? That's fascinating. Tell me about that."

Will checked his watch and rose. They still had a minute or two. Maybe he could take just a quick peek around one of those corners. He said, "Audrey. You want to step into the hallway with me for that private conversation?"

She sent one last glare Meg's way and came to her feet as well. "Sure."

The doorbell pealed and everybody in the kitchen froze. Will said, "That'll be Max."

"He's here?" Olivia's hand flew to her hair. "Now?"

"Early, too." Will slugged back one last gulp of cold coffee and turned to the archway leading into the hall. And froze again. Because there was Jillian, her hand in Hildy's, her eyes huge and pinned to her mother.

Chapter 30

The doorbell rang again and Audrey leapt to her feet, her heart hammering in her ears, her fingers suddenly cold and shaky.

"Will," she said, "why don't you get that?"

He nodded shortly and headed for the door. Hildy drew Jillian aside to let him pass but he paused beside the little girl. He dropped a hand to her thin shoulder, and she turned those huge, searching eyes up to his. He didn't say anything but something passed between them that Audrey couldn't begin to interpret. Then Will headed for the front door and Jillian turned her eyes back to her mother. She didn't move. She didn't blink. She simply stared at Olivia, hope in those giant eyes, resignation in the tight set of those fragile lips.

"Holy *hell*," Olivia snapped before Audrey could even manage a *hey, Jillian, look who turned up in the dead of the night?* "What have you people *done* to her?"

She shoved past Audrey and stalked across the kitchen toward her daughter. Jillian's thin arms twitched like they might open for a hug, then went still. Audrey's heart screamed like a rusty gate but she only leaned around Olivia and smiled at Jillian.

"Good morning, baby," she said. "Your mom's home. Why don't you come have some breakfast?"

"Yeah, eat up, kiddo." Olivia eyed Jillian narrowly as the child sidled past her and made for a stool at the island counter. Meg poked Drew in the ribs and he obligingly scooted over to open up the stool between them. Audrey decided she might not be able to hate Smiley Meg after all. Not completely, anyway. Bummer.

"Hey, word shark," Drew said to Jillian. "If I'd known you were coming, I wouldn't have eaten everybody's breakfast. Sorry." He gave her an utterly insincere grin, and Jillian's lips flickered in response. Audrey watched Meg take in the exchange with a blink of startled comprehension. *Yeah*, she thought, *that's right. There's a sensitive and generous heart operating underneath all that screwball comedy, Smiley Meg. Break it and I will take you the fuck apart.* Meg must've felt Audrey's eyes on her because she looked up and gave her the most inscrutable and dazzling of her smiles. Audrey just gazed back, stone-faced.

"What do you mean, you ate—" Jem said, then broke off. He frowned thunderously down at his empty plate. "Where the *hell* are my eggs?"

"Oh, um." Drew offered him that scalawag grin. "I thought you were finished."

"I'll show you finished, you filthy little—" Jem began but Hildy caught his elbow neatly.

"Temper," she murmured. "It's very chaotic in here." She tipped her head meaningfully toward Jillian and lifted her baby-fine brows. "Let's not add fuel to the fire, hmm?" She released Jem and drifted toward the stove to put on the kettle, a disapproving eyebrow tilted Olivia's way.

Olivia ignored her easily, and said to Audrey, "Cripes, how much weight has the kid lost?"

"None," Audrey said, her smile fixed and plastic as she punched down the toaster button on a couple slices of whole wheat. "She's grown three inches."

"And the bags under her eyes?" Olivia leaned back against the counter, folded her arms and glared. Audrey scooped up some eggs from the pan on the stove and slapped them on a plate. "Those from growing too hard too?"

"No," Jem said, joining them at the counter. "Those are from your mom."

"Those—" Audrey interrupted before Jem and Olivia could escalate, "—are from screaming herself awake and crying herself to sleep twice a night for the last six months. She has night terrors." She slid the plate of eggs onto the counter in front of Jillian. "There you go, sweet pea."

"She won't eat those," Olivia said tightly, her lips white, her eyes hard on her daughter. "She hates eggs."

Drew eyed the plate thoughtfully and Jillian hastily picked up her fork and began shoveling in the eggs. Olivia went a shade paler.

"What the hell?" The toaster shot a couple slices into the air and she caught them automatically. "I've been making you those same eggs for eight years and you've acted like I was trying to poison you every single time!" She tossed the toast to Audrey for buttering and glared at her daughter. "When the hell did you start eating eggs?"

Jillian froze mid-chew, her eyes huge and guilty.

"Well?" Olivia barked, and sounded so much like Jem that even Audrey flinched. "Answer me!"

Audrey held her breath, toast in one hand, butter knife in the other, but that electric moment of demand passed and Jillian didn't fill it. And Audrey knew she wouldn't. Couldn't.

"She can't answer you," Audrey said quietly. She finished buttering the toast, cut it neatly into quarters and tucked them onto the side of Jillian's plate. She pointed her knife at Drew and said, "Don't even think about it."

He held up both hands and sighed like the perpetually and unjustly accused.

"What do you mean, she can't?" Olivia glared around the circle of faces at the island counter. "And don't hand me any more bullshit about hauntings or demonic possession or—"

"Language," Hildy said with a warm smile for Jillian.

"Excuse me?"

"Language," Hildy said, her tone imminently reasonable. "There's a child present."

Olivia sputtered for a moment and Audrey had to hide a grin in her coffee mug. That mom vibe of Hildy's really was something else. She'd had no idea Olivia would be susceptible to such a thing but there was no arguing with the sputter.

Olivia pulled herself together. "Who the hell are you to tell me how to—"

"Language," Hildy said again, this time with a disapproving lift of her brows. "Really, dear, if you can't control yourself, we'll need to have this discussion away from little ears. And that would be a shame after you've been apart so long already but—" She beamed warmly at Olivia. "—I'm afraid I'd have to insist."

Olivia took a moment to digest that one. "You'd have to insist," she repeated slowly. Dangerously.

Hildy inclined her head, serenely unconcerned by the fury slapping hot roses into Olivia's cheeks. Audrey had to hand it to Hildy. The woman was the very definition of unflappable.

Olivia turned to Audrey and hooked a thumb Hildy's way. "Is this bitch for real?"

"All right then." Hildy turned to her daughter. "Meg, would you and Drew mind taking Jillian upstairs?"

"No problem." Meg flashed that dazzling grin of hers and scooped up Jillian's plate. "I'll just grab this before *somebody* eats it out from under you." She gave Drew a pointed look. "Vulture." Jillian glanced at Drew, who managed to look both mournful and hungry at the same time. She turned back to Meg and they shared a look of perfect understanding. Meg put her nose in the air. "Come on, Miss Jillian. Let's finish breakfast upstairs." She marched toward the stairs, and Jillian put her own nose in the air and followed. Drew snatched up Meg's coffee mug and heroically didn't drink it. A sign, Audrey knew, of pure devotion. God, she hoped he pulled himself together. Smiley Meg? Cripes.

"I've got your coffee," he called and hurried after them. "Meg? I've got the coffee!"

Audrey sighed and tuned back in just as Olivia bared her teeth and ripped into Hildy.

"Who the *hell* do you think you are, telling me how to talk in front of my own kid? And what the *fuck* makes you think you can judge me? You don't know me. You don't know *shit* about me, or about this family, or—"

It went on like that for some time. But Hildy, Audrey noted, didn't rise to the bait. She only listened, her face open and tender, as if she were taking some meaning from Olivia's words and tone that nobody else was getting.

Audrey had no idea what the woman was hearing—if anything—but suddenly she understood why Hildy was such a legend in the paranormal community. It was hard to watch this and *not* believe that she had access to some supernatural frequency.

"This is she?" A new voice came from the archway, dark as coffee and heavily accented. "This is the famous Hildy Wise?"

Audrey turned and found Will standing in the doorway next to one of the most beautiful men she'd ever seen in person. The stranger's eyes were hot, liquid and intense, and they were fixed on Olivia.

Will followed his gaze and rolled his eyes. "You only wish," he said. "No, Max, this is—"

Max 'The Blade' Robledo ignored him. He focused on Olivia with a single-minded intensity that sent a hot little shiver up Audrey's thighs. Wow. No wonder Olivia knew who this guy was. He moved across the room with a predatory grace that cut off her sister's furious rant like, well, like a blade. Ha. She could see how the country of Spain might have some trouble letting this one go. She blinked at Will who gave her a faint smile that said *what the hell, let's see where this goes.*

"This," Max breathed, and took Olivia's limp hand from the counter. "This woman." He lifted it to his lips and pressed a reverent kiss to the inside of her wrist. "She is the most magnificent creature I have ever seen, in all my days and all my nights." He raised his head and gave Olivia the eye contact version of a soul kiss. *"Mi salvador,"* he said softly. "My savior."

Olivia gasped audibly when Max's lips touched her wrist and Audrey had to sympathize. Wrist kissing? It was ridiculous and outrageous and impossibly corny. And Max made it work. God, did he.

Will came into the kitchen. "No wonder your career's in the crapper, Max. Your instincts are for shit." He shook his head. "That's not Hildy. That's Olivia Bing, sailor, agitator and prodigal daughter."

Max didn't release Olivia's hand. "Charmed," he

murmured, holding her with those hot eyes and a bold smile. Olivia colored prettily but seemed, Audrey noted with interest, temporarily beyond speech.

"That," Will said, waving toward the other end of the counter, "is Hildy Wise."

Max turned and beheld Hildy in all her maternal glory. He gave Olivia's hand one last tender press, then moved down the counter to take up Hildy's hand with a great deal more reverence and a great deal less sexual energy. "Ah," he said. "But of course. You are the one who will, how do you Americans say? Save my pork?"

"Bacon," Jem informed him. "A guy's pork is a different thing entirely." He frowned at Olivia's still-dreamy face then gave Max a good hard stare. "And if you want to walk out of here under your own steam, you'll keep it to yourself."

"English," Max said with a charming shrug. "Is difficult, no?"

Jem maintained his stony stare. Max refocused on Hildy. "My bacon, then," he said, all earnest eye contact. "You are the one who will save it?"

Hildy tipped her head and considered him for a long moment, eyes narrowed, forehead wrinkled. Audrey could practically see her turning the dials in her head, finding the ghost-channel or whatever it was she did. Or purported to do. Suddenly her face cleared. "Oh, dear," she said, "You *are* in the frying pan, aren't you?"

Max sighed deeply. "You can have no idea."

"Oh, I think I have some." She took her hands back and folded them in front of her with an air of reproof. "And it's your own selfish fault, so what makes you think I have any interest in pulling you out of it?"

Max's mouth dropped open and he shot a quick look at Will. "But I was led to believe..." Will only nodded him back toward Hildy and her disapproval. Max's shoulders slumped. "I do not think this," he said humbly. "I have no right to expect any such thing. But I place myself at your feet, at your mercy. If you in your wisdom see fit to show me grace, I shall mend my ways. You have my word."

"Your word is your vow, young man," Hildy said severely, and Max flinched. "Your word is your honor."

"*Mio Dio*, I know." Max stuffed his hands into his jeans pockets and gazed at the floor. Audrey was all amazement. Hildy Wise had some serious skills. She should be taking notes.

"You made certain promises, Mr. Robledo."

"*Si*. I did."

"Promises you broke."

"*Si*." A whisper this time.

"Promises to your country. To your teammates." Hildy folded her lips and gazed hard at his bent head. "To a woman."

"A woman?" Olivia said, conveniently regaining her powers of speech. "What woman?"

Hildy said, "You should be ashamed of yourself."

Max made a small, pained noise and closed his eyes. She left him standing there, a pitiful island in his sea of shame, and crossed the kitchen to Will. He watched her come, his face hard and closed, eyes bright and curious. He was having, Audrey realized suddenly, the time of his life.

Hildy stopped in front of him. She folded her hands and gazed at him for a long, silent moment. Then she said, "Is this your idea of a test, Mr. Blake?"

Will lifted his shoulders. "Think of it as due diligence."

"You doubt my abilities?" She arched a brow. "*You* of all people?"

Audrey blinked. What had Hildy expected? Blind faith? From *Will*?

He only shrugged again. "What I believe is neither here nor there. You want to bust ghosts for a living? Fine. You can invoice Jem till the cows come home and you'll get no trouble from me." He tucked his fingers into his pockets and held her gaze easily. "But Jillian is a child and, as such, entitled to adult protection." He sent a hard look Olivia's way. "Unfortunately, the kid doesn't know that many adults."

Hildy glanced at Audrey. "She knows a few."

"Not enough," Will said with a hard stare for Jem. "Not

nearly."

Hildy turned considering eyes back to Will. "More than she did."

Will shrugged. "Nothing wrong with an even playing field."

"So this is all coming from your sense of fair play?"

"I've been accused of a lot of things." He smiled at her. "Fair play would be a new one."

"What, then?" Hildy spread her hands. "Why on earth are you concerning yourself to this extent with a child who isn't even yours?"

Will frowned. "Of course she's mine. What else do you call somebody who lives under your roof, eats your food, and steals your books?"

"Drew," Audrey said promptly.

"Thank you." Will didn't break eye contact with Hildy. "My point exactly. More importantly, though? Jillian matters to Audrey, and Audrey matters to me. So, yeah. Do the math on that and I don't care who her parents are. That kid is family." He grinned suddenly. "And you know what we Blakes say about family."

"Family first," Audrey murmured, and he turned that fierce smile on her. Her heart gave a terrified, joyous lurch and she found herself smiling back.

"What we have, we share," he said. "Even the fights."

"Especially the fights," she said and sighed. Seemed like she never shared anything with Will *but* the fighting. And suddenly that felt wrong. Terribly wrong.

"Lucky for me," he said. "I *like* fighting."

Lucky for him? She put a hand to her aching throat. To the exquisite tenderness growing there for him. Lucky for *her*.

Hildy sighed. "This isn't a war, William."

"The hell it's not."

"For heaven's sake." Hildy pressed weary fingers to her forehead. "I'm trying to help the child."

"Jillian's not your ordinary child."

"You'd know," Hildy said softly, and it sounded to Audrey like she was talking about more than Will's genius level IQ. She wondered—not for the first time this morning—what she was missing. Because she was definitely missing something.

"Maybe," Will allowed. "Maybe not." He rocked back on his heels and studied her. "But if you're straight up about this? If you honestly want to help the kid out? You're going to demonstrate right here and now in broad daylight exactly what you intend to do, and on an adult who deserves whatever might be coming to him."

Chapter 31

Hildy folded her arms over her waist and considered him for a long moment. Then she cast a look of deepest loathing over her shoulder at Max. "I would really rather let this young man stew in his juices a little longer."

"Needs must when the devil drives," Will said.

"I've heard that." Hildy sighed. "But as it happens, you're right. Jillian's a child, so her needs come first." Her eyes touched on Olivia, then on Jem. "A child's needs must always come first."

"We *are* putting the kid first!" Jem said. "And if this joker would get the hell out of the way—" He jabbed a thumb Will's way. "—we could have knocked this in the hat months ago!" He scowled at Will. "So why don't you get your goddamn goalie out of my kitchen so we can get down to business?"

"No." Audrey spoke quietly. Jem turned on her but Hildy raised a hand. He snapped his mouth shut to fume silently. Neat trick, Audrey thought. Why hadn't she ever learned to do that?

Hildy lifted curious brows. "Yes, dear?"

A greasy wave of nerves seized her. Hildy had cleared the way—Dad was silent, everybody was waiting. This was her moment. Now was the time to explain exactly why she'd be damned to hell and back before she'd let Jem have his way on this.

She swallowed, hoping to loosen her tight throat. It wouldn't open, and panic scrabbled inside her chest. She couldn't breathe. Because, oh lord, she didn't want this. She didn't want to fight. She just wanted to take Jillian home. Take her home and make her better without dragging out the dirty laundry and flapping it around in front of all these curious faces.

Panic beat frantic wings inside her and she glanced wildly around the kitchen until her eyes met Will's. He stood silently, his face as hard and closed as always, but his eyes were warm. Steady. The sight of him there, solid and unmovable and firmly in her corner, steadied her. *Your fight is my fight.* That was just the way it worked for Will. Family. Love. Whatever you wanted to call it. She might fall but he would always catch her. They might go tumbling into the void, but they'd be there together. *What we have, we share.*

The constriction in her throat eased up, enough to release the words. And it *was* words, she thought wonderingly. It wasn't panic blocking her throat; it was words. She'd been holding onto them for years, if not decades, and they were all clogged up in there. And if she was going to breathe, she had to clear them out. Either that or swallow them down and keep them forever.

"I remember," she said softly. She turned to her dad and spoke only to him. "I remember being Jillian's age. I remember understanding that mom was gone, even before she died. Years before, really. I remember understanding that my mom was gone, and that my dad didn't even see me." Jem scowled, and she waved a hand. "Didn't. Couldn't. I was eight. Let's not split hairs." His eyes skittered down and away from hers. But Audrey didn't look away. She couldn't.

"I remember what it was like to live in a house without filters," she said. "To have words and problems I couldn't possibly comprehend dropped into my imagination like evil little seeds. It might've seemed like a bunch of harmless hocus-pocus to you, Dad. The séances, the exorcisms, the spirit world, whatever. It kept Mom happy—relatively speaking, of course—and out of your hair. But I was just a little kid and I had a damn good imagination. Exceptional, in fact. So good that after a while I had no idea what was real and what was pretend.

"And then she died. Mom died and, God help us, *you* started in with the paranormal crap. Now suddenly my mom is dead and the house really is haunted. Then Olivia has a *baby* and I'm the only one who seems to notice. My God."

She pressed cold fingers to her forehead and gave a ragged laugh. "And I loved that baby but that's not why I slept next to her crib for a year. I slept on Jillian's floor because I didn't want to sleep alone. I was too scared."

She dropped her hand and met his eyes. "I was drowning, Dad. Night after night, nightmare after nightmare, and nobody noticed. Nobody even *saw* me. I was invisible. I was a ghost." She shook her head. "And how's that for irony, right? Everybody's looking for ghosts and there I am, but nobody can see me. And why not? Because they were looking for solutions and I was just another problem." She lifted open palms. "So I stayed invisible. It's easy when you're pretty. Nobody looks very hard."

She sucked in a breath and linked her fingers together on the counter. They weren't shaking, she noted distantly. That was funny. Maybe the trembling was all in her head? "But that's not going to happen to Jillian. Not on my watch. I see her, and I'm going to keep seeing her. Seeing her, loving her, protecting her. So if you want to do this thing?" She looked up, met Jem's eye and held it. "You'll do it Will's way."

"Our way," Will said.

"Our way," she agreed. "Or not at all."

Jem's mouth opened but Hildy said, "I agree completely." Jem sent her a ferocious frown which she placidly ignored. Max cast his eyes heavenward and murmured gratefully in Spanish while Olivia looked on with the strangest air of helplessness. Hildy smiled her approval at Audrey. "Such a fierce little champion." She shifted her gaze back to Will. "You'll have your hands full." She said it like a warning.

"I should be so lucky," he murmured, his eyes still on hers.

"You haven't been," Hildy told him, "but you could be. If you reach for it." She took Will's jaw in the soft cup of her palm, and he froze, startled. She rubbed her thumb over the blade of his cheekbone and said softly, "Courage, dear heart. You're so close." She dropped her hand and sent him a sparkling look that Smiley Meg would have envied. "You've certainly gone the long way round, though, haven't you?"

Audrey's brows shot skyward. That sealed it; she was definitely missing a significant chunk of this conversation. She looked to Will to see if he was getting it but he didn't appear any better off than she was. Hildy, utterly unconcerned by their bewilderment, turned back to Max and his limpid-eyed gratitude.

"You, then." She sighed deeply. "Let's get started, shall we?"

* * *

It was nearly noon when Audrey led Jillian into Cece's old room. It was, as usual, dim and stifling and lousy with flowers. Jillian's nose wrinkled and Audrey said, "I know. Me, too."

She squinted into the scented darkness and found Max on the brocade silk fainting couch her mom had always angled into the bend of the L-shaped room. He lounged across it like some kind of expensive man-blanket—knees wide, elbow hooked over the couch back, one tanned hand spread casually on his knee. A knee, Audrey noted, that was bouncing like a piston. Interesting.

Olivia sat beside him smiling like she'd just been crowned prom queen, her ankles demurely crossed, her hair doing that just-got-laid thing it was so good at. Jem stood at one end of the couch, his arms folded, scowling fixedly at Will, who leaned against the opposite wall. Hildy stood just behind the couch, smiling her gentle smile.

Audrey flapped the door open and shut a few times in a desperate bid for fresh air. "It's a cliché in here," she said. "Can't we open a window or something?"

"Believe me, dear, I wish." Hildy sighed. "I generally prefer to work in the sunlight, too, but I thought this would be best for today." She smiled at Jillian.

"You did?" Audrey gave up on fresh air and let go of the door. "Good heavens, why?"

"So there are no unpleasant surprises later on. I want everything now to be just as it'll be for Jillian." She came around the couch and crouched in front of the little girl. "Everything I do now for Mr. Max, Jillian? We'll do it again for you when we ask your grandma to leave you alone."

Jillian glanced up at Audrey then back at Hildy. She nodded cautiously.

"Your grandma doesn't belong here anymore, honey," Hildy said. "I've told her and told her how beautiful it is across the bridge where souls go, but she's never been there, and she's afraid. She'd rather stay here with you where it's comfortable and interesting and fun, and she's not afraid of anything. She's being rather stubborn about it. You may have noticed?"

Jillian nearly smiled at that, and Audrey's stomach went light. She didn't believe in ghosts, she told herself. She didn't. And she'd made sure Jillian didn't either. The little girl was under strict instructions to take anything Hildy said to her as a metaphor, a kind of story that was helping Grandpa make sense of his grief. But, damn, the woman was convincing.

"That's why I've made this room so dark and stinky," Hildy said. "This was how your grandma liked it best. She felt safe and protected in her little cave, surrounded by her favorite things. Her candles and flowers, her pillows and such." Hildy glanced around the gloomy room and flattened her lips. "It's not to my taste but to each her own, I suppose."

She gave herself a little shake and smiled. "So this is just how it'll be when we do your ceremony later on. It'll help your grandma feel brave and strong, you see, and she'll need all her courage to cross the bridge when we ask her to. Make sense?"

Jillian considered this with grave silence. She peered at Max on the couch, then looked back at Hildy. She gave a tiny nod and Hildy touched her shoulder. "Brave girl." She rose and touched Audrey's shoulder as well. "Brave *girls*, I should say." She nodded them toward a pair of straight-backed chairs set at a discreet distance from the couch. "Why don't you make yourselves comfortable? I'll just see how Meg and Drew are doing, then we'll get started."

Audrey peered into the gloom and found Will behind the chairs, one shoulder to the wall, arms folded. She shot

him a tight look and he gave her a tiny nod. She hoped to
hell they were doing the right thing. She glanced down
reassuringly at Jillian. "Okay here?"

Jillian looked at Will behind them and nodded. She sat
down. Audrey sat next to her and took one cold little hand
inside her own just as Meg appeared in a blast of light. She
marched around the corner from the alcove where Audrey
knew the bed was, a bundle of wires in one hand, a bunch of
miniature electronics in the other, a headlamp blazing on her
forehead.

"Okay," Meg said. "We've got the last of the cameras
disabled." She reached up and clicked off her light. "Sorry,"
she said. "Dark in here."

"You disabled the cameras?" Will's voice was sharp in
the darkness. "Why?"

Drew followed Meg around the corner, similarly lit up,
and with several yards of cabling draped around his neck.
"Max wasn't keen on getting this on film."

Max smiled easily. "My career, it is already—how did
you say, Will?—in the crapper. Yes." He nodded in
satisfaction. "The crapper. That is a good expression."

Drew grinned at him. "So evocative."

"And Americans!" Max shook his head sadly. "They
believe in nothing but work and pluck."

"Pluck?" Meg lifted a brow.

"Is this not the word?" Max gave her a look of melting
earnestness. Drew's grin died. "Like a happy courage?"

"No, it's totally the right word." Meg gave him The
Smile. "Pluck." She shook her head and began sorting out
her electronics into an enormous black case. Drew sent Max
a look of pure dislike, then hurried to her side and helpfully
shone his headlamp into her case.

Max went on blithely. "So situations such as this?" He
waved an encompassing hand. "Such as mine? Pah! They
think it is all *en la cabasa, si*? In my head?" He shrugged.
"And since I have no desire to find myself on YouTube, I
wished to have no cameras."

"As you like," Hildy said. "But I insist on taking an
audio recording, at the very least."

"On it," Meg said, holding up what looked like a tin-foil pouch.

"A faraday bag!" Drew bent for a closer look. "Sweet!"

Meg ripped open the Velcro flap, pulled a hand-sized black plastic rectangle out of the little pouch and hit a button. Evidently satisfied by the way it lit up, she shoved it back into the bag and sealed it up.

"Okay. We're now live and completely impervious to EMF interference. Where do you want it, Mom?"

"Under the couch, I think," Hildy said.

Meg sauntered over to the couch and Audrey said, "I'm sorry, but *what* is that again?"

"It's just a digital audio recorder," Hildy said. "Memory is so unreliable; a playback of events can be extremely useful. The pouch simply ensures that we record only sounds that originate within this room." She smiled. "We certainly don't need to record every cell phone conversation or baby monitor signal floating through the cul de sac, do we?"

Once again Audrey felt like she heard all the words but only got half the intended meaning. But she couldn't quite put her finger on an objection so she just shut her mouth, took Jillian's hand and waited for the show to begin.

Chapter 32

"Are you ready?" Hildy asked Jillian. The little girl nodded, her eyes large and curious but not frightened. Hildy turned to Max. "And you?" she asked. "Have you settled on a totem?" She sent Jillian a sideways look. "A totem is a little something you can hold, small but meaningful, to help you focus."

"I have," Max said.

"It can be a special piece of jewelry, or a lock of hair," Hildy said to Jillian. "A photo of a loved one, or a baby blanket. It can be anything you like, so long as it feels important."

Max held out his hands to Olivia on the couch beside him. He gazed raptly into her face. "I have chosen beauty."

Hildy paused. "Of course you have." She sighed. "All right, then. Beauty it is." She moved to a long, narrow table hugging the back of the couch and busied herself with an assortment of dishes and bowls that Audrey couldn't quite see. "Take her hands in yours, then, Mr. Robledo, and concentrate. Study the angles and the curves of her face. Know it for perfection, and calculate the geometry of that perfection. Be humble before it, and let it wipe your mind clean. Be still. Be empty. Be open."

She picked up an unlit candle—long, slim, its wick virginally white—and touched it lightly to his temple. "I want you to close your eyes, Max," she said. She touched the candle to his other temple. "Close your eyes now, and see."

Will watched Hildy work that skinny table. Her hands were brisk but her voice remained unhurried and gentle. That *mom* vibe of hers thickened and deepened and tugged on Will's inner orphan relentlessly.

237

"I want you to picture a bridge, Max." She was murmuring, and yet her voice carried easily. "It can be any bridge you like. Wooden, stone, marble, rope. It doesn't matter what it looks like, only that you can see it." She took the candle she'd just knighted Max with and screwed it into a simple glass holder on the table. "Can you see it, Max?"

"*Si*, I can."

"Describe it to me." She struck a match and touched it to the candle wick. Light bloomed. "Make me see it, too."

"There were railroad tracks near my home when I was boy," he said slowly, eyes still closed. "Just outside town. They crossed a...how do you say?" He lifted his hands and sketched a deep dip.

"A gorge," Hildy said. She unstoppered a bottle and the fruity scent of really good olive oil slipped underneath the heavy musk of cut flowers. She poured a bit into a dish. "Your bridge spans a gorge?"

"Yes," Max said. "A steep one, with a pretty river twisting along the bottom. The top of the bridge is thick and ugly—black beams and rusty tracks—but underneath it is different. Metal and airy, like so?" Again his hands rose, and he traced thin, delicate arches in the air. "How do you call that in English?"

"A trestle." Hildy opened a drawstring pouch and withdrew something that she crushed between her palms and let fall into another dish. A dusty, piney tang filled the air. Rosemary, Will guessed.

"*Si*," Max said. "A railroad trestle. Up and down, up and down, like long glittery legs walking across the river, safe to the other side." He smiled. "We were to stay away from it, but we never could. It was too beautiful."

"Yes, of course." Hildy opened a tiny vial and shook a bit of powder into yet another dish. Dried garlic, unmistakably. Will didn't know what Hildy's plan was here, but he was suddenly in the mood for pizza.

For God's sake, Bob sighed. *Focus, will you?*

Right. He shifted his attention and reached for Audrey's ocean. It was right there where it always was, lapping evenly and strongly against his consciousness. He wondered if the receiver in his head—or whatever it was that had him hearing Audrey's ocean and chatting with a dead guy—was strong enough to read Jillian, too. Because he'd feel a lot better if he didn't have to guess how the kid was doing, if he could just tune in and *know*.

It took some groping around in the dark of his mind, but eventually he found her. She was small and impossibly delicate, tick-tocking away like a pocket watch. Wound tight, Will thought, but unwinding evenly. Jillian was fine. Happy, Bob?

Oh, thrilled. Now pay attention.

"Olivia, dear," Hildy said. "I'd like you to kneel, please."

Olivia frowned up at her. "Excuse me?"

"Kneel, dear. On the floor in front of Max. At his feet, facing him, if you would."

"Why?"

"You're his totem." Hildy smiled that benign smile of hers but Will thought he heard something faintly evil in her voice. Hildy was enjoying this, putting Olivia on her knees. Nice.

Olivia shot her a skeptical look but scooted off the couch and knelt on the floor at Max's expensive sneakers.

"You get to hold his candle," Hildy informed her.

Now Max grinned. Olivia said, "His what?"

"Candle." Hildy picked up the white candle she'd lit and passed it to Olivia. "Hold this up, please. Near your chin." Olivia took it in strong, tanned hands and sat back on her heels. Her profile came into stark relief, and Will had to admit it—that face of hers really was perfection. He had his concerns about what she hid behind it but he doubted Max's interest reached that deep.

"I want you to open your eyes now, Max," Hildy said. "Open your eyes and focus on the flame. Look into the light. See only the light until the light is all there is. It is the air you breathe, the blood in your veins, the thoughts in your mind, the strength in your limbs. The light is beauty. The light is the bridge. *Your* bridge. Do you see it?"

"*Si.*" His lids had dropped to half-mast, Will saw. "The

light is the bridge."

"Good. Very good, Max." She set her hands on his shoulders, her grip so strong that her fingers sank into the meat of the guy's muscles. Max didn't object, however. His eyes just slammed the rest of the way shut, and his head fell back against the couch like he'd been knocked into an abrupt nap. Olivia gasped and Hildy sent her a quelling look. Olivia snapped her mouth shut, but the candle trembled in her hands, sending huge shadows dancing and leaping against the far wall.

Hildy began kneading Max's shoulders with those small, strong hands. She worked her way down his arms, stretching them wide and leaving them balanced on the couch back, palm-up. When she had him spread-eagled there—all set for his crucifixion, Will thought uneasily—she stepped back. She selected one of the dishes on the thin table between her and the couch, then swept her thumb through it.

"Father God," she said and pressed that thumb to the pulse point on Max's left wrist. She swept her thumb through the dish again, pressed it to his right wrist and said, "Mother God." Will could see two faint, oily thumb prints on each wrist, gleaming strangely in the low light. She dipped again and pressed her thumb to the center of Max's forehead. "Creator God."

The entire room seemed to hold its breath as Hildy dipped her thumb into the dish of crushed rosemary.

"We beg your protection—" She touched his left wrist. "—your mercy—" She touched the right wrist. "—and your light." She pressed her thumb to his forehead. "Shed them now upon this unworthy soul."

She went for the garlic powder next. "Come into him now," she murmured and touched his left wrist. "See all that he is, both hidden and plain." She pressed a powdery thumb to his right pulse point. "Discover that which means him harm." She touched the center of his forehead. Max slumbered on, blissfully checked out to the point that Will half-expected to hear him rip off a nice healthy snore.

Hildy wiped her hands neatly on a folded square of linen, then tipped her head back. She drew in a deep breath and spread her own arms wide, a small, eerie mirror of the man spread out on the couch before and below her. On the wall behind them, however, her shadow loomed huge. Her outflung arms touched everything in the room; nothing was beyond her reach. Will's heart picked up the pace and he shifted on uneasy feet.

What? Bob murmured in his head. *I thought you didn't believe in this shit.*

Will ignored him. Because holy hell, was that a *draft?* He blinked into the darkness surrounding them, searching for an open window, a cracked door. Nothing. He touched an ankle to the air vent in the wall behind him to see if maybe the furnace had kicked on. Nothing there either. Not that he'd expected anything. Jem was a stingy bastard when it came to heat.

Hildy had just thrown her arms out, he told himself. He'd probably caught the back draft.

Sure, Bob said. *You keep on telling yourself that.*

Except that a back draft, he had to admit, would be a temporary thing. A quick waft, over and done. But the air in this room? It was still moving. Faintly, yes, but undeniably. It stirred the hair at the base of his neck, kissed his cheek like a lover. It was circling, he realized sharply. Twisting slowly, deliberately. Clockwise, his brain informed him, and definitely moving fast enough to threaten the candle. Only Olivia's flame was rock steady.

Because there was no wind.

Oh hell. A cold shock of fear ran down his legs. First he was hearing things that didn't exist—ghosts and oceans and clocks, oh my—and now he had a phantom breeze? He really *was* losing his grip.

For God's sake, Bob snapped. *Pay attention.*

Right. He pushed back against the worry and the fear, and forced himself to focus on the moment. On protecting Audrey and Jillian from whatever might come next. He'd deal with his mental health later.

He moved forward, laid one hand on Audrey's shoulder, the other on Jillian's. Audrey's free hand came up to his. She kept her grip on Jillian with the other, completing the circle. Love for her welled up inside him. Family was complicated—his more than most—so what were the chances that he'd fall for a woman who got it? Who not only got it, but *agreed*, instinctively circling the family wagons whenever shit got weird?

Not great, Bob said. *Think about that.*

Will didn't bother to answer. He seriously had to stop engaging in conversation with his imagination.

Jesus Christ, Bob said wearily.

He sent up a brief prayer that he was, indeed, dealing with his imagination and not the early stages of dementia.

"In the name of the Father," Hildy said clearly, and her *voice*—oh holy shit. That was new. Because suddenly her voice was huge. Massive. As deep as the earth, as staggering as the sun. Will barely had time to think *what the fuck?* before it came down on him like a brick to the skull. There was a tremendous crash inside his head, his chest went hollow and he blinked.

It was the strangest sensation. On one hand, he was utterly demolished, everything he knew as himself crushed to a fine, sparkling sand. But on the other hand, he was quite clearly still standing here, one hand on each of his womenfolk, watching Hildy as if nothing had happened.

Which was because nothing *had* happened. He glanced around the room and, sure enough, nobody else was freaking out. And nobody else looked at all shocked or confused by Hildy's little voice bomb. Just him. In fact, they all looked a little glazed. Maybe even bored?

He must have some vulnerability to her particular brand of hocus pocus, he told himself quickly. Maybe it was the orphaned child thing plus her mom vibe?

Or maybe he was losing his mind.

Either way, it was fucking unsettling, like trying to watch two movies at once. Because there was Audrey's hair, a milk-smooth sheet of silver not two feet from his face, for God's sake. He could *see* that. So why could he also feel it licking and whipping across the back of his hand like they were having a day at the damn beach? Why—

The wind leapt abruptly into a howling gale, and it—oh

Christ—it snatched him up. The him that was nothing but a pile of sparkling dust after Hildy's voice bomb, anyway. And then he was twisting and flying with that wind straight into the heart of the hurricane.

Dizziness rushed him and he closed his eyes, concentrated on the solidity of the floor beneath his feet, of his feet inside his shoes. Italian leather, he reminded himself. Hand-cobbled. That was where his feet were. On the ground, on the ground, on the ground.

"In the name of the Mother," Hildy said, and that *voice* cut through the hurricane like a knife. Or maybe her voice *was* the hurricane. Will was rapidly losing his bearings, and his hands were trying desperately to gather into fists. Fight, his monster chanted. Fight, fight, fight.

"In the name of the Creator of All," Hildy boomed and even Will's monster scuttled back into its shell. He forced his eyes to open so his vision could reinforce the reality that the rest of his senses refused. "I call forth from this soul that which stains it."

She dropped her head until her face was no more than six inches above Max's calm, slack one. Will, dizzy and fascinated, watched Hildy drag her hands through the air over Max's body as if gathering something thick and viscous into herself. She brought her arms together with aching slowness, then lifted them until they were high in the air above her head, wrists crossed, hands fisted.

"I call it out," she boomed again. "And I send it *home*."

She flung her arms abruptly forward, as if throwing a soccer ball back into play, and Olivia was her target. Will got one last blast of wind—cold and oily, with a whiff of damp campfire—then Olivia squealed and fumbled her candle. There was a noise in the darkness that suggested she'd tumbled back on her butt. And possibly dripped a bunch of hot wax in her hair.

The lights snapped on and reality came with it. Will found himself standing inexplicably in front of Audrey and Jillian. He hadn't been aware of moving, but he was definitely standing in front of his women folk, feet wide, fists ready. But ready to what? Punch a draft? A voice? He had no idea. But that strange double perception was gone, and so was the wind. Or whatever that had been. He was back to his normal, whole self, and was breathing stale, flower-drenched air that smelled like it hadn't moved in years. And Will was sure of only one thing.

He was no longer losing his grip.

He'd lost it entirely.

He'd lost his mind.

Chapter 33

Drew stood by the door, his hand on the light switch. "Just checking," he said. "Thought we might be burning the house down."

"Good thinking," Will managed.

Jem said, "Did it work? Is the curse gone?"

Max sat on the couch, still spread out like a sacrificial lamb, blinking at the ceiling. "I don't know." He frowned, and began to sit forward. He stopped, winced, then eased his arms down to his sides like they ached. He laid a wrist on each thigh and let his hands dangle loosely between his knees. "I remember the bridge," he said, studying the carpet at his feet. "And I remember the candle—" He blinked at Olivia suddenly, who was still on her bottom in front of the couch. He turned a baffled face up to Hildy. "Why is Olivia on the floor?"

"Well, hell," Olivia said, staring unhappily at a gob of wax in her hair. "How am I going to get that out?"

"But did it *work*?" Jem barked. "Hildy?"

Will—along with everybody else in the room—turned to Hildy. She was, he saw, just a soft-faced housewife again, her massive shadow and that impossible voice fading like a dream, the kind that seems incredibly real when it's happening but that disappears like smoke the instant you wake up. That irretrievable, soul-deep brokenness lingered in Will's memory, though. It lodged itself under his heart like an undetected aneurysm, a weak spot on an artery just waiting to take him out. He stared around the room, his throat hot and tight.

Judging by the blank curiosity in all those faces, he was definitely the only one who'd experienced a mini-cyclone just now. Panic rattled around inside his hollow chest. His

245

brain was the only thing he'd ever had that worked. If it crapped out on him—and all signs were pointing that way— what the hell did he have left?

His knees trembled and he had the ridiculous urge to drop to the floor. To bury his head in Audrey's lap and let her stroke his damaged head until he figured out what the hell he was going to do now. Now that he was broken.

He didn't do it, of course. He didn't even glance her way. He couldn't. Not when he didn't have anything left to offer her. It hurt too much.

Hildy only smiled that placid smile of hers, clasped her hands together at her waist and said, "I believe so." She patted Max's shoulder and Will watched that small, soft hand of hers with a frown. It wasn't small, his troubled brain whispered. And it wasn't soft. It was tough as steel, with a grip like a vise. Implacable, undeniable. He shook himself and blinked and it was just a hand again, the impression of brutal strength wisping away like morning mist. Oh fuck. He put his thumbs to his temples and pressed hard, like he could physically put back whatever Hildy had shaken loose.

Good luck with that, Bob said.

Shut up, he thought savagely. Just shut the fuck up.

"But, really, only time will tell," Hildy said. "You'll have to let us know how things go the next time you're in the goal, Mr. Robledo. The proof is, as they say, in the pudding."

"Yes," Max said absently, rubbing his wrist and studying her with a face that was—for the first time in Will's short history with the guy—utterly free of pretense. "Yes, of course. Pudding."

She patted him again and came across the room to kneel in front of Jillian. Will stepped aside at the very last moment, as if his feet were siding with his whacked brain on the matter of Hildy's harmlessness.

"There, now, dear," Hildy said to the little girl. "How was that? Not too scary, I hope?"

Will watched Jillian shake her head slowly. She pointed a finger to her own chest and Hildy nodded.

"Yes, darling. You'll be next. Are you ready?"

Jillian pointed at Audrey and lifted an eyebrow.

"Yes, of course. Your auntie will be right there."

She pointed to Will next, and her mouth went tight, as if she was expecting a fight. Hildy didn't blink.

"Certainly, love. Will, too."

Confusion flooded him and he frowned down at the kid. She wanted him? What the hell for? Then he glanced at his doubled up fists and thought oh, right. For that. Tough to play effective defense when you're hearing and feeling a bunch of shit that wasn't even there, though. He tried to smooth out the frown before he scared the poor kid—he was scared enough for both of them—but she'd already moved on. She glanced almost involuntarily at her mother. Hildy followed her eyes.

"If you wish," she said softly. "Do you?"

Jillian hesitated, then nodded.

"All right." Hildy patted her little knee. "We'll do yours tonight then. Just the way you'd like."

"Tonight?" Audrey asked sharply. "Why wait for tonight? Why can't we do this now?"

Hildy smiled and put a hand on Jillian's chair back. She pushed halfway to her feet, then staggered sideways.

"Hildy?" Audrey leapt up but Meg was faster. She flew across the room, snatched up her mom's elbow and steadied her.

"Back off, your majesty," she snapped at Audrey. "Can't you see she's exhausted?"

"From what?" Audrey asked, her mouth a perfect *oh* of astonishment.

Meg didn't answer, opting instead to draw her mother gently toward the couch. Hildy moved like she'd aged twenty years in twenty minutes.

"Whoa." Audrey frowned and followed them. "Is she all right?"

"She's fine," Meg said. She nudged Max with a foot and he jumped up hastily. "But right now she needs food, and a lot of it. Hot, greasy, salty." Hildy sank gratefully to the couch and closed her eyes. Meg frowned down at her, lips tight, no smile in sight. "Drew? You want to get on that?"

"How about pizza?" He pulled out his cell and started scrolling. "I've got the craziest craving for pizza."

Will barked out a completely involuntary laugh.

"I know, right?" Drew gave him a sheepish smile. "Not to be weird or anything, but Max, my man, you smell delicious." He turned to Meg. "Is pizza okay?

"Fine."

Audrey pushed past Meg to perch on the edge of the couch next to Hildy. "What's wrong with her?"

"She's exhausted," Meg told her shortly. "It's not all lighting candles and chanting, you know."

Amen, Will thought.

"No?" Audrey cocked a skeptical brow. "Because that's all I saw." She sent a glance around the room. "Or did I miss something? Anybody?"

Drew shrugged, working his phone. "All I saw was Hildy anointing ol' Max there with pizza toppings, and poor Olivia nearly burning herself bald." He sent Olivia a sympathetic look. "Which would've been a shame. You have incredible hair."

Olivia picked at the wax in her hair. "Yeah, thanks."

"Jillian?" Audrey asked with exaggerated politeness. "Dad? Anything?"

Jillian shook her head and Jem scowled. "Some people feel it," he muttered. "Some don't. That doesn't mean nothing happened."

"Right." Audrey looked back at Meg, her lips tight. "How about you? You commune with any spirits today?"

"No, but I never do. Not my gift." She glanced at her mom. "I know the aftermath when I see it, though."

Will followed her glance to Hildy, who sat small and silent on the couch. Her eyes were closed, her lids thin and blue-veined and so very fragile. She looked exactly the way a really good charlatan might intend to look after putting on the show of her life. Utterly wrecked. Wrecked enough to distract Audrey from asking him if *he'd* experienced anything out of the ordinary this fine morning. Like, oh, say, an indoor tornado that had only happened in the confines of his broken mind.

Meg, though? Meg was on top of that shit.

"How about you, Mr. IQ?" she asked, her face shrewd and curious. "You get a whiff of fire and brimstone today?"

"Nope." He blanked his face and met Meg's eyes. "Not me."

She studied him for an endless moment. He studied her back. All those years of being the last bastard to blink were coming in right handy today. "Yeah, okay." She nodded slowly. "Be surprised if you did, actually. It takes a certain brain-to-heart ratio to dial in on this stuff. That's why I'm the techie in this outfit." She sent him one of her warmer smiles. "Too much brain."

Will smiled back. Hoped it didn't look as splintered as he felt. "Story of my life."

On the couch, Hildy stirred and Audrey leaned forward anxiously. "Hildy? Are you okay?"

"Oh, Audrey," Hildy said and sat up. She was still pale, but the smile she offered came pretty close to her usual wattage. Will's inner orphan whimpered pathetically. "You're sweet to worry, but you needn't. I'm not dying. It takes a great deal of energy to traffic between worlds, that's all. And I'm not as young as I used to be. A full belly, a few hours of sleep—"

"Try six," Meg said tightly.

"Six!" Hildy shook her head. "I don't need—"

"Four, at the very least." Meg shot a finger at her. "And don't argue with me or I'll let Drew eat your pizza."

Hildy laughed. "Four, then." She turned back to Audrey. "A little food, a little rest, and I'll be as good as new." She leaned in with a confiding sparkle. "Sex works, too, if you ever need a charge up. Very rejuvenating, spiritually speaking. If you do it right." Audrey goggled at her and Hildy chuckled. She held out her hands to Meg who hauled her to her feet. "Which is not," she said with a sideways glance, "news to you, I imagine."

Meg gave Audrey a sour smile. "Nope. Little Miss Hicky's got that base all covered."

Audrey's eyes flew to his, then dropped to the knot of

his tie. Her cheeks went gorgeously pink, and longing was a hot punch to his gut. He looked away. She wasn't his. She wasn't his now and she never would be. Last night had been a dream—a long shot at best—and it had disappeared the instant his mind snapped free of its moorings and went flying off to neverland. He was nothing but fists now, ungoverned and unreliable, and she'd be better off—safer for sure—if he never looked her way again.

"Oh, for real?" Meg muttered. "She blushes like a prom queen! Gack."

Drew's phone chimed. "Lunch time!" He sighed happily. "I love the internet. Hey, Jilly, want to go on a pizza run?"

Jillian glanced her *can I?* at Audrey who nodded absently. "Go ahead, baby."

Jillian and Drew bounded for the door.

"Come on, Mom," Meg said, her hand gentle on Hildy's shoulder, her eyes hard on Audrey's. "Let's get you into something comfy before lunch."

Hildy allowed Meg to lead her toward the door without protest, but she stopped at Will's elbow. She leaned forward and touched his arm. He suppressed a flinch but it was an effort. "You're conflicted," she said softly. "Afraid."

He shook his head automatically but she hit him with a warm hug of a smile.

"Of course you are, dear. A man like you? I'd be worried if you weren't." She nodded briskly, already looking more like herself. "Bring your questions to lunch. We'll talk."

"Right." He eyed her warily. Non-existent tornadoes were one thing; effortless mind-reading something else entirely. He could see how she'd earned her street cred with the ghost-hunting set. "I'll do that."

"Okay, good chat." Meg tugged her mother toward the door. "Time for lunch now." Hildy gave him one last pat then submitted meekly to Meg's herding. Jem followed them, stopping only to snap, "Lunch!" when he drew level with Max and Olivia, who were still in the corner, murmuring over their entwined hands. Olivia jumped. Max only smiled his slow, hot smile and tucked Olivia's hand through his elbow. He led her through the door, and Jem fell in behind them, glowering darkly at Max's back.

Will put his hands in his pockets, rocked back onto his heels and waited for Audrey to draw level.

"I don't think I understand more than half of what Hildy means when she talks," she said.

"You're doing better than I am, then," he said. "I'm at maybe a third." She gave him a doubtful look and he hurried on before she could start asking questions. "Hey, will you be okay here if I skip lunch?"

"Skip lunch?" She blinked. "Since when does anybody in the Blake house skip lunch? For that matter, since when do you skip the opportunity to get some questions answered?"

"Since never," he admitted. "But it's like you just said—Hildy's answers are never really answers. Plus I've got a few things on my plate I've been pushing toward the back these past few weeks. I really ought to deal with them." This was a dirty lie. There was nothing on his plate more important than her and Jillian. "And since Hildy probably won't be ready to jump back in until after dinner, I thought—"

He let the thought dwindle away suggestively and her eyes filled right up with guilt, exactly as he'd hoped.

"I knew it," she said. "I knew you couldn't possibly have this much free time. Go." She fluttered her hands at him. "Go on. Go to work."

"I could stay," he said quickly. "If you need me—"

"No, no." She patted his forearm. "I'm good. It's fine. You should go."

"If you're sure?"

"I'm sure," she said.

Will fled.

Chapter 34

Will stayed at the office until the sun sank low enough to set the skyline on fire. He stared sightlessly at it until the windows went dark. Until he'd made peace with his decision. He stood, stuffed a random assortment of papers into his laptop case and locked up the office.

Hey we're moving! Bob's voice was snide in his head. *We all done chickening out?*

Will strode down the deserted hallway and punched the elevator button.

"Yep," he said evenly. Right out loud, too, because he was crazy now. Or would be in a few hours. What did he have to lose by talking out loud to the voices in his head? "Let's finish strong, right?"

Oh boy. Sports metaphors. Has it come to this?

"You know," Will mused, "I always hoped that if I went crazy I'd *enjoy* the voices in my head."

For a guy nobody likes, you're awfully fussy about company.

"Fair point."

The elevator doors slid open, splitting his reflection neatly in half. He snorted. That was happening kind of a lot today. He stepped into the carriage, faced the doors and let them zip his reflection back together. Wished it could be just that easy. He smiled, and didn't give one good rip how ugly it was.

So. Where are we going, Will?

"What, you don't know? I thought you were the all-knowing, all-seeing *Bob*."

Maybe I just like this new talking out loud thing. Indulge me. Where are we going?

"You sound worried." The elevator hurtled down a

couple dozen stories. Sinking, sinking, sinking. Bob's silence was pointed. "You don't need to be. I've got this."

Do you?

"Yep. I'm good here." The elevator eased to a stop and Will let the doors split him in half again. "I didn't actually expect a happily ever after, you know."

A trio of lawyers waited politely outside the doors. He showed them his teeth and they blanched. Damn, he was going to miss that. He strode across the lobby, and noted with dark amusement that he wasn't even the only person talking to himself. Hands-free cell phones made everybody look crazy. Or made crazy look like everybody.

This is sounding suspiciously like a farewell speech, William.

"Aw. You going to miss me, Bob?" He hit the street, beeped open his car at the curb and fired it up.

Sure thing, buddy. As soon as you decide to miraculously part ways with your own mind, I'll miss the crap out of you. That on the docket any time soon?

"Would you believe I have it penciled in for this very evening?" He blazed into city traffic, threading the needle with his usual bloodless calculation.

Really. And here I thought I was up to speed on your bad decisions.

"Guess you missed one."

A particularly stupid one, too.

"Hey, it's not the way I'd have ended the story, either, but—" He shrugged and passed a bus by a single coat of paint. Horns blared. "Guess I should've seen it coming. Dead guy moves in and there goes the neighborhood."

I thought we were doing sports metaphors. Now your head's a neighborhood? Maybe you should just tell me what the hell's going on.

"I'm leaving."

The fuck you are. That little girl needs you. She expects you.

"I know. I'll leave after—" He downshifted into an exit ramp and hugged the curve like a lover.

After what? The exorcism, or the hero sex?

His blood ran cold at the very idea of touching Audrey after going another round with Hildy's soul splitter. "After the exorcism," he said. "Before the hero sex."

You're the dumbest smart guy I've ever met.

"Yeah, thanks." He obeyed a stop sign with careful precision and turned into the gated community where he'd begun to lose his mind. Where he'd finish the job shortly.

Never figured you for a coward, though.

Will laughed. "You figured wrong, then. Because I'm scared, Bob. I'm scared shitless."

Of what?

"Losing my mind."

Not a huge loss there, buddy. And I'm talking to you from front-row seats.

"No argument. But I suck at people, and God knows I'm not much to look at. That big ol' brain was all I had." He was talking to himself. He *knew* he was talking to himself, but it was comforting. And the comfort was the weirdest part, considering that what most folks might consider casual conversation had always been sweaty, anxious work for Will. Then his brain had started shedding bits and pieces of itself like a rotting house dropping shingles, and now he was chatting himself up. Maybe his newly-fragile psyche preferred the slower pace.

Or maybe you're just better at being human since Audrey.

He sucked in a jagged breath. Even her name hurt.

"If it's not one thing it's another," he agreed evenly. "Bottom line, though? I've been having trouble putting a hard line between reality and imagination for a while now." He recognized the irony of speaking this truth out loud to the dead guy in his head and smiled humorlessly. "Today's trip through Hildy's little mind-blender didn't do me any favors in that department."

Really shook the ol' foundation, huh?

"And I wasn't the most stable house on the block to begin with." He drove through winding, identical streets at a sedate pace, his memory faultlessly supplying the lefts and rights. "My talents are few and far between, Bob. You take out the smart, and what's left?"

Silence. The damning sort.

"Pain, Bob. I'm good at pain."

Bob sighed. *You do enjoy your punching.*

"And my sanity? It's hanging by a rusty hinge here, buddy. I fully expect Hildy's little freak show tonight to snap it clean off. And when that happens?" He smiled, the same smile that made hardened lawyers backpedal. "Well, somebody could get hurt, couldn't they? And that—" He stopped smiling. "—is not going to happen. Not to Audrey."

Right. Audrey. The love of your life, the delight of your eyes, the reason your heart beats. Let's talk about her. Does she know about this? Because she's a smart cookie, that one. And she seems to like you. Actually— He paused. *I think that girl loves you.*

Had he thought her name hurt? It was nothing to the bright, jagged agony of Audrey's love. Even the idea of it. The idea that happily ever after had been right there, close enough to touch, to smell. To have, to hold, forever.

He closed his eyes, breathed through the pain.

It's possible, Bob went on relentlessly, *just possible that she'd have something useful to say here. Something—and brace yourself now, because this is going to blow your little mind—something that you didn't think of. Imagine! Will, missing something! Ah, the mind boggles. So, yeah. Chew on that. Maybe Audrey can help you. Have you considered asking her?*

Will didn't bother to answer himself. He just pulled into the neat black semi-circle of Audrey's drive. Killed the engine and stared up at the house. At that big black door. He was going to walk through that shiny door with his head intact and his heart full of love. When he walked back out, his head would be shattered. He'd just go ahead and leave his heart behind.

"You haven't been listening, Bob. Pain is all I'm good for anymore. All I have to offer. The least I can do—the very least—is keep it to myself."

He went inside.

* * *

Will was home, thank Christ. Audrey's first instinct was to fling herself into his arms. He hadn't been answering his phone—cell or office—all afternoon, and inconvenience had morphed into worry hours ago. She was going to kill him, of course, but first she wanted to hug the crap out of him.

His face stopped her.

It was cool, shuttered. Distant. That shirt was all knife-edged creases, that tie still high and tight. Nothing unusual in any of that, she admitted even as her feet faltered and her arms dropped. It was the eyes. They were blank. She'd always been able to read the roaring furnace of his brain in those eyes of his, even when it scared her. But this? This emptiness? It was new. Shocking. Worry shifted to fear and it gnawed at her, acidic and insistent.

"Will?" She stopped three feet sooner than she'd intended, halted by the wall of chill surrounding him.

"Hey, Audrey."

She frowned at him. "What's the matter?"

"Nothing." He checked his watch. "Am I late?"

"No." She rubbed the goose bumps on her arms. "No, but I couldn't reach you and—"

"Yeah, my battery died. Sorry about that. I didn't realize."

She tipped her head, wary. She supposed she could demand to see his phone, to prove the lie. Because she knew he was lying. She didn't know how; she just knew. But what was the point of proving it? A guy wanted to lie to you, he was going to lie. Besides, she wasn't about to waste time or energy on details. Not when his eyes looked like that.

"Will," she said again. "What is it?"

He cocked a brow. "What's what?"

"What's the matter?" She stepped uneasily forward. She wanted a closer look at those dead eyes, that tight mouth. "Why do you look like this?"

"Like what?" He didn't blink, didn't fire up, didn't move. Terror shoved fear aside, and crawled up her throat with ugly claws.

"Like the undead."

He barked out a sharp laugh. "The undead?"

"Yeah." She waved a hand in front of his face, fear putting a mean edge on her concern. "The body's still operating, but nobody's driving. Nobody sentient, anyway."

"I said I was sorry."

He said it with a mildness that turned terror into dread. Because nobody liked a good fight better than Will. They were entering body snatchers territory here. "This isn't about the phone, Will."

"No?"

"No." She edged nearer yet. He stepped back. Away from her. "It's about the fact that you're not okay. You're not okay, and you're not talking to me."

He folded his arms and gazed down at her impassively. "Funny. It *feels* like I'm talking."

"Not about anything that matters," she shot back.

He blinked patiently. "What do you want to talk about?"

She stared at him. "About *this*! About you! Where *are* you, Will?"

"Right here."

"The hell you are." She gripped his wool coat in both hands, and shook him. Nothing. Not a flash of hunger or want or even interest. He just let her rap him into the back of the door. She stared, dismayed, then dropped her forehead to his tie. He stiffened as if her touch were a trial, and her heart howled. But she didn't let him go. She only breathed in the dear familiar scent of him, of ink and paper, of buttery leather and reckless speed. Her throat constricted, right down to a damn pinprick. She didn't know how she was even breathing, the pain was that vicious, that pervasive. It was *eating* her, for Christ's sake. Consuming her. She'd had no idea pain could even do that, not until Will had given her his love, then just as inexplicably decided to withhold it.

None of which should surprise her. He didn't need her. She knew that. Had always known it. Why should he? What on earth had she ever done for him? A big fat load of nothing, that's what. So of course he'd leave her whenever it was convenient. Or he got bored. Didn't they always? The minute they got her into bed, they were all about the goodbyes. There just wasn't enough behind the pretty to keep them interested. Why should she expect anything different just because she was in love with this one? Why should he be any different than—

Because this is Will.

Her brain delivered this information with a sharp slap, the kind dealt out to hysterical women in old movies. It knocked her interior monologue right out of its groove, short-circuiting the familiar litany of experience. *Yeah, yeah. You've been loved and left before,* her brain said sternly. *It's the curse of the pretty girl, poor you. But Will saw you. Will knows you. So pull yourself together, knock off the woe-is-me and put the focus where it belongs. Because this guy looks like a bomb went off in front of his face and he can't even hear yet over the ringing in his ears. He needs help. He needs compassion and patience and love. He needs his family. Is that you, or isn't it?*

That's me, she thought without hesitation. God willing, that'll be me forever.

So earn it.

Right. Of course. Nothing good was free, or to be trusted. That actually made her feel better. Will's love was the most precious thing she'd ever been responsible for, with the possible exception of Jillian. She'd feel a whole hell of a lot better if she could point to one single, solitary thing she'd done to deserve it.

She gave herself one more moment with her forehead to Will's chest, pulling the scent of him deep into her lungs, letting it fortify her, letting it fill the dents and dings life had put on her heart. Then she shoved the panic and the pain and the doubt deep down inside herself. She opened her hands, let her flat palms rest against the warm fact of his chest. She slid them up, cupped his nape in both hands and lifted her eyes to his.

"Will," she said. He only gazed back, eyes wary, face closed. Her heart ached. "I'm not going to argue with you."

"Good. Because I really don't have it in me right now."

"Oh, honey." She pressed her lips to one sharp cheek bone, then the other. "You've really had a day, haven't you?"

He went stiffer yet under her hands and her heart wept.
But she didn't pull away. Didn't let him, either. She just
drifted her mouth over to his ear. She put her words right
into it, soft with love, edged with stainless steel courage.
"It's okay, Will. You don't have to tell me what you're
chewing on. But when you do? If you do? Please believe that
I won't give a damn what it is. I'll be on your side
regardless. Because I love you, William. All of you. Every
mean, broken bit. Every gorgeous, loyal shard. You're mine
now. My heart, my soul, my family. And you know what we
say about family around here."

She stepped back, folded her arms and gave him a good,
toothy smile. His head was tipped back against the hard oak
of the door, and he stared sightlessly toward some point
above and behind her head. She told him anyway.

"Family first, that's what we say." And if her voice
trembled a little, well, what the hell. A girl didn't bare her
soul every day. "What we have, we share. The good, the bad
and the ugly. You've fought enough of my fights, God
knows. I stand ready to fight yours. I won't turn from you,
Will. Not now, not ever. I might not be much of an asset, but
whatever I have? Whatever I am? It's yours. All you have to
do is ask." Her smile started to crumple so she cleared her
throat and let it go. "So when you're ready? Just ask.
Please."

Silence. He didn't twitch so much as a muscle. She
wasn't sure he was even still breathing. It wasn't quite the
response she'd hoped for, but she supposed it would do. It
would have to, wouldn't it?

"Hildy wants us all in Cece's room in twenty." She
touched his hand. It was like plastic under hers. "See you
there?"

He nodded and she left.

Chapter 35

You are the stupidest son of a bitch I've ever haunted.

Will didn't know how long he'd stood there, back to the door, head ringing, heart a fiery ball of pain inside him. She loved him. She loved him?

That's what she said, asshole. Not that you deserve it.

"Truer words."

Do we disbelieve her?

"Hardly the point."

He moved like a robot up the stairs. When he got to the top, he stopped. Wondered what he was doing there. He'd hauled his gear out of Cece's room before he'd gone to the office. There was nothing up here for him but Audrey and Jillian. And the demise of his sanity.

I'd argue it's already gone, Bob said. *Because your decision making is for shit.*

"No decisions here, Bob." He turned and went back down the stairs. Headed for the kitchen, thinking vaguely of coffee. "I'm not safe. Love or no love, I refuse to—"

What we have, we share, Bob said coldly. *Even the fights. Especially the fights. Sound familiar, William?*

He shook his head. "Again, not the point."

Exactly the point. Or is that a one-way street for you? Family is only family when somebody else needs something? But not you. Surely not you. Because you're Will! You're so smart and so strong and so dangerous! You can take care of everybody else and *yourself without any help from the lesser folk. Do I have that about right?*

"Please shut up now."

I'm just saying. Why not let somebody help you for a change? Somebody who loves you, and who has a hell of a lot more strength and courage than you're giving her credit for?

Will's entire soul cringed away from the idea of Audrey throwing herself between him and his madness. He stopped talking. Because answering the voices in his head made him sound fucking crazy.

Not crazy. Just stupid.

"Christ's sake," he mumbled and stalked into the kitchen. "Shut up."

Drew pulled his head out of the fridge, a massive slice of pizza in his teeth, the box in his hands. "Nice. I wasn't even talking."

"It was pre-emptive." Will pushed a hand across his mouth, as if he could physically erase his habit of chatting with a dead guy. "I know you."

"Ah. Fair enough." Drew plopped his pizza box onto the island counter and demolished the slice hanging out of his pie hole with impressive speed. He caught sight of Will's face. "Hey, whoa." He pushed the box magnanimously Will's way. "You look like you could use a slice."

"Thanks." He took a slice and began eating mechanically. It was like sawdust in his mouth but to refuse pizza would arouse more suspicion than eating without enthusiasm. "You ready for round two of ghost busters?" he asked before Drew could take the reins of the conversation.

"Yeah, I guess." Drew helped himself to another slice, but his eyes were thoughtful on Will's face. And way sharper than people gave the kid credit for. Will blanked his face with the skill of long practice. "Kind of weird, though, don't you think?"

"What?"

"Hildy ate an entire large pizza for lunch."

He said this in reverent tones and Will tried to inject interest into his voice. "Really?"

"Sawed logs for a solid five hours this afternoon, too." He chewed slowly. "A guy could believe she really was whipped. Like she'd done some hard-core heavy lifting all morning."

"You were there," Will said. "You see or feel anything?"

"Not so much as a goose bump."

"There you have it then."

"Doesn't mean nothing happened."

Will gave him a sideways sneer. "Now you sound like Jem."

"I'm not going to punch you," Drew said easily, "so don't bother trying."

Will sighed.

Fuck, Bob said. *You're disappointed.*

Will hunched. So sue him. He wanted to feel something straightforward and distracting. Pain worked for him. Physical pain, anyway. The other sort was getting old.

He checked his watch. "Looks like it's time to get upstairs."

"Looks like." Drew helped himself to the last slice and folded the box in half. "What about you, Will?"

Will took the box from him and shoved it into the recycling. "What about me?"

"You get a goose bump or two?"

Will looked him dead in the eye. "Why would you think that?"

He shrugged. "It's kind of your MO, isn't it?"

"Seeing dead people?" Will injected a note of scorn into his voice. "Wrong brain-to-heart ratio. Isn't that what your beloved said?"

Drew gave him a melting smile. "Smart as a whip, my Meg. And the legs on that girl, my God! That aside, however? I'm going to disagree with her on this one." He made short work of the last slice of pizza, spoke around a mouthful of Italian sausage. "Because to my way of thinking, your big ol' brain is what makes you *more* likely to see ghosties, not less."

Will's heart thudded cold and heavy in his chest. "How do you mean?"

Drew dusted his hands on his jeans and swallowed manfully. "Seeing what the rest of us don't see? Getting what the rest of us don't get? That's you all over again, big brother." He slapped a hand on Will's shoulder, jolted him out of his frozen dread and into motion. "And—no offense, buddy—but you ran out of here this morning like a cat with your tail on fire."

Or like you'd just seen a ghost.

"Shut up."

Bob chuckled. So did Drew.

"Just putting it out there," Drew said and aimed him toward the stairs. "Could be an interesting evening. You'll have to let me know."

"Yeah," Will mumbled. "I'll do that."

If hell had a smell, he decided five minutes later, it was cut flowers. He stood in Cece's dark, cloying room, breathing through his mouth and trying to convince himself that it was the thick scent of flowers choking him, and not the deep, warm current of love he could hear slipping through Audrey's ocean.

It was like one of those hidden picture deals, her love. Now that he'd heard it, he couldn't *un*hear it. It was just there, warm, steady, welcoming. Inviting. So damn inviting.

She sat on the couch this time rather than in a chair at his hip. She was still close enough for him to see the freckle on her jaw—she only had the one—but too far away for him to touch, and on so many levels. A hysterical chuckle rose up in his throat, all sharp edges and tearing claws, but he choked it back. God, he hoped he could walk out of here tonight under his own steam. Bad enough to lose his marbles. He didn't want to lose his dignity, too.

Not that he was overly attached to that anymore. But he really didn't want Audrey's last memory of him to be of the strait-jacket variety. And he really didn't want to scare Jillian. Not when she'd specifically asked for him to be there. Or as specifically as a kid who didn't talk could ask for shit. He didn't figure she trusted many grown-ups, and with good reason. He'd promised to be here for her, and he'd be damned if he'd break his word. He just prayed to God or fate or whoever was in charge up there that he wouldn't let her down. He knew he was a mixed bag for the people who loved him, for the people he loved. But just this once—this one last time—please God let him be a blessing instead of a curse.

"I had a dream this afternoon," Hildy announced. Will caught himself staring at the perfection of Audrey's profile like a love-sick stalker. He jerked his attention quickly to Hildy.

"A dream?" Audrey asked.

"Yes." She beamed around the circle. "A very helpful one, too. I'd been struggling, you see, with how to address the problem of Jillian's silence."

"Her silence isn't a problem," Audrey pointed out. "It's a solution."

"I know, dear." Hildy touched her shoulder, and turned an approving smile on Jillian. "Talking only makes it worse, doesn't it?" Jillian twitched a shoulder. Hildy folded her hands and turned back to Audrey. "But there's a key difference between breaking a curse as we did this morning and getting rid of an uninvited houseguest as we'll do tonight."

"What kind of difference?" Audrey asked.

"Think of a curse like a mild poison. I simply locate it, draw it out and send it over the bridge. But a soul is a consciousness. Not a whole, functioning person, but near enough for government work. Which means it's best to treat them as such. So when a soul has overstayed her welcome, it's the responsibility of the host—that would be you, Jillian, dear—to tell her so." She lifted open hands. "I can make the bridge, and I can make it as inviting as possible, but the host must speak for herself. She must—absolutely must—be the one to issue the eviction notice."

"Which Jillian can't," Audrey said. "So what are we doing here?"

"Oh, but she can." Hildy beamed. "I dreamed a solution."

"Wonderful," Jem muttered.

"Let's hear it," Drew said. He sounded like he'd just been invited to a party, complete with pony rides. Will wondered momentarily what it would be like to live inside that guy's head. Were there unicorns?

You'd be surprised, Bob said tersely.

Will filed that away for future consideration while

Hildy looked to Meg. Meg produced a whiteboard the size of a child's desk and presented it to her mother. "The totem," she said.

"The totem?" Jem's brows sank low over his eyes.

"The totem," Hildy said with satisfaction. She took the board and came to sit on the couch, sandwiching Jillian between her hip and Audrey's. "Now I know you're not overly fond of the touchy-feely," she said to the child, "but I wonder if you'll indulge me."

Jillian nodded cautiously. Hildy's smile was brilliantly approving. "Will you sit on your auntie's lap for me?"

Jillian studied Hildy's face as if looking for hidden clues, then glanced at Audrey. Audrey shrugged and opened her arms. "Just try not to crush me with your immense weight, huh?"

Jillian grinned and scooted up onto her lap.

"Okay." Audrey threaded her arms under Jillian's and stroked the child's chin as if it were a second head she'd just sprouted. "Hmm. Now what, I wonder?" Jillian wrinkled her nose and swatted at Audrey's hands. "Pardon me," Audrey said. "I believe my nose itches. I must scratch it." She patted around until she found Jillian's nose and gave it a good scrub. "Yes, that feels much better." Jillian swatted at Audrey's hands again, her face alight with silent laughter this time. Audrey tucked her hands under her thighs and met Hildy's eyes over Jillian's head. Her face clearly said *This is me meeting you halfway, lady. It's your turn now. You better show up.*

Will's love was an acidic churn inside him. He wondered if the heart was like the appendix—nothing you thought much about until it ruptured on you, then say hello to pain, infection and possible death. He smiled, bitterly amused by the thought.

Hildy stood and offered the whiteboard to Audrey. "Will you hold this, dear? On Jillian's lap, perhaps angled so she can write on it? Perfect!"

She pulled a couple of markers from her sweater pocket and handed them to Jillian. "I wasn't sure which color would best match your mood tonight, so I brought an assortment."

Jillian sorted through them. Uncapped one, sniffed it. Capped it again, plucked up another. She held it over the board and arched a questioning brow Hildy's way.

"Certainly, dear," Hildy said. "Take it for a test drive."

Jillian swept it across the whiteboard, and color streaked behind it. The same violet, Will noted, as her eyes. As Audrey's eyes. His heart whimpered pitifully. He ignored it. Jillian nodded decisively and Hildy smiled.

"All right. You have your voice." She handed over a small square of white toweling. "Your eraser, should you choose to rephrase at any point in the night."

Jillian took it in her left hand, kept the marker in her right. She lifted her brows, a silent *are we ready here?*

Hildy glanced around the room. "Is everybody set?"

"I'm good," Drew said. He grinned at Jillian. "Knock 'em dead, kiddo."

"Oh my God," Meg muttered, pained. "Dead jokes."

"I've *been* ready," Jem said. "For the past decade."

Olivia just shrugged from her chair in the corner. She looked markedly less enthusiastic about this evening's activities than she had about the morning's. Then again this morning she'd been Beauty, not a neglectful mother watching her kid depend on other people.

"Ready as we'll ever be," Audrey said and pressed a quick kiss to the top of Jillian's head.

Hildy glanced at Will. He stretched his mouth into his usual ghastly parody of a smile. "Ditto. Pull the trigger."

She folded her lips down, as if torn between speaking and silence. "As you like," she said finally.

Will didn't like anything about it, honestly.

Except for being a fucking martyr. You love that shit.

He wondered idly if the Bob situation would get better or worse after tonight.

How could I possibly make your situation worse? You're doing a bang-up job of that all by yourself. Bob indulged in a damning pause. *As usual.*

Hildy's gear was set up on a rolling cart by the wall this time, and she wheeled it over to the couch. She perched on the edge of a cushion between Audrey and the cart. "So,

Jillian," she said. "Tell me about your bridge."

Jillian hesitated, her marker suspended an inch above the board, and Will could read her question as easily as if she'd spoken it out loud. Evidently Hildy could as well.

"However you like, dear," she said. "Pictures, words, free-form. Just make me see it, too."

Jillian's focus went inward, then her marker came down. Will stuck to the perimeter but circled the room until he was behind the couch and could see the whiteboard over Audrey's shoulder. The child's printing was small and tightly spaced, as if she were afraid of running out of room before she ran out of words.

And it *was* words. Of course it was. Words were her most powerful tool, her best weapon. Words were what made her *her*. They were the vehicle for all those lovely ideas, the medium that delivered her cherished stories, and she loved them for that. So of course she would choose words. And would choose silence as the ultimate withdrawal. He understood that with every functioning brain cell he had left.

Hildy leaned in and peered at the board. "Interesting," she said. "I didn't know you were a C. S. Lewis fan."

Will frowned and leaned in himself. He'd have put good money on Jillian's bridge being either the bridge into Hogwarts from *Harry Potter* (the one Seamus Finnegan had blown up so spectacularly in book seven) or the one from *The Fellowship of the Ring*, (the scene of Gandalf's famous *You shall not pass* speech). Evidently, she'd chosen neither. He squinted at her whiteboard.

My bridge is a closet, she'd written. *The kind that stands up by itself, not the kind that's in the wall. A wardrobe. It has four feet shaped like lion's paws, and has two doors. Each one has a black metal lion's head in the middle, roaring, with a ring in its mouth for pulling the doors open. They open out like arms. It's big—taller than Drew—and old. Made out of wood, and carved with fruit and leaves and vines and stuff. It looks normal but feels important. Full. Maybe dangerous but like you want to open it at the same time. It smells like fur coats and mothballs.*

"Huh," Will said under his breath. "Narnia."

"*The Lion, The Witch and the Wardrobe*," Audrey said, a smile in her voice. "I loved the Narnia Chronicles when I was a kid. Where did you find them?"

In the dresser in my room, Jillian wrote. The Horse and His Boy *wasn't very good, was it?*

Audrey laughed and Will smiled at the sound of it. "Nope. But the *Voyage of the Dawn Treader* is a classic. Reepicheep rules." She rested her cheek on Jillian's hair. "So this wardrobe of yours. It goes somewhere? Somewhere that's not Narnia, I assume?"

Yes. The bridge is in it. The bridge to the place where souls go. It works for anybody who believes.

"Just like in the book," Audrey murmured.

"Do you believe, Jillian?" Hildy asked.

Jillian's marker hesitated for the first time. She gazed at Hildy for a long moment, then wrote slowly. *I don't see her or hear her, not like—* She flashed a look around the room, her eyes touching her mother scowling in the corner, then bouncing off Will hovering behind the couch. *—like other people do. But I feel her. She's in my dreams. Not like HER, like a person, but it's her anyway. I can just tell. She comes when I'm asleep and she takes me...*

"Where does she take you?" Hildy asked softly. "What does she show you?"

Chapter 36

It's a room. Now Jillian was scribbling madly, as if she'd finally decided to let it all out, everything that she knew damn well sounded crazy and would make her aunt do that worried, pinchy face more than she already did. That would make all the gentle-voiced doctors exchange looks over her head and behind her back. That would end up with her swallowing a bunch of pills that made her feel dopey and slow. She was right where he was, Will realized abruptly. Right at the end of don't-give-a-fuck lane, ready to end this shit once and for all.

She takes me to a room. I don't know what room, or where, just a room. Different every time. But it's always cold. It's really cold and something's there. I don't know what. I can't see anything, I can't hear anything. I can't tell what's wrong but I know it anyway. Something there is WRONG. It's bad. It's cold and angry and it hates me. It hates me and wants to hurt me. And she keeps it in the closet. There's always a closet.

Will thought about the closet just around the corner, the one filled with Cece's death and Audrey's pain and God only knew what else. He closed his eyes against the shuddering reality of Jillian's nightly terrors. Then he forced himself to open his eyes and keep up with Jillian's marker.

She keeps taking me there and showing it to me, that DOOR. She makes me want to open it. But I DON'T want to open it. I DON'T. But I do. She makes me want to. I can see my hand reaching for it, and I know that if I open it, whatever's in there will rip me up like a sheet of paper, and I'll be over. But I can't stop myself. I try not to argue or ask her to stop because that only makes it worse. It makes her laugh, and that's awful. I can't hear it but I KNOW she's laughing and it's awful. But when I can't help it anymore, when I see my hand reach for the door handle anyway, I scream. I don't do words but I can't help screaming. I scream and scream and scream and Audrey comes for me. She can't see or hear or feel the bad thing in the closet, or the cold thing in the room, but she finds me. She finds me and pulls me up. She's when I start to feel warm again.

Will saw Audrey's shoulders heave up with a sudden, involuntary breath—a sob?—then shudder back down. But she was utterly silent. Hildy nodded slowly. "So you picked a closet of your own for the bridge," she said. "A good closet?"

Jillian shrugged and wrote, *She has a thing for closets. I thought maybe she'd go easier if my bridge was inside one.*

Audrey swallowed audibly, and turned sharply to the side. It gave Will her profile and he could see the unnatural brightness of her eyes, even from a few yards away. She blinked hard and rubbed her cheek against Jillian's hair.

"Smart girl," Hildy said. "Let's see if that's true, shall we?"

She unstoppered her olive oil, crushed her rosemary, poured out her garlic powder. She adjusted her cart, rubbed her hands to warm them and reached for Jillian.

Suddenly Will was off the wall, tight up behind the sofa, the skinny console table Hildy had worked from that morning biting into his thighs. The urge to hurdle the sofa back, to put himself and his fists between this woman's hands and those he loved was desperate and overpowering. He throttled it back by the thinnest of margins.

He stepped back. Put a nice, easy foot of space between himself and the table. He wanted to leave, oh God, he wanted to run, but then Hildy's hands were on Jillian and his feet refused to go anywhere. He was here for the duration, good or bad. He would not leave this child or this woman. Not until it was over and they were safe. And then he would leave. To keep them that way.

"Father God," Hildy murmured, and it began.

In less time than Will thought possible, Hildy had blown through the anointing portion of the show. Jillian's head fell back onto Audrey's shoulder, her lids low, her face calm, her hand still wrapped loosely around that violet marker she'd chosen. He could hear her breathing, deeply, evenly. He reached farther, listened differently, eased the dial on that receiver in his head and latched onto the tick-tock of her energy. Her presence. Her life force. Whatever. He shifted, uncomfortable with his own woo-woo. He could almost hear Drew's laughing voice: *Somebody's been watching his Dr. Phil.*

He set his teeth and listened to Jillian tick steadily away, the delicate machinery of her mind and spirit evidently in good repair. He spun the dial a little farther, allowed himself the luxury of tuning in to Audrey's ocean one last time. It wasn't as serene as Jillian's ticking, but that was to be expected. She was nervous. He could hear it in the anxious swirl and twist of her waves, as if they were breaking on rocks instead of smooth sand. But there was nothing alarming in it. Not unless you counted the warm and precious undercurrent of the love she bore for him. Because that, he could hear. He couldn't stop hearing it. It was the foundation of each wave, underpinning each advance and retreat, singing to him like glory. He gave himself a moment—one single aching moment—to savor it, then tuned back in to the tick-tocking.

"Jillian," Hildy said softly. "Jillian, can you hear me?"

Jillian didn't move but her fingers tightened around her marker. She wrote *yes.*

"Erase your board, dear. Make it clean and blank."

Her left hand came up obediently and wiped the board clear with that square of white fabric Hildy had given her. An oily thumbprint gleamed on the fragile inner curve of her wrist.

"Now put your wardrobe on it."

She printed *WARDROBE* in the center of the board in small, neat letters. It looked vulnerable there, so small and alone, and fear spurted up in Will in a hot, startling surge. Not fear for himself, but fear for her. She was just like her printing, so small and neat and breakable.

"I'm going to make the bridge now, dear," Hildy said.

"I'm going to make the bridge inside your wardrobe."

She clasped her hands together in front of her waist, bowed her head and appeared to drop into a brief nap. Will snapped upright, like somebody'd hit him with an electric cattle prod. Because, oh fuck, here it came.

The air in the room began to circle, clockwise, always clockwise. The slim white candle on Hildy's cart burned steadily on, impervious to the breeze that didn't exist. It kissed his cheek anyway, a demented lover cycling up for some serious fun and games. He waited for the soul-rending boom of that voice again, and terror gripped the back of his neck with cold fingers. But it was Bob he heard in his head. Just Bob.

Don't panic on me now, buddy. Now's when we listen. Listen hard, like your life depends on it. Because it probably does.

He put the heel of one shoe onto the toe of the other and ground down hard. Hard enough to have pain running bright and hot up his shin. It cut through the panic trying to rise up between him and what was left of his reason, and allowed him to reach for the dial inside his head. If Bob thought there was something for him to hear in this, he was determined to find it. What else did he have to do? Panic like a little girl?

That's the spirit, Bob said. *Now shut up and listen.*

He eased the dial left. Then right. He strained to hear but there was nothing. Nothing but the hungry, accelerating whine of the gathering storm. It was a hungry growl, a salivating gnash. It was—

His nape prickled and awareness struck him with a hollow, quivering thud. It was hiding something.

He had no idea what it was, only knew with absolute certainty that it was there. That a terrible threat was crouched down inside the shrieking wind, in the eye of the hurricane. It was stalking, circling, *coming*. Oh good Christ, what *was* it?

Keep listening, Will. Listen harder. Listen like you don't know the answers.

The answers? Holy hell, he didn't even know the question. His hands were shaking. In real life, or on the imaginary knob in his head? Who knew? Shaking was shaking. But he forced the bottled breath out of his lungs and eased the dial through the spectrum. He got to the end and stopped, his mouth sour with fear. What now, Bob? What the hell now?

Don't stop there, Bob whispered. *Just because it's as far as you've ever gone doesn't mean it's the end. Push harder, Will. Reach, goddamn it.*

So he reached. Nausea churned inside him, and sweat slicked his palms. But he pushed. And pushed. And—just like in a dream when the impossible suddenly slides into the possible—the knob gave. It eased a degree past the end, into beyond. And the wind—that wild, terrifying storm that had shattered him, scattered him earlier that morning, the howling gale that camouflaged this hellish unknown creeping ever closer—changed. The wild roar abruptly rearranged itself into...

Music? Yes, that was music. Dazzled, he traced the contours of it with his inner ear. The tune was high and piping, dancing mischievously over a throbbing heartbeat of a bass line. It was fecund and rich, that beat. Dazzling and compelling. It was a symphony, and it vibrated through him in deep, stunning waves.

And it was shaped, he understood somehow, like a cone. A trumpet. A morning glory. Its mouth was open to the ceiling, soft and inviting, and its edges brushed the walls, all four. It swirled and gathered and *sang*, pulling everything down, down, down into the dark mystery of its center. Into that pulsing, magnetic heartbeat that suggested gauges and gears and impossible perfection.

Curiosity ratcheted upward, became a driving, desperate compulsion inside him. A ravening appetite, an impossible itch. He strained toward those enchanting depths. He wanted to *hear*. He wanted to *know*. He'd been born a question, and now the answer was right *there*. If he could just lean in a little farther...

No touching! Bob barked suddenly, and some dim slice of his consciousness reported pain. Will came back to himself with a slow blink, and saw that he'd pressed himself up against the sofa table hard enough to put a couple of righteous Charlie horses in his thighs. His hand was stretched toward the whiteboard in Audrey's hands. Toward Jillian's neat, firm printing in its center.

WARDROBE.

Because if you leaned in far enough, he realized with a pale shock, you'd fall right into it. Into the jaws of that glorious machinery. Into the vortex. Into the heart of the storm (song). Which wasn't a storm *or* a song so much as an invitation. An invitation to a terrible knowledge. The kind guaranteed to separate a guy from his heartbeat.

It was, he understood suddenly, the bridge.

Hildy had made the bridge inside Jillian's wardrobe, exactly as she'd said she would. And his soul yearned toward it.

Well, Christ. It wasn't his brain that was slipping. It was his fucking soul. All those years of desperate self-loathing, all those acts of self-sabotage? Evidently they hadn't been in vain. He'd spent years deliberately damaging himself, slicing through the bonds of goodness and conscience in an effort to feel something. Anything. And it was now clear that he'd succeeded. His goddamn soul was hanging by a rusty hinge at this point, so tenuously attached to Will that the bridge— which, according to Hildy, only tugged on souls turned loose—was tugging on his. Hard.

And while he'd be one hell of a loose cannon without a functioning intellect, he wouldn't be a loose *anything* without a soul. He'd just be done.

No wonder Bob was on edge.

Bob sighed. *You don't know the half of it.*

He switched feet, mashed his other toe with his own heel and welcomed the hot spurt of pain that proved his soul was still chained to his body. That he was still at the wheel of them both. He'd stay there as long as he possibly could. But the sound of Hildy's bridge was...God, it was magnetic. Seductive. It pulled on him with greedy hands and he marveled that Cece had been able to resist it so long.

It takes cold purpose and a dedication to the mission, remember? Bob whispered. *That bitch wants her revenge.*

She won't cross that bridge until her pain is everybody's pain. Until Jem is good and fucking broken. He paused. *Or until you make her.*

Me?

Bob laughed that rough laugh of his. *Why do you think you're here, buddy? For your good looks?*

That *would* be a new one. He frowned. How the hell was he supposed to do it, though? It wasn't like you could grab a *sound*. Plus he'd never actually even heard Cece. How the hell was he supposed to find her?

Oh, wait for it. You won't miss her.

Right. He set his jaw and waited, trying not to hear that terrible/wonderful song filling his ears and tugging on his soul.

"It's your turn now, Jillian," Hildy said. She was as calm as ever, though Will could sense the strain in her voice. Like she was holding something terrifically heavy but trying to be cool for the kid, like it was no big deal. Evidently this bridge of hers was a limited-time-only offer. "Time to show Cece the door. Go ahead and write it down. Tell her you want her to leave."

Will watched Jillian grip the marker until her nail beds turned white. Audrey held the board, her chin hooked over the child's shoulder with a loose relaxation completely at odds with the tense set of her shoulders, the stiff line of her spine. If Will wanted to, he could probably count her vertebrae through her shirt. She was braced, he saw, for something she couldn't see, feel or sense. Something was coming at the child she loved and she, by God, was going to stand between them. Just as soon as she figured out what it was, and from what direction it might attack.

Tenderness for her swept through him, a deep and solemn current that was—in its own way—as shattering as Hildy's hurricane (bridge.) It lifted everything inside him from its place and set it down again in slow motion, and in just a slightly different order. It left him feeling oddly newborn—all wet and bloody and off-balance.

That's love for you, Bob said. *Believe me, I know. Knew. Enjoy it while you can. It's different from this side.*

Will didn't know what to make of that, and he didn't have time to dwell on it. Because Jillian had started to write.

The words came out of the marker in her small, tidy printing. *I want you to leave now, Grandma. I want you to cross the bridge. I want you to leave now, Grandma. I want you to cross the bridge. I want you to leave now, Grandma...*

She wrote it over and over again, and for a minute—two minutes? Five? Ten?—nothing happened. She just wrote and wrote, until the board began to look more purple than white. And still her hand flew steadily on, not a pause or a misspelling. Just the firm, flat command. Leave.

Will kept one hand on the dial in his head, though. Easing it through the known spectrum and pushing hard on either end, wondering if Cece were there, just beyond the range of his expectations. He was dimly aware of everybody else in the room, of a strange slackness in their faces. Like they were awake, but not. He didn't waste any energy wondering about it. He dialed on.

And then he heard it. He heard something. A snapping, a popping. Faint and far away but marching closer. He leaned hard on the dial, pushed until sweat gathered on his brow, dampened the line of his spine. Then the volume came up with a sudden, vicious roar, and it knocked him back. It shoved the air from his lungs in a hard, scorched huff.

Fire. Invisible but encompassing, it rushed and crackled around him like demented laughter, ripping up the walls, devouring the drapes. It gushed and danced, a deafening howl of static, a rumble and roar that filled his head, and made the seams in his skull creak dangerously. It had knocked him back, and now it rocked him forward, unhinged his knees. He slapped his hands onto the table and sagged.

Bob said grimly, *Hey, Cece.*

He flailed blindly for the volume control, found it by pure luck and dragged it to low. His knees still felt like water but he managed to pry his eyes open. And saw Jillian's left hand snap open with a jerky twitch, like it had been seized by a malevolent puppet master.

A shock of horror sang through Will's head and the joints of his skull creaked again, louder this time. It was like his brain, his soul, whatever, was being scooped out of his physical being with a melon baller, Christ. But he didn't look away. He couldn't.

Her eraser fluttered to the floor like a white flag of surrender and that *hand* scrabbled through the pile of markers forgotten on her lap. It seized up the red one and lifted it to her mouth. Her teeth opened, snapped down on the cap and yanked it off. The cap dropped numbly from her lips and the marker came down to the board.

Her right hand continued its dogged litany—*I want you to leave, Grandma. I want you to cross the bridge.* The word WARDROBE stood in the center of it all like a pulsing, living island. But her left hand landed on top of all that neat purple printing with a deliberate thump.

NO.

Chapter 37

NO, Cece wrote with Jillian's hand. *NO. NO. NO. NO NO NO NO...*

An odd clicking sound edged under the roar and crackle of Cece's fire, and for a moment, Will took it for Jillian's tick-tock. Then he realized it was her teeth. They were snapping convulsively together, as if she'd been tossed into a tub of ice water and her body was desperately fighting to warm itself. He reached for her tick-tock and there it was, but oh God, it was skipping beats. Gears were grinding, springs twisting.

And it showed. Her right hand faltered, the printing slowed, those valiant purple letters fell out of round. He could see her trembling now, her whole tiny body vibrating with effort. Or terror. Likely both. Her right hand went weak, faint, but the left hand only grew stronger. It flew over the board, spilling ink like blood and obscuring the small purple command.

NO NO NO NO NO NO NO

"What the hell?" Jem stepped up, but slowly. His eyes were vague but his hands were hard fists at his sides. He stared at the board for a long, uncomprehending moment, then his lips peeled back to reveal those blinding white teeth. "God damn it, Cece," he snarled. A vein bulged in the center of his forehead. "What the fuck is wrong with you? This is a *kid*. You want a fight? I'll give you one. But you leave her out of it."

Jillian's head snapped side to side and her right hand fell away from the board completely. Her left flew gleefully across the surface, streaking red ink behind it, somehow always managing to avoid the WARDROBE singing in the center. Audrey moaned faintly. Her eyes jerked behind

closed lids and Will knew—knew without knowing quite
how he knew—that the bridge had cast its spell again. Just
like it had this morning.

People weren't supposed to look straight at that kind of
thing, weren't supposed to hear that song up close. Not while
there was significant living yet to do. Will glanced around
the circle of faces and found everything from slack stares
(Drew) to uneasy sleep (Audrey) to sleep walkers (Jem.) But
without exception everybody's consciousness had taken a
little vacay. Everybody's but his, probably because his soul
was some kind of low-hanging fruit. And they wouldn't be
back, he knew, until Hildy's bridge dissolved.

Which side would Cece be on when it did, he
wondered?

"You just leave the kid out of it," Jem growled again.

I won't, Cece wrote wildly with Jillian's hijacked hand.
*Just try to make me and see what happens. Hate you, hate
you, hate—*

The vein beat madly in Jem's forehead and terror
buzzed around him like bees swarming murderously up from
the hive. His hazy eyes tracked that red marker dripping
hate, his muscles tensed, the tendons in the backs of his
hands rose up slowly as his fists gathered again.

—take her anytime I want, forever and ever and ever—

Jillian threw her head back. It hit Audrey's shoulder
with a meaty thunk. Her mouth jacked open, wide and
desperate and useless, like she was searching for air and
finding none. As if she were drowning. She arched and
twisted, her heels drumming the front of the couch. She was
strangling, Will thought dumbly. Cece was killing her.

Audrey didn't let her go. Not even in her fugue state.
She let go of the board with one hand and lashed an arm
around the child's waist, as if somebody were trying to wrest
the little girl away. She pressed her cheek to Jillian's thin,
shuddering shoulder. "Jillian," she mumbled. "Jillian, baby,
I'm here. Can you feel me? I'm right here. Reach for me,
baby, come back."

Red ink slashed viciously on.

...want me to go, I'll go. But I'll take her with me. Not

279

all of her, though. Oh, no, only some. I'll leave you the husk, the stupid staring shell. Damaged, broken, bleeding, just the way you left me. Ignore that, *you fuck...*

Jem roared. He knocked the board out of Audrey's grip and seized Jillian by the upper arms. He jerked her up, shook her like a dirty rag and bellowed through bared teeth. "Get the fuck *out*, Cece! You get *gone*! You're not wanted here!"

Jillian was utterly stiff inside the bracket of Jem's cruel fists, but that silent howl on her frozen mouth broke. Her lips curled up and shot out a high crackle of laughter. It jolted from her in machine-gun bursts of madness, macabre streamers of bloody sound. It was Cece laughing. Cold sluiced down Will's back from his collar to his heels and his wobbly knees went numb. Jem dropped the child like she'd vomited on him, and Will couldn't blame him. It was toxic, that laughter, broken and wrong and poisonous.

She hit the floor and crumpled, a used paper bag of a child in a too-big shirt, still and broken. Then she hunched and gained her hands and knees. Her body swayed jerkily, seeking its center of balance like something newborn trying out its legs for the first time. She rose up, leading with the shoulder blades, her head hanging down below the withers like some kind of unholy marionette. Horror crashed against his eardrums in heavy, deafening pulses, paralyzed him. He watched, frozen, as she turned her face up to Jem's. Hair hung over her face in lank strings and she leered up at him, the laugh a soft hiss this time, like a snake through dry grass.

Jem's teeth snapped together, and the swarm of his terror merged into the metallic clang of his fury, creating a single dark beat of unreasoning purpose. It drove his hand up, gathered it into a lethal fist. And Will understood that the man had reached his limit. Blown by it, really, and landed in territory where the only option left was destroying whatever sought to destroy him, and in whatever form it took.

Even a child.

Jillian's chin came up, and Cece's leer spread across her delicate face. Her tongue lolled out like a dog's and Cece sat her up, inviting—no, *welcoming*—Jem's rage. His violence. The damage he was about to do to the precious and fragile package she'd wrapped herself in.

"No," Will said. But his voice was lost in the twisting wind, in the buzzing clang of Jem's fury and fear, in that terrible/wonderful symphony still singing underneath it all. Everybody else remained slack and paralyzed, under the bridge's protective spell. Nobody was riding to the rescue here, Will realized numbly. Nobody coming but him. Just me, he thought. That's why I'm here. That's what I'm for.

His tongue was slow, his lips thick. He cleared his throat, tried again.

"No," he said. Louder this time. "Jem! Stop!"

Jem's fist hesitated at the zenith of its backswing, and he stared at Will, his eyes hazed with sleep and bright with violence. Jillian's head ratcheted his way too, but awkwardly, as if she were fighting for control of it. Her ticking came to him for a brief moment, unsteady and broken. Her eyes met his and for a fraction of a second, that face was hers, only hers. Her eyes were huge, filled with terror and grief, but her mouth trembled open.

"Will?"

He'd never heard her voice, but he knew it was hers. Jillian's. He knew it like he knew his own name, even when that name was nothing but a broken plea. And it *was* a plea. Her clock wasn't just winding down; it was dying. She had strength enough for one word, and she'd chosen his name.

It split him open, shattered his horrified paralysis. But it shattered Jem's paralysis as well, and his fist came down like a hammer. It accelerated through its downward arc, gaining speed from its own weight. It fairly whistled through the thick air, though Will experienced it in cold-blooded slow motion. He himself was already airborne, vaulting the couch and the table in a single boost, the way he and his brothers used to jump fences back when they were kids in Texas. He observed Jem's fist coming down, calculated its trajectory with cold, precise eyes and got his shoulder under the blow before it (broke her fucking jaw) connected.

A snarl gushed up from that well of violence and pain inside him, peeled his lips back and made a wrecking ball of his own fist. A wrecking ball that he sent crashing into Jem's jutting chin with a roar of satisfaction. (said I was going to do that, promised myself, fuck it felt good.)

Jem went down like a sack of concrete.

Cece's fire roared like a nuclear blast. It filled his head, the shriek of her appetite for destruction denied. It scoured out his skull and incinerated his lungs. His vision flickered out, and then there was nothing. No light, no walls, no room. There was only pain, and it was huge. Vast. Planetary. And Will was trapped in orbit. He circled and cycled, the pain rising and withdrawing, and he flew helplessly from crest to bloody crest. And all the time that fire *laughed*. Cece laughed.

Some dimly functioning bit of his brain snatched this information up and Will realized that she wasn't just enjoying his pain. She was *eating* it. Feeding on it. Growing stronger and harder and more dangerous.

But you're good at pain, Bob whispered in his head. *Aren't you?*

Well, hey, he thought vaguely, give the man a cigar. Bob had a point. He *was* good at pain.

He came around slowly. Bitch packed one hell of a punch but his brain was crawling back to its feet inside his skull. The room was still gone for him, everything was gone except that strange control panel in his head where the first lights had begun to flicker back on.

He checked his mental map. It was there, but barely. There were only four points on it, and they were audio only. He had Cece's fire to the north, Jillian's clock to the east, Audrey's ocean to the west, and the bridge (song) to the south. Will's body was the compass rose in the center, a pulsing heartbeat of pain pointing every which way.

He aimed his mind at the pain, and oh, yeah, holy hell, he was on fire. His nerve endings reported this in no uncertain terms, and advised unconsciousness. Retreat! She wants your pain? Let her have it! What do we want with this shit? Time to check out!

Will ignored that sage advice. Instead, he sucked in a breath and lowered himself into the agony like a guy easing himself into a boiling bath. He put himself right into the heart of the flow, and diverted it like a human dam. It switched courses with a cooperative gush, flooded into his mind with a red roar. And shocked his brain into that cold, rational place that only pain took him.

Above him, Cece gave an enraged roar. His mind's eye filled with a picture of her fire fountaining up the walls, ripping into the ceiling. Will smiled around teeth that felt sharp and shattered. He'd turned off the tap while she was still drinking, and she was pissed.

"Oh fuck you," he said. "It's my pain."

He let her rage and reached for the knob on the control panel in his head. He eased it—carefully, so carefully!—toward Audrey's frequency, toward the swirl and rush of her. She was still there, thank Christ. Choppy and anxious, but still moving in and out like clockwork. Speaking of which...

He dialed in on Jillian's clock. It jerked along, sluggish and slowing but not silent. Not yet. Damn, that kid had grit. Relief and pride drove back the leading edge of his pain, brought it down to a trickle.

Cece screamed her dismay, but it was thinner than before. More fearful than furious. Memory chimed inside his head. What had Hildy said? That it took a tremendous amount of energy to resist the bridge once you were dead? Cece needed juice, and plenty of it, but Will had just kicked her out of the all-you-can-hurt buffet. He cocked an ear to her howls. Definitely weaker. Weak enough to get sucked across the bridge against her will?

Only one way to find out.

He eased the dial in his head toward the bridge. It was still there as well, still singing its terrible invitation. But even as Will listened, the volume dropped. It grew faint, distant. Oh hell, oh damn, oh fuck. Hildy was getting tired, too.

It's not enough, Bob said skeptically. *Cece's off her game but not that far. She won't go, not for that.*

No, Will knew, she wouldn't.

Not unless somebody took her across.

The idea whispered itself across his mind, pushed down tentative roots and took hold.

He could cross the bridge, and take Cece with him. It

sang to him, that idea. Tugged on him. Pulled him. Why shouldn't he?

It would be death, Bob said flatly. *The End, all caps. You know that, right?*

Well, yeah. But that was why he was here, wasn't it? Silence.

Plus, he'd finally get to *know*.

Know what?

Everything. Every answer to every question his restless, relentless brain had ever posed. And when all the questions had answers, wasn't it possible—just possible—that his brain would finally shut the fuck up and leave him in peace?

What about Audrey?

The pain level jacked up again but Will embraced it. Let it feed his resolve. Because yeah, leaving Audrey would hurt. A lot. An epic, immeasurable amount. But wasn't this exactly what he'd hoped for? Prayed for? For some opportunity to atone for all the damage he'd done in his life? Because, Jesus, he'd done a lot of damage over the years, and had all the regrets to show for it. Particularly where Audrey was concerned.

But giving his life to protect the woman he loved and the child she held precious? Trading his pathetic future to free them from the poisonous prison of Cece's hate? That wouldn't be one of them. That would be a privilege. An honor. As deaths went, it would be a good one. Damn good. Better than he had any right to expect, honestly.

So now you're an army of one? Such a fucking martyr.

Will ignored this and focused on the pain. It roared through him, sending his mind to that place of cold, bright clarity. He located Cece's greedy, furious fire, then pinpointed Hildy's bridge and that terrible/wonderful song pulsing from it. He found himself, an insignificant bit of self-contained agony. He calculated the distance between them, figured trajectory, velocity, force. Laid out the path. Then he crept quietly toward Cece, slid invisibly behind her raging flames. Then he opened his arms and embraced the fire.

Chapter 38

She arched and bucked against his grip, a roaring crescendo of fiery hate that used to be a woman. A mother. Audrey's mother. And then the fire...oh God, it wasn't just in his arms. It was *inside* him, hot and devouring, and he heard his mind (soul?) ripping slowly free of its moorings.

So, he thought dimly. This was dying.

Audrey's ocean murmured sadly, and regret ached inside him like the broken teeth inside his mouth. He should have said he loved her. When she'd said earlier that she loved him? He should have manned up and said *I love you, too*. He wondered if he'd take that fresh mistake across the bridge with him, or if he'd get to leave it behind with all the rest.

Only one way to find out.

He wrapped his arms around the fire (himself) and staggered toward the bridge (song) crying and weeping in the distance. He labored toward it for endless minutes (seconds? Hours?), listening only to the crackle of fire in his head and the rending inside his body. (Bones breaking, muscle shredding, spirit flying.)

And then he was there, trembling on the edge. One more step, one more push and he'd drop over the edge into everything/nothing. Into the answers and the empty. Into forever, into space.

He stopped on that razor sharp precipice and thought, *Audrey*. He'd take that terrible step but he wanted to make sure that the shape of her name was in his mouth and the sound of her ocean was in his ears when he did. If he got to take anything with him, he wanted it to be that.

He crouched for the leap, his shaking legs far past the limits of their endurance under this burden of pain and fire.

But Cece had been lying in wait for this moment of human hesitation, and she unleashed the last of her strength in a mighty heave. Will's grip faltered and he shouted out in fury and terror.

And then he was flying, shooting backward, away from the bridge, away from the fire. He was sailing through cold space, fists still swinging uselessly while the bridge's song faded in the distance.

He hit Audrey's ocean with a terrific crash, smashing through the deceptive glitter of her surface at high speed. She closed over him with a wet slap, and swallowed him into her depths. He sifted slowly down into the complicated tangle of her tides.

Will, they murmured as they rocked him. *Will, Will, Will.*

I'm sorry, he told them. Told her. *So sorry. I did my best but it wasn't enough. I wasn't enough. I never have been.*

She didn't answer, only rocked him with soft arms. He felt himself suspended inside her, swaying slowly like green weeds in the deep. Her currents drifted over him like gentle fingers, seeking, testing, pressing. Tapping at his widows like an unexpected visitor who wants to come in.

Shame filled him, thick and familiar, and he wanted to hide from her. He was broken, defeated, worthless. She shouldn't see him this way. But even as the thought took shape in his mind, he yearned toward the sound of her voice.

Will, she whispered again. *Will.*

I'm here. His heart screamed what his voice wouldn't say. I'm right here. Find me, Audrey. Please find me. I'm so alone.

And he was. He'd had his brothers in every minute of every day his whole life, but deep inside some grim mental cellar, it had always been just him and his monster. Him and his fear. Unloved, unwanted, unchosen.

Will, Audrey murmured sadly, her currents still tapping and nudging and seeking. *Will.*

Except...Audrey had chosen him, hadn't she? She'd chosen him, and beautifully, using the only language he was sure to understand: *You've fought enough of my fights, God knows. I stand ready to fight yours. Whatever I have? Whatever I am? It's yours. All you have to do is ask.*

But he hadn't asked. Hot shame filled his throat at the memory. And why hadn't he? Habit, maybe. Alone was a hell of a lot easier to swallow when you chose it. When you didn't have to face the ugly fact that nobody had chosen *you*. Except that Audrey *had* chosen him.

And he'd said no.

He'd told himself that it was for her own good, that he was protecting her. But he understood now that he'd only been protecting himself. He'd been facing a fight he knew he couldn't win, and he hadn't wanted her to witness his defeat. Hadn't wanted to risk watching her love turn to disappointment or, worse, disgust. He had enough courage to die for her, he realized with a twist of bitter shame, just not enough to live *with* her. Not truly and fully.

And it was too late to change that. Death was coming for him, and soon. He was too broken for anything else. He had perhaps a handful of heartbeats left to him.

So, no, he couldn't change the way he'd lived his life. But he could change the way he faced his death. He didn't have to be alone. Not anymore. Not with her strength and straightforward courage swirling all around him, circling, nudging, waiting. All he had to do was invite her in. All he had to do was ask.

He licked his cracked lips and tasted blood. Felt the jagged edges of his broken teeth against his tongue. His charred lungs tried to refuse him but he managed a shallow breath. It hurt but he savored the pain, the stinging proof that his soul and his mind were still attached to his body, however tenuously.

"Audrey," he whispered, releasing the breath—his last?—on the beauty of her name. It was agony and it was art. It was pure love, and it filled the wreck of his body from top to bottom. "I'm so afraid. I don't think I can do this alone. I need—" *Help. Love. Forgiveness. Strength. Courage.* "—you." Because she was all those things. She was everything. "I need you, Audrey. Just you. Please."

For one suspended moment, there was nothing. No sound, no movement. His heart fell utterly still in his chest and he wondered if it were too late. If it were already over. If he was already—

She crashed into him like joy, like sunshine, like a speeding train he'd never seen coming. Suddenly she was *inside* him, the bass rumble of her ocean invading his very cells. It vibrated through his bones, rattled his teeth. Waves smashed over his head, merging and mounting, rearing up and hammering down. A single startled cry ripped from his throat, and he shattered. Simply exploded, and the shrapnel flew into her ocean like a school of darting silvery fish.

For a long moment, he simply hung there, stunned by his own brokenness, unable to grasp where or even *what* he was.

Then he heard her. He heard her and he remembered.

Will, she crooned, and her voice was all around him. It was *inside* him, swirling and spinning through all those new and shocking spaces where he'd once had only darkness and fear. *Oh, Will. Don't be afraid. I have you. I won't let you fall.*

"Audrey." Joy uncurled inside him, small and green and precious. "Audrey, you came."

Always.

"I kind of fell apart."

I know. I caught you.

"Is that what happened?"

You were so brave, Will. You fought so hard.

"I was scared shitless."

You were alone. You don't have to be.

"I don't want to be. Never again. Stay with me, Audrey."

I can do better than that.

"What—"

He broke off as all that straightforward energy of hers flashed through him again, as it lifted and buoyed him. She was putting him back together, he realized with dawning wonder. With every wave, every ripple, every eddy, she knit his bones and stitched his flesh. She was healing him.

Renewing him.

Energy surged and flowed in his veins. But it wasn't his, not precisely. It wasn't the old, black-edged drive he was used to, but it wasn't the constant motion and purpose of her ocean, either. It was, he realized slowly, some hybrid of the two, some powerful and unexpected harmony born of their two utterly separate songs twining together.

His heart swelled inside him and he offered it up to the song. To her. To what they were together. That small green joy inside him flowered, and he felt his soul slip back into the repaired husk of his body. Felt her lash it down tight and strong. His brain surged back to full power, and the control panel in his head lit up like Vegas.

Cece's howl came with it, filled up his head with a red roar like ground glass. He staggered back from it, fumbled for the volume control but her ugly chaos echoed inside his skull without mercy no matter how low he dragged it. Blood lust kindled inside his mind and his hands gathered into fists.

"We have to deal with her, Audrey."

No argument, she said and her voice came from *inside* him. Like she lived in his cells now. Maybe she did. He smiled at the idea, and his teeth felt smooth and shiny and whole.

But fighting isn't the answer, she whispered. *She's like Olivia, remember? She likes that crap. It only makes her stronger. We need some other way to get her across that bridge.*

"Oh, hell. The bridge." He closed his eyes and strained to catch the soul-deep reverberation of the bridge's song. It was still there but weak. So weak. "Hildy's fading out. She's not going to be able to hold it open much longer. We have to get Cece to cross. Now."

How?

"Give me a minute."

An idea germinated slowly in his mind, and he reached for it. Willed it out of the fuzz and into focus. He stared blindly at the control panel in his head and strained toward this maybe-solution until he was sweaty and trembling.

Will?

"I think I have something."

Great. Lay it on me.

"Don't freak out, okay?"

About what?

"Things are about to get weird."

And here we were having such a nice calm evening.

"Just brace yourself, okay?" He paused. "Hey, Bob?"

Right here, buddy.

Audrey's silence was sharp and shocked.

"We need your help, Bob."

Of course you do.

"Can you do something for us?"

Bob heaved a long-suffering sigh. *I can do anything I want. How many times do I have to tell you that? I am not your imagination, you self-centered dickwad.*

Audrey made a muffled noise that might've been a startled laugh.

"It's kind of a big ask."

What do you think I'm here for, William?

Will paused. He hadn't thought about that. He'd spent a lot of time thinking about what he himself was here for, but not Bob.

That's because you're not as smart as you think you are. But maybe you're not quite as dumb as I think you are, either. Now let's hear this plan of yours.

"It's time for Cece to go home, Bob. Tonight. If we can amp up the bridge, if Audrey and I between us can make it fucking *sing*, can you take Cece across?"

There was a long, tense silence.

Finally Bob said, *Of course I can. But you're going to owe me. And you're going to miss me.*

"I already do, on both counts."

No shit, kid. Bob laughed his gravelly laugh. *Are you ready to do this thing?*

A pang of regret took Will by surprise. "I really am going to miss you, Bob."

Don't get weepy on me now, Nancy.

"Like I would." Will eyed the control panel in his head. "There's no crying in baseball."

You are such *a chick sometimes.*

"Are you ready, or do you want to trade insults a little longer? You know, for old times' sake?"

Just crank the volume, son.

"Cranking on three."

He closed his eyes and felt for Audrey. She vibrated under his skin, swam through his blood, buzzed in his cells, infusing him with courage and energy and strength.

"One."

He reached for the master volume slider. His hand shook but he drew on the endless swirl of Audrey's ocean and steadied it.

"Two."

The hair on his arms stood up.

"Three."

He jacked the volume slider to the top of its range.

The bridge exploded in song.

It blasted him backward, and he tumbled ass over teakettle through Audrey's ocean. The song was a mad demand now, ringing and singing and shoving everybody willy-nilly toward the dark machinery at its center. Audrey's ocean crashed wildly, monster waves battering at jagged cliffs as it slid downhill. Jillian's clock bonged like Big Ben, reverberating through his skull with molar-rattling strength. Cece's fire roared upward in a mushroom cloud of rage. The earth itself tilted, and they were all sliding down, down, down, toward the hungry maw of the bridge.

Then Bob's voice came down like a massive hammer.

Sounds like three to me. Well, kids, it's been fun. Drop me a postcard some time.

Cece's fire gave an anguished howl, then snapped off like somebody had cut her power source. That inexorable gravity snapped off, too, and Will flew abruptly up, like he'd been fired from a sling shot. He broke the surface of Audrey's ocean at the speed of light, and then he was flying through air that was shockingly cold and utterly black.

He slammed head-first into a brick wall of light and shattered.

Chapter 39

When Will came to, he was lying on Cece's bedroom floor. He became aware, slowly, of three things.

First, everything ached. His joints were at least a million years old.

Second, Jillian was parked at his elbow. He could hear her there, tick-tocking along like an itty-bitty soldier. Damn, he was proud of that kid.

Third? His head was in Audrey's lap.

Items number one and two faded into obscurity.

His head was in Audrey's lap.

Her fingers danced over his brow, and her ocean stirred anxiously. "Will?" The back of her knuckles feathered across his cheek and he sighed involuntarily. "Will? Time to wake up, sweetie. Come on, now."

Sweetie? He struggled with lids that weighed a ton apiece but it was worth the effort. Audrey's face, perfect and worried, hovered above his, her violet eyes wide and tense.

"Hey," he said, and smiled.

She barked out one of those odd laugh/sobs he was coming to love and shoved him off her lap. His head hit the carpet with a thud and she flung herself across his chest. He closed his eyes and savored the warm weight of her, patting her back and murmuring nonsense while her tears soaked his shirt. Something warm and golden filled his soul from the bottom up and he thought, *hey, I think that's happiness*. He smiled again, and for the first time in his life, it didn't feel foreign on his lips.

"Will?"

He turned toward this new voice and found Jillian kneeling beside his elbow, Audrey's hair sprinkled across her lap.

"Well, hey, look who's talking now," he said and, without thinking, opened his free arm to her. Jillian didn't hesitate. She scooted down into the cradle of his elbow, put her head on his shoulder and threw her free arm over her sobbing aunt.

"You saved me," she said.

"Well, your auntie saved me," he murmured, his fingers drifting over Audrey's back, his eyes sliding shut again. "It seemed only fair."

Silence reigned for a long blessed moment, and sleep tugged on Will with sticky fingers.

Jillian said, "Will?"

"Hmm?" He was so tired. Even talking was an effort.

"Who's Bob?"

"Good question," he said, and fell down, down, down into sleep.

* * *

They slept the clock around, Will and Audrey and Jillian. They staggered down to the kitchen the next day around mid-afternoon to wolf down enormous plates of spaghetti, then staggered back to their beds.

It was nearly two a.m. when Audrey woke up with a jerk in her sister's old room, heart pumping, adrenaline screaming. She'd thrown back the covers and shot to her feet before she realized that she was hearing a running faucet, not a screaming child. Olivia must be in the bathroom. She peered into the darkness and, sure enough, the twin bed across the room was empty.

She shivered and considered getting back under the blankets. Jem's thermostat convictions didn't exactly encourage nocturnal wanderings. Then again, she was already up. It wouldn't hurt to look in on Jillian. Just to make sure.

She eased the door open and slid into the dark hall.

The door to Jillian's room stood open, and a figure loomed just outside the threshold. Tall, silent, watchful. Protective. Her heart squeezed and she tiptoed down the carpet.

"How does she sound?" she murmured, sliding an arm

around Will's waist and fitting herself into his side.

He glanced down at her, his eyes startled. "What makes you think I'm listening to her?"

She smiled. "Oh, please. You love that kid. And when you love somebody, you can hear them. I know this from personal experience." She rested her head on his shoulder and turned her gaze to the lump of slumbering child under the quilts. "So? What does she sound like to you?"

For a moment it was silent, and she thought he'd hold out on her. Then he said, "She's a tiny little clock."

"A clock, huh?"

"Yeah." He sighed, relaxing into her. Into this new nakedness between them. She accepted the warm weight of his trust with gratitude. "She's got these itty bitty gears and springs, all delicate and complex. She's so damn breakable, Audrey."

"Tell me about it." She shook her head in perfect understanding. "But she's running fine?"

"Yeah. Like, uh, clockwork."

Audrey snorted out a smothered laugh.

"For now, anyway." He tossed a glance toward the bathroom where Olivia's sink continued to run.

"Yeah," she said. "For now."

She felt more than saw Will frown down at her. "Hey, about that," he began. "About Olivia—"

"No," Audrey said with a certainty that surprised her. "Whatever happens, happens."

"There are legal options here, Audrey," he said. "We could—"

"No," she said again. "I love her, Will, and I want to keep her. But she has a mother, and it's not me. And I can't put her through whatever it would take to change that." She shook her head. "I won't. So if Olivia takes her, she takes her. It won't break me. Not this time. But I'll be right here when she comes back, ready to love her and keep her, and be whatever she needs. She'll be fine, Will. And so will I."

He didn't say anything, but she felt his lips on her hair. She rubbed her cheek against his shoulder, savored the warm strength of him.

Finally she said, "What are you doing up, anyway? Is Drew a kicker, or a blanket hog?"

"Worse." He sighed wearily. "He's a snuggler."

She laughed.

"Lucky for me, though, he took off when Hildy did."

She drew back to stare up at him. "Hildy's gone?"

"There was a spiritual emergency or something." He waved a vague hand. "She took off and Meg went with her. Drew volunteered himself as chauffeur and bag man. Of course."

"Did he now?" She grinned and put one finger on the shallow groove of his abs. Drew it downward. Slowly. He stopped breathing for a gratifyingly long moment. "So you have that big cold bed all to yourself?"

"Well, yeah." He covered her hand—now toying with the waistband of his shorts—with his. Glanced into the darkness beyond the open door. "But Jillian—"

"—is fine." She threaded her fingers through his and drew him away from the door. She eased it closed.

"Audrey," he began, "we don't have to—"

"I know. I want to." She led him down the hallway until they were standing outside the closed door to her mother's old room. "You know why?"

He shook his head, fascination and curiosity chasing each other over the dangerous beauty of his face.

"Because I'm yours. And you're mine." She took his other hand and knitted their fingers together. "Wherever you are? That's where I want to be."

He frowned gravely down at her, his brain spinning madly behind his eyes. Love for him bloomed messily under her breastbone.

"Ah, Will." She grinned up at him. "You're having a hard time digesting this, aren't you?"

He looked away. "It isn't that I don't believe you—"

She snuggled herself into the taut heat of him. He gave a hiss of pained appreciation, and it started a fire low and sweet inside her. "You know what I think?"

His throat worked. "What?"

"I think you should stop thinking." She came up on her

toes and put her mouth beside his ear. The paper-and-ink scent of him wrapped itself around her, tugged her closer. "I think you should stop thinking and listen."

"I *am* listening," he told her tightly. "I—"

"Not with your ears." She nipped at his lobe just to make sure he was paying attention. She snuggled herself into the hot press of his hips and smiled. He was. He was definitely paying attention. "Listen with your heart, Will. Listen with your body and your soul and that weird-ass antennae in your head that thinks I'm an ocean."

She drifted her lips along the knife-edge of his cheekbone to his waiting mouth. Nibbled at the corner. "Listen to *me*, Will. Listen to this."

She took his mouth with hers, with aching deliberation and quiet joy. With pure, blistering love. She traced his lips with her tongue, worshipping each gentle dip, each dangerous curve. Wonder rolled over her, tangled with gratitude and streaked with heat.

I love you.

His hands came together in the small of her back, still joined with her own. She found herself arched into him, helpless, and desire kicked hard in her belly. It slipped into her bloodstream as the wordy scent of him filled her lungs, and she made a hot, needful sound into his mouth.

I love you.

She pressed herself hungrily into him. The doorknob bumped her arm and she shook a hand free to twist it open. They spilled into his room. No, into her mother's room, where her heart had been broken so many times.

He stiffened under her hands. "Audrey, no. Not here. We don't have to—"

"Will, look." She took his hand in hers and peered around. There wasn't a single flower in sight, and the heavy curtains were gone. Moonlight shone onto the floor through the naked windows. "Oh, Will, look." She smiled up at him. "She's gone. There's nothing here that can hurt me. Not anymore. I don't pretend to understand how you did whatever you did earlier, but I'm grateful. No, *screw* grateful. I'm in awe."

Dull color mounted his cheeks and he looked away. "Geez, Audrey, I didn't—"

"You did. You slayed my dragon." She waited until he looked at her again and said, "You're a soldier, Will. You went to war for me. You shed your blood for me. For me and Jillian. And we love you for it. For being exactly what you are." She smiled crookedly. "Whatever that is."

"Audrey—"

"Still thinking." She sighed with mock weariness. "Why are you still thinking? You need to *listen*, William." She hooked a finger into the collar of his t-shirt and drew him to the bed. She nudged him down, spread him across that ocean of sheets.

"I'm not saying you're a knight in shining armor," she told him, and tugged off his t-shirt. Her breath caught in her lungs. His stark beauty simply robbed her of words, left her with only an exquisite ache in her throat and a humble gratitude for the gift of him. For this taut, tough body. For this powerful mind. For this ancient and heroic heart. All of them hers, now and forever.

"Good," he said and stacked his hands behind his head to peer at her in the darkness. "Because I'm not."

She cleared her throat. "I know that." She slid her hands up his thighs and stripped off his shorts. Hunger uncurled inside her, hot and ready, and she grinned up at him. "Your weaponry is unparalleled, though."

He snorted out a laugh and delight arrowed through her. She loved making Will laugh. She shimmied out of her own clothes and crawled onto the bed beside him. Wondered where to start. Moonlight kissed him, silvered every elegant line of that lean, spare body.

He came up on one elbow, his face suddenly grim. "Good God, Audrey. Look what I did to you."

She followed his gaze to her collar bone, to the mark he'd put there with his mouth and his teeth. She touched it with fond fingers.

"I do," she said. "I look at it all the time. I love seeing it there."

She pressed him gently back down, and came over him,

braced on her elbows and knees. Her hair hung down like a curtain and she touched her lips to the mark she'd left on him, in the hollow of his throat where his pulse beat madly. "I love this one, too. I did this to you, Will."

He made some kind of noise she couldn't interpret.

"And I love the piece of you that marked me. I love the fists and the teeth and the mean." She licked her way along his collar bone, and bit lightly at the meat of his shoulder. The noise he made this time was less sorrow, more hunger. She smiled against his skin. "I love it when you snap your leash and take me like I'm plunder. It's kind of hot." She moved back to his chest, found the groove of his abdomen with her tongue. Ran it downward and his hips jerked upward. Desire roared through her veins and she slid lower yet toward the hot thrust of his desire. "Very piratical. I like pirates. Did I ever mention?"

He made some noise that could be construed as a no.

"Hmm. Well, I do."

She took him into her mouth and he whimpered. *Whimpered.* Triumph broke over her like a wave, and lust crashed in behind it. Because Will's surrender was the hottest thing she'd ever seen. He lay sprawled under her, the strongest man she'd ever known, utterly vulnerable. His eyes were closed, his face pained, his body whip-tight and shuddering under her touch. At her command.

She took her time. She worshipped his body with her mouth, her hands, her skin. She helped herself to the leashed strength and the gorgeous generosity of him, discovered him, tasted him, savored him.

I love you.

And when they were both gasping, when they were both shaking, she rose up over him and took him into her. She took him into her body and she invited him into her soul. She rode him until he broke under her like the sea under a storm. Until she, too, shattered. Until they were both lost, wrecked, reborn.

They lay there in a pool of cool moonlight, tangled in the sheets like shipwreck survivors washed up on the beach. His heart thudded hard and damp under her palm, constant and true and forever. She patted it fondly, utterly beyond speech.

I love you.

His arm tightened around her. "I love you too," he murmured.

Epilogue

Several hours later, Will woke to a room full of sunshine and a bed to himself. He followed Audrey's ocean to the kitchen. He found her facing off with Jem, the coffee maker between them like a long-suffering Switzerland. Of course. Evidently Kitchen Smackdown was a Bing family tradition. A tradition he'd have to get used to now that Audrey was family.

Family.

It glowed inside him like a secret ember. Audrey was his family. He couldn't wait to make it official. Even if he got Jem in the bargain.

"What do you mean, she's gone?" Audrey snapped at Jem.

"Gone?" Will's heart stopped. "Jillian?"

"God, no." Jem rolled his eyes. "Olivia. She left the kid behind." He smirked. "Again."

Audrey glared at him. "What did you *do*, Dad?"

"Coffee first." Jem folded his arms and gave her that sharky smile of his. "Then chit-chat."

Audrey glared at him, then turned to Will. "He did something."

"I can see that." He gave Jem a wary once-over, but the guy was exactly as usual. Minus the buzz of fear. "To Olivia?"

"I assume so." Audrey pointed to a piece of paper on the island counter. "Check that out."

She set her jaw and made coffee in record time while Will read. By the time she'd plunked a mug down in front of her dad, Will was sitting on a stool, knees weak, wonder unspooling inside him.

"She signed over custody of Jillian," he said faintly.

"Yep." Jem lifted his mug with an air of deep satisfaction.

"To Audrey."

"Sure did." Jem flashed those brilliantly white teeth.

"And me." Will swallowed. "Jointly."

"Didn't see that one coming," Jem admitted. "Olivia always was good at loop holes." He shrugged philosophically and went back to his coffee. "But, hey, a guy can't predict everything." He smiled smugly. "Just most things."

"And you predicted this?" Audrey shook Olivia's letter at him.

"Not hard to do. Not when you know your kid. And I know mine." He sat back, fully caffeinated now and prepared to expound. "See, Olivia? She's all flash and dazzle. Lives for drama. Good in a fight but doesn't know how to knuckle under and get the day-to-day work done. And raising kids?" He lifted shaggy eyebrows. "That's day-to-day shit. Endless details, God." He waved a hand. "Olivia isn't cut out for that." He lifted his mug toward Audrey. "But you are. You're all about the lists and the chores and the charts. Boring as hell—"

"Gosh, thanks, Dad," Audrey said dryly.

"—but that's parenting for you. And you were going to fight her for it."

"I wasn't, actually."

Jem's brows shot up in genuine surprise. "You weren't?"

"Nope."

"Why the hell not?" He frowned ferociously. "You love that kid."

"Yep. So much that I'd rather let her go than turn her childhood into some endless battle between me and her mom. She's a kid, not a wishbone."

"Well, hell," Jem grumbled. "Wish I'd known that earlier. Could've saved myself some—" He cut himself off. "Worry." He cleared his throat. "Saved myself some worry."

Audrey narrowed her eyes. "What did you *do*, Dad?"

"Nothing." He lifted innocent shoulders. "Well, not

much. I just got in touch with good ol' Max The Blade and suggested that he might want to consider hiring a personal assistant for World Cup season. You know, somebody to go on the road with him, smooth out the details, make his life pleasant. Let him really focus on his work between the goalposts, you know?"

Will smiled. He might like Jem after all.

Audrey considered this. "And you suggested that Olivia would be ideal for such a position? Our Olivia? The one who isn't so good with details?"

He shrugged. "I might've dropped her name, sure."

Will leaned in. "Or you might've offered to fund this position, should it go to the right candidate."

Jem gave him the side eye. "It's possible."

"And in return?" Will prompted.

"And in return," Jem said, "Max discovered that he was deeply reluctant to separate a mother from her only child. So reluctant, in fact, that he might refuse to go to contract unless Olivia named a legal guardian." He glanced at Audrey. "That was when I mentioned *your* name. You're welcome, by the way." He gave Will a skeptical up-and-down. "I don't know how you got involved. Olivia's a strange bird sometimes." He shrugged. Then his brows came down and he aimed a dangerous finger Will's way. "But if you think I'm about to let my only grandchild witness the two of you living in sin—"

"Oh my God, Dad." Audrey's hands were on her cheeks—her very pink cheeks, Will noticed with interest.

"—you've got another think coming," Jem finished. "So you can either suit up for legal action or put a ring on it. Those are the options, son. Choose wisely."

Will checked his watch. "The ring should be here in about twenty."

"It better be." Jem grunted and went back to his coffee. "Now where's my damn paper?"

Audrey said, "What?"

Jem said, "The newspaper. Where is it?"

"I was talking to him." She pointed at Will like she'd never seen him before. "The guy you just threatened with legal action if he didn't marry me."

"Oh, him." Jem snorted. "Right." He took his coffee mug and rose. "Paper's probably out front still. Some butler you are." But he patted her shoulder on his way to the door.

"What's this now?" Audrey said as her dad wandered off. Her face was white, her eyes enormous. "Something about a ring in twenty minutes?"

"If Drew makes good time." Joy unfolded slow and golden inside him and he grinned at her. "I asked him to get my mom's wedding ring out of the safe at home." He tucked his hands into his pockets and studied her. "It doesn't have to be *the* ring. You can pick out whatever you like. But you said it yourself last night. I'm yours." He shrugged helplessly. "You're mine. I want my ring on your finger. Now." He shifted uncomfortably. Was he starting to sweat? He felt sweaty. "Yesterday."

Her ocean lapped and rolled and twisted, all chaos and white-caps. But even so, he could hear that undercurrent of love—solid, steady, true—ringing through. Christ, he was making a hash of this.

He felt for the place Bob used to occupy in his head and found a rapidly closing gap. Grief pooled under his heart, thick and bittersweet. Bob had called him a lot of things, starting with *goatfucker* and ending with *kid*. Bunch of uncomplimentary stuff in between, too. But right before the end, he'd called him son.

Son.

His inner orphan wept. Damn, he was going to miss that guy. He'd been foul-mouthed and abusive, but very instructive. He could almost hear him now: *What the fuck are you doing, son? Is there a proposal in there somewhere?*

Good God. There wasn't.

He raked both hands through his hair and blew out a long breath. When he opened his eyes again, Audrey was still standing there, looking like he'd hit her on the head with a hammer.

"Audrey." He stepped forward, took her hands in his and frowned down at her. "I'm going to screw this up for the rest of my life. Are you really ready to deal with that?"

She blinked, and color bloomed in her cheeks. A smile trembled on that beautiful mouth. Her ocean curled softly in his ears. "I'm a bossy, sarcastic butler with an eight-year-old plus-one who might be smarter than you are. Are you really ready to deal with that?"

Gratitude and love swamped him. "I'll do my best."

She beamed up at him. "Then so will I."

He sucked in a breath. "Will you marry me, Audrey? Will you be my family? You and Jillian both?"

"Yes." Her ocean roared in his ears. Roared and leapt and frolicked. She lifted her mouth to his, and he tasted salt. For an instant, he thought it *was* her ocean, then he realized he was tasting her tears. Or his. Who knew? Did it matter?

"Your fight is my fight, Will." She murmured it against his lips. "What we have, we share. Forever and forever and forever."

"I love you," he said, his throat aching, his heart full.

She rubbed her cheek against his. "I think it's the same thing."

"Yeah." His heart went ahead and overflowed. "It is."

About the Author

Susan Sey lives and writes in St. Paul, Minnesota, with her wonderful husband, their two charming children and a whole lot of snow. In addition to producing smart, sexy contemporary romances on an annual basis, Susan is also the proud owner of a filthy house, a broken oven and a cranky van whose off-and-on relationship with the check engine light is driving her crackers.

She loves ice cream, her family and happy endings, though not necessarily in that order. She does not enjoy laundry, failure or mowing the lawn, but rises to the occasion as necessary.

Want to connect with Susan? You can find her at www.susansey.com, where it's just a hop, skip and a click to finding her on Facebook, Twitter, the Romance Bandits, Red Door Reads, and signing up for her newsletter.

Or you can just shoot her an email at susan@susansey.com. She loves a good letter.

www.ingramcontent.com/pod-product-compliance
Lightning Source LLC
Chambersburg PA
CBHW020912200626
46814CB00001BA/298